SHE WAS NO LONGER MIRIAM.

She was the Dance, and the elf was the Dance, and as her sword came up, waving in and out of the shifting pattern of life and death, the elf's blade was leaping forward once again. Effortlessly she blocked . . . and counterattacked.

Sword to sword, face to face, they fought in the middle of the clearing, dancing in and out, matching speed for speed and strength for strength.

Miriam knew this was just a lesson. Soon shc would no longer be the Dance. She would be the Warrior, ready for the real thing. She would be the Death of an enemy. . . .

STRANDS OF STARLIGHT

STRANDS OF STARLIGHT

by
Gael Baudino

A SIGNET BOOK

NEW AMERICAN LIBRARY

A DIVISION OF PENGUIN BOOKS USA INC.

SIGNET TRADEMARK REG. U.S. PAT. OFF. AND FOREIGN COUNTRIES
REGISTERED TRADEMARK—MARCA REGISTRADA
HECHO EN DRESDEN, TN, USA

SIGNET, SIGNET CLASSIC, MENTOR, ONYX, PLUME,
MERIDIAN and NAL BOOKS are published by New American
Library, a division of Penguin Books USA Inc., 1633 Broadway,
New York, New York 10019

First Printing, November, 1989

1 2 3 4 5 6 7 8 9

PRINTED IN THE UNITED STATES OF AMERICA

This is for Mirya

"Et ades sera l'alba!"

PART ONE

Planh

Chapter One

Rain.

It fell steadily on the city of Hypprux, a promise of the coming spring, but a cold, grudging one to be sure. The men who were repairing the roof of the cathedral had given up shortly after noon, and the shopkeepers had admitted defeat only a little while later, packing up their wares with numbed fingers, trudging into their homes soaked and shivering. The church bells had only recently rung nones, but the flickering glow of rushlights and tallow dips was already seeping through the cracks of shuttered windows on this dark February day.

George Darci made his way along Domino Crossing. Wind now. The almost-sleet stung his eyes and he paused to wipe his face on his sleeve and pull his hood up a little further. He did not often visit Hypprux, and somehow, with the rain and the cold and the lack of people on the streets, he had become thoroughly lost. Standing in the porch of a small, run-down church, he peered up through the drops, searching for landmarks. Thomas had mentioned in his letter that there had been changes in the city, but surely something had to be familiar.

He made out the spires of the cathedral that poked up above the rooftops, and at last the towers of the Chateau. Wading through the river of mud and sewage that was now flowing down the street, he took the next turning, his steps confident, crossed a small market square that lay deserted in the wet, smiled when he at last found the Street of Saint Lazarus, broad and familiar, tripped over some scaffolding that was lying across the way, and went sprawling.

The cobblestones were hard, cold, and covered with muck; and as he lay, half-stunned, he was glad for the first time since he had left the inn that the streets were empty. People were always inclined to laugh when a fat man took a tumble, but if there were no people, there would be no laughter. He caught his breath, grimacing at the filth that now covered him, and began to struggle to his feet.

A sharp pain in his ankle sent him into the filth again. "Oh, dear . . ." He managed to sit up. Even through the thick leather of his boot, the swelling was already perceptible. "By Our Lady . . ."

Walking was out of the question. So was rising. Crawling was, at best, doubtful. It seemed that he would have to sit in the street until the evening watchmen made their rounds. But considering the wretched weather, George would not have been surprised if they skipped the whole business and stayed in a warm, dry tavern with some pretty girls. He could possibly spend the night in the open and catch a fever.

The rain pattered down. He had to laugh at himself. "George Darci," he said under his breath, "mayor of Saint Blaise, dead of a broken ankle."

He saw a dark shape move along the other side of the street, under cover of the overhanging balconies. "Ho there!" he cried. "Can you help me?"

The shape halted.

"You, boy! Come help me and I'll give you some money. I'm hurt."

It started forward slowly. "I know you're hurt, curse it." The voice was a rough soprano, and a small, dark girl came and knelt at his side. "Hold still."

"What?"

"I said *hold still*. Don't keep me." Her hair was coarse and matted with the rain, and her sharp black eyes caught his and silenced him. "I don't have time for talk. I wish I hadn't found you, but I've no choice in this now." She was shaking.

Her hands came down on George's ankle, and he felt a sudden surge of warmth, like the flash of a sunbeam. The pain vanished.

The girl rose, trembling fiercely, and turned away. George caught her arm.

She tried to pull away. "You're healed. Leave me alone." Her face was cut and bruised. George saw blood on her arms and realized that there was blood pooling around her feet also.

He stared. She was badly wounded. "Who did this to you?"

"Let go of me."

"Who did this?" He was shouting, outraged. The girl was small, thin, not more than thirteen by the look of her. Who could possibly—

She stopped pulling and looked him full in the face. Her black eyes seemed those of an animal about to chew its leg off in order to escape a trap. "Bishop Aloysius Cranby did this to me. Are you satisfied now?" She bit the words off one by one. "You owe me your life, or at least your foot. Pray say nothing to anyone about this."

He sat, stunned, for a moment, then got slowly to his feet. There was no pain. His whole leg felt better than new. "I want to help you."

"Then let me go, damn you."

George thought quickly. "Here, please," he said, fumbling at his purse. "Take this. Go in peace. Forgive me for troubling you." He filled her hands with coins, hesitated, took off his cloak, and fastened it about her.

She stared at the coins, looked up at him. "Why?"

"You healed me."

"I didn't have any choice. I never have any choice."

"Go child. Find someone to tend you. May you find happiness."

She turned away in silence. In a moment the green cloak was indistinguishable among the shadows of a cold, dark afternoon. George looked after her for many minutes, heedless of the icy rain. For the second time in his life, he had been saved by one persecuted by the Church.

She was cold and wet, and the pain in her legs, already intolerable, was getting worse.

She dragged herself into a church porch and propped herself against a pillar that someone had rudely marked with green paint. This was not the best place in which to take shelter, but her vision was blurring with the pain, and she could ill afford to push herself further. If she were lucky, her escape would not be noticed for another hour, when the

inquisitors came to question her again. It was just possible
that she could make the gates of the city. She might have a
chance . . . if her legs did not give out.

It was too dark to see clearly, so she permitted herself a
look at her calves. They had stopped short of breaking her
shinbones, but not by much. Perhaps that would have been
next. As it was, she would scar badly.

She permitted herself a harsh laugh. She was worried
about scarring? Of the body? How ludicrous!

She left the porch and moved on. Her vision blurred again,
and she grabbed for a wall to steady herself. "My name is
Miriam." She forced herself through the litany that had
shored up her sanity during hours of questioning and torture. "My name is Miriam. I have black hair. I have black
eyes." She coughed, tasted blood. "My name in Miriam—"

The coins the fat man had given her weighed her down,
and she was inclined to throw them away. But she would
need money, possibly a great deal of it. Her wounds were
many, and deep. The fat man was right: she had to find
someone to tend her. She would have to pay if she wanted
to survive.

She pushed off from the wall, stumbled down the street.
Ironically, the weight of her purse could keep her from making the gate at all.

In the haze of pain, she took a wrong turn and wound up
looking down Street Gran Pont. Even through the rain, she
could see the Chateau, walled and guarded, illuminated by
torches and bright lamps. But she had escaped from it.

You won't take me alive again.

Reeling, she turned away and tottered along the street
toward the city gate, the cold rain stinging her face and
soaking her even through the fat man's heavy cloak.

She was within sight of the gate when her legs finally gave
out. She fell, but she felt nothing by then.

George eased back in the tub, letting the hot water lap at
the nape of his neck, watching the steam fantasies in the
air. After a minute, he lifted his foot and propped it on the
wet wood above the water. His once-broken ankle showed

not a sign of injury. Whoever that stranger lass was, her powers were remarkable.

"Well, George, you're still wet, but you look considerably better than when you came to my door. Don't you people from the Free Towns believe in cloaks?" Thomas a'Verne stroked a short, gray beard and grinned at him from the doorway.

"I feel considerably better, thank you, Thomas. And, yes, we believe in cloaks."

"But not in the rain."

"True. Not in the rain." George picked up a bath brush and scrubbed at his foot. The smell of raw sewage was fading slowly from the back of his throat. He never could quite understand: Saint Blaise coped with the problem quite effectively. So why not Hypprux? With a glance at Thomas, he flicked the brush expertly, sending a shower of drops in the direction of his father-in-law.

Thomas was sixty-three, but nimble enough to dodge. "Next time, George, I'll make sure the bath is cold."

George looked toward the window. Outside, the rain still fell. "It *was* cold, Thomas."

The nobleman handed George a towel. "What happened?"

"I fell and hurt my ankle," George said as he dried off.

"Remarkable recovery."

"Yes, remarkable."

"Ready for dinner?"

"Quite. Shall I wear the towel, or are we being formal?"

The fur-lined robe was much better than the towel, and the two men ate dinner alone in the large hall of Thomas's house. Over the fireplace hung a portrait of the nobleman's long-dead wife. The house was very quiet save for their voices and the sound of the rain.

Thomas helped George to some pork roast and filled his wine cup. The older man's voice was casual when he said: "And how are my daughter and grandaughter?

"Right as rain, Thomas." George looked at the window. Outside, the icy rain was still falling.

Thomas laughed. "Better than that, I hope."

"Anne couldn't come with me because of the weather. Her lungs are still weak from that fever she had last year."

George broke off a large piece of bread. "But otherwise she's fine. Did you know she's learning to read?"

"Really?" Thomas thought for a moment. "I suppose it's all for the best, though I don't know what I would have said fifteen years ago if my new son told me he was going to turn my daughter into a scholar."

"I had nothing to do with it. She made the decision herself when she was arranging for a tutor for Janet. Now they sit together with Otto, spelling out their letters."

"Janet too?"

"Janet too. You'd be proud to see her, Thomas. Thirteen years old, straight and tall like you. Mind as quick as a squirrel. She argues with Otto in Latin—Barbara, Celarent, Darii, Ferio—and gets the better of him."

"Thirteen . . ." Thomas mused as he cut into his pork. "They grow up fast. Have you . . . have you thought about a suitable marriage for her?"

"I've spoken with Janet and with Anne about it. Janet would like to wait until she's a little older. Maybe eighteen." George had been buttering a piece of bread, but his words reminded him of the stranger lass in the street. He frowned suddenly.

"George?"

"It's nothing. A thought, no more."

"Something happened tonight. I should have sent a servant."

"No. It's quite all right." He thought for a moment. "I broke my ankle. I thought I would surely spend the night on the street."

"Your ankle is fine." Thomas's voice was grave. Outside, in the distance, someone began blowing a horn, and they could hear the faint clang of a metal gong.

George refilled his cup with raisin wine. Simply, he told Thomas of the girl, of what she had done.

Thomas cast his eyes to the ceiling. "George," he said. "You're a fool. You have a heart of gold, though, and I'm sure you'll go directly to heaven after the Inquisition burns you at the stake."

"She was hurt."

"And newly escaped from the keep, I daresay." The horn

and gong continued their clamor. Thomas cocked his head. "The alarm. She's been missed."

"I hope she gets away. She didn't want any help from me, though. So I gave her money and my cloak—"

Thomas went the color of his beard. "You what? Your cloak, man? Sweet Jesus, have you no sense? If she's taken with that cloak, you'll be implicated. I can't save you from the Inquisition, George."

"I don't expect you to. I'll tell them it was stolen."

"And Aloysius Cranby will, of course, believe you. Of course. And you the mayor of the chief of the Free Towns."

The gong continued to sound. "What does that have to do with it?"

Thomas returned to his pork. "Some things have changed here in the last two years, George. That's why I asked you to come. Bishop Cranby, everyone suspects, wants to be a cardinal eventually. There is also the possibility that he has his eye on the papacy."

George snorted. "Aloysius Cranby? He has no qualifications for such things."

"Remember his mentor. Jaques Fournier became Benedict the Twelfth on the strength of his work against the Cathar heresy thirty years ago. Cranby wants to use the same stepping-stone: the Inquisition."

"What does that have to do with the Free Towns?"

Thomas popped a piece of pork into his mouth, chewed for a minute, and washed it down with wine before replying. "Had much dealing with the Elves recently, George?"

George stared. "How—"

"Rumor spreads quickly. Now, I don't see any strange light in your eyes, so that part of the story must be false. But there's always a shred of truth in these tales, and Cranby's heard them. And to top it all off, one of Cranby's associates disappeared down in Saint Brigid about two years ago. Arba . . . Alda . . . what was his name?"

"Alban. Jaques Alban. Nasty individual. Was not liked at all. There's a local lad, though, has the cure in Saint Brigid now."

"But don't you see, George? Human dealing with Elves, and a priest disappears. What does it sound like to Cranby? Or rather, what can Cranby make it sound like?"

George put down his knife. "All right, Thomas. What's happening that I should know about?"

Thomas rose and went to the window. Outside, the gong had died away, but the horn continued to sound. "My position gives me access to information that . . . well . . . numerous people wish I did not have. Sometimes I wish I did not have it myself. If Aloysius Cranby stamped out heresy in an entire region of this country, his eventual claim to the papacy would be strengthened. Clement the Sixth has to die sometime." He shrugged, his chain of office glinting in the candlelight. "Avignon is a nice place to live, I hear."

"There's no heresy in the Free Towns."

"Not in your opinion. But in your opinion there's no heresy in a little bedraggled healer girl either." Thomas crossed to George's side, put a fatherly hand on his shoulder. "There's talk of a crusade against the Free Towns." His voice was old and dry. "Nothing definite yet, but . . ."

"But what?" George demanded. "Cranby wants the papacy? Well, let him work for it. Benedict the Twelfth investigated a real heresy. He didn't fabricate it. It takes more to make a heresy than the greed of one churchman."

"True. It takes the greed of one churchman combined with the greed of many barons."

"You don't mean to tell me that your fellow barons are supporting this idiocy!"

"Not supporting," said Thomas. "Not quite. But times have been uncertain. The Plague took its toll in the rest of the continent the last three years, and the war between England and France looks to be a long one. The barons of Adria are interested in a . . . financial cushion. The Free Towns are well run, wealthy, comfortable, productive—"

"And independent," snapped George. "We threw the last overlord out a century ago and want no more of them. The barons will have their hands full if they try to annex us."

"But if the barons and the Church work together? With the full force of God's spiritual representative on earth condemning the heretical Free Towns?"

George found himself calculating strengths. Yes, the Free Towns could fall. A condemnation by the Church could bring just enough of an uncertainty into the hearts of the people that they might give in. Damn that Cranby. "You're chamberlain of Hypprux, Thomas,'' he said. ''You lead the baronial council. Can you stop them?''

''There's nothing to stop quite yet. Any action on my part would be premature at this time. There are only whispered words among some of the barons—and I don't even know which ones. Only one name has come up for certain: Roger of Aurverelle. He holds the lands just to the north of the Towns. If I made a fuss about this now, I might be branded a daft old man.'' Thomas rubbed his beard. ''And that might be true.''

''Hardly.''

Thomas looked sad as he returned to his chair and picked up his knife. ''The old ways are dying, George. We seem to be entering into a period of . . . what? Hopelessness? The Church has become secular, the nobility has forsaken its duty of protecting the lower classes, the Elves have been persecuted into near extinction—and I could be burned for saying that. Now France and England have been at war for over a decade.'' He sighed. ''It looks like dark days ahead. And what place does an old traditionalist like myself have in them? Soon I'll be joining my Judith, and I hope the Lord will judge me mercifully for my stubbornness.''

The horn was still sounding outside. George looked at the window.

''I hope she got away,'' he said softly.

Miriam was facedown in the street when she came to herself, lying inches from a deep puddle of dirty water. The rain had pattered on, and she was soaked, chilled, and certain that a fever would find her soon. In the distance, a horn was blowing, and a monotonous clanging told her that the Chateau had been roused, that guards were on their way, that she would soon be a prisoner once more.

No. Never.

Healing the fat man had sapped her strength. She should not have stopped for him, but she did not wield her power: it wielded her. It had thwarted her life, brought her to the point of death, threatened to destroy her small chance of escape. Ironically, it could do nothing about her own wounds.

Voices in the distance. Fear drove her to her feet and

through the rain. The gate was ahead, but how to pass the guards? And what to do once she was out, anyway?

The sound of horn and gong grew louder, mixed with the cries of many men. Doors were being pounded upon, householders questioned, women and men driven into the street while their belongings were searched. Miriam heard a scream in the distance, followed by a cry of pain.

"Pain?" she mumbled. "It is pain you have? Bitch, you don't know what pain is."

The alarm had reached the guards at the gate, and as Miriam fell into the shadows of a rubbish heap, the soldiers came running out of the gatehouse to meet their comrades. She lay in the dark, unnoticed, as they passed her by.

She stared fuzzily at the gatehouse. Had they all left? Was the gate, for the moment, unattended? In what kind of jest did a mocking God dangle this hope before her?

She tottered down the street clutching the fat man's cloak about her. Her purse was heavy, the wet cloak heavier still. The glare of torches blinded her failing sight, and she had to feel her way up to the portcullis bars that prevented entry . . . or exit. The iron was rusty and scraped her fingers as she sought in vain for a latch. Then she remembered: it took two men to turn the large wheel that raised the grating.

Voices. Horns. Gongs. Screams.

Expecting at any moment to feel hands upon her, she groped at the portcullis, searching for a way out. She had little time. The men were returning. She could hear them, booted feet on cobblestones, harsh voices.

She stuck her head through one of the openings, wishing that she could simply squeeze through like the child that everyone always called her—when they did not call her witch. It was not until her shoulder slid through the iron lattice that she realized she *could.* She was a small, thin woman, and starvation and ill use had made her thinner yet. The portcullis had been designed to bar full-sized adults and armed men: it would not hold her. Working quickly and desperately, she untied her purse and pushed it through another opening, pulled off the cloak, and dragged herself through the bars. She thought for a moment to leave the cloak, but then turned and drew it after her. The heavy fabric came reluctantly at first, then loosed itself and tumbled her to the ground in a small heap of cloth and blood.

She lay stunned, but she could not afford to remain where she was. Crawling, dragging herself, she made her way out of the range of the gatehouse torches, down into the ditch that bordered the road.

You'll never take me alive again. The thought hammered at her. *Never.* She continued crawling, half-unconscious, half-blind, cold and wet, but free.

Chapter Two

Miriam's hands were sore. She did not recall that the torturer had touched her hands, but they were sore, and sticky with her blood. Maybe the gate . . . Gate? Of the keep? Of the city? She could not quite remember. Lying half in, half out of the slimy water of a ditch, she came to consciousness slowly, realized that it was morning, that the rain had stopped.

The sky was a cold blue, and the chill wind blowing from the west made the gray weeds at the edge of the ditch tremble. Miriam pulled herself up to the level of the road, grimacing as the effort opened the wounds in her legs and rubbed mud into her inexplicably raw hands.

She parted the weeds and peered up and down the road. Where was Hypprux? For that matter, where was anything? The road stretched, empty and bare, in both directions, and there was not a sign of a dwelling, much less of a city. The land was open and rolling, patched with small stands of trees that lifted bare branches into the warmthless sunlight, but covered mainly by the dry, matted grass of winter pastureland.

Surprise numbed her pain for a moment. She looked at her hands. "How far did I come?" she wondered aloud. "Did I crawl all night?"

High above, a crow called as it balanced on a tenuous updraft.

Miriam looked up, shading her eyes. "Go away," she said. "I'm not dead. Bad luck for you." She had been propped on her elbows, but now her strength failed again and she collapsed. She guessed that she must be hungry, though that sensation was buried by the pain in her legs. That was probably for the best: she had no food, and little hope of getting any. She wondered if she was thirsty also. No way of telling. She might have prayed, but enough had been done to her in the name of religion that she had no intention of looking to God for anything save a chance to spit in His face.

A flapping of wings. The crow alighted a few feet from her face, stalked over, and peered into her eyes.

"Go away, dammit," she snarled. "You'll have to wait."

The bird clucked at her and shook its head, then quietly began nosing about among the stones and mud. Miriam heard the creak of wagon wheels.

She had to move again, but her limbs, tortured and torn, fatigued beyond their tolerance, would not respond. She struggled, but she could do no more than rock back and forth in the mud. Flies buzzed about her ears, attracted by her blood. She could not even turn her head to the wagon's approach.

The wheels came closer. The crow flew up, crying harshly. The wagon stopped.

"Dear God." It was a woman's voice. In a moment, gentle hands were on her and a matronly face came into view. "Oh, dear God. You poor child . . ."

"I'm not a child," she managed. "I'm eighteen. I'm not a child."

The woman held a flask to Miriam's lips. "Drink. You'll be all right now. You're safe."

Miriam looked at her incredulously. But she drank.

"My name is Mika," said the woman. "I'll take care of you. I'm traveling toward my home, south of Furze, and I'll take you with me. You'll be safe there."

"Don't be stupid."

Mika seemed unperturbed, as though she were used to the blunt responses of the injured. "I can guess who you are, child. Hypprux is buzzing with the story of your escape. But the soldiers think you're still in the city, and they're not searching the roads yet. It's a miracle you made it this far. You must have crawled all night. We're three leagues from the city, and you're almost dead."

"Why don't I just get it over with, then?"

"Hush, child." Mika lifted Miriam easily and put her in the small cart. A shaggy red pony eyed her curiously.

"Come, Esau," Mika called as she took the reins. "Let's take this little one somewhere where I can tend her wounds. Find us dry ground and sweet water."

Miriam lay amid sacks and cushions. The sunlight felt warm now that she was out of the wind, and the fat man's dark green cloak began to dry with an odor of wet wool. Fatigue reduced the pain in her legs to a dull ache.

She was asleep by the time Mika stopped, and did not awaken until the sun had slipped behind the Aleser Mountains and the first stars had appeared. Miriam found that she had been washed, bandaged, and dressed in dry clothes that were much too large for her. Mika had kindled a small fire. The sound of a rushing stream was in the air.

Mika heard her stir, brought her food, and helped her to sit up. Miriam looked at the gruel in the wooden bowl she had been handed. "What is this?"

Mika smiled. "Horrible stuff. Tastes awful. Eat it."

Her hands clumsy with pain and bandages, Miriam wielded the spoon with difficulty, but she managed. She would have been offended if Mika had offered to help, but the older woman did not. The gruel was not at all bad, Miriam decided. Halfway through the bowl, she asked, "Where are we?"

"About a day's journey from Hypprux," said Mika. "Ypris is about a league farther down the road, but I didn't want to risk an inn. Someone with your wounds might attract attention."

"I attract attention, anyway."

"Be easy, child."

Miriam dropped the spoon. "I'm not a child. I'm tired of being called one." She indicated her legs. "Would the Church do this to a child?" she demanded.

Mika looked at her for some time before replying. "That . . . and worse."

"Who are you, anyway? What are you doing out on the road? Are you some kind of a witch?"

Mika shook her head wearily. "I'm a midwife. I do some healing, too. I've a knack with herbs and poultices, but some plants never make it as far down as Furze or even Belroi. None of my ladies are near term this month, so I went shopping."

"Why are you helping me?"

"You're hurt."

"That's no reason." Miriam found that she was suddenly hungry. She picked up the spoon again and began shoveling the gruel down her throat. "I was hurt in the dungeon in Hypprux and no one helped me," she said between mouthfuls.

"I don't work in Hypprux. I don't work for the Church. I've watched a midwife or two burned, and I'm in some danger myself. A hazard of the trade. But if I don't attract attention, I'll survive, and so will my ladies." Esau the pony nickered, and Mika rose and went to him. From the deepening darkness outside the firclight her words came back: "You're someone who heals. That's enough for me. I don't agree with the Church when it says that anyone with gifts beyond the usual has to get them from demons." Mika came back to the fire. "Besides, you must have some good patronage: it's not every condemned woman that goes around wearing a cloak with the badges of Saint Blaise and the Free Towns on it."

The cloak was hanging on the low branches of a tree near the fire. The wool was almost dry, and embroidered at the collar with precise stitches were the blazons Mika had named. Miriam stared at them, their threads of red and blue, silver and gold flashing in the firelight. "I didn't know. I found him in the street when I was escaping. He'd broken his ankle."

Mika put an arm about her. "And in spite of your danger you healed him? A godly act."

Miriam jerked away. "God had nothing to do with it. I'd just as soon have left him in the rain. I had to heal him."

Mika looked at her, puzzled.

"Don't you understand?" said Miriam. "I've no control over my powers. If I see illness, wounds, injuries, I have to cure. I have no choice." Her hands were hurting, and she realized that she had clenched them into fists. "I tried to stop myself once. I . . . I must have fainted from the pain. People around me said that I was screaming. I . . . can't . . . live like that."

Mika stared.

"And I can't do a thing for myself. The power doesn't

affect me." Miriam looked at her bandaged hands, then at Mika. She froze. "What's that? Your arm . . . ?"

"What? I burned my arm this evening heating water for your gruel." Mika looked at the scald. "It's not serious. Don't worry."

The power flared up Miriam's spine, white-hot, like molten iron. She stiffened, teeth clenched, then stumbled toward Mika. "Give me your arm."

"Child, don't trouble yourself. It's nothing. Really. You have to rest."

"Give me your arm!" Without waiting, Miriam tore the bandages from her hands and seized the midwife's arm. The power was searing along her back, and she could almost see light somewhere behind her eyes just before it let go. There was a flash, and then the midwife was looking at her arm again, this time almost in fear.

"It's gone. The scald's gone."

Miriam wavered where she stood. The world swam about her. "Of course it's gone. It never works by half measures. I've healed plague. I've reattached severed legs. I can't do any different."

Mika reached for her with an unmarked arm. "Child."

"I'm not a child. And *don't touch me.*"

Mika drew back, startled, and Miriam toppled to the ground.

Fever found the little healer that night, and the next day she lay delirious in Mika's wagon as the midwife drove south along the road that led to Belroi and the great dairy lands. The land rolled away, spotted with trees, crossed by streams that rushed toward the River Bergren. The scent of cows and goats was strong, but Miriam stared uncomprehendingly at the sky, scrabbled among the blankets, and now and then whimpered when the pain in her hands and legs overcame her.

Mika was hurrying. The herbs she had with her were not adequate to stem Miriam's fever, and she could not stop for help along the way. Her supplies and her medicines were at her house, so she urged her little pony onward.

Esau found his own way down the road, and she looked over her shoulder to reassure herself that Miriam was as

well as could be expected. But something about the healer
held her gaze.

Sometimes she thought she could see into people's hearts
and catch a glimpse of what the future might hold. Times
like this made her think so, for as she looked at the little
woman whose black hair lay matted and soaked with fever
sweat, she thought she saw more: a gleam about her, and a
flash of red gold around her head. For an instant, she thought
of night skies, and of stars that shone clear and cold in the
darkness.

The vision persisted for a moment more, then faded. Mika
lifted her head. In the distance, Malvern Forest spread like
a dark cloak upon the land, stretching for many leagues to
the south and west. The dairymen of this region shunned it,
and kept their herds from it, saying it was a forest full of
magic, that Elves lived there, that it was best for God-fearing
folk to stay away. But the old tales that mentioned the Elves
also mentioned the stars, and told of a light shining about
eleven faces that was like that of moonlight and starlight
mingled.

Miriam moaned, struggled, clutched at the cloak with
bandaged hands. Mika tucked the warm wool around the
girl. The vision of the stars had faded. Miriam was once
again no more than a little, battered healer. Yet the midwife
could not help but wonder about the meaning of the vision.
The Elves? What could those terrible, immortal creatures
have to do with this girl?

A crow called overhead, and Mika shook herself out of
her thoughts. There was no time for daydreaming. She had
to take Miriam home. Quickly.

"I'm . . ." Miriam mumbled in her delirium. Mika
urged Esau forward, but the noise of the cart wheels could
not drown out the words she had heard over and over again,
words the little healer had obviously uttered many times,
in rising pain and desperation: "I'm not a witch. I don't
know anything. I healed them, that's all. I can't help it. I
have black eyes. I have black hair. I don't know anything.
Please . . ."

George Darci, mayor of Saint Blaise, waited in the ves-
tibule while the serving girl climbed the stairs to the upper

floor. The words of Thomas a'Verne had wrung his thoughts for two days. There was not much to fight against at present, only whispered words and meetings that the participants—churchman and baron—described as merely "informal." He did not have much hope that this visit would achieve anything, but he was determined to try.

The top panel of the front door was open and let in the sounds of the street, the February crop of flies, and the dust. "Pies," came the call. "I have good pies."

"Karl of the Green Man Inn has opened a cask of this wine. Whoever wants to buy come along please!"

"Pasties!"

George waited. Pies, wine, pasties. The bells had rung sext. Time for food. He was hungry, and his head ached with worry. But he waited.

The girl came back down the stairs. "M'lord will see you, sir."

George followed her back up the stairs and entered the study of Paul delMari, tenth baron of his house. Though he was the same age as George, he looked older, and he had a chronic tic over his right eye. A half-empty decanter of wine stood at a nearby table, along with an untouched plate of lunch.

Paul rose, took George's hand. "I haven't seen you in some time, George. What has it been? Ah . . . ten years?"

"More like fifteen. I have a lot to occupy me in Saint Blaise."

Paul waved him toward a seat. "Quiet life and peaceful nights, I should say," said Paul. "I should like something like that to occupy me for a while."

George smiled. "I rather do feel like the country mouse here in Hypprux." He was watching the baron. *He's nervous. He doesn't want me here.*

Paul poured himself a cup of wine, offered some to George, who politely declined. Wine on an empty stomach would be a mistake. "Oh, we're busy here. Very busy. Running about and getting nowhere. How is the family?"

George told Paul a little, recounted bits of news. Janet's birth. The Two-Score-and-Five Fair. Anne's illness. He spoke to fill the void and to entertain Paul, no more. The real business would come soon enough. George had never before called upon the bond that linked him to Paul del-Mari, and he wondered if what he wanted might not strain the link beyond breaking.

"So all in all," the mayor concluded, "life goes on in Saint Blaise . . . in the Free Towns as a whole, I should say."

"Good . . . good . . ." Paul fidgeted.

Several moments of uneasy silence. George coughed. Paul poured another cup of wine and downed it. George rose and strolled to the window that overlooked the street.

"Pies! Come buy my pies!"

"Karl of the . . ."

George turned around. "Trade between the Towns and the northern cities has been increasing steadily. At the century fair in Maris, our people accounted for at least one-quarter of the taxes to the city. Free Town goods are popular in the north."

"It's easy enough to see why." Paul rubbed at his tic. "The quality is excellent. Your guilds are fair. They provide good training and good standards."

"They've been left alone to work as they see fit," George said simply. "Their pride spurs them to perfection."

Paul laughed dryly. "That, and the fact that every artisan in Adria that's worth anything flees to the Towns."

George shrugged and returned to the street scene. "Freedom . . ."

"Somewhat dangerous freedom . . ."

"Pies! I have pies!"

George went back to his seat. "You have to admit, Paul, that it's producing good results."

"Still, each man has his place in God's plan," said Paul. "And the Free Towns disturb the balance. You know that, George. It's only a matter of time before—" He stopped short, stared straight ahead for a moment, then appeared to find something wrong with the buckle of his belt.

"Before what, Paul?" George waited, watching.

Paul said nothing for some time. Finally: "Before God's plan becomes manifest."

"That wasn't what you were going to say originally."

Paul poured more wine. "I don't know what you have in mind, George."

George sighed. It was time. "We're milk brothers, Paul. We sucked the same breast when we were little ones. We played together in the streets of Hypprux, and later on, you stood beside me when I married Anne. Now I need to ask you some questions. About the Free Towns."

"I'm sure you know infinitely more about the Free Towns than I, George."

"On the contrary. When the name Aloysius Cranby comes up, my knowledge fails."

"The bishop? What—"

"Come now, Paul. I've heard that Cranby has some interest in the Free Towns. I have some interest in them also. What can you tell me?"

Paul mopped his forehead with his free hand, though it was not at all warm in the room. "There's been some talk."

"That's what everyone tells me," said George. "I had hoped for more from you."

"Well, that's all there is," said Paul. "Talk. Don't blame me for such things. You're the ones that are getting involved in heresy."

"Heresy?"

"Dealings with the Elves. My God, George, what are you doing down there? Jaques Alban disappeared, and now everyone hears stories about you and some Elf in the woods, and about odd dealings down in Saint Brigid. What can you expect? Why do you have to go and bother the Immortals? Haven't they given us enough trouble?"

"I hadn't heard that the Elves had been any trouble at all," said George evenly. "On the contrary. It's the Church and the baronage that have given the Elves the problems."

"Don't talk that way, George. They're demons."

"Horse shit."

"Well, you can horse-shit your way right out of the Free Towns, then." Paul nearly shouted. He caught himself. When he spoke again, his tone was normal. "Cranby is talking to the council one by one. He's feeling for support. There's been no action, nor any talk of action."

"How are the barons reacting?"

"Some moderately favor the idea of a crusade and annexation, but you know as well as I that favoring an idea and favoring the Church with men and horses are two different things."

"Do they really think there's heresy in the Free Towns?"

"Not at all. Their interest is purely economic." His tone was a little too casual. "The Free Towns are wealthy, productive, and the land is fertile. A plum ripe for the picking, but a plum fenced in by thorns. You people in the Free Towns fought like devils when you threw out Baron David a'Freux, and the barons will weigh the value of the Free Towns against what it might take to win them. I'm sure they will decide against Cranby's plan for that reason."

"What about the fact that the Church is active in this?"

"Oh, well, the Church . . . you know . . ."

"I don't know. Could it be that the idea of spiritual sanctions by the Church has never crossed the minds of the barons?"

"I . . . suppose such a thing could raise a little more support than simple greed. We all have to die someday. I would rather not be condemned to the pit."

"And has Aloysius Cranby spoken to you, Paul?"

Paul looked at George, said nothing. After a while, the baron dropped his eyes and studied the parquetry floor.

"Paul? How do you stand in this?"

"I have no desire for annexation. . . ."

"But?" George did not consider himself an imposing figure. He was plump, round-faced, altogether too jolly looking to inspire fear or respect. But he tried. He stood, drew himself up straight. "But?"

Paul raised his eyes, but could not look directly at George. "I . . . I have to think of my soul," he said. "I'm a good Christian. If I protested, I could be condemned myself. My wife . . . my children . . ." He fell silent, licked his lips.

George rubbed his face. His headache had grown worse. "Thank you, Paul. I'll say good-bye now. I trust that our bond will be enough for you not to say anything of our talk to Bishop Cranby. Or to Roger of Aurverelle."

Paul started. "Roger of— How did you know?"

"How does anyone know anything in this damned city?" George snapped. "The wind . . . the dogs . . . the farting of birds . . . Suffice to say that I know. All right?"

"I won't say anything," said Paul. "It would be dangerous for me to admit that I even met with you at all."

"Good. Thank you. God be with you, Paul." George
bowed without shaking hands, found his own way down the
stairs and out into the street.

"Pasties! Good hot pasties!"

He was not hungry.

Chapter Three

"What's this?"

The soldier leaned over the side of the cart. Mika turned around and nearly gasped: she had thought Miriam completely hidden, but the healer had obviously thrashed about enough that her coverings had been dislodged.

The soldier looked up inquiringly. The cold wind caught the red scarf about his neck and whipped it out straight. Belroi glittered in the bright, morning sun, and the waters of River Malvern were deep and cold.

"My daughter," explained the midwife. "She's been ill."

"Sure." The soldier glanced at Miriam again. "Doesn't look a thing like you."

"She took after her father."

"Sure." The man did not look so much suspicious as lecherous.

Mika sat up in her seat. Prostituting an injured girl for a ride across the river was not what she had in mind this morning. "Is there some problem, m'lord?" She addressed him in the tone of a mother, with an edge to the rising inflection.

"No problem at all, unless you want to make one." He sounded unimpressed. "You're just two women and you got no men with you. Now, I'm a man who could use a little comfort this cold morning. Do you want to get across this river?"

His words were not without threat: Belroi lay on a tongue of land south of the juncture of two great rivers, Malvern and Bergren, and its ferry was the only crossing for several leagues. To the south of Belroi was open land, and another day's journey to Furze, where Mika kept her house. But first the river had to be crossed.

"Of course I want to get across this river," said the midwife tartly. "I have a sick daughter, and she needs to come home and be tended. I've given you the three-penny toll, and you have no reason to keep us from our journey."

The soldier looked at Miriam again. "Scrawny," he said with some distaste.

"Consumption does that to people."

The man blinked. "Consumption?" He looked a little shaken.

"Yes," said Mika. "We were visiting our folk around Lake Onella, and the air of the marshes is not good. The fog comes up at night."

His mouth tightened. "I was born near Lake Onella," he said flatly. "There aren't any marshes there."

Mother of Mercy, thought Mika. Just let us over. "What do you want?"

"Wake her up."

"She's ill."

"Consumption, eh?"

Behind Mika, a dark man with a cartful of geese shouted angrily: "Will you hurry up? I have a market to get to!"

The soldier looked at him. "You won't get to anything quick if you don't shut up." He turned back to Mika. "Wake her up."

Miriam stirred.

"I'll report you," said Mika. She felt sick. There was nothing she could do. The soldier was correct: two commoner women without patronage or defense had no recourse. She could cause a commotion, but it would do no more than call attention to Miriam. But the thought of what the soldier had in mind . . . "This is barbarous—"

"So it's barbarous. So report me."

"Give . . ." Miriam fumbled under the blankets, her teeth clenched in pain. "Give him this." Mika realized that she was hunting for her purse.

Reaching down to the bag that still bulged with George's gratitude, Mika came up with two gold florins, each stamped with the ensign of Saint Blaise. She put them into the hand of the soldier. "Enough? May we cross?"

"Lady, you just bought me ten girls, all prettier than your

daughter. Or whatever she is.'' He laughed and waved Mika and her cart onto the ferry. ''Pass.''

Mika urged Esau onto the wooden deck. ''Pass yourself, you devil,'' she muttered. ''You'll have a fine time explaining how you came by that much Free Town money.'' Miriam had opened her eyes. ''It's all right, child,'' said the midwife. ''You're safe.''

''I'm not . . . a child.'' Miriam shuddered, then lay still, her face buried in George's cloak. Her head swam, and the rocking of the ferry in the swift stream did not help, but she was aware of the slap of waves against the pier, the call of ducks, the cries of fishermen and rivermen. She was aware, too, of what the soldier had wanted, and of Mika's attempts to thwart him. Anyone else, she thought, would have given her up, glad to be rid of her. But Mika . . . not Mika . . .

She summoned her strength and managed to roll over. She saw the upper stories of houses, painted balconies, windows. The air was damp, but the buildings shielded the streets from the wind, and the sun was warming the town a little. Maybe spring would come after all.

''Where are we?'' she managed, her voice hoarse with three days of fever.

''Belroi,'' said Mika. ''Another day and we'll be home.''

''I heard you back at the ferry. Thank you.'' She said the words with an effort. Thanks were not something she had occasion to tender very often in her life. *What does she want? She must want something.*

The cart rattled along the cobbled streets. ''How do you feel?''

Miriam heard the passage and talk of many people: men and women, the voices of street vendors, the screams of playing children. ''My legs hurt.''

''The fever must be abating. I found wormwood day before last. You were beyond feeling any pain in your legs by then, I'll tell you.''

''Is that what I'm tasting? It's awful. . . .''

''Hmmm.'' Mika took a turning and breathed easier when the south gate came into view. ''Odd. You didn't complain when I forced it down your throat that night. Lie still and sleep. You need to rest.''

Miriam did not reply, but she did not sleep, either. She watched the buildings pass, saw the immense bulk of the cathedral that lifted marble pinnacles toward heaven, saw, at last, the roof of the gatehouse pass over her.

Then they were out on the open road again, the stray houses and outbuildings of the great dairy city thinning quickly into pasture land. Miriam watched the sky and the wheeling crows for some time, lifted a bandaged hand and rubbed her face.

"What do you want, Mika?" she asked.

The midwife was not flustered by the question. "You," she said. "Alive."

"Why?"

"We've been over that before."

"Christian charity isn't a reason."

"Reasons can be as plentiful as blackberries and mean even less. Why must I have a reason?"

"Because . . ." Miriam pushed herself up, frowning at the pain in her hands. "That soldier back at the ferry wanted me. Those people I saw on their balconies want their fine houses and their rich clothes. The local bishop wants his big cathedral. Sinner, saint, pope, prince: everyone wants something. And you're no different. So don't say otherwise."

Mika allowed Esau to find his own pace. The shaggy little pony plodded on. Miriam looked out at the bare landscape: stripped trees, dry grass. "What about you?" said the midwife. "What do you want?"

"Who cares?"

"I care."

Miriam said nothing for some time. The wagon creaked and Esau snorted, and those were the only sounds. The land was open and bare, stretching from nowhere to nowhere and back again. If her life were a landscape, this was it. Eight years before, she had stumbled through the streets of Maris, ten years old and homeless, her eyes nearly swollen shut from tears. She had stopped crying, but that was the only change.

"I want . . . I want people to leave me alone." The emptiness of the pastures suddenly frightened her. Was that all? Was that her life? Her tongue loosened. "I want to be able to walk into a marketplace and not worry that the Church is going to drag me off before I can say an Ave Maria. I want a . . . a home. I want a mother who won't throw me out of the house because I can heal like I do. I want . . ." The fever must have weakened her, because she felt her throat constricting. There was dampness in her eyes, but she fought the emotion down.

"Those are good things to want," said Mika. "I can't supply freedom from the Church or from other people, and I can't change the past, but I can supply a home. Will that be sufficient?"

"You're still not telling me why?"

"Do I have to? Well then, let this be my reason: when I found you by the side of the road you were bloody and broken and wet, and you look about thirteen, which is how old my Esther was when they dragged her from the river . . . bloody and broken . . . and . . . wet . . . except that you're alive and she—"

Miriam could feel that the midwife was weeping. "I'm not your daughter," she said.

"That's not the point," said Mika softly. "I couldn't save her. But I could save you. I do what I can."

"I won't be able to stay with you."

"As long as you like, child."

Miriam flared. "I'm not a child, dammit."

Mika looked over her shoulder. "I don't know what else to call you," she said. "You never told me your name."

Miriam saw kindness in her eyes and wished that she could acknowledge it, but her heart had grown cold, as though the iron of the blades that had torn her legs had imparted something of themselves to it. She looked away quickly, back at the landscape, and noticed that it was not totally empty: there were trees, low shrubs, even an occasional house. And to the west was the dark forest of Malvern, and beyond that the mountains.

"My name is Miriam," she said.

Miriam said little more the rest of the day. Toward evening, they came in sight of Furze, but Mika was still unwilling to risk an inn, and they spent a third night by the side of the road. Miriam fell asleep over a supper of gruel and a little salt meat. The weather was cold, but the dark green cloak was warm.

Mika's house was set back a distance from the road, overlooked by two tall oak trees, and surrounded by well-tended gardens. Winter was not yet done, but there were green shoots poking up and even a spot of color here and there at the borders where an optimistic crocus was blooming. The house itself was good and sturdy, of woven willow carefully plastered with mud. The crucks supporting the roof were tall and straight, and the thatch had recently been beaten in.

Mika helped Miriam to the door and began loosing the latch fastening. "Jeanne has been here today," she said. "Smell the straw? I told her I'd be home. She's always doing things like that for others." She swung open the door to reveal a clean, well-kept room. There was fresh litter and herbs on the earth floor, and the fire on the hearth had been carefully banked.

Miriam smelled something else, too. "Fresh bread! Who is Jeanne? A neighbor?"

Mika put some cushions by the fire and made Miriam comfortable while she talked. "A neighbor, yes. Her sister is due in another month or so, and Jeanne is helping her." She straightened, hands on hips, and surveyed the house. "And taking care of her midwife, too, I see. Here, ch— Miriam, have some bread, and I'll be back as soon as I've seen to Esau." She put the basket of fragrant loaves by the small woman and went back out into the yard. Miriam heard the creak of the cart and the whinny of the pony as he was unharnessed and led away to a full manger.

She was hungry, but she left the bread untouched and stood up, blanket clutched around her shoulders. The house was like any other—hearth and kitchen, barrel and bench— and as such could not but remind her of the home she had left eight years ago. She did not remember it very well: it was no more than a vague recollection of a kinder time. But she did not require specific memories, for to describe it she needed only to enumerate those things that she wanted and did not have. Safety. Continuity. Surety. Company. And— if she dared even think of such a thing—love.

Still wobbly, Miriam moved about the house, peering at

walls, hangings. Smoked hams dangled from the kitchen beams, and the pantry was stocked not only with roots and sacks of grain but (yes, Jeanne had been here, too) with apples fresh out of storage, wrinkled but sweet, and a large Bergren cheese. One wall was all shelves crammed with pots and jars capped with parchment and leather, each neatly labeled in a firm, even hand. Miriam squinted at the letters for a moment. She could not read, but she guessed that they were Mika's medicines.

The idea of resorting to herbs and infusions seemed strange to her. She had always been able to heal by a touch. For a moment, she smiled wryly. If she had used herbs, if she had only clumsy and inconsistent methods with which to work, she would not be hunted, her legs would be unmarked, and she would have to worry far less about winding up at the stake. As it was, her gift demanded no effort, on her part or that of the sick, and the cure was instantaneous. Such efficiency was not rewarded.

She sat down on a stool, bandaged hands to her face. She could not hope. She had given up hoping. Oh, she might hide for a time, but before long her reputation would spread—as it always did—and the Church would hear about her. Aloysius Cranby would arrive with his court and his questions, and she would be taken . . . back to Hypprux . . . .

She cried out involuntarily, wishing she could kill a certain churchman.

Don't hope, Miriam. Just survive.

"Miriam?" Mika stood in the doorway.

"I was just remembering something."

"The Chateau?"

She shrugged. "And Bishop Cranby."

Mika closed the door, went to the hearth, and stirred up the fire. "I meant what I said on the road. You're safe here. You can stay."

"And you want to train me as a midwife."

Under Mika's hand, the flames quickened, stirred, crackled among the dry sticks. "If you'd like that," she said. "My last apprentice went off to Belroi with a new husband before the snows came."

"It won't work."

"What makes you so sure of that?" Mika opened the pantry door and smiled. "That Jeanne." She took out the apples and the cheese and began slicing them.

"I told you: I can't control my power. If I see any illness, I have to cure it. Don't you understand? I have no choice. People talk."

"Not if they love you."

"Don't talk to me about love." Miriam pulled at her bandages, examined the raw skin of her hands, wrinkled her nose. "People can't love someone who does miracles."

"They can love someone who heals."

"There's a difference. A big one."

Mika let the argument hang. "Do you want to study midwifery?"

Miriam stood, made her way back to the cushions by the fire, accepted a plate of bread and cheese from Mika. "I'll do what I have to to earn my keep." Hopes and fantasies swam in her mind. She shoved them down with an effort. "Will that be enough?"

Mika smiled softly. "I suppose it will have to do." She sounded disappointed. "I suppose it would be difficult to train a porcupine as a midwife."

There was hurt in the midwife's voice. Miriam paused with a piece of cheese in her hand. She had hardly said one kind word to the woman who had picked her up from the road, cared for her, nursed her, and taken her into her house. "I'm sorry, Mika. I'm not used to this. Maybe I should just go my own way. You shouldn't be so burdened."

Mika sat beside her. There was a hint of a tear in the corner of her eye, and her face looked lined and sad. "Child," she said, and silenced Miriam's objection with a glance. "You need rest, and healing. And I'm afraid your heart needs healing, too; but I don't know how to help you there. Maybe someday, somewhere . . ." She looked past Miriam, as though she were remembering something. "Maybe you'll find an ending. But for now, listen to your midwife: don't make any decisions until you're well. There will be time enough for decisions later on."

There was a lump in Miriam's throat. "Please," she said. "Can I lie down?"

Without comment, Mika fixed a pallet for her in the corner, close enough to the fire for warmth, but far enough away for privacy. Miriam curled up under the comforter. Hands to her face, she shuddered, muffling her sobs in the thick dressings around her palms and fingers.

After a while, she slept, and Mika silently replaced the bandages that Miriam had soaked with her tears.

Chapter Four

To His Holiness, the Most Gracious Holy Father Clement VI, from his obedient servant Aloysius Cranby, Bishop of Hypprux, *benedicite*:

As we enter into the Lenten season, renouncing worldly pleasure and frivolity so as to comprehend better the Mystery of Our Savior's death and resurrection, the people of the city of Hypprux and the land of Adria extend their heartfelt wishes for Your Holiness's continued good health, and their thanks for Your Holiness's wise and just rule.

In the letter that Your Holiness sent to me last autumn, I was requested to provide an account of my see (given unto my care by my friend, and Your Holiness's predecessor, Benedict) with regard to a most evil and pernicious heresy that has taken root here. In these grave days, we of Holy Mother Church are much assailed by Satan, as is evidenced by the spread of heretical beliefs. My friend, Jaques Fournier, (who later graced the Throne of Peter as Benedict XII) well distinguished himself in eradicating the despised Cathars in the Pyrenees: and I can but hope in my own way to carry on his work.

In this land of Adria, which my friend Benedict XII gave into my care when he raised me to the rank of bishop, I have found heresy of two sorts: ordinary and extraordinary. That is, beliefs and practices brought about by Satan's penetration into the hearts and minds of common people, and those brought about by Satan and his representatives manifesting in material form. In describing this latter evil I am, of course, referring to those demons whom the vulgar call the Elves.

Of ordinary heresy, much has been written, argued, and accomplished, both in Adria and in other parts of Europe. Holy Mother Church has done much to differentiate between those sects devoted solely to the greater glory of God (such as the Minorite Friars and the Franciscans) and those in service of the Great Enemy. By the grace of God, Catharism is no more. The notorious Knights Templar are dead. Unfortunately, the Fraticelli, the Spirituals, and the abominable Beghards still persist from year to year.

I have fought these latter heresies in Adria, and have, to a great extent, succeeded in extirpating them. News has reached me that there are some small villages deep in the Aleser Mountains where the Fraticelli still find refuge, but I am confident, Holy Father, that their days are numbered.

But as it grieves me to speak of such evils, it grieves me even more to speak of the extraordinary heresy brought by the Elves. You asked me to enumerate, Holy Father, the nature of this heresy, and to tell you something of its beliefs, so that God's truth may be better known by its contrast to such lies and abominations.

The Elves are still with us, and though their race declines, they are yet capable of leading God's children astray with their magic and their voices, for it is rightly said that an Elf can confuse black and white merely by speaking of them, so subtle and devious is that pernicious race of forest-dwelling demons.

Of the preaching of the Elves I can enumerate many errors. I have painstakingly collected numerous reports, gathered from the far corners of Adria, in order to present a list of their lies. Such information is difficult to come by, for there are few who will admit to hearing the Elves preach, and such information as I have comes only after intense and rigorous questioning. Although their errors are legion, there are five main heresies of which they are guilty:

1. The Elves deny the existence of evil in the world. They cunningly attempt to disguise their service to Satan by stating that he does not exist, that he is but a fancy invented by Holy Church so as to terrify people and make them subject to her will. As to what reasons exist for death and misfortune, they are silent.

2. The Elves deny the finitude of the material world. They preach against belief in the Last Judgment. They deny also the omnipotence of God, saying that He is by nature limited. Thus do these demons turn the uni-

verse upside down: the world will go on forever, but
God, the Creator of that world, will not.

3. They revere women, and treat them with respect,
ascribing various noble virtues to the daughters of Eve,
thus more easily to ensnare our women and make them
subject to their inhuman wills. For woman is ever
ready to listen to sweet lies, being by nature weaker
and more susceptible to error and to the lusts of the
flesh, and so do the Elves and devils corrupt even the
most seemingly chaste women.

4. They deny the sinfulness of the material world in
general and of fornication in particular, holding that
what is natural to the body cannot be evil.

5. It is well-known that the Elves worship a woman,
consummating their rites in obscene blasphemies.
Furthermore, they claim that this woman-god of theirs
is tangible, and that she can be perceived by the be-
liever directly, before death, and that this perception
can be constant and joyful.

Such are the errors promulgated by the Elves that
the greater truth of Holy Mother Church might shine
more brightly. I trust that Your Holiness will approve
of my most rigorous actions against these foul beliefs
as did Your Holiness's predecessor, Benedict. Therefore, in Christian love and charity, and in the fraternal
spirt of our Most Holy Mother the Church, I wish
Your Holiness a blessed Easter and do humbly request
that Bartholomew of Onella, the good cleric who bears
this missive, be treated well and sent back to me as
soon as Your Holiness deems it fit.

Dated this Twenty-Eighth day of the month of February, in the Year of Our Lord 1350.

The weather slowly turned warmer. By the beginning of
Lent the clouds were dropping what was definitely rain; and,
come mid-March, the sun was melting even the stubborn
snow to the north of Mika's house.

Miriam was still mending. While she insisted on her share
of the housework, she spent the lengthening afternoons on
the split-log bench by the west wall of the house, warming
herself in the sun, watching the lower slopes of the Aleser
Mountains shake off their white coats while Malvern Forest
took on hues of soft green. The heat soothed her aching

joints, and Mika's ointments faded the deep wounds on her legs to a network of reddened welts.

Mika was often away, for her skill in midwifery was such that she was in great demand in the houses of both rich and poor. Miriam learned that the good midwife had been granted a monthly stipend from the local overlord, Paul delMari; but when Miriam had mentioned it, Mika laughed. "Baron Paul thinks he can buy everyone," she said. "Furze is big enough for me, but if he wants to pay me to live here, I won't complain. Nor will my ladies." She chuckled again. "Nor will his. What a fine big boy she had last week!"

But Furze was half a league away, and when Mika was gone, the house was quiet and still, the only sound that of the wind in the branches of the oak trees. The crocuses were blooming fiercely. The daffodils were up, and the tulips also. Miriam sat amid a torrent of color, lapped in a comforter, and it seemed that here, in a little hamlet south of Furze, she had found an end to her fears.

For a time. She reminded herself of that. For a time.

But for now here were flowers, and a bright sun, and a blue sky. The neighbors, bluff, earthy people who had little to do with formality, accepted her within a week, and it was not unusual for Jeanne or Agnes or even Robert or Charles to stop at the door and ask after her, the women more often than not bringing something to eat for Mika's little cousin, the men bowing, their hoes or shovels or picks over their shoulders and their voices rough but friendly.

Miriam spoke politely in return, and she even learned not to start in fear at a knock on the door. But she usually kept her eyes averted as much from an instinctive aversion to forming attachments as from a real and immediate fear that she would see something—a cut, a bruise, a skin infection— anything that would awaken her slumbering power and send it climbing up her spine in a rush of white heat. Then these same neighbors would shun her and talk among themselves about the horror that had come to dwell among them. And word would spread, widening like the ripples left by the leap of a fish, until it reached Hypprux, and Cranby, and the Inquisition.

It can't last.

She drowsed in the warming sun, bits and pieces of her

imprisonment drifting into her thoughts and startling her out
of sleep: the soldiers, impassive; the torturer, grim and tac-
iturn; Aloysius Cranby, passionate, ironic, and insinuating
by turns.

Elves? She knew nothing about Elves. She healed, that
was all. There was nothing else. What did Elves have to do
with it? They lived in Malvern Forest, sheltered from the
same persecuting Church that captured and tortured small
healer girls. Elves?

If Aloysius Cranby wanted information about the Elves,
he should ask someone from the Free Towns. Certainly the
bishop had heard the same stories as she. The mayor of
Saint Blaise, it was said, went out and danced with the Immortals on Midsummer Eve, and there was even a rumor
that elven magic had turned a particularly troublesome priest
into a pig. One could hear about it any market day in the
square. Why did Cranby have to bother her?

"Let that bitch's whelp deal with the Free Towns," she
muttered, shoving the memories down. "Then he can leave
me alone." She closed her eyes only to be awakened a short
time later by a gruff voice calling her name.

She cried out, flailing with her arms for a moment, but it
was only Robert, husband of Jeanne's sister, Clare. "I'm
sorry, Miriam," he said as she gathered the comforter about
herself. "Din't mean to scare you."

"It's all right, Robert. Is there something wrong?"

"It's Clare sent me over to see Mika. Her water broke
last night but she han't started labor. She's still dropsied,
too. The herbs han't helped much."

"Mika's out with Petronella," said Miriam. "It's her first.
It'll take a while. I'll send Mika over when she returns."

"I'm worried."

"Clare will be fine," said Miriam, though she did not
know much about the woman who had been in last-month
confinement since Miriam had come to Mika's house.

Robert wrung his cap in his hands. "She's late, she's
dropsied, she's han a headache for the last week, and her
water . . ." He fell silent, almost embarrassed.

"What about her water?" Miriam felt the barest stirrings
of heat along her spine.

" 'Twas green and slimy," Robert blurted out. "Like pea

soup. Not clear like Mika said it would be. Flecks of black in't, too.''

The heat stirred a little more. Miriam tried to ignore it. "I'll send Mika over right away."

"Thank'ee," said Robert. He turned away, still wringing his cap, the broad back of his tunic streaked with sweat and dirt. Miriam watched him go, and the heat in her spine faded. Probably no more than the comforter and the sun, she decided.

But she did not go back to sleep. The water green? Flecks of black? Mika had talked a little about midwifery, and as far as Miriam knew, such symptoms meant trouble. For a moment, she wished that she had accepted Mika's offer of training. She could go and see Clare and maybe bring aid of some sort . . . .

She stood up, arms folded and pressed to her belly as if to shield her from the thoughts. Training? Aid? Was she some kind of a fool? When Mika's training failed, would she then reach out with preternatural abilities and cure, regardless of the consequences? And when word got back to Cranby, would she then cheerfully climb up on the rack, stick her legs once more into the clamps, skip blithely down the street to the stake?

You'll have to handle it yourself, Clare. God—or whoever—be with you. I'll tell Mika. It can't last. It never lasts, but I'll hold out as long as I can.

Mika returned in the evening. The sun has already dropped below the mountains. Venus glittered in the west.

The midwife looked tired. The silver in her dark braids seemed more prominent than usual, the lines in her face deeper. Miriam noticed that her hands were shaking as she sliced cheese and smoked meat. "You needn't tell me about Clare," she said. "I stopped on the way home."

"How is she?"

"It's hard to tell. There's danger anytime the water breaks and the baby doesn't follow after. But Clare's late, too." She filled a cup with cider and sat down on the padded lid of a clothes chest. "So the labor will be a long one. But the water was green with black in it. It means the baby's not happy there in her belly. And the dropsy. And now she's been with headache.''

"What does it mean?" Miriam felt, again, the slightest flash of heat up her spine.

Mika shrugged. "Can't say for sure. Clare might start tomorrow morning and have no problems at all. Then again, all this might be adding up to . . . I don't know. Anything." Mika was staring at the shuttered window where the last vestiges of twilight shone through the cracks. A tear trickled down her cheek.

"Mika?" Miriam was alarmed. "Did—"

"I lost Petronella's girl. She was breech, and the cord was tangled. I . . . just couldn't get the child out in time. Oh . . . the sweet little thing. A face like her mother's." Mika put her own face in her hands.

Miriam was beside her in a moment, ignoring the pains in her joints. "Mika . . ." She stopped, unable to say a word. Eight years of bitterness filled her mouth with sand. Babies died. Of course they did. So did adults. So did healers. What difference did it make?

But Mika's shoulders were shaking, and Miriam knew that to some, it did indeed make a difference. There were those in the world who, like Aloysius Cranby, took life; and there were those who, like Mika, desired to give it, who reached out to the ill, the old, the newborn to find at times their hands empty, their grasp not large enough, their reach just short of the goal.

"It happens, Mika," she managed.

"It does," whispered the midwife. "But I always wonder: if I'd done something different, been wiser, seen more . . . maybe . . ."

"Don't blame yourself."

"Who should I blame? God? The devil?" The midwife raised her head and blinked at the healer. "Times like these, I don't know, Miriam. Times like these, I envy you."

"Don't envy me. Just look at my legs. Don't envy me."

Mika did not seem to hear. "And now Clare seems to be having difficulty. Mother of God, be with me!"

Miriam rubbed her shoulders, made her eat and lie down. Clare's husband might come at any time for her, and she needed to be rested. When she was sure the midwife was asleep, she banked the fire, extinguished the lamps, and sat in the darkness, listening to Mika's slow, even breathing.

Crows were flying south over the roofs of Hypprux, circling about the cathedral spires, counterpointing the bells ringing terce with their croaking descants. They flitted past the weavers' guildhall, paused above the market to eye the breads and cheeses, then passed on, wings beating heavily, making toward the faint dark line of the southern horizon that was Malvern Forest.

For a moment, their shadows fell on Roger of Aurverelle's city house that stood near the walls of the Chateau, snuggling up against that seat of power as though it pressed an ear to the door of a council chamber. It stretched all the way from High Baron's Street to Trinity Street, white, new-painted, and ornamented with grotesques and with emblems of its owner's interest: a stag running from the hunter's arrow, a bear cornered by hounds, a falcon in flight, the arms of the city of Hypprux.

George Darci paused before the gate. The arms of Hypprux. Why Hypprux? Roger's lands lay to the south, adjacent to the Free Towns. He had his own arms. Why did he display those of Hypprux?

When George entered, the porter was already waiting for him. "I am sorry, Your Honor," the man said in his French accent. "The master is not in today."

George pressed his lips together, fought for his temper. It was not, after all, the porter's fault. "This is the sixth time in as many weeks that your master has been unavailable," he said finally. "Tell me, my man, is he *ever* available?"

"Begging your pardon, Your Honor," said the porter. "He took it in his head to go hunting. He set off toward his lands early this morning."

George contemplated his boots. He had stayed in Hypprux too long, and the odors of the city—garbage, sewage, the omnipresent stench of the retting pools—were rank in the back of his throat. He wanted to go home, back to Saint Blaise, away from all this bowing and scraping and intrigue. He wanted to crawl into bed with Anne, laugh and giggle with her as they always did during lovemaking. Roger was gone? So much more the excuse to return to the Free Towns, talk to the burghers about the threat, take Janet out to gather flowers, and maybe—if it was not asking overmuch—see Terrill again. How long had it been? A year? Well, everybody knew Elves did not like cities.

He realized the porter was waiting for a response. "Will I be able to find your master at his estate in Aurverelle?"

"By Notre Dame I do not know, Your Honor. Sometimes the baron goes off into the forest alone for many days."

"Very well. Thank you." He started to leave, but turned again. "Why does your master display the arms of Hypprux?"

"Ah, sir," said the porter. "His half-sister married Enguerrand, Baron of Hypprux. Baron Roger is most anxious for good relations with his brother-in-law."

"Thank you," said George. "God be with you, sir." He went out to the street. Stag, bear, falcon, and the city arms. Hunting, hunting, hunting . . . and hunting.

Chapter Five

It was Robert who came for Mika, the big man standing in the doorway with the cold wind tearing at his hair. Clare had, he said solemnly, gone into labor at last.

Miriam watched as Mika took up her bundle of supplies and the pot of herbal infusion she had kept ready. "I'll be back late," said the midwife as she went toward the door.

The healer stood. "I'm . . ."

Mika and Robert paused at her tone. Outside, the wind blew fiercely. Miriam picked up the dark green cloak and wrapped it around her. It hung on her like a tent, but she fastened the clasp and tucked up the hems. "I'm going with you."

"Child . . . you can't. . . ." Mika shook her head vehemently. "It may be difficult." She stole a glance at Robert. His usually impassive peasant face showed strain and worry. His doting on Clare was almost a local joke.

"I'm coming. You'll probably need . . . an apprentice . . . or someone. . . ."

"Child—"

"I'm not a child!" Miriam flung the words at her like a sword. Mika looked again at Robert, then at Miriam.

"All right," Mika said at last. Her voice was small, fragile, nearly drowned out by the wind.

Robert led them out of the house and down the road, the wind driving bits of trees and clouds of dust like hailstones and rain. Mika put her arm around Miriam to steady the tottering healer. "Why?" she said into Miriam's ear. "You can't do this. It's dangerous."

"I could say the same to you."

"Answer me!"

A gust kicked at them. Miriam stumbled both from the

wind and from the flash of white heat that flickered for an instant at the base of her spine. She clung to Mika. "I saw what happened when you lost Petronella's girl," she said. "I . . . I don't want that to happen again."

"It could bring the Inquisition."

"I'll take the chance."

"Miriam!"

"Dammit, Mika, just do your bloody job and we won't have to worry about it. All right?"

Mika flinched and said nothing more.

Robert's was a farmer's house—rock, wood, and mud—lying at the edge of the hamlet, looking out across the new-plowed fields that stretched off toward the west. The wind buffeted it, and its thatched roof seemed about to blow away at any moment. " 'Tis a hard wind for this time a year," said Robert as they crossed the yard. "I think she'll hold, though." A cry, half of surprise, half of pain, drifted from the hut, and he stopped and fell silent, his eyes moist.

The fire was building in Miriam's spine. She stifled it, and it turned into a pool of magma in the small of her back. Was Clare in such condition that even out here . . . ?

"I'll take care of her," Mika was saying to Robert.

"By Our Lady," he returned with a clumsy bow, "I'll thank'ee for't." He straightened and turned away. "I'll be with Kyle," he called over his shoulder.

There was another brief cry. Mika took Miriam by the arm and pounded on the door. "The midwife," she called, and the door was jerked open by Jeanne. The sturdy woman hustled them in and helped them off with their cloaks.

Because of the wind, the shutters were closed, and Miriam blinked while her eyes adjusted to the dim light. Some of the other women of the village were there, sitting around the fire, knitting, sewing, making swaddling bands. Then she saw Clare lying on a pallet on the other side of the room, and the flash up her spine nearly sent her staggering.

The woman was grossly bloated from the dropsy, and her face was pale and damp with sweat. When she saw Mika, she extended a puffy hand. Her fingers looked like sausages.

"Boil water," said the midwife to Jeanne. She reached into her bundle and extracted a package of herbs. "And brew up some of this. It's raspberry leaf and parsley. You know what I need.''

"Aye."

"And bring me something so I can wash my hands, please."

While Jeanne was hurrying for a basin, Mika sat down next to Clare. The laboring woman was dazed. "Mika?"

"I'm here, child."

"I'm cold. . . ."

The midwife put a hand on Clare's forehead. Miriam did not have to see the shake of her head to know that Clare was fevered. She knew also the mother's heart was racing. The power flickered along her spine. Brutally, she shoved it down again. The magma pool grew larger.

Let Mika do it. She can handle it. That's what she's here for. She tried to reassure the power, but the fire only grew. She looked at the circle of women around the hearth. One of them, gray-haired and grandmotherly, patted an empty place on the bench. Miriam shook her head. *Mika, please don't fail.*

The midwife washed her hands carefully and examined Clare. "Pain?" she murmured.

"I . . . I . . ." Clare made an indefinite gesture at her chest. Mika looked alarmed. Clare let her bloated arm fall to the side and stared blankly at the ceiling. A long contraction shuddered down her belly.

"Jeanne, Miriam," snapped the midwife. "Some cold cloths for her forehead."

Jeanne brought them, but Miriam pulled herself away from thoughts of the power and took the basin from her. The room was wavering in her sight as she wrung out a cloth and placed it on Clare's brow. The mother's eyes flickered.

Mika was wiping her hands. "I think the baby's in a good position," she said. "I won't be able to tell for certain for a while." Her face was pale.

"What is it?" said Miriam.

"The baby's in trouble," the midwife whispered. "There's little I can do right now. Pray."

"Pray?" It had been years since she had prayed. She could not start now, not here in this house with a roomful of women, a delirious mother, and the white fire of her healing battering her from within.

Jeanne brought the tea. Clare was hardly able to swallow. Mika gave it to her in minute sips after stirring in a little honey, then sat down by the pallet and wiped Clare's face periodically with the cool cloth, murmuring reassuringly. She was obviously waiting.

The conversations among the women by the fire started up again, soft words about children, housekeeping, husbands, and Clare. There was an element of worry in their tones to be sure, but there was also confidence. Mika was here. She could do anything.

Hours passed. Outside, the sun crawled toward the horizon. Inside, Clare was still delirious, now in heavy labor, crying out in a vague voice when the pain became too great. Mika bathed Clare's face, felt the muscles of her belly, tried to get her to drink a little more of the infusion.

Miriam sat beside Mika, the magma burning through her back, a white haze of pain creeping into her vision. Her hands shook. Toward evening, Mika turned to her. "Maybe you'd better go."

"It's too late for that."

Jeanne brought more cool cloths. Mika waved her aside and bent over Clare, who was, between contractions, tossing back and forth on the sweat-soaked pallet.

"I can feel the baby's head," she said softly to Miriam. "It's not breech. So that means toxemia. Mother of God, I wish it were breech!"

Just then, Clare shuddered, and her face, already blank, lost all expression. Mika slid a hand beneath the mother's knee, elevated it, and gave it a slight blow just below the kneecap. The leg jerked in a massive reflex, the foot swinging high toward the ceiling once, then again. The twitches died away slowly.

"Jesus—"

"Mika?"

Mika was already reaching into her bundle. She came up with a short, thick stick. "Miriam, you'll have to—"

The midwife was cut short by a sudden spasm in Clare. It was not a contraction. It grew quickly, massively, spreading through her body, twisting it, wringing it. Clare's head slammed down on the pallet, her back arching. Mika shoved the stick into Clare's mouth just as her jaws snapped shut, splintering the wood. Clare moaned as she writhed on the pallet, shuddering terribly.

"Miriam, hold her," Mika snapped as she grabbed and pinned Clare's legs. Without thinking, the little healer flung herself across Clare's head and shoulders, fighting against muscles that were clenching the woman's entire body. A froth of spittle grew around Clare's mouth, and her gasps sprayed flecks of spume into Miriam's face. She hardly noticed: the fire was climbing rapidly.

Abruptly, the seizure passed, and the woman went limp and unconscious. Miriam lay on her, exhausted. The women by the fire had fallen silent, and she heard only the crackling of the fire, the wind, and the sound of blood dripping from the pallet.

Mika straightened. "Jeanne," she said. "By my bundle is a pot of ergot infusion. Put some in a cup."

Jeanne was staring at the pallet. Blood was pooling rapidly around the unconscious Clare, soaking the matting, dripping to the floor in a thin stream.

"Jeanne!"

Jeanne fumbled with the pot and a cup.

"I . . . don't understand," Miriam forced the words out. "What's happening?" The power was white-hot now, flooding her mind, blanketing her sight.

Mika moved with terrible purpose. She snatched the cup of infusion from Jeanne, then turned around and pulled Miriam off the hemorrhaging woman. "She's bleeding to death, Miriam," she said. Her voice was like ice. "The fit tore the afterbirth away from her womb. Jeanne, you'd best run fetch the priest."

The peasant woman threw the door open and set off at a run.

Blood dripped steadily, soaking the rushes on the earth floor, puddling, spreading. Mika forced Clare's mouth open and tried to make her drink the ergot tea, but she would not awaken, would not swallow. "Clare. Clare! Swallow! Dear God!"

The women had stood, and were huddled together now

by the fire, watching silently. *"Ave Maria,"* one said, *"gratia plena, Dominus Tecum . . ."*

"Clare! Drink, please. . . . If we can get your little one out, your womb will close and you'll both live. Clare . . ."

Miriam heard it all from within her small crucible of light and pain. The power had broken free of her spine and had flooded her, streaming through her body, burning terribly, each muscle and nerve and fiber igniting in turn, blazing white-hot.

Too late. She could not stop it. If Clare was, by a miracle, restored, it would fade, but otherwise it would go on and on like this until Miriam herself passed out, screaming, as she had that one day when she had seen the leper in the hills outside Maris. She had no choice but to shriek in agony or submit and be violated once again.

She was sitting on the floor by the pallet. The pool of blood lapped at her scarred legs.

There were footsteps on the path outside, and the door was flung open again. The deep tones of the priest's voice made Miriam shudder, and she dragged herself to hands and knees. "Get him out of here," she cried. "Get him away!"

"How dare you—"

She could not see his face, could not see anything. She got to her feet and shoved him aside blindly, her outstretched hands groping for the bleeding woman. "Get him away. Mika!"

"Miriam! No!"

She nearly laughed. Mika might as well deny a thunderstorm, or a flood, or a forest fire. She was screaming now, the white fire tearing the sounds from her lips in ragged hunks. Near fainting, she bumped into the edge of the pallet and fell forward onto soft, dropsied, fevered flesh. She smelled the rank odor of old sweat, the ripe stench of growing death. "Get him out of here," she cried again.

And she let the power have its way with her.

There was a change in the air, a sudden cry, a flash of white light. The world spun. Then the fire faded from her body, and when Miriam came to herself, she heard the wail of a newborn child.

"A girl, Clare," Mika was saying. "You have a daughter."

* * *

"I have to leave," said Miriam. She was crumpled into a corner of Mika's kitchen like a rag doll that some child had carelessly flung down. There was a dark, metallic taste in her mouth, as if she had bitten a sword blade, and her belly ached, though not from hunger. She watched blankly as Mika put together a cold dinner.

"I know," said the midwife tiredly. "I know. I saw the priest's face."

Miriam gave a short, bitter laugh that had no feeling behind it. "At least he didn't pick me up and throw me on the fire then and there. He was almost funny. He looked like a fish, puffing and blowing."

Mika turned around with a platter of dried fruit and smoked meat. "Why did you do it? You . . . you *knew* the birth would be difficult."

"Yes." Miriam stirred from the corner, got up, and cleared a seat for Mika. The two women sat down and Mika said a blessing. Miriam sat with her hands folded. She did not believe in God anymore. She believed in nothing save her power, and she wished that she could deny that also.

"So?" said Mika after they had started to eat.

Absently, Miriam put food into her mouth, chewed, and swallowed. "I'm stupid. I actually started to care about you, Mika. You and your ladies and your babies. When I saw you broken down about Petronella's girl, I couldn't bring myself to stand by and watch it happen again. That's all. I didn't want you to cry again, because I'd feel bad. Selfish as usual. So I helped. So I'll have to leave now. It'll look better for you, too: you can say you put me out when you found out I was a demon . . . or a witch . . . or whatever it is I'm supposed to be. God knows, I can't possibly be human."

"Don't talk that way."

"All right. I won't."

The wind was still blowing strongly. Mika rose, went to the window, and fiddled with the shutter fastening as though envisioning a small, frail healer traveling alone and in such weather. "Where will you go?" she said at last.

"I don't know. I don't particularly care. Certainly not to Hypprux."

Mika was silent for a time. "What about the Free Towns?"

"Good as anything, I suppose." Miriam chewed listlessly at a piece of bread. The safety was gone. The drowsy afternoons on Mika's bench were gone. So were the quiet evenings on the fire. The women would not be bringing food anymore, nor the men bowing. It was over.

"I'm serious," said Mika. "There are . . . stories . . . about the Free Towns."

"Stories. Of course. The Elves turned a priest into a pig. The mayor of Saint Blaise goes out and dances with Immortals. The village of Saint Brigid floats in the air every Lammas Eve. Sure."

"Have you looked at that cloak you've been wearing?"

Miriam glanced at it. The blazons of the Free Towns and Saint Blaise glistened in the firelight.

"You healed that man in Hypprux," Mika continued, "and he helped you. He *helped* you. He didn't run away."

"Up until I healed him, he couldn't. He had a broken ankle." Still, Miriam was considering. Elves were said to visit Saint Brigid with regularity. She did not know whether or not to believe the stories, but something was going on down in the Free Towns, or else the stories would not have started up.

Her gifts might be tolerated there. Surely the Free Towns could not be any worse than the rest of Adria.

"Let it be the Free Towns, then," she said. "I'll see if Saint Brigid is interested in burning a healer."

Mika looked stricken. "Please . . ." Her voice broke. "Please don't say things like that."

Lifting her head, Miriam saw the tears in the older woman's eyes, realized how deeply Mika would miss her.

Her vision blurred and she buried her face in her hands, and Mika came to her and folded her in her arms.

She spent the next week preparing to leave. Her legs still ached, but they were essentially healed; and the last scabs had fallen off her hands a week before. Mika sewed an extra gown for her and packaged enough food for several days on the road. Miriam looked at the bundle. "It'a a little large for me to carry."

"Don't worry about the size. You'll be taking Esau."

"Esau?" The shaggy red pony lived in a small stable at one side of Mika's house, his only task being to draw the cart when it was needed. "I can't take Esau."

"You need a mount, and I can always prevail upon Baron Paul to supply another horse." Mika met her eyes. "I can give very little to you. Please take what I can give."

In the end, Miriam took the pony, and Mika saw her off just at dawn. The bells of Furze were ringing prime, and the weather was clear and cold.

"Follow the road," said the midwife. "It's in fairly good repair. You might pass a house or two before you get to Saint Brigid, but if you have any problems, mention my name. They all know me. Even the bandits."

Miriam nodded. She unfastened the green cloak. "I'd better leave this with you. The emblems might cause trouble. They're too easily recognized."

Mika took the cloak and glanced at the gooseflesh on Miriam's arms. "Wait." She turned and went into the house.

Miriam looked off toward the forest. She would be traveling around the southern end of Malvern in order to reach Saint Brigid, but she was not overly worried about venturing onto the isolated roads alone: thieves and ruffians avoided Malvern to a large extent, and there was not enough traffic upon the south roads to make brigandry a profitable venture.

Mika returned, a bundle under her arm. She shook it out. It was a thick cloak, sized for a young girl . . . or for a tiny healer woman. "Here," she said, fastening it about Miriam. "It belonged to my Esther. She never got a chance to wear it, and . . . for some reason, I've kept it. I think . . . I think I kept it for you."

The cloak was soft and warm. The two women embraced for a long time.

Then the road took Miriam away to the south and west. She knew without looking that Mika was standing in the road, watching after her for many minutes, watching even after she was out of sight.

Departures again. Always departures. There could be no returns. She was a piece of straw blown by the wind, always moving, the wind itself for the most part heedless of her presence. Just so much chaff, she was, to be consigned eventually to the flames.

She winced at the thought.

There were two houses along the way, small steadings surrounded by farmland, but she passed them by without incident. She spent the nights by herself, curled up on a pile of bracken near Esau, the blue cloak wrapped warmly about her. As she dozed off, she wondered what Mika was doing, remembered the warm house she had left, recalled the homely smells of fresh bread and dried herbs.

On the third day, there were signs that a village was ahead: a house or two sheltering in the eaves of the forest that, green and gold with spring, now bordered the road. She saw fields, and a stray cow looked at her with large brown eyes. She estimated that she would reach Saint Brigid by evening.

But toward noon, she heard a groan of pain from the forest, and she reined in her pony. White flame flickered along her spine. The sound had not come from very far away, no doubt just from the other side of the first ranks of trees. Prudence told her to go on, that the village was near, but prudence was fighting against the power, and there was no contest.

She bent her head for a moment. Another groan. The heat rose. "All right. All right. I'm coming," she muttered bitterly. She dismounted and took Esau's bridle in her hand.

About ten yards into the trees, she came upon an unconscious man, his arm nearly torn off at the shoulder. From the look of his other wounds, she judged that he had been mauled by a bear. The fellow, though, looked as though he would have been a match for any bear: he was huge, dressed in hunter's garments of leather, strongly muscled, deeply tanned. But his hands were not those of a laboring man, and his weapons had a well-used look.

Blood was pouring from the stump of his arm, and Miriam's spine turned into molten iron. Dizzy, she let Esau's bridle fall and staggered forward. Kneeling beside the stranger, she took out her eating knife and cut away cloth and leather so that she could touch the wounds. He was badly hurt in other ways—ribs crushed, flesh cut and mangled by the bear's claws—but the arm was killing him. She felt the power rising, felt the familiar haze of heat and light.

"I don't want this," she murmured, but the power was forcing her, taking her against her will once again. Sucking in a breath, she seized shoulder and arm and brought them together.

Then she was conscious only of the torrent of fire that ran through her being, and jaw clenched to keep back the scream, she let the power that was her master do as it would.

Afterward, she sat back on her heels, drained, blinking at the trees, her thoughts scattered until called together by the movements of the man she had healed.

Huge, unwashed, his garments caked with dirt, he looked the proper ruffian. Only his hands did not conform to the role. He pulled himself up, touched his restored arm, and stared at her. "And who are you, my pretty maid?" he said.

Miriam was mildly surprised: his accent was that of the northern part of the country. But she felt uneasy, too. "A traveler," she said. "I healed you just now."

"Oh?" He laughed. "Did I have need of healing?"

"Your arm was torn off," she said abruptly. "Next time, pick on a smaller bear." She got up and turned to take up Esau's bridle.

She was seized roughly from behind. She tried to whirl around to beat him off, to grab for her knife, but she was tiny, untrained in fighting, and he was a large man, a match for a bear. One, two cuffs from his massive hands and her senses were reeling.

He was tearing at her clothes now, the clasp of her cloak giving way suddenly and her gown ripping free at the shoulder and down the side. Her anger erupted, as white-hot as her power. Even the Inquisition had not treated her so. Then men in Hypprux had been too frightened.

Not so this stranger. He smacked her again to loosen her thighs, and before she slid into unconsciousness, she felt the pain as she was forced.

Chapter Six

The pain drove Miriam to her senses in the late afternoon. She was lying faceup among the trees, and the leaves and spring flowers fluttered quietly and incongruously in the breeze. She focused on them, tried to ignore the fire in her groin, and managed to pull herself to her feet without crying aloud.

My name is Miriam. I have black hair.

She was alone save for Esau. Dark blood was streaking down her thighs, and she could sense that it was not going to stop on its own. She wished she could heal herself.

I have black eyes. . . .

She stumbled to her ripped garments and knotted them clumsily about herself. Esau's brown eyes stared into hers as though he understood her plight, and he crouched slightly as she pulled herself onto his back and collapsed across the saddle, one foot finding a purchase in a stirrup.

My name is Miriam. . . .

"The road, Esau," she whispered, patting his rump.

He picked his way through the trees, and when he reached the road, she set him on a course toward the village she knew was ahead. She tried to stay conscious, but vertigo made it difficult to judge whether or not she was succeeding.

The pain hammered through her body, and her face throbbed where it had been struck, but she would not weep. She would not cry anymore. The Church had persecuted her, her power had violated her, and now on top of those rapes was piled yet another, and the outrage fused with the pent-up anger of eight years of running, eight years of hiding.

She was going to find the man who had raped her. She could not touch the Church, she could not stifle her power or the persecutions it brought upon her, but she could deal with *him*. He was going to suffer and die. She held on to that thought, saving the rage, gathering the hate, storing them away for the future.

I have black hair. . . .

Although Esau plodded along steadily, the miles to the village seemed endless. The bleeding was weakening her, and the ground blurred and darkened. She was vaguely aware that the pony had rounded a bend when she heard shouts of surprise. Lifting her head, she made out a walled village. Two men were running toward her.

"Esau," she whispered. "Stop."

She loosened her foot in the stirrup. Some obscure element of pride made her want to stand on her own feet, but her legs betrayed her. When she slid off Esau's back, she collapsed in the dust of the road.

Commotion. Voices. She was nearly blind with pain and blood loss, but she felt herself lifted by strong, gentle arms. "Please," she mumbled. "Please don't hurt me." She was fainting again, dizziness spiraling up around her.

"I'll take her to the priest's house, David," someone said. "You run and get Varden. She needs a healer."

I am a healer.

But she could not heal herself, and the darkness was taking her too far away in any case.

Miriam opened her eyes. The room was quiet, and the only illumination was that of a fire burning on the hearth. Dark, carved beams crossed the ceiling, their shadows flickering as the flames crackled and snapped.

The pain was gone, replaced by a warmth that had settled into her body as though flesh and bone were glowing with a soft, golden light. *I've been healed,* she thought. *Healed by someone with great power.*

Somewhere in the distance, a door closed. Footsteps approached, then receded. Another door, and then once more only the crackling of the fire that warmed the room and echoed the light within her. She was almost inclined to close her eyes and drift off to sleep, but her memory was returning—the man, the sharp blows, the pain—and she shuddered.

When she turned her head, she found she was not alone. A young man was sitting in a chair by the bed. He was dressed simply in green and gray, and his dark hair fell smoothly to his shoulders. His face was gentle, almost womanly.

"Hello," he said. "My name is Varden."

She was looking at his eyes. They reflected the firelight, but there was something more to them, something that seemed to fill their depths. Starlight, maybe. "Miriam," she whispered, still staring. "You . . . healed me?"

"I did," said Varden. "I have that talent, among others."

She turned her face into the pillow for a moment and sighed. The pain was no longer with her, but the memory clung to her mind, a tangled montage of grasping hands and leering faces. She felt unclean and empty, both.

Varden leaned forward. His tunic was open at the throat, and a pendant in the form of a moon and rayed star swung free, glittering in the firelight. "I understand," he said. His voice was sad.

"You can't understand." Her hands clenched on the comforter. "I want to kill him. I want him dead. I'd just healed him, and to repay me—" She broke off suddenly, white-faced.

"I know of your power," he said simply. "And you know of mine. Why do you fear?"

She was still wary. "Where am I?"

"This village is called Saint Brigid. It is the southernmost of the Free Towns. You are in the priest's house."

Beyond Varden, she made out a bench, a table, chairs. Moonlight shone in through a window of glass, glinting on the lozenge-shaped panes and on a crucifix on one wall. "You don't look like a priest."

"Kay is the village priest. Andrew the carpenter brought you here." Varden sat back, watching her. "Kay's attitudes about those who are . . . different . . . are much more enlightened than those of his Church, and many folk here are not unused to such powers as you possess. You will find this village a haven."

A few hours ago, she would have considered his words an invitation to paradise. But that was all gone now. The montage came back, and her hands shook with her rage. Eight years—and now this. Varden laid a cool hand on her forehead. "Peace."

The memory did not go away, but it eased, and she was able to master it. She wondered at him. Varden's touch was effortless, almost casual. He and his powers were one. His eyes held her, deep blue and filled with that strange starlight.

"Who are you?" she whispered, mouth dry.

"A healer, like yourself."

"That's not all you are."

A slight smile played at the corners of his mouth. "Maybe." He withdrew his hand. "How do you feel?"

He was evading her question by asking his own, but she did not press him any more than she would have prodded a lion. Held by those frighteningly gentle eyes, she looked away only with an effort.

"How do I feel?" Her voice was harsh. "Angry. There's only one way I'm going to find healing." Holding up her hands, she examined them. They were, like the rest of her, tiny. They were not used to holding any weapon larger than the small eating knife she carried. She felt weak and helpless, but hate and anger were burning inside her as hotly as the power ever had. "Somehow . . . somehow I'm going to kill him."

"Some paths are closed to us," Varden said gently.

"That's easy for you to say: you weren't raped."

He rose and went to the window. He looked up at the moon as if taking counsel, and the light wound around him in a soft shimmer. When he turned around, she was conscious again of his eyes. "Among my people, Miriam, the ways of healing involve more than closing wounds and casting out disease. We try to bring comfort and strength. As I healed you, my mind touched yours, and I lived through your violation. Believe me: I understand."

"Then how can you stand there and talk to me about barred paths?" she cried. "That's not human."

He returned to his chair in silence. The starlight flashed in his eyes. Miriam felt uneasy, and as the silence lengthened, she clenched her hands on the coverlet again, afraid to ask that last, direct question.

A quiet tap at the door broke the spell. "Come," said Varden, his voice pitched just loud enough to carry.

A slight man in a rumpled soutane entered with a tray. His thin, fair hair barely showed his tonsure. "I heard voices," he said cheerily. "I brought our maiden some dinner."

Miriam flinched. Her maidenhood could not have been farther fled.

The priest stood over her and tried to smile reassuringly. "I am Kay," he said. "How is it with you, mistress?"

"Well . . . my body is healed."

He failed to catch the implication. "I have some soup, if you are hungry."

She was not, but his young face was so earnest that she sat up and ate a few spoonfuls to please him. Kay hovered, resting a hand on Varden's shoulder. "God bless you, my friend," he said softly. "Thank you for coming."

"Could I do otherwise, Kay?"

Kay smiled at him and turned to Miriam. "Mistress," he said, "you are welcome in my house. You may stay as long as you wish, and you may come and go as you please." He spoke with the rustic formality of a peasant. This, Miriam decided, was no city-bred clerk, educated in some northern town and given a pleasant and comfortable cure because of high-ranking friends. Kay was obviously a man of the country, and was just as obviously glad of it.

Miriam nodded slightly. With Kay present, Varden was more distinctly different, the light in his eyes more evident. "Thank you," she managed.

But she had heard the words before. Mika had said them. *You're welcome here. You're safe here. As long as you want.* Of course. Until her power flared and she—

She stopped short, her train of thought utterly demolished. Varden, himself a healer, had said she was safe. And it was Kay, a priest, who had offered her sanctuary.

The Free Towns. My God. And maybe this place floats every Lammas Eve after all. . . .

Kay was bowing to her. "I must go," he said. "Vespers is well overdue, and tonight I have some special concerns."

"What? Me?"

Her tone made him frown slightly. "I had . . . I had thought to pray for strength for you." He looked uncertain.

"Don't bother. I appreciate the thought, but don't bother. I don't want anything from your God or your Church."

She expected him to become enraged, but he only looked sad. "As you wish," he said. He touched Varden's shoulder again. "God bless, my friend."

"The Hand of the Lady be on you, Kay."

Kay closed the door behind him. "I pray you, Miriam: speak more kindly to Kay," said Varden. "He is a good man."

His calm rankled her, and her words to Kay had made her bold. "And what about you, Varden? Are you a good *man?* Or something else?"

He said nothing for a moment. She might have commented on the weather. "What would you know, Mistress Healer?" His voice was quiet, but he could not have been more terrifying had he shouted.

She dropped her eyes. "Nothing . . . at present, Varden. Thank you for healing me. I'm not sure you did any good, though: I have to kill him now, and I'm not sure I can. You probably should have let me die."

"Be at peace." He laid a hand on her forehead. "Sleep now. You have traveled far, and my powers cannot achieve everything. Sleep." Though soothing, his words carried the essence of command, and she obeyed.

She slept fitfully, wandering through labyrinthine corridors of dream, trapped by doorways bricked up with montages of groping hands, leering faces, pain, blood. She awakened frequently throughout the night, not knowing where she was, crying out, falling back into nightmare as though she were a swimmer too storm-tossed to pull herself onto shore.

Varden remained by her bed; and when, infrequently, her dreams parted enough for her to peer out into consciousness, she saw him, his eyes shimmering with the stars. Once, in the hours just before dawn, she fled into consciousness with a shriek and found herself clinging to Varden, her cheek pressed against his tunic.

"You are safe here, beloved," he said, laying her back down. "There is nothing here that will harm you. Rest."

After that, her dreams were more tranquil, and she had glimpses of starlit lakes and sunlit forests. For an instant before she awoke, she saw a grassy plain under a night sky. A woman walked there, robed in blue and silver.

Miriam blinked at the pale morning light that washed the room. For a few minutes, she was too groggy to remember anything, and she was content to know that she was in a soft bed and that there was a fire on the hearth.

Then memory returned. She winced, her stomach cramped, and the white-hot anger blazed up again.

Rolling over, fists balled beneath the pillow, she gritted her teeth and fought. She had to control her anger. There was a task before her now, and she had to think, to plan. Somewhere, sometime, she would find the stranger; somehow she would kill him. She had run too long. She would no longer be a victim for the world. The change started now.

The hammering in her temples subsided slowly, and she sat up. Varden was gone. Fresh clothing lay neatly folded on the table. A pitcher of water and a basin sat beside it.

Resolve had calmed her, and she rose, washed, and dressed herself in the simple blue gown that had been left for her. Someone had estimated her size very well, though the style seemed more fitting for a young girl than for a woman who had been battered by life for most of a decade. The flowered trim on the hems seemed superfluous, even frivolous, but at the same time it comforted her, as though the idea that a seamstress had thought to adorn clothing so innocently implied that somewhere, innocence was safe.

She found her bundle at the foot of the bed, and she dug through it for the brush Mika had given her, then took a moment at the mirror by the door and ripped at the stubborn tangles in her hair.

Innocence. Had she ever been innocent? Fear alone had dominated her existence since she had first lifted her infant hands and cured a playmate's cut. Fear blotted out everything. Even her parents had been afraid, and eight years ago, in fear, they had put her out of the house.

She looked again at the gown. It was an unkind reminder of what she had never possessed. Such innocence was safe here in Saint Brigid, perhaps, but it had best stay far away from little vagabond healers lest it be blasted.

A distant knocking. The sound of muffled voices.

She listened at the door and distinguished Kay's cheerful tenor and a woman's gentler inflections. "No, she's not up yet," the priest was saying. "But I expect her soon. There's a hot breakfast waiting for her."

"Did she spend a hard night?" It was a girl's voice, actually, firm and clear, with a touch of water in it.

"Varden sat with her."

"Bless him. Mother sent these along with her best wishes."

Miriam lifted the latch and stepped into a short hall that ran to left and right. There was light to the left and she could see a small kitchen.

"Is that you, my child?" called Kay.

She winced at the *my child*. "Yes."

When she entered the kitchen she found Kay and a girl of perhaps thirteen years. "Miriam," said Kay, "this is Charity. She's the daughter of Andrew—the man who carried you here."

Miriam knew without asking whose gown she wore. "Hello," she said softly, staring at her.

"Blessed be," said Charity. Her voice was sweet, and she wore her dark hair long, almost reaching to her waist. Blue eyes, like mountain lakes, regarded her quietly. She curtsied as though Miriam were gentry.

"I . . ." Miriam felt uncomfortable under the gaze of those blue eyes. Innocence. "Thank you for the gown."

Charity smiled. "I'm glad I was able to help." She laughed. "I'm also glad we're the same size." She was holding a cloth-covered basket, and she lifted it slightly. "Mother sent some bread."

"Elizabeth is the best baker this side of the mountains," Kay explained. "Eating her bread is like . . . is like . . ." He had lifted his hands in preparation for the simile, but it did not come. He furrowed his brow. "It's . . . uh . . . very good. Very good indeed."

"I will assume your guest is hungry, Kay," Charity prompted.

Kay clapped a hand to his head. "There I go. My child,"

he said as Miriam winced again, "you must forgive me. Please, come sit down." He pulled a chair away from the split-log table.

It was a good, hearty breakfast: porridge and fresh milk and bread and honey, and Miriam felt her stomach begin to unclench. Charity sat beside her and served her, and although Miriam found that embarrassing, the presence of the girl was strangely comforting.

Miriam found herself watching her. There was more to Charity than was usual for a girl of thirteen years, but what it was, she could not say.

Priests who were not normal, children who were not normal . . . Miriam wondered what was going on in the Free Towns. *That's not human,* she had said, but Kay and Charity were quite human . . . and quite out of the ordinary.

"What became of Varden?" she asked as calmly as she could.

Kay answered between mouthfuls. "Oh, he went away, back to the forest to be with his people. He said you'd gotten through the worst of the night and that he really couldn't do anything more. He left a while before dawn."

"To be . . . with his people."

"Yes." Kay was unflustered.

"Where are you from, Miriam?" said Charity as she refilled Miriam's cup with milk.

Miriam glanced between Kay and Charity, wondering what the officers of the Church would do with what she was seeing and hearing. After a moment, she dropped her eyes and shrugged. "Everywhere."

"I've always wanted to meet someone from everywhere," said Charity with a smile. "It's so dreary to be from one particular place."

Miriam wondered at first if she were being ridiculed, but Charity's smile was honest and open. Her stomach unclenched a little more. "I was born in a village near Maris. My father was a fisherman. I guess . . . I guess I've tried to forget anything more than that."

"Did you lose your parents."

"You might say that." In truth, she had lost them the first time the power had taken her. She had been only three then, but the final rupture seven years later had been a mere technicality.

Charity's eyes were sympathetic. "I'm sorry," she said.

"I've wandered about. I never stay anyplace for very long. People . . ." Miriam wondered how much she could say. "People become afraid of me. I'm . . . I'm a healer."

Kay was unperturbed. "Varden mentioned that. You're welcome in Saint Brigid." He started to butter a piece of bread.

Miriam found his nonchalance irritating. "Doesn't your Church take a dim view of people like me, Kay? I had a fine time with your friend Aloysius Cranby—"

"Aloysius Cranby is no friend of mine," Kay said bluntly. "I was ordained by Augustine delAzri of Maris. I stay away from Hypprux."

"Well, my powers are supposed to come from the devil."

Kay was still buttering the dark bread, and his movements became agitated. "Some people are fools," he said. "They should get down on their knees and praise God for people like you. Healing coming from the devil indeed! And Who was it that made lame beggars walk and blind men see?" The bread slipped out of his hand and skittered across the table. Kay peered at it. "It does always land with the buttered side down, doesn't it?"

Miriam smiled in spite of herself.

"I think of them as city dwellers," Kay resumed, peeling up the slice and then mumbling through it. "Noses buried in their books while the sun shines and the flowers bloom about them. They've never gone out and gotten their hands dirty, never really looked at a sunset or watched a tree grow."

"How did you ever become a priest?"

"I wanted to serve God," said Kay. "Not gold. Not the bishops and the cardinals, not Rome—nor Avignon either. I grew up out here among the fields, and I always knew there was magic about. No one had to tell me. At school, I simply kept my mouth shut." He smiled at her with the expression of an angel who had just purloined the largest, reddest, juiciest apple from a neighbor's tree.

"This place is a miracle," she said. *But I can't ever enjoy it.*

Kay was working on another piece of bread. "Yes," he mused, "I suppose you'd say that there is something about Saint Brigid. Of course there have been ups and downs. If you'd come here a few years ago, my child, you'd have found a different reception."

Miriam stifled her instinctive retort. "Why is that?"

"My predecessor, Jaques Alban, was an associate of Bishop Cranby, and held to most of his views. How he was ever given this town as a cure, I'll never know. He certainly never fit in." Kay rambled on. "Saint Brigid was a rather unhappy town for several years, but Alban, fortunately, disappeared one day."

Miriam thought for a moment. "Was he the one the Elves turned into a pig?"

Kay looked uncomfortable. "Uh . . . wherever did you hear that?"

"Up north. It's a popular little tale."

"Well, Alban disappeared one day. . . ."

Charity sighed softly. "It's sad."

Kay shrugged. "Alban did some good in the end, though his motives were not the best. He rebuilt the church, and he made sure that he had a fine large house to live in. This one. Comfortable . . . and capable of taking in wandering healers." He looked at Miriam.

She understood the unspoken question. "Thank you," she said. "I appreciate your hospitality. If I could repay you in some way—maybe keep your house for you—I would like to stay for a while."

"You're welcome to stay as long as you want," said Kay. "As for the housekeeping . . . we can talk about that later."

Miriam was surprised when she looked at Charity. The girl's eyes were wide, and she was smiling broadly, as though the news that Miriam would be staying in Saint Brigid was a cause for great joy.

Chapter Seven

Saint Brigid lay nestled against the southwest corner of Malvern Forest, separated from the trees by a bow shot or two of tilled fields and pasture. It was a neat, orderly town, its walls and streets well kept, its houses trim and sturdy. The tidy streets meandered off as streets will do, but within a few weeks Miriam could find her way about as well as any native.

She had, without further comment, taken over the housework, though Kay lived so simply that there was not much of it other than the basic tasks of washing, sweeping, and cooking . . . and Kay did some of those himself anyway. He urged her to get out of the house as much as she could, obviously hoping that fresh air and sunshine would cheer her up. Miriam had no such hopes herself, but she acceded to his wishes. She rambled through the town and the fields around it, becoming, day by day, a familiar figure to the village folk.

The days warmed. Spring was taking hold for certain, the fields greening with crops, the forest shining with new leaves, the meadows bright with flowers. But Miriam paid little attention. Arms folded inside the sleeves of one of Charity's gowns, she kept her eyes on the ground as she wandered. Her mind was far away, searching for a path that would lead her to a certain large man.

She had made some inquiries and had found that no one in the town knew him. Indeed, his accent had been of the north. She might have thought him a common wanderer, but for his hands: they were not those of a vagabond or a soldier. Something else . . .

She was treated well by the people of the village. There was an openheartedness about them, and they seemed to forgive Miriam her dark looks and her scowls, but their kindness made the healer reflect bitterly upon the irony of her circumstances. Hunted, pursued, tormented for most of her adult life, she had come now to a place of love and safety. And she would have to leave. And it was not the Church that would drive her away: it was herself. Full now to the brim with impotent rage, she could not accept any haven, no matter how inviting.

And it was indeed inviting. The village folk accepted her as family, and Charity treated her like a sister. Miriam had not been in town a week before the girl had taken her off to visit friends, relations, people who were dear to her. What time Charity had to herself, she spent with Miriam, trying in whatever way she could to lighten the cloud that hung over the healer.

"Charity," Miriam said once as the girl gleefully tugged at her sleeve. "I need to be alone."

"No, you don't" said Charity, her blue eyes bright. "You've been alone too much. You need to play."

"Play? Dear God . . ."

"Come on."

They gathered flowers for the statue of the Lady in the church. They listened to the roar of the river to the north of the town as it bounded over boulders and under the stone bridge. They climbed among the rocks of the foothills of the Aleser Mountains.

There was a depth to Charity. Miriam had seen it before, but it manifested itself most strongly when the girl was engaged in frivolity. It was as though Charity had long ago realized how precious and transient her youth was and had determined that while she could, she would drain that cup, refill it, and drink again.

But even in those hours Charity gave her, the obsession burned in the back of Miriam's mind. She wanted the man dead. She wanted him dead by her own hand. She wanted to feel the impact of sword on flesh, see the living man cleft by cold steel, and know it was her arm that guided the blade. Despite the townsfolk, despite Charity, Miriam's rage and anger drove her through the lengthening days.

One morning, near the middle of April, Kay asked her gently if perhaps she brooded a little too much.

She glared at him across the breakfast table. "What am I suppose to do, dammit? Laugh? Sing about it? Tra-la-la, I've been raped, and the man's off having a fine time."

Kay flushed with embarrassment. "I only meant to help."

Miriam caught herself and took a deep breath. "I'm sorry, Kay. I've no reason to be cruel to you."

"Maybe if you got your mind off it?"

"Charity's been trying. I'm not sure I want my mind off it. Somehow, I'm going to kill him. That's what I want."

"I was thinking of some distractions."

"What do you suggest?" She stared sullenly at the table.

"Would you like to learn to read and write?"

She lifted her eyes.

Kay shrugged uncomfortably. "After Bishop Cranby, I can't blame you for having no great love for such as me. But—by Our Lady, Miriam, I'm a priest. I'm here to help. I'm supposed to bring aid and comfort." His eyes were moist.

She stared at him. "Why are you all doing this?" she demanded suddenly. "You're driving me mad."

"Miriam?"

She dropped her bread, spread her hands. "Everywhere I go, people are terrified of me, and now all of a sudden I'm adopted by an entire town. Everyone says hello to me. Your father carries me across the street when it's muddy. Charity's friend Roxanne is making me clothes. For nothing. For . . . for love!"

Kay blinked. "Is it so incomprehensible that people can be kind to one another?"

"People aren't kind. You talk of kindness? Talk to the torturer that put those blades into my legs. Have him tell you about kindness. People are horrible. I know that for a fact. Now, what in hell is going on in Saint Brigid?"

Kay was silent for some time. Light and air spilled in from the unshuttered windows: yesterday's rain had brought a softness to the morning. "Maybe we've just learned a few things here in Saint Brigid," he said at last. "Maybe we've learned that people are important. Not because they can tithe, or pay scutage, or build castles, or make brass candlesticks, or anything like that. Just because they're people.

And if they care about one another, then that's important, too.''

She eyed him. "That's crazy."

Kay shrugged. "Maybe. But Saint Brigid is a different town than it was ten years ago. And it's because of just that."

"What changed it? The . . . the Elves?"

Kay went to the pot of water boiling over the fire and tossed in a handful of peppermint leaves. "Probably," he said. "They were there, out in the forest, and they helped us a number of times. Think of that, Miriam. Humans have been persecuting Elves for centuries, and yet they helped us!"

Miriam stared at the piece of bread she had let fall. "Varden's an Elf, isn't he?" The young man had been to Kay's house many times. How was Miriam feeling? Was there anything he could do for her? And always those starlit eyes watched her as though he were waiting for something.

"Yes, he is."

"And he healed me."

"You know that."

"Why?"

"Because that's what Elves do. Help and heal. Aid and comfort. That's really what everybody should do. Varden's been pounding that into my head ever since I took up this cure, and I'm finally beginning to understand him."

"Help and heal. Sure. And get burned."

"Not here." Kay poked a floating piece of peppermint down to the bottom of the pot, filled a mug, and drank.

"What about the Inquisition?"

Kay grimaced. "We keep our own counsel here in the Free Towns. Jaques Alban was the only outsider to have a Free Town cure in many years."

Miriam's eyes glinted. "And he disappeared."

Kay shook his head. "He went against the grain of the town. He just vanished one day."

"Turned into a pig?"

Kay said nothing.

There were hurried footsteps outside, and a quick knock on the door. Kay glanced at Miriam, who had flinched at the sound, and swung it open. "God bless you, Roxanne," he said to the tall, dark woman who stood there. "Is something wrong?"

"It's your brother, Michael," she said. "There's been an accident at the forge. Some tackle fell and crushed his foot. Varden's away in the forest. I'm doing what I can, but I'm limited."

Miriam felt her stomach start to churn.

"Mick . . ." The priest was stunned.

"Is Miriam here?"

"Yes . . . of course," said Kay. He motioned Roxanne in.

Miriam knew her a little. Roxanne had measured her for some new clothes a few days before. Black-eyed, good-looking, she was skilled both at her trade of weaving and in the use of herbs. She functioned as midwife for many of the women of Saint Brigid. Charity was extremely fond of her.

"Miriam," said Roxanne softly, "Varden has told me of your powers. He's also told me of your reluctance to use them. Normally, I would send for him, but he's away, and Michael's foot is badly damaged. So I have come to ask you if you would heal Michael."

Since she had come to Saint Brigid, she had tried to ignore her power, never looking closely at anyone for fear that she would see some injury or disease that would set it off. Following so closely upon her rape, the surge of healing would have been not only a reminder, but also a rape in itself, for in its own way, it used her just as brutally as had the stranger.

But hard as Miriam's heart was, it was not hard enough. "I'll come," she said, cursing herself. She rose and went to her room to fetch her cloak. As she fastened the garment, she looked into the mirror by the door. Black eyes, black hair, jaw set. Hard. Too hard. She did not fit here in Saint Brigid. She thought about Mika and the house she kept on the outskirts of Furze.

"Why did I ever think it could be better?" she said.

But her reflection tightened its jaw and would not answer.

Kay came with them, saying nothing. Roxanne had long legs, and Miriam and the priest had to hurry to keep up with her. Together, they crossed the broad village common, went down the street toward the barless gates of the town, and entered Francis's house through the wide doors of the smithy.

The big smith was standing in the hallway, his arm around Anna, one of this daughters. They both regarded Miriam with a sense of relief. "Thank the Blessed Mother yer here," said Francis. "Hester's in wi' Mick, and tha boy's trying a brave face, but his foot wants otherwise."

Miriam was already feeling the power. "Take me to him." *I don't want this. I want out.*

Roxanne led her down the hall and into a small chamber. Michael lay on a pallet against one wall. His mother was beside him, bathing his forehead with cool water. The boy was sixteen and sturdy, with a stubble of beard frosting his cheeks, but his face was white. A glance at the blood-soaked bandages about his left foot told Miriam his pain had to be terrific.

Out of habit, she fought the power. "H-how did it happen?"

Michael answered. " 'Twas my own stupid fault, little mistress," he whispered, trying for a grin. "I should a fixed tha peg that held tha tackle last week, but this head a' mine won't hold anything in't."

"Shh," said Hester. "Don't blame yourself, Mick."

"Ah, ma . . . I'm surprised I can breathe and eat at tha same time." He shuddered suddenly, clenched his teeth.

Roxanne bent to Miriam's ear. "I gave him some herbs to ease the pain. I hope that will not interfere with your work."

Miriam nearly laughed. Would that anything could interfere! Her spine was hot, the power surging up her back in waves of fire. She let her cloak fall to the floor and staggered forward, her head splitting. "I'll . . . I'll . . ."

Roxanne took hold of her shoulders, and miraculously, the power settled into a controlled, even flow. "Easy," said Roxanne. "You've never had help with this, I see. Let it flow, but stand away from it, and direct it as you wish."

Miriam looked up, astonished. "What are you doing?"

"Helping as I can." There was moonlight in Roxanne's eyes. "Be at peace. There's no sense in hurting yourself."

With Roxanne holding her still, Miriam stepped forward and removed Michael's bandages. His foot had been pulped by the heavy pulleys. The toes were a mass of crushed flesh and bone, the ankle twisted and cracked in many places. Miriam stared. She could actually see what she was healing. Recalling Roxanne's words, she laid her hands on the foot.

White light. Michael gasped. "Oh!" said Hester as though a chipmunk had run up and sat in her lap.

Roxanne gave Miriam's shoulders a gentle squeeze. "Good work," said the weaver. "Very good."

The healer shook her head to clear it of the flash. She felt very well, with none of the half-drugged grogginess her power usually left behind it. It had been almost pleasurable.

Francis and Anna had come to watch, and when Miriam turned around, they were smiling. Hester and Michael regarded her fondly. Roxanne was openly admiring. Kay grinned broadly. "No one's afraid of this?" she demanded. "I just put his foot back together, and no one's afraid?"

"Wi' sha we be afraid?" said Francis.

She shook her head, bewildered. "Never mind . . . just, never mind." Dazed, she picked up her cloak and wandered out of the room and down the hall.

Francis came after her. "Mistress Healer." Miriam stopped, and the big man went down on one knee before her. "I thank ye humbly, mistress. I'm greatly in yer debt. If there's anything I can do for ye, I'll be dard glad t' do it."

"You're not afraid," she said blankly.

"Afraid? This in't the first time we've been touched by healing powers. Some years ago, Varden fixed me hands once, he did, after that old hag of a Leather Woman burned them. And I dinna know Varden then, nor he me. But he came nathaless. And how sha I be afraid a such godly workings?"

"But people are always afraid," she said. "And then the Inquisition comes, and they . . ." She put her hands to her face. The power had not dazed her. It was the love that had done it.

Francis face darkened a little. "Speak na' of that here," he said. "That Jaques Alban was one a' them, I'm certain.

Wi', he tried to force David tha carver to work for him. Imagine that! 'Tis a mercy a' God that Alban is no more.''

Miriam pulled herself out of the daze enough to ask: "What happened to him?" Kay had never answered her question.

"I din know. Got lost. Wandered awa. Whate'er. But y'see, mistress. We ha' little love for sic as that here. Be easy. Lord, Miriam, it's as though one of the Elves ha' come to live wi' us!"

"I'm not an Elf." She looked up to see Roxanne and the others standing around them. "I'm not an Elf, and I'm not a witch." Roxanne seemed almost wistful. "I just heal, that's all. And I don't understand any of this."

Almost in terror, she made her way out to the street. She ran all the way to her room in Kay's house, slammed the door, and buried herself in the bedclothes as though blankets and comforters could shield her from the acceptance that had found her.

Chapter Eight

Miriam heard the front door open and close. A minute later there was a tap at her door.

"Go away." She huddled herself into a ball.

"Miriam." Roxanne's voice was gentle. "I'm not going away."

"Then you can stay out in the hall for all I care," snapped the healer. "Everyone in Saint Brigid is so concerned about me, it's making me sick. Charity drags me off to play, Kay wants to teach me to read, now you're here. What are you supposed to be? My confessor?"

"No." Roxanne swung the door open. "I'm your priestess."

Miriam looked up. Roxanne was a tall woman, but now she seemed taller, and her eyes held a depth of wisdom that made Miriam almost afraid.

"Are you . . . are you an Elf, too?" said the healer.

Roxanne shook her head. "I'm mortal, like you, though I've learned a few things from Varden's folk."

"What do you want?"

"I want to help, if I can. Saint Brigid must be strange to you. Charity is young, and maybe she's too exuberant. Can we talk?"

Miriam shrugged. "You're here."

"True. But it's still your choice."

Miriam worked her mouth for a while, then swung her legs over the edge of the bed and sat up. "All right."

Roxanne dragged a chair over. "You probably have some questions about this village," she said.

"Not anymore. Kay told me the whole tale over breakfast. The Elves came to Saint Brigid, and now everything's love and kindness."

Roxanne smiled slightly.

"Go ahead. Laugh at me."

"I'm not laughing," said the weaver. She sat down, leaned back. "May I tell you something about yourself?"

"That I have an evil temper, and that I'm a nasty little bitch? Go right ahead."

Roxanne appeared to be looking out the window at a willow tree that, new-leafed, swayed gently and dappled the floor with shadow. "We grow up, and we get used to living as we do. I'm tall and broad-shouldered—always have been—and my mother saw nothing wrong with me wearing boys' clothes and climbing up into the mountains with the village lads when I was little. I still climb upon occasion. I'm used to it. If I had to give it up, I'd be unhappy, and probably quite irritable."

"What does this have to do with me?"

"Everything, Miriam. You're used to being hunted, pursued, and in fear of your life. Regardless of whether or not all that was pleasant, it's still what you're used to and now it's all changed. I can understand why you act the way you do. What I am asking is that you understand it also."

There was respect in Roxanne's voice. She sounded like a teacher, one who honored her student as much as she expected to be honored in return. Her gown was simple, dark, girdled by a woven cord of black and silver, and Miriam noticed an ebony-handled knife at her side. Roxanne had called herself a priestess, and though Miriam did not know what she had meant by it, she admitted to herself that the weaver seemed to be deserving of the title.

After a while, Miriam spoke. "All right. So I understand. It doesn't help much. Is everyone in this town so damned accepting of Elves, healers, and—Lord knows—witches?"

Roxanne toyed with the end of her cord. "The Elves are known by sight in the town. Varden often comes, and occasionally one of the eleven ladies comes with him. No one is afraid, but only a few in Saint Brigid know the Elves well. Andrew the carpenter and his wife Elizabeth and their family often entertain Varden. Likewise David the carver and Charlotte who live on the edge of Malvern. Kay, of course. Charity, whom Andrew and Elizabeth adopted six years ago, is much loved by the Elves."

"And you?"

"Varden is my lover. And I am his."

"The Church would call you a witch."

Roxanne smiled, but sadly. "I am a witch, Miriam. But not in the way the Church thinks, and not because I took an elven lover. Long before the Church came to this land, my ancestors worshiped a Goddess. When the Church came to power, it declared that the old beliefs should die and be forgotten. Churchmen preached that witches did great evil, and they should be destroyed. The persecutions have gone on for a long time, and will continue for a long time to come."

"Don't talk to me about persecutions." Miriam had been shaken by Roxanne's admission, but was determined not to show it.

Roxanne nodded slowly. "Very well, I won't. Let's just say that I am one of only two in Saint Brigid who keep the old ways. Not many know what I am. Most know me as weaver, herbalist, and midwife. But the Elves, and Kay, and Charity and her family know that I am a witch, a priestess of my Goddess."

"And Kay tolerates this?"

"He comes to me for advice, and I go to him. Our paths are different, but they lead to the same goal. Kay says mass and administers the sacraments, and I bless the crops and call the rain when it's needed."

"And blast an occasional priest?"

Roxanne laughed merrily. "Alban? No. Though I confess I was tempted."

"Well, someone did some blasting. Francis said something about an old hag. Was she a witch, too?"

"We called her the Leather Woman because she made bits of harness and tackle for a living. She worked magic, but she wasn't a witch. Nor was she particularly happy. She was crippled and deformed, and she had spent her childhood being ridiculed and her adulthood being feared. Once, she struck at Francis, and Varden healed him. Later on, she disappeared."

"It seems that unpleasant people have a way of disappearing in this town. What did the Elves turn her into? A butterfly? Am I next?'' Miriam laughed harshly. ''Maybe I could convince them to make me a warrior.''

Roxanne regarded her appraisingly. ''It would be a difficult path, Miriam,'' she said at last. ''Before you ask for anything, make sure you know exactly what it is you want.''

Miriam was puzzled. ''What are you talking about?''

Roxanne shook her head slowly. ''I have a gown I must fit to you, Miriam,'' she said. ''Will you come to my house? I can have it ready by tomorrow morning if we do this today.''

Miriam had the feeling that Roxanne had told her as much as she wanted, but not as much as she could. ''I'll come,'' she said, still wondering what the witch had meant. For a moment, she thought about being a tall, strong warrior, about hunting down her rapist and killing him. She laughed ruefully to herself. Another barred path, another sealed door.

But Miriam suddenly found herself wondering: Was it so barred? Was it so sealed?

What had happened to Jaques Alban? And what about the Leather Woman?

Kay made his way up the street, his arms folded in his sleeves and his soutane flapping in the breezes that came down from the north. There was a good, hearty scent of forest in the air, as if Old Malvern were cupping the village gently in its gnarled hands and wishing it a blessed spring.

He stopped at the low fence that surrounded Andrew's house. Elizabeth waved at him from the doorway. ''Andrew's in the shop,'' she called. Philip, her youngest, dodged around her, vaulted the fence, and took off down the street. ''Philip! Use the gate!'' But he was already gone, and she laughed.

Kay laughed, too, and went round the corner of the house. Andrew was hammering pegs into a bench leg. A pot of glue sat beside him on the floor. He looked up at Kay's approach. ''God Bless,'' said Kay.

''Be at peace,'' said Andrew. There were wood chips and sawdust in his sandy hair and he shook them out. ''Is it that time already? The morning went quickly.''

''Very quickly,'' said Kay. ''My brother lost and found

his foot at the forge between prime and terce." Andrew looked puzzled. "There was an accident," explained Kay. "Some pulleys fell on his foot."

"Dear Lady! Is he all right?"

"Roxanne came for Miriam. She healed him."

Andrew smiled. He took a rag and cleaned his hands of glue. "Bless her. Is she feeling better then?"

"I don't think so," said Kay. "She ran off after it all. Roxanne followed. She might be able to help. Woman to woman and all that."

"I hope so." Andrew opened the door into the house. "I'm off now, Elizabeth. I'll be home for supper." He blew her a kiss.

As they crossed the fields on their way to the forest, Kay noted that the crops were coming along fine. Of course they were. With Roxanne in the village and the Elves in the forest, could they do otherwise?

"She's such a mite of a girl," said Andrew as they approached the trees. "No bigger than Charity. I remember thinking that when I found her on the road. And the thought of someone mistreating Charity like that . . . well . . ."

The carpenter was a quiet, gentle man, but Kay noticed that his lips were pressed together, his fists clenched.

"That time's long past," said the priest. "No one is mistreating Charity—or Miriam—now."

"I don't understand it," said the carpenter. "I just don't. Poor Miriam. I wish her well."

"We all do," said Kay. "How is Charity? How are her studies?"

"Oh," said Andrew with a laugh, "she's fine. And since Roxanne took her on, she's been better than fine. She's growing up, looking like the lovely woman I know she'll be. She's like a butterfly: always cheering people up wherever she goes. But she can't tell me much about her studies. It's all secret. Only witches can know, and I've no desire to become a witch."

"I can see why," said Kay seriously. "After all, you're almost an Elf already."

The two men looked at each other and laughed. "Hardly," said Andrew. "Although Varden did say it could

rub off. Look at Roxanne. For that matter, look at Charity.''
His eyes twinkled. ''Or yourself, Kay.''

They approached a small house that was nearly hidden
among the first ranks of trees. The facade had been carefully carved to look like a part of the forest, and it was
difficult to tell where Malvern left off and the house began.

A dark-haired woman opened the door before Kay had a
chance to knock. ''Come in an' be welcome,'' she said.
''David's waiting. Varden's already here.''

''Elves are always so prompt,'' said Kay.

''How are Ma and Da?'' said the woman.

''Fine, Charlotte, though we nearly lost a brother this
morning.'' In a few words, Kay told his sister of the incident at the forge.

''Why, bless her,'' said Charlotte. ''I knew she had a
good streak in her a league wide. Mick's all right then?''

''Good as a new nail. He ate a pound of meat and a loaf
of bread to settle his nerves . . . so he said.'' Kay chuckled.
''And now he's back at work.''

''I should go an' visit Miriam,'' said Charlotte. ''To thank
her.''

Kay shrugged. ''It might be best to wait.''

Charlotte nodded. ''I understand. Go on into the shop,
then. I'll have some beer for you all in a jiffy.''

Kay and Andrew went through the house and into David's
workroom. The carver and Varden were standing in front
of two large, canvas-draped panels, chatting.

David was a thin man with a sharp nose. ''Hello, hello,''
he said when he saw the new arrivals. ''I'm very glad you
could come.'' He rubbed his hands together gleefully.
''Normally, I don't show anybody my work until it's finished, but I think you'll all enjoy this.'' He paused, considered, and added: ''Or be dreadfully offended. I'm not sure
which.''

Charlotte bustled in with the beer. She handed out the
mugs, took one herself, and sat down on a bench to watch.

David begun untying the ropes that held the canvas in
place on the panels. ''You all remember Jaques Alban and
how he wanted me to carve a crucifix for the church—''

Kay spoke up from behind his beer. ''It's come to my

attention, David my son, that we still have only a blank
wooden cross over the altar.''

David paused. ''And when the roof beams finally fall in,
we'll still have only a blank wooden cross.'' He spoke
lightly, but the memory obviously pained him. Kay quickly
apologized.

''Never mind,'' said the carver, waving his hand as if to
chase off an annoying fly. He pulled several knots loose.
''But that's why we have a statue of the Lady in the church
instead. Kay asked me, though, as a favor, if I might carve
some panels to go behind the altar. And as a favor, I agreed.
Providing, of course, that I chose the subject matter.''

''Being very naive and foolish,'' said Kay, who was starting to worry, ''I assumed David would carve something
edifying. From the lives of the saints, or something like
that.''

''Well,'' said David. ''Something like that.'' He reached
back to his belt, pulled out a knife, and sawed through the
bindings. ''Anyway, since I wound up working for the
Church after all, I decided to commemorate the first attempt.'' He climbed up a ladder to the top of the panels,
cut the last knot, and held the canvas with his hands. ''The
final finishing will take a little while, but I wanted to get
some opinions.'' They were all waiting. David shrugged a
little. ''Well, here it is.''

He dropped the canvas.

Varden smiled. Kay put his hand to his mouth. Andrew
laughed.

''Are you really taller than Varden?'' said Andrew. ''Or
is that vanity?''

''I made them stand back-to-back,'' said Charlotte.
''David's taller.''

''How about Alban?'' Andrew pointed.

''Oh,'' said David. ''I don't really remember how tall he
was. So I guessed. Varden and I were *both* taller than him
when Varden was through, though.''

Kay still had his hand over his mouth. He was not sure
what to say.

''Kay?'' David sounded worried.

Kay dropped his hand after a while. ''They're . . .

lovely," he said. "It will take some getting used to. And it'll remind me to watch my step."

"I meant no offense."

"None taken." Kay stepped a little closer, looked at the first, then at the second panel.

"Varden?"

The Elf was smiling. "Your style has changed since that day. Did you know that, David? I do not think any of your folk could carve as you do now."

David blushed. "I can't take any credit for that. I mean . . . after all, when . . . when She's touched you like that. . . ." His voice trailed off, and he looked sheepish. "Do you like it?"

"It is beautiful," said the Elf. "Is it appropriate, though, for a church? What say you, Kay?"

Kay shrugged. He felt outnumbered. Sometimes he wished that his God were not so exclusive and demanding. "I can't say that it's inappropriate," he said truthfully. "And if people laugh during my sermons now, I can blame it on the panels."

David sighed. "Good. You'll have these by Yule. I don't want to rush them."

Kay was examining one part of the second panel. Gently, hesitantly, he reached out and touched one figure in particular. Sometimes he wished . . .

"Varden." The Elf came to him. Kay indicated the figure, set off from the rest of the scene by a field of stars. "Is that really what She looks like?"

The Elf was silent for a while. "To David. Everyone sees Her a little differently, Kay."

"Is there any chance . . ." Kay faltered, felt his face grow hot. "I mean . . . could I . . . ?"

Varden understood. "Someday, my friend."

Andrew stayed to visit with David and Charlotte. Varden and Kay walked toward the village together. "I heard what you said about Miriam," said the Elf.

"About her healing Michael? I must say I was glad."

"For Michael?"

"For both. I didn't want to lose my brother. And . . . as for Miriam . . ."

"Has she been a trial to you?" Varden spoke quietly, understandingly.

Kay shrugged. "I do the best I can, Varden."

"You do very well. You are a credit to your race and to your priesthood."

"She might be improving."

"She might," said the Elf. "But then again, she probably is not. Is that not what you mean, Kay?"

The priest shoved his hands into his sleeves. "Are you reading my mind, Varden?"

"The tone of your voice tells me of your doubts." Varden glanced at him, eyes flashing.

Kay rubbed at his beardless cheeks. Varden always talked about healing and helping, but what could one do when someone was so firmly set against both? "I worry, Varden. I lose sleep at night. There's so much anger and rage and despair in her that I wonder sometimes if I'm going to go to her room some morning and find that she's hanged herself."

"I do not think you need worry about that, my friend," said Varden. "She is too determined to survive at all costs, if only out of spite. But despair, anger, rage: all of those can combine, as we both know, to produce a life that is much, much worse than any death."

"Like the Leather Woman."

"Think of it."

"I try not to. I was only fourteen at the time, but I still remember Da's hands. I can't imagine the amount of hate that must have gone into her spell in order to do that."

"But, my friend, consider her now."

"Kay stopped in the middle of the field, almost frightened. "What are you saying?"

Varden folded his arms. The light in his eyes was troubled. "When I healed Miriam, I linked with her. I felt as she felt, knew what she knew, was raped along with her."

Kay waited.

"Roxanne has taught me a great deal," said the Elf. "My people know compassion. I have learned pity. I do not know if that is a good thing. But I saw something else when I healed Miriam: she is on some kind of path. She has something to do, and she cannot do it out of despair or anger."

"What does she have to do?"

"I do not know, Kay. I can see only so far."

Kay exploded. "Varden, what you're talking about is madness."

Varden eyed him. "At present, my friend, I am not talking about anything. We must wait and see what Miriam does."

Kay heard a shout and turned to see Charity running toward them, skirts flying, hair loose and streaming. She was laughing.

He sighed. A butterfly.

Chapter Nine

If Kay noticed that Miriam of a sudden grew quieter and more thoughtful, he did not say anything, and she was glad of that. She needed time to think slowly, to put together snatches of information, to acquire more.

Jaques Alban.

There were a thousand fates that could have befallen him. He could have become lost in the forest. He could have decided—and Miriam would have sympathized with him—that Saint Brigid was simply too much to handle and fled. He might even have been murdered by a villager who had reached the limits of his tolerance. But there was also that one other possibility: that the Elves had indeed intervened, that Jaques Alban was no more because he now rooted among the ferns and wild turnips of Malvern Forest, transformed by inhuman energies into a pig.

Where before her anger had been a hot cloud in her brain, it was now a focused lance of fire aimed directly at the heart of the man who had raped her, fueled by an almost mad hope that—

She hardly wanted to think it, much less utter it. It was too fragile. It might scatter like leaves before the wind, or disperse like smoke. Before she put it into words, she had to be absolutely certain.

Varden worried her. That first evening when, newly healed, she had awakened in bed, his words to her had been of reconciliation to her fate. Her only link with the Elves, her only chance at success, Varden would probably oppose her plan. But he had said that he had touched her mind, had linked with her, had himself lived through her violation. Surely that meant something. Surely that would be some leverage for her, a flaw in that seemingly impenetrable tranquillity in which he wrapped himself.

He came to the priest's house one morning, looking for her; and he found her in the stable tending Esau. The little pony had not seen much traveling in the last six weeks, but he seemed content to be made much of by the village children who took him for rides out to the forest and back.

"Blessings upon you this day," said the Elf. "How is the good beast?"

Miriam looked up from brushing Esau's shaggy red coat. "Good morning," she said. "He's well." It occurred to her that she should be more polite to Varden, if only because he had healed her—not to mention her ulterior motives. She attempted a smile, but it came out crooked.

The Elf did not appear to notice. "Good." He stood just inside the door of the stable, waiting.

"I'm . . . I'll be done here in a minute, Varden. Did you want something?"

"Will you walk with me today, my lady?"

My lady. The title made her eyes narrow. In the course of her life, she had been *child, girl, wench, healer, bitch,* occasionally *mistress,* but never *my lady.* "Where?"

"Into the forest. I would that you see something this day."

"What's today?"

"Beltaine," said the Elf. "Or so Roxanne would call it. My people call it something else."

Esau snorted as though to tell her that she had not finished brushing him and he was feeling lopsided. "Roxanne mentioned that you two are lovers," she said as she went back to work. "Is that true?"

Varden lifted an eyebrow at the change in subject. "It is, Miriam. That is well-known in the village."

"But it's not well-known that she's a witch."

"That is so."

"What would happen if people found out?"

"Possibly some might fear," he said. "I daresay, though, that if Saint Brigid can accustom herself to Elves—and to healers—she can also accept a witch." His starlit eyes were on her. She wondered how far Alban had pushed the Elves.

"Well," she said, "I don't think that will happen."

"Nor do I."

She finished up Esau with several broad strokes. "I'll come with you. Let me clean up."

Varden bowed slightly and stood aside as she went into the house. In her room, she poured water from pitcher to basin and washed off the horsey smell of the stables. As she dried herself, she looked at the pole near the bed where the two gowns that Roxanne had made for her were hanging. The witch had finished them a week ago, but Miriam had not yet worn either. She was about to pass them by again, but after hesitating, she took one down and pulled it on.

It was the deep green of dark forest leaves, and Roxanne had woven a trim of meadow flowers into the hems. It fit her perfectly, even flattered her, and it reminded her of Charity's clothing. But Charity was bright: pure colors and vivid flowers. Miriam was subdued, the colors muted. Charity was the butterfly, Miriam the moth.

She wondered for a moment what bright, elven flame was luring her, and to what end.

Varden was waiting at the front door. He bowed and offered his arm, and she took it. Together they went through the town and out across the fields to the forest, but Miriam stopped at the edge of the wood, eyeing the shadows beneath the leaves.

"Are you afraid?" said Varden.

"The last time I entered this forest, I wound up wishing I hadn't."

"Be at peace. You are safe here."

"Where are we going?"

"I want to show you something."

His courtesy was impeccable. She was suspicious. "Is this how Jaques Alban disappeared?"

Varden blinked. "Alban? Why do you speak of him?"

His words might have concealed nothing . . . or everything. Miriam shrugged. "You said Roxanne calls today Beltaine. What do you call it?"

"*Arae a Circa*," he said. "Day of Renewal."

"What renewal?"

"I will show you. Come. Please."

After a moment, she nodded. The trees surrounded them, the path twisted and turned, and the ground was spotted with shadow and sunlight. The air was alive with spring, scented with the odor of leaf and blossom.

And Miriam sensed the bond between Varden and the forest. *His* forest, she might have said. Tree and flower, stone and earth, he was a part of them all, and they of him. His garb of gray and green, foreign as it was in the town, fit in among the mossy trunks and rippling streams, and if he touched a bush or a branch, it was with the air of greeting family and friends.

A sparrow hawk dropped out of the sky as they crossed a meadow, and it swooped across the grass and lit in a tree. "Blessings," said Varden, and the bird nodded its head, then mounted into the sky with quick wing beats.

The path rose slowly, ascending a gentle slope that gradually turned into a small hill. At the top was a cluster of beech and poplar trees.

The morning was well along when they finished their climb. Miriam gasped at the sight that lay below and before her, for on one side of the hill, the trees fell away to give a clear view to the northeast. Malvern Forest stretched off for miles, an apparently endless sea of tossing, gleaming leaves, the young sun glinting and shimmering in the greenery and the fresh, morning breeze singing through the myriad branches.

Spring was at its peak, ripe with the newness of a reborn world. This was a time of flower and leaf, but not of fruit. The harvest was still only an expectation, still merely potential. The world reveled in its youth.

Varden stood beside Miriam. "We call the day *Arae a Circa*, that is, Day of Renewal. This is a time when new paths are chosen, new decisions are made, changes in life are contemplated." Miriam turned to him and stared: his already feminine face had softened even more. He looked like a woman.

The sunlight wove about him in a shimmering aura. He stooped to pick a flower, straightened, and proffered it to her. She took it, but she held it uncomfortably, as though it were a symbol of something she was not certain she wanted.

"You've brought me to holy ground," she said.

"Holy?" said Varden. His face still held the glow of

womanhood. "This place is cherished by my people. Perhaps that is the same thing."

"Why are we here?"

"Renewal," he said. "I come at this time of year to find it, and I thought that, maybe, you might also."

She lifted her eyes, but this time she looked beyond the forest. Malvern did not go on forever. In the direction she faced, it gave way to the dairy lands of Adria. To the north was Hypprux, and Aloysius Cranby .·. . and many memories. Farther was Maris, where she was born. Memories again.

And somewhere out there walked the man she wanted to kill, who was, in a sense, emblematic of her entire life of violation and pain.

"There's only one way I'm going to find renewal," she said.

"How will you do that, Miriam? Are you skilled with a sword?"

"I can learn."

"Can you not forget?"

She nearly snarled at him. Forget? Forget eighteen years? Forget her entire existence? "No."

"Can you not leave it in the past, go on and not look back?"

"No!" The word bounced off the surrounding trees and fell into silence. "Somehow . . . I'm going to find him and kill him. There's no renewal for me until then."

"My lady—"

"Dammit, Varden: he took my soul. I want it back."

"Will killing him restore your soul?"

The aura shone about him, shading into hues of blue and silver. Miriam was struck by the thought of the powers he wielded, and she felt cold at the thought of what she contemplated asking. "You helped me before," she said. "Will you help me now?"

"I am not sure that there is help for me to give. What kind of help could I give you?"

She nearly asked him, then and there, but she stifled the words. Instead she said: "You want me to give up? Should I settle down, Varden? Find a nice man to marry a nasty little woman with scarred legs and a heart to match? You touched my mind. Do you think I can? Do you?"

His voice was so soft as to be inaudible, but she saw his lips move. "I do not."

She turned her back on the endlessly rolling forest, dropped the flower. "Then don't expect me to find renewal out here. For me, renewal comes at the tip of a sword."

"Perhaps it will, Miriam." The voice startled her: it did not sound at all like Varden. She looked. He was wrapped in thought, the aura still bright about him, his garments no longer green and gray, but shining blue and silver. She seemed to see beyond him then, to a grassy plain that lay bathed in starlight.

The aura faltered, shifted, faded. "I am sorry I have inconvenienced you," Varden said simply.

"Thanks for trying to help," she said. "You shouldn't, though. Not this way, at least."

"It was something I had to do."

"Why?"

"I told you," he said as they descended the hill. "When I healed you, I felt what you feel. I know your pain. This is how my people deal with the year's accumulated sorrow. We renew. We restore ourselves."

"So you've forgotten all about it now?"

"I have not. I have put it into perspective. Pain strikes, and it departs. Winter is followed by spring, which leads to summer. All things must pass, even the Elves."

"Even my anger?"

"Even that, unless the world is changed."

"It'll change."

Varden was silent.

They continued. The sun climbed toward the zenith, and the day grew warm. When they came in sight of the town, Miriam saw that buntings had been unfurled from the balconies and towers. Green, red, blue, they flapped and rippled in the breeze. "What's going on?"

"The first of May," said Varden. "Roxanne honors her Goddess, the Elves renew and offer homage to the Lady, and human folk praise the holiness of the Virgin." He smiled as he looked at the pennants and streamers. "And who is to say? All three might be the same."

"You're very open-minded."

"Is there another way?" he said gently.

His words irritated her. "Tell me," she said. "Were you so damned accepting of everything when Jaques Alban was priest?"

"It was difficult at times."

"Or impossible?"

"It was difficult, no more," said Varden. "Nothing is impossible: there are merely differing degrees of probability. Alban was a trial, to be sure. He threatened Andrew, and he attempted to extort a crucifix from David."

"What did he do?" They had halted at the edge of the forest.

The Elf looked at her as though he guessed the reason for her questions, but he answered. "Andrew was our first friend in Saint Brigid. I helped him out of some . . . difficulty. We grew to love him and his family."

"Was that when he and Elizabeth adopted Charity?"

Varden looked uneasy. "It was about that time," he said. "A year later, Alban came to know of our friendship and threatened Andrew with greater excommunication—he was, of course, a friend of Aloysius Cranby and could arrange such things—unless Andrew contributed his work to the building of the new church. Andrew was going to capitulate, but Francis the smith threatened Alban in return. The smith is not a religious man. I imagine that if the Church's devil came to his house, Francis would beat him senseless with his heaviest hammer. Which is, I believe, what he threatened to do to Alban. Alban dropped his threat."

Miriam sensed that she was near something. "What did you do for Andrew? In the beginning, I mean. Did it have anything to do with Charity?"

Varden simply looked at her for a minute. The light in his eyes flickered. "Do you love Charity?" he said.

Miriam shrugged. "She's a nice girl."

"I think you care more than that."

"All right: yes, I like her. She's been very kind to me."

"I will say this," said the Elf. "We helped Andrew, and Andrew helped Charity. I will say no more."

You don't have to. That's enough . . . for now. Aloud,

she said: "So what about Alban and David? Francis said something about it."

Miriam felt Varden's glance as though it were a physical touch. For a moment, he examined her, and she began to fear that she had pressed her questioning too far.

But he appeared to reach some decision. "Once again, Alban wanted work for his church. A crucifix. David is famous throughout the land for his woodcarving—"

"Yes," said Miriam. "I've seen the statue in the church."

"Have you really?"

There was an odd tone in his voice. She could not fathom it. A silence grew. "It's . . . it's the Virgin . . . isn't it?"

"I suppose it could be." Varden smiled softly and went on. "David has a sister in a convent to the north. Alban threatened her."

"But David didn't carve the crucifix."

"He did not. Alban disappeared about that time, and his threats went with him."

"Very convenient."

Varden merely looked at her.

"Alban makes trouble, and he vanishes," said Miriam. "Just like that. And Roxanne mentioned an old hag—the Leather Woman—who cast spells on villagers. And she disappeared. Just like that. It sounds like Saint Brigid has become a very happy town since the Elves arrived."

"Would you have me answer any other questions, Miriam?" Again, he sounded as though he knew why she was asking.

Again she was tempted, very tempted, to voice her desire. But no, not yet. Too soon. She was now more confident that her suspicions about Alban were true, but she had to be sure. And there was also the question of the Leather Woman. Charity? What could an old hag, long vanished, have to do with Charity?

In answer, a thought came into her head, but she dismissed it as foolish, almost insane.

Varden was looking at her. Examining her. Sizing her up.

Varden floated among the stars.

He had but to stretch out his mind a little to feel the limits of the universe. The moon was there, and the sun, and seas of stars that floated in the void like vast whirlpools. Saint Brigid was there, too, and he cast his awareness through the streets of the town, staying in the present, ignoring for the moment what could happen, what might come to be.

The streets were bright with torches and lamps, and the balconies were hung with tapestries and hangings. Andrew and Elizabeth ran hand in hand toward the common, pausing, as though they were newly wed, for a long kiss in the darkness of a porch. On the common, a cooking fire had been built, and Kay stirred a huge pot of stew, tasting it with a beatific smile on his face, snapping his fingers with delight when words failed him. Francis played the viele, and people danced; and Michael had become a bit of a juggler, and he did not drop the balls too often.

Varden touched a familiar house, entered. Roxanne was donning elven garb, tucking the gray breeches into soft boots and belting her tunic loosely. Her dark hair fell in waves and curls. He smiled. She felt his presence.

"Varden?"

Here, beloved.

"I'm almost ready. Are you not coming?"

I will be along, Sana. I have some work to do.

"Will you be long?"

Not long at all. He touched her cheek, and she smiled.

"I'll meet you at the edge of the forest."

He kissed her, and then his awareness left her house. Silently, he felt along the street and took a turning, noting as he did that the folk of Saint Brigid were dancing a long dance on the common. Francis played his viele, and Harry had joined in on a musette. Couple by couple, the villagers spun down the green and back again, split apart and rejoined. Francis whooped.

Only the real for now, not the potential.

A star called him, bright blue white and shining, but he continued down the street and slid into Kay's house. Down the hall. An oaken door. Miriam lay on her bed, eyes unclosed, wrapped in a comforter. Her face was hard, and Varden saw the pain of the past and the present in it, as well as the massive horror that had come to dominate both and thereby threaten the future. He almost turned away to seek reassurance among the stars, but he stayed, watching Miriam, reliving the rape, stepping through it moment by moment, possibility by possibility.

He explored the alternatives, followed the strands of probability that led away from the event, found that most led to madness, the rest to death. This present, this present alone, with Miriam lying in Kay's house wrapped in a comforter, brooding on hate and revenge, had been the only future that continued for any length of time. There was meaning in that.

He twisted his consciousness, looked into the future. He did not know fear, but what he saw there was unsettling, for the lattices of the possible blurred into the infinite and unpredictable.

He turned back to the young woman on the bed. He knew what she wanted, knew also that she would eventually ask for it, but did not know what he would say in return.

Someone knocked on the front door. Miriam flinched. Varden saw the cascade of memories: soldiers, armed men, shouting people, the dungeon at Hypprux, the blades. . . .

He pulled away from her thoughts, filtered through the wall, and saw Charity enter. "Miriam," she called.

Miriam did not stir.

Charity ran down the hall and knocked at the door. "Miriam."

"Yes," said the healer at last. "I'm here."

Charity threw the door open. "Come on, Miriam. Everyone's having a good time on the common, and you're lying in bed."

"I don't know how to dance."

"Or to laugh either, I imagine." Charity pulled the comforter off Miriam. "I'm not leaving you here. You're coming out, and you're going to sit with my family and me, and maybe father will dance with you. He's very good. And you don't have to be afraid of him."

"I'm not afraid." Miriam was looking strangely at Charity. Varden saw her thoughts. The Leather Woman. What had happened to the Leather Woman? What had she to do with Charity?

His heart was cold. A thought, and the house vanished. The stars were about him. He went toward the blue-white flame that called, threw himself into it, stood then on a grassy plain that went on forever. The starlight tingled through him, and he went down on one knee before the Lady who stood there.

"I do not know what to do," he said simply.

"I cannot tell you." Her eyes flashed with the depth of a million universes: past, present, and potential.

"I cannot read the future. There is too much of it. Who is Miriam that she brings so many futures with her?"

"She is on a path, Varden."

"But where is she going, My Lady?"

She shook her head slightly. "You know I cannot answer. Miriam makes her path as she lives. You will counsel, and I will love, but she will decide."

"And if she asks me?" He spread his hands slightly.

"Then that is your own path. And you will decide." She touched his head. "My child."

After a while he opened his eyes to the fields around Saint Brigid. The stars were clear and bright, and he felt their light merge with that of the shimmer about him.

"*Elthia Calasiuove*," he murmured.

Chapter Ten

The letters and words Miriam learned from Kay were helping her, but not in any way that the good priest had intended. By mid-June, she had filled several wax tablets with her clumsy writing, setting down a record of the hidden workings of Saint Brigid: the tales no one would tell directly, the stories that filtered to her only in bits and snatches.

She sat up into the night and went over what she had. The weather was warm, and the windows of her room were open to let in air. A moth fluttered about the flame of the candle on the table, and the letters danced with the flickering light. Miriam read slowly, quietly, her voice a steady whisper.

The Leather Woman had been first. She had lived in Saint Brigid for nearly eighty years, a crippled, embittered, leather worker who practiced magic against those she hated. She killed most of a flock of sheep when its shepherd made fun of her. She withered crops. She caused sickness.

Andrew the carpenter tried to help her. Francis assisted him, and lost his hands as a result. Varden healed Francis. Around Christmas of 1343, the old woman disappeared. Her house had been left deserted, her belongings untouched. No corpse. No explanation.

And then, again around Christmas of 1343, Charity had been found by Andrew in the bracken near the Leather Woman's hut. The carpenter and his wife adopted the homeless child.

Miriam leaned back in her chair, her eyes following the moth for a moment. Coincidence? Chance? She wondered. Varden had said that he had helped Andrew, who in turn had helped Charity. But Andrew's efforts had been directed at the Leather Woman, not at Charity, and Varden had healed Francis, not Andrew. How had that helped Charity?

Inscribed in wax, the words made her suspicions take on shape and substance; but they also kept her alert to contradictions, whether in the stories of the villagers or in her own theories. 1343 . . .

And then Jaques Alban. 1348. Varden's story about David and the crucifix had been corroborated by several villagers, including the woodcarver himself. David was a thin man with a sharp nose, whose hands seemed always to be groping for a chisel and a mallet. His earnest blue eyes had bored into Miriam's face as he had told her his story.

But he said that he did not know what happened to Alban. And just then, his earnest blue eyes shifted a little. Dissembling was not easy for the honest carver.

What Miriam wanted was someone who would stand before her and say straight out: *Yes, Alban became a pig. And Charity used to be an old hag who cast spells.* Only then could she confront Varden and demand that she be given consideration and help.

The moth fluttered and danced about the flame.

Miriam watched it. "Change me, Varden," she said slowly, whispering still. "Change me. Make me strong. Make me bigger. Make me able to fight."

The moth flicked about, circled the flame, and dived in. It crackled and hissed as it was immolated.

Charity came to the priest's house clad in a light blue summer gown, an empty basket on her arm. "Blessed be, Kay! Is Miriam home?"

Miriam was sweeping the floor. Kay swung the door wide. The scent of a midsummer morning spilled in.

Charity stepped across the threshold lightly. "Can you come to the forest with me, Miriam? I'm gathering flowers for Roxanne."

"Flowers? You mean herbs?"

"No. Flowers. It's the solstice, and we both want flowers."

Kay laughed. "I don't hear any of this, of course," he said. "Hmmph. Godless pagans."

Charity wrinkled her nose at him. "Hmmph. Goddessless Christians."

"Will I be seeing you at Mass anymore after tonight?" The priest's voice was hearty, but Miriam heard the underlying sadness.

Charity smiled and kissed him on the cheek. "Of course you will, Kay. All paths lead to the same ending. Just be sure you leave the statue of the Lady right where it is."

"Have no fear." He bent and hugged her. "And good luck to you."

Miriam had doffed her apron. "What's tonight?"

Charity blushed, but her lake-blue eyes sparkled. "Tonight I become a priestess. Roxanne will lead me through the Mysteries."

Kay smiled fondly. "As I said, I don't hear any of this."

Miriam turned to the priest. "Aren't you worried at all, Kay?"

He shrugged. "No. Not at all."

"What about the Inquisition?"

"I carry the knowledge I have to my grave," said Kay soberly.

"Or to the stake?"

"If it's God's will, yes. Sometimes we have to suffer and die to save something precious."

Charity spoke. "Roxanne and I would do the same for Kay."

Miriam remembered her suspicions. Could it really be? She peered into Charity's eyes for the hundredth time, trying to see some trace of another life there. The Leather Woman? Miriam had asked once about the girl's earliest memories, but Charity remembered nothing of her life before Andrew found her in the heather and snow. And her eyes were clear, untroubled, loving.

Innocent.

Miriam felt a pang and looked away. How could she think such a thing? Could she not leave Charity to her youth? Was she going to sacrifice that innocence and love to the revenge she sought?

"Miriam," said Charity. "Can you come?"

"Yes," she said hoarsely. "Yes. Just a minute. A memory, nothing more. It'll pass."

Charity put an arm around her. "Poor Miriam. Find peace, please, Miriam. We all love you."

Miriam's eyes ached, but tears were a long time gone. She could not weep anymore. But neither could she pursue Charity's past. Leave it, she told herself. Charity is as she is. Leave her alone. Just enjoy her for what she brings to everyone.

They went out toward the forest together, Charity singing as they walked. Miriam did not recognize the language. Italian?

"Elvish," said Charity. "Varden and Roxanne taught it to me. You can do it as a hocket, where everyone alternates singing the words and the song goes round and round."

The sun was bright, the crops head-high or higher, The road opened out, turned, and they saw the forest. "I'd think you'd get dizzy," said Miriam.

"Oh, no. It's fun. Roxanne and Varden and I sang it last Beltaine, and when we got it up to speed, we were holding a circle of starlight in our hands."

The road north skirted the trees. Miriam noticed a small house in the forest and wondered that she had seen it at all, for it was carefully carved and decorated so as to resemble the leaves, trunks, and branches around it. "What's that?"

"You must be getting used to Saint Brigid, Miriam." Charity laughed. "Outsiders usually don't see it. It's David and Charlotte's house. David built it years ago when he wanted to be a recluse."

Miriam stopped in the road.

"Is something wrong, Miriam?"

She would not touch Charity, would not mar the sanctity of her youth and love with her own soiled heart. Alban, though. Maybe Alban would be enough. "Could you go ahead, Charity? I think I'd like to stop in on David a moment. I'll catch up with you."

Charity shrugged. "All right, Miriam. Don't be long, please. I want to show you a patch of wood roses I've found." She gave her a kiss and went off down the road.

As Miriam approached the door of the house, she heard the sound of singing from the back. She recalled that Charlotte had been in the market square that morning. Good fortune: David was alone in his workshop.

She went around to the back of the house. David was still singing:

*"Alma redemptoris Mater, quae pervia cáeli
Porta manes et Stella Maris, succurre cadenti. . . ."*

She knocked at the back door and the hymn stopped. She heard tools being laid down, and the carver opened the door. "Miriam! Blessings! How are you today?"

"I'm fine, David. I was passing by. Might I stop in for a moment? I've heard so much about your carvings."

He waved her in. "I'm just doing some fine finishing on a piece for the church. You're welcome to sit a bit. Charlotte's gone to market. She'll be back by noon."

Off to one side were two panels, faced just now away from her. Wood chips and dust were scattered around them.

It was a tidy, well-designed workroom, with tools arranged neatly on shelves, a large table, and plenty of light. Near one wall was a carving in high relief of a cityscape. David saw Miriam looking at it.

"I did it for a nobleman in Maris," he said. "It's a view of the city from his window. He had a charcoal sketch sent down to me. I think it's a good rendering."

David was innately modest. Miriam could almost see the river move and the ocean sparkle in the sun. But in the distance, at the tip of a rocky headland that reached out and sheltered the city's harbor, was a small hamlet. Merely a jumble of houses and barns. Her birthplace. She turned away quickly. "It's lovely."

David snorted. "And it'll probably stay here in Saint Brigid. The man died just as I finished it, and his heirs are so busy fighting over his lands and holdings that they don't have time to send someone to collect it. I'll keep it for them."

Miriam was a little shaken. "I hope . . . I hope I'm not interrupting your work."

"I needed to put down my tools for a minute anyway."

"You said you were doing something for the church. Some panels?"

"Oh, yes," said David.

"I'm surprised you want to have anything to do with the Church after . . . after your dealings with Alban."

David looked a little uncomfortable. "Kay isn't Alban."

"But it's the same Church, isn't it?"

"Actually," said the carver, "it isn't. That statue of the Lady wasn't there when Alban was priest in Saint Brigid."

"Does that make a difference?" She tried to sound as though her questions were prompted only by friendly curiosity, but the effect was strained. She did not have the skill.

"Haven't you looked at it?"

"Of course I've looked at it. I've been in there once or twice. Actually, I'm surprised you can stand to be in the church at all. After what I've been through, I usually stay away from churches. I don't believe in it anymore. How do you do it?"

David pulled up a stool and sat down, fiddling idly with the hem of his coarse tunic. He shrugged.

Miriam watched him for a moment. "What really happened to Alban?"

"He went away."

"You're lying, David."

The carver lifted his head and glared at her. Miriam wondered if she saw a shimmer in his intense blue eyes. "What's so important about what happened to a fat priest?"

"The Elves changed him, didn't they?"

David went pale.

"They turned him into a pig, didn't they?"

David gritted his teeth. After a while he said: "Alban vanished."

"It was Varden changed him, wasn't it?" Nervous, she crossed the room to the window and looked out, half-afraid that the Elf was listening.

"Why are you asking these questions?"

"Because I want to know for sure," she cried. "I keep hearing all these hints, all these whispered half-truths. I want to know what they add up to. I need to be certain, because . . . because . . ." She turned back to David and was confronted by the tall panels, intricately carved and partly burnished now with all the skill of a master carver. The pictures leaped out at her. The figures were almost alive. The water almost—no, did indeed move. The clouds floated in the sky. Varden and David stood together as a fat priest ran off into an interlacing of forest trees. Stags, foxes, birds . . . all creation looked on in surprise. In Varden's hand was a staff, and it was pointed at the priest.

And the other panel was much the same, save that the figure of the priest had been replaced with that of a pig.

Miriam stood, frozen. "It's true," she whispered.

David had buried his face in his hands. "Yes, it's true. All of it. Varden tried to persuade Alban to give up his demands, but Alban was too stubborn to back down. Elves don't like to take life, and it seemed more appropriate for Alban, anyway."

"Why didn't anyone just tell me?"

"Not everyone knows. Many people in Saint Brigid think it's just a story. I felt safe doing the panels because of that."

Miriam looked at the panels again. The world had just changed. Everything had just changed. "I'm sorry I'm so mean, David," she said. "But I have to kill a man. And you've just given me a key to a locked door."

She left the house. If she was quick, she could find Charity and ask the girl to take her to Varden. The thought of what she might do then made her giddy with both anticipation and fear. Alban had felt the touch of those elven energies. What had been in his mind when, of a sudden, his body had been seized and reshaped? What was it like? Where was he now?

She had gone some distance down the road when she realized that she was hearing screams. With a chill, she recognized Charity's voice.

"Varden! Miriam!"

The little healer found a path into the forest and set off at a run. Branches slashed at her face and tore at her gown. Charity continued to cry out.

The screams cut off suddenly. Miriam rounded a turning and stopped short. Ten yards away was the man who had raped her, and he was squared off against Varden. The Elf had set himself in a low guard stance. He was unarmed. His opponent held a sword.

Crumpled against the trees at one side of the clearing, her gown torn at the shoulder, was Charity. The girl was breathing in ragged gasps, and her hands were clutched against her belly. Near her was the basket, half-full of wood roses and violets, crushed and trampled.

The man's gaze flicked to Miriam, and then back to Varden. "I'm glad to see you so well, my pretty healer."

She nearly threw herself at him, but she knew it was useless. *Another score, you bastard.*

Charity was obviously injured, and the power started rising up Miriam's spine. She had learned a little from Roxanne, though, and she managed to keep her head clear.

"Attend to Charity, Miriam," said Varden calmly.

Miriam forced herself to move around the perimeter of the clearing. The man's gaze flicked back to her, and Varden moved, flashing into action in the space of a heartbeat. The man did not have time to swing the sword, but his own reactions were quick enough that he ducked out of the way and slammed his elbow into the Elf's ribs.

Varden's momentum carried him past his opponent. When he rolled back up to his feet again, his face was pale. Miriam's power burned hotter: the Elf had been injured.

As had Charity. Miriam knelt beside the girl and held her, but Charity did not appear to notice. Miriam could not tell exactly what had been done to her. Almost anything, given the girl's condition. Charity was calm, intelligent, and strong in her own way, but she could not stand against a sudden, brutal, unprovoked attack.

Movement. Miriam looked up to see the man swinging his sword at Varden. The Elf rolled out of the way and struck for his eyes. The man screamed, but he ripped back and down with the sword and opened Varden's side.

Blood was suddenly everywhere, and the Elf staggered back, face pale, teeth clenched. But as the man approached for a final blow, Varden's hand found a stout tree branch and, before the sword could fall, sent it crashing into the man's skull. The man reeled. Varden collapsed.

When the man regained his balance, he stepped forward to finish off the Elf. Miriam's anger eclipsed even the heat in her spine. This was her rapist, and she was watching him do away with the being who had healed her, shown her kindness, brought her a vision of heaven that, even though she had refused it, she at least recognized.

Without knowing what she would do, she let go of Charity, rose, and threw herself on his broad back. Locking her legs around his neck, she tore at his face, at his eyes, felt blood start to flow under her fingers.

She was screaming, clawing, biting at his scalp and ears. She was vaguely aware that he had dropped his sword and that his hands were reaching for her. She cursed him, but he plucked her off his head as though she were a hat and flung her across the clearing.

She hit the ground in a red haze of pain and hate, and she heard his laughter. Pushing herself up on her elbows, she watched him approach. His face was a mass of blood and welts.

"Ah, little one, don't you like me?"

But she saw that behind him, impossibly, Varden was struggling to his feet, holding the dropped sword. His skin was ashen from blood loss, and she had no idea where he derived the strength to do such a thing. By human standards, he should have been dead already.

The Elf drew himself up straight, blood still pumping from his rent side. The man became aware that Miriam's attention was elsewhere, and he started to turn.

Varden's voice rang out suddenly, clear and bright, like a glitter of cold steel. *"Elthia!"* He raised the sword and threw it, and it turned over once in the air and buried itself in the man's shoulder. As the giant spun around with the impact, the Elf sprawled face-forward onto the grass.

Miriam could not believe it: *the man was still standing.* He looked at the blade, then, "Later, mistress," he whispered. He turned and made his way off into the forest.

"I'm going to kill you," she screamed, but she had been screaming too much, and her voice was so hoarse that she could bearly hear herself.

Charity lay a few feet away from her, unconscious. Miriam attempted to crawl toward the girl and discovered that her right leg was not working. Blurry with power, she pulled back her skirt and found her knee bent at an odd angle. *Broken,* she thought fuzzily.

But that was not important. Charity was nearby, and she dragged herself across the grass, the power flaming along her spine.

When she laid her hands on the girl and let the energy go, it was as though a sun had kindled in her head, and when it was over, she fell away, mostly blind, mostly deaf, hardly capable of feeling anything.

He must have hurt her inside. He probably beat her. I have to kill him.

Something was tugging at her mind, though, pulling her away from Charity. She remembered Varden.

It can't be. He's dead.

Blasted by her power, her leg shattered, she nonetheless crawled across the clearing, dirt caking her face, her brain on fire. When she reached the Elf, she would have sworn that he was dead. But the power demanded, and the power got its way regardless of her wishes, her thoughts, or her denials.

She fell on top of him. The incandescence struck.

Chapter Eleven

For some time after her vision returned and cleared, Miriam thought she was back in the forest, recovering from the rape, bleeding onto the ground, the drone of swarming flies loud in her ears. But she heard voices speaking Elvish, and though she did not understand that language, the smooth, liquid sounds of the words calmed her, told her that the rape was in the past. She lived in Saint Brigid now, with Kay, and she had . . . had friends. A miracle. The whole town. And—

Charity. Varden.

Miriam flailed out and tried to push herself up. She caught a glimpse of a broad clearing, of people clad in green and gray, but her coordination failed her and she fell back.

Someone came to kneel beside her, and a hand passed across her forehead. She became conscious of a familiar warm glow, and a calm, young face came into view.

Her visitor smiled shyly. "I am Talla," she said. Her hair was a dark mass of curls that caught the light in sparks of red. Her eyes were blue and filled with starlight. "Be at peace."

Miriam croaked out the words: "Charity. Varden."

"Both are well," said the Elfmaid. "Your powers are great, healer."

The sound of harp strings hung for a moment in the clearing, a cascading arpeggio that seemed to make the sky itself shimmer and ripple like a wind-stirred pond. Miriam's thoughts wandered off into the blazing light that had burst in her mind when she had laid hands on Varden. She shook her head, tried to hold on to the present.

Light. Radiance. Stars. Suns. The essence of illumination, and yet more. There was something behind it, something that she wanted to see again, though she did not remember what it was.

She stared at the sky. Light . . .

She struggled. "Please," she said to Talla. "Help me up."

The Elf lifted her. Miriam sat on the ground, her face in her hands, pulling the soft air into her lungs. *I'm here. My name is Miriam. I have black hair. I have black eyes.*

The light subsided to a gentle radiance in the back of her mind. Talla was peering into her face. "I'm sorry," Miriam said. "I'm not myself."

The Elf put her hands to Miriam's temples and leaned forward until their foreheads touched. The light flickered, and Miriam had a vision of stars shining serenely in a night sky. She sighed and relaxed. Her hands dropped into her lap. Softness wrapped around her and cradled her for several minutes.

"Where are we?" she said.

Talla's voice came to her as if within her mind. "We are in the forest, among my people. We became aware of Varden's plight and came looking."

"Did you find . . . him?"

"We did not. He had a horse nearby."

A horse. No ordinary brigand then. And those hands. It did not make sense. Nothing did.

She shook herself slightly, and Talla's hands fell away. The clearing came back, and she saw clearly the shimmer about the people in gray and green. The odor of baking bread mixed with the scent of leaves and pine needles, and someone was playing the harp she had heard earlier. After a minute, a maid's sweet voice soared up in Elvish.

Talla closed her eyes and listened, a slight smile on her lips. The song wound on like a river of silver, and it reminded Miriam a little of what she had sensed behind the blinding light.

"What do the words mean?" she said.

"It is a song for this day," said Talla. "It is about fulfillment, and about the cycles that weave through our lives. Natil is singing it for Charity: her music has the power to heal the mind, and Charity needs that at present."

"Charity . . . was she . . . did that bastard . . . ?"

Talla laid a hand on Miriam's arm. "Be at peace, friend. Charity is badly shaken, but she is otherwise well. Sana— Roxanne—is on her way here, and we have sent for Andrew and Elizabeth." She looked off into the distance as though her thoughts were elsewhere. "They should be here soon."

The light in Miriam's mind flared a little, and she saw Charity's parents moving through the forest. Andrew's face was set, his eyes hard with worry. Elizabeth looked much the same, and she was wearing a red kerchief.

The vision faded. She dismissed it as a passing fancy, but Talla was looking at her curiously. "Are you well, Mistress Healer?"

"I'm fine. Where's Charity? Where's Varden?"

"Behind you," came his voice, and she turned. He still looked pale, and he was leaning on a stick, but his eyes were calm. "My deepest thanks." He smiled thinly and went down on one knee before her.

Miriam's eyes suddenly filled with tears. "I saw you. You were dead. I couldn't have brought you back. You were dead."

"Your powers are great, Miriam."

"I can't bring you people back from the dead." She was still weeping.

"I was not dead. It is difficult to kill an Elf."

"It's not impossible."

"That is so."

She wiped her eyes on a sleeve and shook her head in disbelief. "You're immortal. But you were willing to throw it all away for a human."

He laughed quietly. "I love Charity. Sometimes we must battle for those things we hold dear. And that is certainly not what I would consider to be throwing my life away."

She wiped at her eyes again. "I couldn't do that. I couldn't love anyone that much."

"Indeed?"

"I don't care enough about anyone for that."

"All right."

She had the suspicion that he was amused, and she finally realized that she had been crying, that her sleeve was damp with tears. She could not weep, but she had wept nonetheless. "Will you please stop kneeling to me?" she snapped.

"I would rather you rose first."

She glared at him. "Talla, please help me up." Her legs were unsteady, but she managed to stand, and Varden stood also. He was visibly gaining strength with each minute, and when he took a deep breath, Miriam saw, again, the light. There was about him an unquenchable inner joy that seemed to be awakened simply by the air, the sky, the sunlight; and the radiance that had become a part of her responded to it.

Roxanne stepped into the clearing, clad as an Elf, looking as much like one, Miriam thought, as any human could. Her dark hair danced as she ran to Varden, and they embraced. "Thank the Lady you're safe," she murmured into his shoulder.

"Thank Miriam also, beloved," said the Elf. "I had almost passed over, but she healed me."

Roxanne turned to Miriam. Moonlight was in her eyes, and Miriam saw wellsprings of power within her. And she saw more. . . .

The witch held out her hands, and Miriam, without thinking, took them. "My thanks to you, maiden," said Roxanne, and there was respect and love in the title. Miriam stammered an acknowledgment, but she was held by her interior vision. She knew suddenly that Roxanne was pregnant, that the child was Varden's, and a boy. She did not have to ask: she was certain.

Varden was speaking to Roxanne. "Go to Charity, beloved. I am well, and you have her initiation to think of."

Roxanne nodded, bent, and kissed Miriam's forehead, then went off with Talla to the other side of the clearing where the harper was still playing. There, two humans were just then stepping out of the trees. Charity's voice rang out: "Mother! Father!"

Miriam saw the girl then: slender, slight, her dark hair loose and flowing. She stood up and stretched out her hands to Elizabeth and Andrew, then ran to them and flung herself into their arms.

Miriam felt a pang. She was remembering her own mother and father, and that terrible day when she had seen them for the last time, their faces filled with something very different from love and concern. She dropped her eyes and was about to turn away when a stray thought made her look more closely at Charity's mother. Elizabeth was indeed wearing a red kerchief.

Varden slipped an arm about her shoulders. "You are disturbed," he said quietly.

She lowered her eyes. In the back of her mind the light churned into a sea of luminescence. "There's something wrong with me. I saw Elizabeth and Andrew before they arrived. As though they were out in the forest."

"Have you ever healed an Elf before?"

"Miriam!" Charity's voice. The girl was waving at her. Miriam waved back absently, turned to Varden. "What do you mean?"

He touched her shoulder. "When I healed you, my mind touched yours. When you healed me, even though you were unconscious of it, your mind . . ." He smiled slightly. "You see partly as we do now. Think of it as a gift."

"Gift?" she flared. "I don't need any more gifts. The one I've got brings me nothing but trouble. I need someone dead, that's what I need." But she remembered what she had forced out of David that morning, and she fell silent. Charity arrived just then and threw her arms about Miriam's neck.

Feeling awkward, Miriam held her. Charity was shining with light and health, her scars and memory healed by Natil's magic. But when she lifted her head, Miriam suddenly saw a depth in the girl that went back far beyond thirteen summers, that stretched off into another lifetime.

Elizabeth and Andrew stood before her. Andrew was not a large man, but he was well-muscled. He was also gentle, almost shy, and as he stood with damp eyes for a moment, he bowed deeply. "I didn't know," he said, "that when I carried you to the village, Miriam, I was also bearing my daughter's life."

"We owe you a great deal, Mistress Healer," said Elizabeth.

Miriam was still shaken by what she had seen. The Leather Woman. And even Charity did not know. "You don't owe me anything," she stammered. "No one does, except for . . . for someone who owes me a life." She turned to Varden. "I can't stay here," she blurted, and tears were blurring her vision as she ran for the edge of the clearing.

Varden caught up with her before she had gone more than a few yards into the trees. She was hurrying as though pursued, but he fell into step beside her without apparent effort.

"If you wish to go home," he said, "you ought to turn around." She noticed that he no longer needed his stick.

"I'm all right, thank you."

"That may be, but the village is to the west. We are traveling east." There was no mockery in his voice.

She stopped short and whirled on him. "What do you want of me?" she demanded.

"I would help you, if I could."

"If you really want to help, you could—" She caught herself. Was she ready to say that? Was she ready to face the Elf's reaction? "You could . . . teach me how to fight," she finished lamely. "I've never seen anything like what you did. If that bastard hadn't had a sword, you'd probably have finished him."

Varden flinched as though she had accused him of a crime. "I would not have killed him. I would have stopped him from injuring any of us, but I would not have killed him." He shook his head. "In any case, fighting is not my talent. I could not teach it."

"Maybe someone else, then?"

"Some of us are so skilled. Still, you are oversmall for such work."

Miriam looked him full in the face. Did he know of her desire? Was he, in some subtle elven way, already seeking to counter an argument that might be presented in the future?

Nothing is impossible, he had said. *There are merely differing levels of probability.*

But if that were true, then it was also possible that she could gain the stature and strength necessary to kill the man who had raped her. And suddenly she became aware that his tone could have meant *anything,* that he could just as well have been encouraging her request as seeking an escape from it.

Varden's eyes were deep, starlit, immortal. He had seen much. What was he seeing now?

She was almost frightened. "I'm sorry, Varden. I can't do anything else, though." Was she talking about her hate, or about the request that she had not, as yet, uttered? She herself was not sure.

"I understand," he said after a minute.

Understand? Understand what? The future seemed to split into a lattice of plexed potentials, each one subsequently riven into further probable outcomes, and each one of those . . .

Her mind reeled. "Varden," she whispered, putting her hands to her head, "help me. I can't stand this."

He touched her lightly on the head, and the futures settled, folded back into themselves, faded into a shimmer.

"Take me home, please," she said when she could speak again.

"Will you not stay an hour or so with us? You have not eaten today. We would like to have your company."

"I don't see how you can stand me." She wanted to be away. She wanted to run home and lock herself in her room at the priest's house. She needed darkness and solitude, and she was glad Jaques Alban had built a house that allowed her a private room before he disappeared.

Disappeared? No. He was turned into a pig by . . . by Varden. And Charity . . .

"We would like to help. All of us," said Varden softly. His words held two meanings again.

She considered. Was he, then, offering? "All right," she said after a time. "I'll go with you. Maybe I can find something I'm looking for."

Double meanings.

Chapter Twelve

There was food and wine and music. Natil was a skilled harper, and although Miriam did not understand the language of her songs, the sounds themselves made pictures in her mind. The Elf was singing of the day again, of fulfillment, of completion, and the music filled the clearing as the wine filled Miriam's cup: clear, sparkling, infused with the good, strong warmth of the day, flavored with flower and fruit, touched with the radiance of the stars.

The sun passed the zenith and began to drop slowly toward the western treetops, and it was late afternoon when Varden escorted Miriam back to the priest's house. Miriam opened the door and turned to Varden. The Elf regarded her quietly. "Will you stop in for a bit, Varden?" she said.

"My lady," he said, "Charity is to be initiated tonight, and I would like to spend some time with her before Roxanne takes her into Circle."

"This won't take long." She tried to keep her voice even, but it shook.

After a moment, he nodded and followed her into the house. Miriam brought the fire up and heated water, and the Elf sat at the big table, a shaft of sunlight falling on him through one of the high windows.

Miriam made peppermint infusion and filled two cups. "I need your help," she said, setting one before Varden.

The Elf regarded the cup and the woman before he answered. "I offered help before," he said, "and you refused. I have no power on the path you have chosen."

"Ah, but you do."

"What is it you wish?" He sat back, away from her, hands resting on the arms of the chair. He looked completely off guard. But Miriam knew that he saw many futures and knew their possible outcomes. How could he ever be taken by surprise? Even her careful maneuvering seemed to her now to be the actions of a fool.

She plunged in. "You and your people have the power to transform living beings." Even to her own ears it sounded like an accusation.

Varden passed a hand over his face. "All right," he said softly, as though to himself. When he looked up again, he said: "What has given you that idea?"

"This is no idea, Varden. Elves lie badly, so don't try. I know about Jaques Alban and I know about—" She caught herself. No, not Charity. "I . . . I . . . know what happened to him."

Varden averted his eyes.

"It's true, isn't it? *Isn't it?*" She was out of her chair, leaning across the table as far as she could, the steam from Varden's cup rising into her face.

The Elf did not speak for some time. The starlight blazed in his eyes as though he were watching the crossing and recrossing of the many futures, evaluating their new pattern, finding both hope and fear.

"Well?"

"It is true."

"Then you can transform me."

"What are you asking?" The question was almost formal.

She considered carefully. "I'm asking . . ." She felt the light in his gaze. "I'm asking for what I need. Strength and stature. I assume I can find someone among your people who can teach me the way of the sword. But I need to . . . to change."

"Miriam, I—"

"Will you do it?"

He hesitated, still weighing the futures.

"Varden, dammit, you said you'd help. Now I tell you how you can, and you sit there. Are you going to back down after I saved your life?"

"Miriam . . ."

"Cranby and the Inquisition broke my body, Varden, but he took my soul. I want it back. I can't get it back without your help."

"But this way?" he finally burst out. "Magic of that potency is dangerous. Any magic is, but this kind especially so. It cannot be totally controlled. It takes strange forms. There is no telling in what other ways you might be changed.''

"I'll take my chances.''

"But—''?

"Varden, one thing I'm sure of: I can't continue like this.''

"Please do not ask me, Miriam.''

He could do it. She knew he could. "Varden, it's necessary.''

"There are always alternatives.''

"Sometimes there aren't. You've been with Roxanne enough—my God, she's carrying your child—you should know by now that humans are different from Elves. Your people are immortal. You can wait. You can heal. My people die. We don't have time. I can't live like this. I have to do something. You can help me. Or is all your talk about healing and comfort just so much horse shit?''

He merely looked at her.

She realized that she had been shouting. "Varden,'' she said quietly, "Jaques Alban was a nasty bastard, but you didn't kill him. Who knows, he might be happier as a pig than he ever was as a man. The Leather Woman . . .''

The Elf stiffened.

Miriam forced herself to continue. "The Leather Woman was an evil old hag who killed sheep and blasted Francis's hands off. And . . .'' The words stuck in her throat. "And . . .'' *Leave Charity alone. Leave her!* "And . . .'' Her eyes teared. "You helped her, that's all. And she'd been evil.'' She was still crying, not at her own plight, but at that of the Leather Woman. "And I haven't done anything except get tortured and raped. *So why the hell won't you help me?*''

Varden was shaking. Letting his hands fall into his lap, he closed his eyes. "Dear Lady.''

The door latch slid back with a sharp clatter, and Kay stepped into the room carrying a basket of vegetables. He smiled cheerily. "Good afternoon!''

Varden regarded him hollowly. "Be at peace, Kay.''

Kay caught the tone of his voice. "You should take your own advice, my friend. What's happened?"

"Oh, nothing much," said Miriam, angered by the intrusion. "Charity was almost raped this morning by the same son of a bitch that did me, Varden was almost killed, and now he's balking at a simple request that I be transformed magically. Nothing at all."

Her words went by quickly, and the priest stood in shock for a moment. He set down his basket and hung his cloak on the wooden peg by the door. Varden shifted in his chair as though moving a weight from one shoulder to another without actually getting rid of any of it.

"Then the brute is still about," said Kay tonelessly. Varden offered him his untouched tea. The priest took a swallow without appearing to be aware of what he was doing, then suddenly came to himself. "What happened? Is Charity all right? Varden?"

"We are well," said the Elf. "Charity was beaten, but she has been healed in body and in spirit. I am myself sound, by Miriam's power."

"And the brute?"

"He could well be dead."

"Don't bet on it," said Miriam. "I don't believe he can be killed without tearing him limb from limb." She turned to the priest. "He had a sword sticking through him. And he walked away. *He walked away!*"

Kay looked back and forth between the two of them.

"Miriam is probably right," Varden admitted.

"And he'll be back," said Miriam.

Kay set down the cup and wrung his hands. "Child," he said, "please: give up the idea of killing him."

"Why?" Miriam struck her hand on the tabletop, but her small fist made only a small sound. "Why should I? Give me one good reason."

Kay stared. Varden spoke. "I have warned her of the dangers."

"Varden!" cried the priest. "Surely you don't mean to . . ." He groped for words. "It's madness. Verily, verily madness." He spread his hands helplessly.

"When I healed Miriam," said the Elf, "I lived not only

through her rape, but also her life. I am not sure that I can call this madness.''

''But—''

''Have you ever been tortured, Kay? Raped? Persecuted?''

The priest opened his mouth to speak, considered, then shut it. Miriam looked to Varden. Was he defending her position? Then that must mean . . .

The Elf turned to Miriam. ''Is this what you want?''

''It is,'' she said without hesitation.

''Do you ask without coercion, of your own free will?''

''Yes, I do.''

''Do you freely accept the consequences of your actions, knowing that, if granted, your wish may prove to be of questionable worth?''

''I do.''

Varden regarded her for some time. The fire crackled on the hearth. Miriam saw the light in his eyes, saw the shimmer that surrounded him. He was not human. His ways were his own. The power he wielded was that of the stars themselves, and she knew that as it reshaped her, it would reshape the multitude of future possibilities toward different and maybe improbable outcomes. But defiant and demanding though she was, she knew what Varden saw in the depths of her being: a creature—in pain, tortured with the horror of the past and the fear of the future, living in the hell of the present—asking for release, for healing, for aid, for comfort.

His words shook her. ''Tonight,'' he said calmly. ''It must be tonight. Fast until midnight, taking only water. I will come for you then, if you are still resolved.''

''I—'' So soon? So quickly? She felt as though, bathing in the ocean, she looked up to see an immense wave towering over her, already falling, collapsing on her with the weight of worlds.

The Elf stood. ''If you are still resolved.''

She drew herself up. ''I'll be ready.''

Varden went to the door. ''Remember, you may be changed greatly.''

Her stomach felt queasy. ''I'm not afraid.''

''This is the Day of Completion,'' said the Elf. ''*Arae a*

Olora. It is fitting that we act tonight. You could not find renewal in one form, so perhaps you will find fulfillment in another."

"I don't care about fulfillment. I want that bastard dead."

He held her in the starlight of his eyes for a moment, then bowed and departed.

Stars.

Varden floated among them, letting their cool, tranquil energies cleanse him of the worry that had clung to his thoughts for many days. There was no place for worry any longer. Miriam had decided, and he had decided, and the futures had shifted, the intricate lattices of potential changing even as he watched. They would change still more that night.

Now he had to prepare, and he let his awareness expand to the limits of all that was, feeling through starfield after starfield, sweeping through nebulae and then beyond to the beginning of the involution that would take him back to himself again. He found Miriam there, not only as she was, but also as she had been, and as she would be, might be, could be. Carefully, touching nothing, he examined the intricate weave of her existence.

He had not lied: the magic would be unpredictable. He hoped that he could keep the changes within reasonable limits, but one could never be certain. Universes hinged upon the mere turning of a leaf; how much more then upon the transformation of a human life?

In the corner of his mind, he saw other lattices: other lives, other beings, other existences that intersected Miriam, combined with her, and were influenced by her actions. More than usual. Many more. It was as though . . .

The lattices flickered and changed with the actions and decisions of a million lives. Villages, towns, cities, countries pivoted upon Miriam of Maris, their convoluted futures depending upon her continued existence. And if he did not change her—and he saw it clearly: waves, movements building in the webs—then that existence was doubtful.

He left the lattices and stood on a grassy plain, faced the Woman who stood there.

"Is everything forced, My Lady?" he said. "I have seen humans play a game called chess, and I have noted that only the first move is made in freedom, for all the rest depend upon the one before. There are many variations, but one player forces the hand of the other with increasing frequency until there is victory and defeat."

"And how big is the chessboard that you play upon, Varden?"

"Truly, it is infinite, My Lady."

"And what does that mean?"

He looked into Her eyes and smiled. "That anything is possible. Given but two choices, seek then a third."

"You have been with humans much, my child. Does your knowledge of them weigh upon you?"

He sat down at her feet, rested his chin in his hands. "There is much that I wish I did not know," he admitted. "And yet it is nonetheless good that I know it. And I love Roxanne. We all do. We call her Sana, after the gleam of the knife she carries."

"She is very close to Me. I think that, after she bears her child, you could bring her here."

Varden blinked, surprised. "She is not elven."

"Nor is she fully human anymore." Her eyes twinkled. "Such is the danger in dealing with Elves."

"My Lady, I would ask You of Miriam. She has chosen."

"I know."

"I have examined the futures. I do not understand them."

"Has Miriam chosen rightly in your opinion?"

"I believe she thinks she has."

"But has she?"

"My Lady, the futures . . ."

"Do what you think is right. That is all I can tell you. Futures, like lives, evolve, grow, change. The unexpected is a part of life. Is, indeed, life itself. The Elves know the past, the present, and they can see the many futures. But the Elves should not believe that they can compass the infinite in their knowledge." She smiled. "How well *do* you know Me, Varden?"

He was silent for some time. "There is so much that bears

upon Miriam. I do not understand it. I am . . . almost afraid.''

Her love was infinite, unconditional, and now it washed over him like a sea of light, swirled his thoughts out to the edges of existence, bore him gently back to himself.

"Fear not, my child,'' she said. "Should your strength fail this night, I am You.''

And when he opened his eyes, he could see by the stars that it was almost midnight. He stood up slowly and walked into the village.

Chapter Thirteen

Varden's knock was soft, but Miriam caught her breath at the sound, and her hands tightened on the arms of her chair as Kay opened the door.

"Blessings," said the Elf.

"God bless," returned the priest. "You're . . . you're going to do it?"

"If Miriam is willing."

Miriam tried to stop her hands from shaking by thinking of the man in the forest, by reminding herself that this was the first step toward her confrontation with him. "I'm willing," she said, but there was a catch in her voice.

"Come then, child, and be at peace."

For once, she did not feel an upsurge of protest at being called a child. She set the cup aside and went toward the door. Kay stood aside to let her pass, but she saw the tears in his eyes.

"Please be careful, Miriam," he said softly.

"I'll be all right." But her words were not enough, and the priest still wept. "Kay, I'll be back."

"I know."

But Miriam knew that this was a departure for her, and not only for the night. Patterns were shifting: subtly, massively. The world could change, would change. In a way greater than she could imagine, she was leaving Kay.

She went down on her knees before him. "Kay," she said softly, "will you bless me?"

Kay seemed to understand. He made the sign of the cross over her. *"Benedicat vos omnipotens Deus, Pater, et Filius, et Spiritus Sanctus. Amen."*

She rose. "Good-bye, Kay."

Varden started off into the darkness, and Miriam turned to follow, but Kay spoke.

"Miriam."

She stopped, looked back.

"Someday I'll need your blessing," said the priest. "I hope you'll give it to me."

She wondered at his words. "I will, Kay."

And she went off with Varden.

The night was warm, and the Elf led her along hidden paths in the forest. As she held on to his hand with numb fingers, she recalled that this was the night Charity was to be made witch and priestess, and she wondered with what feelings the girl approached that less tangible but no less potent transformation.

The paths wound on. Varden guided her effortlessly through the darkness under the trees. The tales said that Elves could see in the night, and with this living tale gripping her lightly by the arm, telling her to watch for overhanging branches, Miriam was inclined to believe them.

Without warning, they entered a clearing, and the flood of moonlight was blinding. The air here was sweet, the grass lush, and in the center of the open expanse was a low, rectangular block of stone that looked to be granite.

Varden led her to it. "Take off your clothes and lie down."

She did so as he bent and opened a bundle that lay near the stone. She felt not at all self-conscious about appearing naked before him. Any thought of it was masked by apprehension: modesty seemed a paltry thing in view of what was about to happen.

The moon glared down at her as if in judgment. She returned the glance evenly. "I'm not afraid," she whispered.

Varden stepped up to the stone. He now wore a deep blue robe bordered with a filigree of silver. In his hand he held a staff of pale wood. The Elf's face looked sad, concerned. He still seemed to be weighing one terrible choice against another, hoping that the balance would not tip toward tragedy. Closing his eyes, he whispered something to himself in his own language; and with the understanding that the light in her mind had given her, Miriam caught a brief glimpse of a woman robed in blue and silver, a crescent moon behind her and a star in her hand.

Varden finished his prayer and looked down at the small

woman who was dwarfed by the granite slab. "Are you prepared?"

"I am."

"Do you, Miriam of Maris, accept this working as being of your own asking, by and of your own free will, and do you accept the consequences, having had the possible dangers explained to you?"

It was her last chance to back out. For a moment, the thoughts tumbled through her mind: *I could be deformed. I might be in pain for the rest of my life. Anything could happen. Anything.* But she knew Varden, and deep within herself she believed in the power of the Elves.

His eyes were on her. She took a deep breath. "I accept freely and of my own will."

Varden nodded gravely and rested a hand on her forehead. Relaxation flooded into her body, as though every nerve and muscle fiber had been oiled, warmed, and massaged into limpness. She sighed softly and almost drifted off into sleep, but the Elf's voice brought her back.

"The blessing of the Lady be upon you and within you, now and always."

"Varden," she said suddenly. "Varden, whatever happens, thank you."

He smiled softly. "Be at peace."

"I'm afraid I haven't given you much peace since we met."

"Do you still wish to pursue this course?"

"I can't do anything else."

He sighed, bowed his head for a moment, then gestured toward the moon. It hung at the zenith, full and round, though she did not recall that it had been in that phase when she had left Kay's house. "This is the Night of Completion, Miriam," he said. "Watch the moon. Relax and let her light fill you. Let it protect you. Let it empower you."

She shifted her gaze to the shining disk, breathed regularly, felt as though she were herself glowing. Varden stepped out of her vision, but the quality of light changed and she realized that his staff was brightening.

She kept her eyes on the moon.

A tightness gripped her. She could not have moved if she had wanted to. She could not even blink. Eyes locked on the moon, she felt herself drawn toward it. It grew larger, filling the sky and her vision, the white light blazing through her, harrowing her soul and mind with a seething glory.

She wanted to close her eyes, to look away, but she might have been stone for all the movement she was capable of.

I trust Varden. I trust the Elves. But I'm scared. . . .

She heard the sea, the sound growing as rapidly as had the light, the waves rising about her until, invisibly, they overtopped the stone and flooded her, turning the moon into a featureless sky of white mist.

She nearly lost consciousness, but the thought of being unaware terrified her into full cognizance, and she realized she was looking into the mist-shrouded face of a woman. Green-eyed, with red-gold hair, she smiled at Miriam and reached toward her with a strong hand.

"I'm not afraid," Miriam said, extending a hand; and in her mind, a voice answered her: *Good*. Their hands met and gripped. The strange woman smiled again, and her lips silently formed the syllables of Miriam's name just before, fingers tightening for an instant, she swept forward and merged with her.

A jolt racked Miriam's body as though she had been struck, and the white mist fled from her sight. The stars appeared, shining, glorious, their brilliance as razor-keen as a warrior's sword. Transfixed by their light, she saw, unfolding like a flower before her, an infinite complex of futures in which all potentials and possibilities were bound and connected by a vast web of starlight. It went on and on, each future merging with another and with yet another, a convoluted knot of maybes, and might-bes, and . . . and . . .

. . . and one *reality*.

She screamed, muscles spasming as she rolled to the side, fetal, fighting for sight, for thought. A river of starlight poured over her. Something widened within her, and the light flooded in. *Varden! Help me! Please!"*

A hand came down on her head, and her spasms stopped abruptly. "Be at peace . . . Miriam."

She lay for some time, waiting for her heart to calm. Behind her closed eyes, the stars shone, and the tenuous arm of a nebula shimmered in the distance.

Her thoughts slowed gradually, and she forced herself to feel the stone beneath her, to replay the day's events, to relink with the world. "My name is Miriam," she said, repeating the familiar litany. "I have black hair. I have black eyes. I—"

She broke off suddenly and opened her eyes. A few inches from her face, her hand was lying on the granite slab. Gingerly, she flexed it, turned it, touched the stone, watched the fingers move according to her will.

But she did not recognize the hand at all.

It was still obviously the hand of a woman, but that was all she could find in common with it. Large, strong, it looked very capable of wielding a sword. The fingers were long and tapering. In the moonlight they looked carved out of ivory.

"Varden, am I—" Her voice caught. It was different now: an even, smooth contralto instead of a rough soprano. "Am I . . . changed?"

She rolled onto her back and looked up at him.

Varden did not flinch at the sight of her. "You are, Miriam. Greatly." He mustered a reassuring smile.

She sighed with relief. Inwardly, she tried to sense herself, how she felt, how she was different. After a moment's hesitation, she pushed herself off the stone and stood. She realized that she was considerably taller now, and the world tumbled for a moment while she reoriented herself.

"How do you feel?" said the Elf.

"I feel . . ." She stretched, lifting her arms toward the stars. The night wind blew cool and fresh on her body. The moon glimmered on her pale skin and scintillated in the strands of her long, red-gold hair. "I feel wonderful. What do I look like?"

Varden eyed her up and down. "There is a mirror in your room at Kay's house," he said. "Fear not: you are not deformed."

She felt too healthy to have considered the possibility. The air, the moonlight, the clearing—the world was suddenly intoxicating. She wanted to run, to leap, to push her new being to its furthest limits.

Varden doffed his robe and rolled it carefully. "How are your . . . memories?"

She caught his meaning. "You want to know if I've forgotten why I did this."

"Sometimes a working like this brings a renewal of the spirit as well as of the body."

"I remember everything, Varden."

"I understand."

"Do you?"

The Elf was silent.

"If you can't find a teacher for me, I'll find one myself."

Varden shook his head. "One of my folk, Terrill, has offered to help you. He has some . . . painful memories of his own." Her face must have indicated her question, for he added, "Did you think our lives are always blissful? We have our own sorrows from before your histories began."

"Varden," Miriam said as gently as she could. "I'm grateful. This is something I have to do. I'm sorry it has to be like this." Her new voice was liquid, capable of inflections she had thought impossible.

Varden passed a hand across his face as if to banish painful thoughts, then took something from the bundle by the slab. "Here is a gown that will fit you. You should go home now and sleep."

She donned the garment reluctantly. "I won't be able to fight in clothes like this."

"You will have what you need. Elves are known for being ingenious." She wondered if she heard humor in his voice. He gestured toward the trees. "Come."

As he guided her through the forest once more, Miriam saw the previously invisible branches and paths clearly, as if by cloudy daylight. She halted, staring at Varden. Colors had shifted into blues and lavenders, and the Elf shone with a radiance more pronounced than she had ever noticed.

"Miriam?"

"I can see you." When she closed her eyes to rub them—as if that might make her newfound vision more familiar—she noticed that the darkness behind her closed lids was still full of stars. She might have been gazing at a night sky. "What . . . what's happened to me?"

"I told you that the change would be unpredictable."

Unnerved, she opened her eyes. "What's wrong with me?"

"Nothing is wrong with you. You can see in the dark."

The stars flashed within her. She held up her hands. About them was a faint light, as of an aura, flickering in soft hues of violet and indigo. "That's all?"

He took her hand comfortingly. "Miriam—"

"Give me a moment." Swallowing her fear, she closed her eyes again and confronted her inner sky. She did not recognize any of the constellations, but the points of light were clear, steady, and surprisingly comforting. "I'll be all right."

Varden spoke slowly. "What are you . . . looking at?"

"Stars."

"Elthia."

"I said I'll be all right." Feeling better, she opened her eyes.

Varden's face was set. Lifting his hand slowly, he touched her head, her face, ran his fingers back through her hair, brushed past her left ear. He stopped, breathed, removed his hand.

"You are well, Miriam," he said softly. "Blessings upon you."

"Thank you, Varden." She shook her hair back into place. "I'll just have to get used to this."

It was still some hours before dawn when Kay jerked open the door in response to Varden's knock. The good soul had obviously been waiting up. His eyes were red with fatigue and tears, but they widened when Miriam stepped into the room.

"Miriam?" His voice was a whisper.

"Yes, Kay."

His shoulders sagged, and he wiped at his eyes. "By Our Lady," he said. "A tall, lovely woman walks into my house and tells me she is the child I blessed a few hours ago."

Lovely? She touched her smooth face, wondering.

Varden spoke. "Do you have anything to eat, Kay?"

"There is something hot ready for you both."

Miriam still held her hand to her face. "Could I . . . could I go to my room for a minute? I want to look in a mirror." Lovely. The word made her uncomfortable.

"I'll dish up while you do," said Kay. He was staring unabashedly.

Miriam went down the short corridor and entered her room. As calmly as she could, she faced the mirror. Kay had used the right word. The stranger in the glass was exquisite: a finely featured oval face, immaculately complexioned; eyes that flashed like clear emeralds; hair the color of red gold. She looked nobly born. Beautiful. Lovely.

She turned away quickly, trembling. She had not thought of this. She had known that she would be changed, and she had prepared herself for a different face. But not this. Not beautiful.

She held up her hands. They were as well formed as the rest of her, and she did not doubt that should she remove her robe and examine her naked body with a critical eye, she would find the same masterful sculpting.

Varden entered quietly and stood behind her. "The meal is ready. You should eat something."

Dropping her hands, she turned around. "What did you do to me?"

He looked puzzled. "I do not understand."

"Look at me!" Her fists were clenched.

He looked her up and down. "I still do not understand."

"I'm beautiful!"

"That is so." The Elf looked bewildered.

She collapsed into a chair, covering her face. "I don't know how to . . . I . . . I can't understand it." She choked out the words. "Did you plan this?"

"I did not," he said. "I was most concerned with keeping your appearance as normal as possible. As I said, results are unpredictable. For that reason, many of my people do not like to use magic for any purpose."

She tore her hands from her face and shook them in frustration. "How am I supposed to live like this? I'm used to being plain."

"Miriam,' he said gently, "you are also used to being small, weak, and at the mercy of those about you. I will tell you this: when I wielded the energies that reshaped your body, I felt another Will influencing them. Take that as you wish."

"I'm afraid I'm no friend to religion."

"I am sorry."

Sighing, she rubbed her face. "All right. I'll live." She

rose and went once again to the glass, plucked bemusedly at her waist-length hair. "Terrill will teach me, you say?"

"He has so promised."

"Good." There was something familiar about her new face, something she could not exactly define. With a shrug, she gave up and turned back to the Elf. "Let's not let the food get cold." She tried to sound offhand, but her voice was tense.

They ate in silence. Kay sat at the table along with them and nursed a cup of peppermint tea while he watched Miriam. She was too preoccupied with herself to notice. She would stop in midbite to stare at her hand, or pause to examine the way she held a cup or broke off a piece of bread.

Varden insisted that she go to bed after the meal, but though she protested that she was not tired, she allowed herself at last to be escorted to her room. Kay wished her a good night and extinguished the candles, but the latter action made little difference to Miriam's new eyes. For a time she lay awake, wondering how she was to sleep when darkness was no longer dark to her.

She touched her face again. Like Charity, she had been reborn. Unlike Charity, she had retained her memory. The thought crossed her mind that she would now be even more attractive to her rapist, and her hands clenched on the sheets.

She would have her vengeance. She would have his life. She would.

When she closed her eyes, she was confronted by the night sky, stars gleaming serenely in the velvet dark. The vision calmed her, and she slept.

PART TWO

Tenso

Chapter Fourteen

The woman sat on a stool in the middle of the small, hot room, staring at her hands. Or maybe at the floor. Flies buzzed near the ceiling. Hoyle scratched at his tonsure and examined the tablet on the table before him. "This is her?"

"Yes, brother," said the guard at the door. "We brought her in this morning. One of the fish sellers in the market took the money to the Jew's house to see if it was good. We got a description—"

"And tracked her down. Yes, I see." The woman had not looked up. Her gown had too many colors in it, so more than likely she was violating one sumptuary law or another, but Hoyle was not concerned about that. He picked up the gold florin that lay by the tablet. The ensign of Saint Blaise winked at him.

"She's well-known," said the guard.

"By you and all your fellows, I'd guess," said Hoyle. He could not see why. Doubtless she had talents. He felt a stirring in his groin, ignored it.

"What's your name?" he demanded.

The woman did not reply for a moment. "Denise," she said sullenly.

"You're a whore."

Again a pause. Again a sullen answer. "Yes."

Hoyle was irritated. He decided to prod her into some respect. "And a witch, too."

He got his reaction. Denise's head snapped up. "Oh, no, my lord. I—"

"Silence." He tossed the coin onto the floor before her. "You used that to buy fish for your household. Free Town money. Everyone knows about the Free Towns. How long have you been having dealings with Saint Blaise?"

She stared at the florin. "I han't anything to do with Saint Blaise. That's a florin. Like any other."

"Ha." He picked up the tablet and pretended to study it. "It's nothing like any other." He dropped the tablet on the tabletop. "It's witch money."

"My lord—"

"You've had intercourse with demons."

"No! No, never!"

"Then why do you pay for fish with infernal currency?"

"How was I to know what currency it was?" The woman was panicking, her hands clenched white-knuckled against her belly. "I din't get it from the devil. Holy Mother! I'm a good Christian!"

Hoyle snorted. "A good Christian who fornicates for a living. How amusing. Very well, where did you get it?"

"A soldier gave it me." She was telling the truth, Hoyle knew. She was too frightened to do otherwise.

"Where?"

"Right here in Belroi. He got his money's worth, too. But he wan't any devil."

"I have only your word for that. The word of a witch . . . pah!"

"I'm na a witch!"

Hoyle sat down slowly, took a stylus and a fresh tablet. "Describe the man," he said. "Who was this so-called soldier who gave you the money?"

She did not know his name, but she described him, the words tumbling out of her mouth. Hoyle jotted notes. The guard in the room started. "But that's Roderick!"

"Roderick?" said Hoyle.

"He has the ferry watch every three days. Quite a hell-raiser. It's said the priests shudder when he comes to confess."

Hoyle stifled a chuckle, turned it into a frown. "Well, I have only this whore's word for it. She might be trying to implicate an honest man. Go and tell Roderick I want to see him this evening. I will attend to this woman."

The guard left. Hoyle eyed the prisoner. She was not at all attractive, so she had to have some talents. He felt the stirring in his groin again. "I find myself wondering if your story is true," he said. "There might be something you can do to convince me that you're not lying."

The woman looked up at him, frightened, eyes pleading.

A falcon tipped and sidled among the high airs above Adria, her plumage red gold in the sunlight, her green eyes bright and searching. Below her, the land unfurled like a long, intricate tapestry patched with farmland and forest, worked with the silver tracery of rivers and streams.

And beyond this Adria that lay from horizon to horizon there were others—many others—unfolding one out of another like the petals of a rose; and strands of starlight joined them all. And even the passage of a gold florin from the hand of a soldier to the hand of a prostitute shifted and tipped the pattern of the many Adrias just as the falcon slid and banked among the currents of air that bore her ever higher.

The universe revolved. Worlds shifted.

Miriam dreamed, floating in a soft womb of oblivion. She heard faint voices, but she flew higher without answering. There was only one voice she would answer right now.

"She's been in coma for two days, Varden."

"I believe it is necessary, Kay."

"Do you . . . do you see that . . . around her?"

"I do."

"What does it mean?"

"I do not know, my friend."

"Varden, what did you do to her?"

The voices faded as the stars surrounded her. The falcon's wings cut the starlight as they had the wind, their feathers shining silver white. There was a star calling to her, and for a moment, she hung above it, poised, spreading her wings to stall ever so slightly, her eyes flashing with anticipation . . .

. . . and she stooped, a bright bolt of feather and bone and blood that hurtled into the stellar flame. It roared about her for a moment; then she settled softly onto the arm of the Lady who stood on a grassy plain beneath a glittering sky.

"Have you come so soon, child?" she said, stroking the

sleek feathers. "But then, you have a great heart, and your soul has wings, so perhaps this is not unexpected."

The falcon blinked at Her, knowing only that she was home, that she wanted to stay, that the eyes that met hers, that flashed starlight and moonlight both, that held the many universes in their depth, were eyes that would never turn from her.

"Be at peace, child," said the Lady. "But return to your friends, lest they grieve."

The falcon preened nervously.

"Fear not. You will be back, and you will have full knowledge then. Go now."

With infinite strength and gentleness both, the Lady lofted the bird into the sky. Again the falcon's wings bit starlight, again she soared aloft. But there was horror where she had to go, and the memories came back.

Miriam stirred. "Varden . . ."

He was beside her instantly. "I am here, beloved."

"Varden, they want to hurt me . . . they want to kill me . . . please help me."

He took her hand quietly, stroked it, clasped it. The shimmer about her body flickered. The Elf touched it as though it were a mist, then brought his hand to her face, felt the soft, cool skin.

"Varden . . ."

"Sleep, my lady," he said. "All will be well. Morning rolls toward us, and the Dawn Star waits at the edge of the world."

He sang to her for a minute, the elven language flowing like water, the melody as even and strong as the tides of the sea. She quieted then, and Varden tucked her arm under the sheet and stood up.

"Will she be all right?" said Kay.

"She will."

"Varden, this is the third night."

"It is to be expected," said the Elf. "Miriam has been reborn in body, and maybe a little in soul, too. Such transformations demand at least a retroactive gestation."

"You're taking this pretty calmly."

"There is no other way, my friend. Fear not." He glanced at the sleeping woman appraisingly. "She will awaken with the dawn. Have a good breakfast for her. She will be hungry.''

Kay shook his head in amazement, but he followed the Elf out to the kitchen. Varden opened the front door. The sounds and odors of night entered the room. ''You're leaving?'' said Kay.

''Our vigil is ended. Miriam will be ready tomorrow morning. I am going to talk to Terrill.''

The priest rubbed his cheek. ''Terrill. That's the fellow who's going to teach my girl how to kill?''

''Kay,'' Varden said gently, ''Miriam is not yours, nor is she mine. She belongs to herself. I told you that she is on a path. Who knows where she will have to go in order to follow it? Pray to your Lord that yours will be easier . . . as I pray to my Lady.''

The night air made the candle in Kay's hand flicker. He winced as a rivulet of hot wax found his skin.

''All right,'' he said. ''God be with you, Varden.''

''The hand of the Lady be on you, Kay,'' said the Elf, touching his forehead. He closed the door behind him.

And Miriam dreamed. Starlight.

Mika was not sleeping well these nights. Over the years, she had trained herself to fall asleep quickly, to snatch as much rest as she could before she was called out to attend a laboring woman, but the ability was failing her now. Eyes unclosed, she stared into the darkness as the night crawled slowly toward morning.

She wondered if her sleeplessness was not perhaps for a reason. Maybe one of her ladies was going to begin labor prematurely and her midwife's intuition was responding. Maybe someone was coming down the road right now, sent to bring her to the side of a woman who needed her.

Her eyes felt dry, and there was a whiteness in her mind: emblems of the insomnia afflicting her these nights. The summer heat was not helping. Sweating, she unbarred the door and went out into her garden.

Sitting on the bench, head tilted back against the warm wall, she looked up to the stars that shone brightly in the dark sky, their light tingling almost palpably on her face.

They reminded her of something, something she had seen before.

She shut her eyes for a minute while she grappled with the memory. It was important for some reason that she recall it right now, as though there would be a gap in the pattern of life and living that she suddenly sensed around her if she did not. She opened her eyes, the stars blazed down at her, and the recollection at last settled into her mind.

Starlight.

She remembered Miriam again. She did frequently, for though the girl had spent only a few weeks with her, she still thought of her as being a part of the household. This was the corner where she slept. And this was the plate and cup she used. Here is the chest where the dark green cloak of the Free Towns is folded.

But this time there came to her not a recollection of Miriam as she had been—housemate, helper, almost daughter— but the all-but-faded memory of the vision that had surrounded the healer when she lay, feverish, in the back of the wagon north of Belroi. Mika had seen stars then, too.

There: the pattern was complete. For a moment, the night had paused, waiting for Mika to remember, and now that she had, it continued on its way. The stars burned, wheeling slowly in the sky.

But why? Why now? What pattern had she, for a moment, entered? Lifting her head, she looked off into the darkness, almost expecting to hear a familiar step on the road. "Miriam?" she called hesitantly.

But aside from the hoot of the owl and the chirping of crickets, there was no answer, unless it was the clear, cool, twinkling of the many stars.

George Darci awakened to find Anne's arms wrapped around him and her blond head pillowed on his shoulder. Her hair lay like a tumble of gold silk across the bedclothes. He sighed contentedly. It was nice to wake up in such a way. It made the dark clouds on the horizon seem less dark. He smiled at her, kissed her forehead.

"Umph," she said sleepily, and she snuggled a little closer. Outside, the first light of dawn was growing, and it glowed in through the unshuttered window. A skylark fluttered to the sill, perched, and surveyed the room.

George nodded to it. "Good morning," he said. "If you were a burgher of Saint Blaise, would you defend your city and not mealymouth about niceties of Christian doctrine? You understand, I ask as one mayor to another."

"Hmm?" said Anne.

"We have a visitor."

She lifted her head and smiled at the bird, then fell back to George's shoulder. "Have I told you today that I love you?"

"Let me see. . . ." George pretended to think. "Well, it's morning, just dawn. No, I don't think you've had time."

"Well then, I love you."

"I love you also, my sweet." George looked back to the window. "If you see Terrill somewhere," he said to the bird, "could you please tell him that I need his advice?"

There was a burst of laughter from the next room, a high, girlish giggle, and a clap of hands. The skylark took wing.

"You'd better come tell us, love," called George. "We'd like to start out the day with a bit of mirth, too."

The curtain that covered the doorway was pushed aside, and a young woman who looked much like Anne peered in anxiously. "I'm sorry, Father. Did I wake you?"

"Not at all. What's so funny, Janet?"

She was holding a book in the crook of one arm. It was a large, heavy tome, bound in thick covers. "Otto gave me this to read. It's about rhetoric. He thinks it will improve my Latin. I suppose he may be right, but there are some good stories in here. Listen." She opened the book and translated. " 'Six centuries after the birth of Our Lord, the learned monks of Hibernia, Gabundus and Terentius, argued for fifteen days and fifteen nights the vocative of *ego*, and in the end, unable to agree, they attacked one another with hand and with weapon.' Imagine that!" She laughed again. "Maybe they should have just called themselves Gabundus and Terentius!"

Anne chuckled. "It would have been easier, I suppose." She nuzzled at George's cheek. "Janet, would you please go back to your studies? Your father and I are going to make love."

"Really?" said George. "I didn't know that."

"Ummm. You do now." She crawled on top of him, stared into his face, and—very deliberately, very sloppily, very noisily—licked the tip of his nose. Their laughter drowned out the whisper of the falling curtain.

Although it was only midmorning, the day was already hot. The tilled fields around Aurverelle sent up their odors of manure and mulch and filled the air with humidity; and the heat seeped along the narrow streets of the town as Bartholomew shouldered his way through the throngs that had come for market day.

As he went, he looked at faces, listened to voices. He had a good memory for such things, and it was a useful talent. He was also quite a mimic—though that was not quite so useful—and could imitate even Baron Roger himself, drawing himself up and crashing about the room like a great bear, thundering curses and imprecations. The bishop would laugh heartily at him, though Baron Roger was never present at such times. For good reason.

But the bishop and the comforts of Hypprux were far off, and Bartholomew was indulging in more than a little self-pity as he presented himself at the entrance to the castle complex.

"Brother Bartholomew to see Baron Roger."

The guard lounged back, pursed his lips. "Baron Roger's not seeing no one."

A trickle of sweat wound down Bartholomew's temple. "I'm bearing messages from Bishop Aloysius Cranby."

"Oh?"

The friar pulled out a signet ring. The guard took it and whistled. "Quite a chunk of gold, that."

"Quite," said Bartholomew, steaming. "May I see the baron?"

"He's not seeing no one, I told you," said the guard. "He's sick. Not seeing no one."

"Will you at least tell him that I'm here in town? It's rather important. Bishop Cranby—"

"I don't care much 'bout Bishop Cranby myself," said the guard, handing back the signet, "though he does keep nice rings. But if you're with him, you're welcome. Talk to the steward in the front house. But Baron Roger won't see you for a while.''

"What's wrong with him? Fever?''

"I dunno. Maybe. Something with his arm, too, I think. None of my business. Anyway, go on.''

Still sweating, Bartholomew tucked the ring back into his pouch. Food was near, and drink, and—please, God!—some place where he could strip off this Dominican habit and flounder in a pool of reasonably cool water like a great, pink whale . . . or maybe even like a bear.

Chapter Fifteen

Terrill was tall, fair-haired, and his eyes held a calm grimness that seemed to evaluate dispassionately everything that they focused upon. His actions were sharp, quick, well defined—like the sword that hung from his belt. His voice was clear, his intonation firm and factual.

He showed up at the door of the priest's house in the late morning and asked for Miriam. Kay hesitated for a moment, then called her. When she appeared, Terrill handed her a bundle and asked her to put on the clothing it contained.

As he talked, he was watching her, and Miriam, though she was clothed, felt more naked before him than she had when nude before Varden. Every movement, every shift of her weight, even the way she held the bundle was, she thought, being examined and memorized for future reference. She searched his face for reactions, but his reserve was impenetrable.

She took the bundle back to her room in order to change, leaving Terrill waiting at the door. He would not come in, thank you very much. Perhaps some other time. Be at peace.

The clothes he had brought were light, simple, of green and gray, with a belt and boots of soft leather. It seemed to be the standard dress of Elves, male or female, for not only Varden and Terrill wore it, but Natil and Talla—Roxanne too, Miriam recalled—had also been garbed in the same way.

She tied the belt loosely, as it seemed meant to be, and tucked the legs of her breeches into the tops of the soft boots so that they bloused at the knee. She peered at herself in the mirror. Her face and body were still strange to her, but she was starting to learn what she looked like. Maybe the three days she had spent asleep had made some difference, though she remembered nothing of them.

The elven garb fit her exactly, flattered her, and again she was struck by a sense of familiarity about herself. She puzzled over it for a minute, then shrugged it off. After giving her hair a quick brush and tying it back loosely, she padded down the corridor, her boots almost noiseless on the tile floor.

Terrill's eyes flickered for a moment when he saw her. Touching his forehead with both hands, he bowed.

"Terrill," said Kay suddenly.

"My good father?" said the Elf. Dispassion and respect blended seamlessly in his voice.

"You'll take care of Miriam, won't you?"

The Elf looked him up and down, weighing, balancing, reading in the priest's eyes what had not been uttered aloud. Finally, he nodded tersely. "Fear not."

Without another word, he led Miriam down the street toward the village gate. Kay looked nervously after them, drying a plate that had lost all its moisture a quarter of an hour before.

Outside, Miriam felt self-conscious. Villagers stared at her without recognition. It chilled her. She had known these people for months, and now she was a stranger to them. How could she explain? What had she given up in return for a new body and a chance at a new fate?

They crossed the fields, the trees closed about them, and for a minute or two Miriam thought that Terrill was leading her back to the site of her transformation. But the path twisted oddly, and after a short time they entered a different clearing. It was level and carpeted with grass. Wildflowers were scattered about, their colors bright and clear.

Leaning against a tree were two wooden practice swords. Terrill took up one of them. "We will not do much today. I want to come to know you a little and watch you handle this. You are tall for a human woman, but not overtall. So I will be teaching you to fight like an Elf: deft, quick. We are slender, as are you, and depend upon lightness of foot rather than brute strength."

She nodded. There did not seem to be much to say.

Terrill walked a dozen yards from her, turned suddenly,

and tossed her the sword. The wooden blade tumbled gracefully in the noon light.

Without thinking, she caught it properly, her hand settling
on the grip comfortably but firmly. The Elf's eyebrows lifted
for a moment, but he sat down cross-legged where he was.
"Hold it," he said. "Play with it. Feel it. But remember
this: even a wooden sword is a weapon. Respect it. I once
cut a man through the spine with a wooden sword."

There was a hauntedness about his eyes as he spoke, but
no further information was forthcoming. He gestured for
her to proceed, leaned back on his elbows, and stretched
out his legs, relaxed.

Left standing here in this clearing with a practice sword,
told to do something indefinite, she felt again self-conscious,
momentarily overwhelmed by the difficulty of the path she
had chosen. But she had a sudden flash of a leering face,
felt the grip of a new-healed hand and arm, and hate welled
up. Instinctively she raised the sword and cut through the
air in a graceful, sweeping arc, her feet taking up the follow-
through just so, coming to rest lightly and ready to move
again.

Risking a glance at the Elf, she found that not only had
his eyebrows lifted, but his eyes had widened also. But his
calm resettled. "That was done in anger," he said simply.

"Yes. That's true."

"It is not a good way to fight. Anger quickens response,
lends strength, but is not a reliable ally."

"It's why I'm here."

"True," said Terrill, "and it is why I am here. You will
eventually ask me whether you are ready to fight the man
who raped you. I will tell you something then, but I will
tell you this now: when you can love him as you kill him,
then you will be ready."

She nearly dropped the sword. "But that's crazy," she
cried. "That's not human—" She caught herself, felt a little
cold inside. Terrill only looked at her, appraising, examining, analyzing.

"Proceed," he said.

It went on that way for several hours: Miriam moving as
best she could with the wooden sword, Terrill's dispassionate voice advising, commenting, pointing out her faults.

This did not seem fair to her, for she knew nothing of swordplay, and she finally whirled on him. "All right, dammit, what's the *right* way to do this?"

Terrill remained relaxed. Miriam doubted that he had moved at all since he had stretched out. He glanced at the sun. "We will get to that."

"How am I supposed to learn anything this way?"

"I said that I would teach you. That is what I am doing. Do you want to give up?"

She glared at him. "Never."

"I did not think so. I will think about you tonight, about what I have seen. Tomorrow, you will work harder."

Miriam wondered if that were possible. She was tired, hungry, dripping with sweat. A headache was beginning to pound through her left temple. She shook her head and leaned on the sword.

Terrill rose and came to her, put a hand lightly on her shoulder. "Be at peace. You did well. Now, stand up straight."

Fighting her fatigue, she did so, and Terrill stared into her eyes.

"Close your eyes, Miriam," he said. "Find your stars."

She was among them in a moment, relieved. The firmament within her was quiet and peaceful, but the Elf's next words startled her.

"Where is my hand?"

"What?"

"Where is my hand?"

"I can't see your hand."

"I did not ask you to look for it. I asked you where it is. Now, again. Do not open your eyes. Where is my hand? My right hand."

"I don't know."

"You do, but you are trying to see it." His voice gentled. "Relax first. Feel your body. Feel the ground beneath you, the sun on your head, the sword in your hand. Do not look: feel them."

Trembling, she stared at the stars. They comforted her, slowed her heart, let her do as Terrill had asked.

The warm grip of the sword, damp with her sweat. The

bright, westering sun in her fine hair. She moved her toes, felt the supple boots around them, and below, the grass.

"Center yourself," said Terrill. "You know who you are. Say your name to yourself."

Miriam.

"Now . . ." Terrill's voice was soft, soothing. "You are here, and I am here, and we both stand upon the same earth, we breathe the same air. I am holding out my right hand. All you have to do is put the blade of that wooden sword in my palm. Do it."

She hesitated. Feeling . . . the stars . . . the sun . . .

"Miriam," he said sharply, "do it. Do it now!"

The tone in his voice jolted her into action. The sky shimmered and vanished: she was back in the clearing, the tip of her wooden sword resting in the palm of Terrill's right hand.

She staggered, caught herself, lowered the sword. "How?"

Terrill nodded approvingly. "I said that I would teach you to fight like an Elf. That is what I am doing."

"But this? What is this?"

"We will come to that." He folded his arms and bowed. "Your powers are great."

"I've only got one power, and I wouldn't call it great."

"Ah, but that was before. Varden told me of some of your changes, and I myself am finding others. It is well."

He held out his hand for the sword. She gave it to him and he leaned it back against the tree. Its companion had remained untouched throughout the afternoon.

"I will take you home now."

He led her away from the clearing, back the way they had come. When they stepped out of the forest, Terrill bowed to her, touching his forehead as he did so, and told her to expect him at midmorning the next day. He left then, fading into the green leaves and brown trunks almost immediately, and only Miriam's strangely augmented vision allowed her to see him beyond the first few yards.

She shut her eyes. The stars were still there, shining brightly, and she realized that the light she had found in her mind after she had healed Varden was with her still, but that it had, as a result of her transformation, surged forward and enveloped her totally. Before, she had seen it only in an obscure fashion, but now, clearly: it was the stars, brilliant, flashing.

She opened her eyes, realized that a skylark was sitting on a branch a few feet from her, watching. "If you're looking for Terrill," she said suddenly, "he went home."

The bird blinked, cocked its head, and fluttered off. Miriam turned toward the town, padding softly down the road, rubbing her aching temple.

She passed several townsfolk that she knew well, but they merely stared at her curiously and without recognition. She greeted them by name, but they looked bewildered. She felt a pang, and her stomach cramped as she thought about revealing herself.

Shadows were lengthening as she made her way down the street toward Kay's house. She heard the sound of steady pounding from the smithy. Francis was at work.

The smith stood at the anvil, sooty and bronzed, his black beard glistening with sweat in the ruddy light of the forge. Miriam's passage attracted his attention. "Greetings, mistress." He looked up, and his eyes widened. "Blessings on ye, Fair One. What brings ye t' Saint Brigid?"

She might as well begin with Francis. She shook her head ruefully, reached up, and pulled free the thong that had held back her hair. The red-gold waves tumbled over her shoulders. "I'm going to Kay's house," she said in her clear voice. "I live there. I'm Miriam, Francis."

He looked as though he had been struck with his own hammer. "Miriam! I'd heard . . . that is . . . Kay said . . ."

"It's me."

Unthinkingly, he crossed himself. She turned her head away, reminded too much of the fear she had inspired in other places, for other reasons.

Her transformation had not come cheaply. Francis smiled nervously, and she could feel the confusion in his mind. She could not blame him. Were their positions reversed, she would probably react in much the same way.

She wept silently. Francis had been kind and gentle to her, had carried her across the street when it was muddy, had knelt before her to offer his thanks when she had healed Michael. Was it, then, all gone now?

Someone tugged at her sleeve. She looked down into Charity's lake-blue eyes.

"Hello, Miriam," said the young woman, and she smiled and stretched her arms. Miriam blinked at her through her tears, knelt, and held her.

With the insight given to her by the stars, Miriam sensed a change in Charity. She was still innocent, still alive and vibrant with her youth, but she seemed deeper now, as if her innocence and vigor had grown, rooted themselves deep into the world, sent up branches that reached up to embrace the moon and stars.

But there was too much to be felt here and now. This, Miriam realized, was what was important: this time, this embrace, this heartfelt kiss in the middle of a dusty street in Saint Brigid. Charity was here, and Miriam was here, and the sun shone on both. Miriam needed the present, and in Charity's love she found it.

"Varden told me," said Charity, her smile bright, "but he didn't describe you well enough. You're beautiful."

Miriam blushed and dropped her eyes.

"You look . . ." Charity's hands tightened on her arms for a moment. "You look like an Elf."

Miriam shook her head. "It's the clothing."

"No, it's you."

She touched her face. The skin was soft, unlined. She looked at her hand. Slender, with long, tapering fingers. Agile. Deft. Elven? "I suppose you could think so, Charity," she said, faltering.

They stared at one another in silence, and Miriam felt a terrible strangeness in their meeting like this: clad in flesh with which they had not been born, wearing forms other than nature had given them.

"Will you come to my house and have supper with my family?" said Charity. "Roxanne will be there. And Kay. We'd like to welcome you back."

Miriam nodded after a moment, wiped at her tears, and stood up. They were about to go off together when Francis came forward, cleaning his hands on a rag. Miriam searched his eyes and found worry and concern, and yes, a little fear, but less than she had expected. He stood before her, dipped his head slightly by way of a bow.

"Mistress Miriam."

There was a gulf between them, but Francis was trying, on his side, to bridge it. Still holding Charity's hand, Miriam bowed in return. The starlight was with her, filling her, and she was conscious again of the sun, the sky, the earth, aware of her connection with them and with this man before her. The cramp in her stomach eased a little.

"Mistress . . . blessings on ye. Forgive me. . . ."

"I understand, Francis. I suppose I'm a little frightening now."

He shook his head as if grappling with uncustomary thoughts. "It's na that, mistress . . . or may be 't is. I canna say I'm na afraid, but then I was afraid a' Varden when I first met him, and maybe I sha take a lesson from our maiden here and na fear what I dana' understand."

"Thank you, Francis."

"It's na more'n your due, Miriam."

"You still have a home, Miriam," said Charity.

The tears were coming again. Francis was trying, and others, she thought, might try also. "My thanks to you both," she choked. Leaning forward, she kissed Francis lightly on the cheek. "Blessings upon you, Master Smith."

He grinned. "Lord, Miriam, 'tis as though one a tha Fair Ones ha' come to stay wi' us!"

She smiled thinly. The comparison bothered her.

Chapter Sixteen

It was not the same. It could never be the same. Miriam's life in Saint Brigid continued, she still kept house for Kay, still shopped in the market, still waved at acquaintances in the street; but there was a difference now. She could not call it fear, and she could not call it discomfort or uneasiness, for the difference was not any one of those in particular, though it contained a little of all three.

Maybe, she thought, lying awake late into the warm summer nights, her pillow bunched up against the headboard so as to eke a few more inches out of an almost too-short mattress—maybe it was awe. A bedraggled, ugly little woman had been transformed into a tall, slender beauty. Something out of a romance or a fable. But the events of romances and fables were supposed to stay off in some other land or far distant time. They had no business breaking into the real world of brooms, horse dung, nails, and scabies.

So she could not blame the townsfolk in the slightest if there was more silence in the market than usual when she appeared with her basket, could not find fault with a bit of stammering on the part of Francis or Hester or Harry or Paul, could not be bitter when Kay—yes, even Kay—stared at her abstractedly and—she thought—a little sadly.

To be sure, Andrew and Elizabeth did not seem put out in the slightest by her appearance, nor did Charity and Roxanne. But on the whole, she had lost the easy acceptance she had found in Saint Brigid, and once again she took to wandering alone, treading the road out to the edge of the forest, sitting on a fallen log, and staring into the trees.

Terrill came for her every other day, and his methodology became no less opaque or frustrating. Weeks went by during which she never even saw a sword, wooden or otherwise, save the one that hung, sheathed; from Terrill's belt.

The Elf was forcing her, instead, to concentrate on an intricate series of what seemed to be dance movements. He would demonstrate and ask her to imitate him, apparently willing to go over a particular turn of the hands for hours until she did it properly. He did not explain, he simply demanded that she learn.

The dance was full of turns and twists, of steps and retreats. Even when performed at top speed, it took several minutes to finish, and Terrill drove her to perfect her form.

"Don't I have this hand sweep right?"

"Very good. Now, about your feet . . ."

It went on, the days spun by, and in her opinion she made little progress. The hot sun of August burned down on the barley harvest by the time Terrill watched her fumble through the dance in its entirety, unaided. When she finished and bowed to him, he nodded and pronounced her form "reasonable."

Her patience finally broke. "I thought you were going to teach me how to fight."

"I am. Have you studied before?"

"Well . . . no . . ."

"Then accept this as it is." He smiled thinly, held up his hands in a starting position. "Let us go over the second section."

And so her lesson continued. And as always, at the end of the day, when she was hot and sweaty, when her knees seemed ready to crumble beneath her, Terrill told her to stand up straight, relax, and close her eyes.

Her stars had become clearer with time. She saw depth in her interior sky, and she had found that if she concentrated, she could search out one particular point of light and hold it in her mind. Within her now was a limitless expanse of breadth, height, and depth. And all she had to do was close her eyes.

"Where is my hand?" said Terrill.

"What exactly am I seeing, Terrill?"

A moment of silence. Soft currents of energy swept among the stars. She sighed, her knees stopped shaking and her shoulders dropped as the muscles untensed all at once. "How am I to understand your question?" said the Elf.

"Are these real stars?"

"They are."

"But where am I when I'm here?"

Another silence. "Where is my hand?"

"Why, here, of course," she said, touching it with her own. "But—"

"I will explain later. Now is not the time."

At her next lesson, Terrill handed her a wooden sword once again, and to her surprise, he himself took up another. Within minutes, she found that her reflexes had been sharpened by Terrill's incomprehensible exercises, her instincts trained without her realizing it. Soon the Elf was standing before her, lashing out at her uncertain defenses, and though more often than not she wound up tumbled into the grass, she forced herself to her feet again. She endured, and she learned.

For hours he pushed her, driving her back and forth across the clearing, commenting with disinterest on her form at the same time as his sword found weaknesses in her guard. At last he stopped and waited for her to crawl to her feet and face him again. He permitted himself one of his rare smiles. "You are doing well."

"You always say that, Terrill," she panted.

"It is always true. Rest now. You have earned it." He sat down on the grass, calm, dry, with scarcely a hair out of place.

Miriam collapsed in a sweaty heap. "So that's what it was for?"

"It?"

"The dance. It was for fighting, wasn't it?"

"I could say that. You were transformed, true, but your muscles were untrained. The movements you have learned correct your deficiencies. I could tell you that. But it would be only a partial truth."

"Wasn't that the whole point, though?"

"Close your eyes," he said abruptly. "Find your stars. No, you need not stand. But sit up straight, for I will not have you slouching like a human."

She blinked at him, then shrugged and did as he requested.

"All right, good." She heard this voice in her mind. Terrill was among the stars also, and the vision linked them. "There is a skylark flying northwest of here, just passing a tall pine tree with a lightning scar down its side. Feel it."

"I don't understand." She had learned by now that she did not have to speak out loud at times like this. She merely thought the words.

"It is difficult to explain, as there are no words for such ideas in your language. That is part of what I am trying to teach you now."

Shrugging mentally, she tried to become aware of the meadow and forest around her, but received only a confused mass of impressions and images.

"Start simply, Miriam. Feel the grass beneath you. Feel the air. Hear the sounds about you. Then expand from that."

She did so, and her awareness spread outward like ripples in a pond. She felt the forest, the many branches and leaves, the movement of sap beneath bark. She could tell tree from tree and stone from stone as she could her right hand from her left.

Northwest was directly behind her, but she sensed the pine tree, tall and straight, a white-lightning scar streaking its length. "Where's the bird?"

"Moving," said Terrill. "Reach with your mind."

He helped her, stretching her awareness until she could, suddenly, pick out a small, flying bundle of feathers. The skylark fluttered toward the branch of an oak, seemed to think better of landing, turned, and doubled back toward the clearing.

"Now," said Terrill, "feel this: the skylark is but one small part of the pattern—the dance, if you will—that is this forest. What it does, alters the larger pattern. You saw it decide not to alight. Something will happen because of that. The consequences may be large or small, but nothing—be aware of that: nothing—is unnoticed in the dance that goes on about us ceaselessly. And we also are a part of it. Now come back and open your eyes."

When she had refocused, he nodded at her. "Your powers are great."

"You keep telling me that."

"It remains true."

"What about the fighting dance?"

He sighed at her single-mindedness. "The dance that you know is pattern. Everything is a pattern, even fighting. What the dance that you know teaches is not only fighting, but knowledge of the Dance that you do not know, but which you will have to learn. Of the latter, you just saw a small part."

She shook her head. "But what does that have to do with fighting?"

"Everything, Miriam," The sadness crossed his face.

"It doesn't make any sense to me. Fighting is fighting, isn't it? Whether it's against the Church or against that . . . that bastard . . ." Her mouth tightened.

"You think too much about your hate."

"What am I supposed to do?" She flared at his reprimand. She was here for a purpose. One purpose. One only. What did patterns have to do with it? "Love him?"

"What you are supposed to do, Miriam, is become fully human . . . or whatever. . . ."

There was an odd tone in his voice. "Or whatever? What do you mean?"

He did not seem to hear her question. "Look at your hands. You are a healer. How do you reconcile that with that sword you have been using?"

"Are you saying I should quit?"

"I am saying that you must know yourself. And as you are a part of the Dance around you, you must know that also. Did you seriously think that swordplay was going to be a simple matter of hacking meat until it stopped moving?"

Her patience fled. "What are you trying to do to me?"

He was unruffled. He smiled again, sadly. "Teach you."

Just then the skylark swept into the clearing, plummeting out of the sky like a feathered projectile, and alighted on Terrill's shoulder with a flutter of wings. The Elf did not start. He looked at the bird as though it spoke to him.

Miriam blinked, and the thought came to her unbidden: *A part of the pattern . . .*

* *

When Terrill had put the practice sword into her hand that morning, Miriam had felt elated; but as she entered Saint Brigid that afternoon, the heat of the day shimmering up from the unpaved street, she found that her feelings were mixed. Yes, she was learning to fight, but Terrill's explanations had taken away the elation. Patterns? What did patterns have to do with it?

When you can love him as you kill him, then you will be ready.

She flinched. She did not want to love anyone, particularly the stranger in the forest. How could Terrill say such a thing after Varden had nearly been killed? One of his own kind! Was that the price she had to pay in order to learn from him?

"Too damned high," she muttered, scuffing down the street and across the common. Upset and agitated, she plumped herself down on the grass and closed her eyes, looking for peace. The stars burned at her, calmed her.

Idly, she let her awareness grow. She felt the houses and the shops, sensed the people around her, recognized Francis at his forge, Andrew in his shop, and others she knew by name or by face.

But she came upon something unexpected. There was pain nearby, and grief, and tears. The touch of those emotions startled her back into herself, and when she opened her eyes, she heard, very faintly, the shrill yipping of an animal in pain.

She rose. Her long legs carried her quickly down one street and then another, across an open field, and finally to a small orchard of old apple trees that stood by the village wall closest to the river. There were children there, their faces drawn at the sight of the three-month-old puppy that writhed in the dust as it screamed its pain and bewilderment into the hot afternoon air, its left hind leg bent at a crazy angle.

These were no city children of the north, raised amid violence and pain and inured to the sight of suffering. If the people of the Free Towns were different, then so were their sons and daughters. The Elves had come to this village, and they had brought with them something gentle, something healing.

Healing.

One face turned toward her as she hurried up. It was Philip, Andrew's youngest. "We were climbing in the trees," he said hoarsely as the puppy screamed on and on. "And Deborah wanted to bring the puppy. He slipped from her hands when she was quite up."

Something was stirring in Miriam, but it was not her power, and it was not in her spine. It was something else, and it was in her heart. The puppy shrieked and yipped, but she pushed her way through the little knot of children, stooped, and took the dog into her arms. She felt it clearly: a small part of the world around her that hurt without cause, a part that she could soothe. She straightened, and when she looked at the faces of the children, she saw hope.

"What are you going to do, Miriam? Can you . . . ?"

The dog screamed again and tried to fling itself out of her grasp. "Yes," she said, wondering why she said it, astonished at this sudden upwelling of compassion. "I can."

With her mind on the stars, she reached into herself. The power flowed like a warm, sweet river, flooding her mind with soft light. When the flash faded, the puppy blinked at her, astonished. It sniffed its leg suspiciously, then licked her hand and went to sleep in her arms with a small *grrff*.

The children stood for a moment in silence, then cheered. Miriam scarcely heard them. In the wash of peace that surged into the void left by the power, she felt the light of the stars, strong and tranquil, saw, among them, a lattice-work, a web of possibility that encompassed and held infinity within its strands. It blazed at her, inundated her with knowledge of the pattern, of the Dance.

Yes, it was there. Yes, it changed with every decision, with every action. And Miriam as she was once and Miriam as she was now were parts of it, essential to it, just like the children standing around her, their faces awed and happy both, just like the sleeping puppy in her arms.

The strands flashed, then faded. Terrill was right. Everything participated in the Dance. It was not something one could accept or deny: it simply was.

Almost blind with starlight, she pushed the puppy into Philip's hands and stumbled back across the field. Patterns.

Patterns. Everything was patterns. Something would happen—had already happened—because of what she had done.

When she reached the priest's house, she closed the door behind her and wiped at her eyes. Kay rounded the corner from the hall, the sleeves of his soutane rolled up and a broom in his hand. He looked at her carefully. "Are you not well, Miriam? Did your lesson go badly?"

Something had indeed happened, she knew. It had to do with her heart. It had widened once when she had been transformed, and now it had widened again, reaching out to contain child and puppy and town and forest. She wondered if it might not continue to widen until it contained the universe.

Terrill will be pleased, she thought, trembling.

"Miriam? Is something wrong?"

She wiped her eyes again. "I'm not sure," she said. "Maybe. Maybe it's right. I don't know."

Her dreams that night were a whirl of images. She seemed to fly like a falcon, spiraling up until all of Adria lay below her. She saw fields and mountains and rivers and forests, and she saw also the scattering of houses and cities, the works of human beings that crisscrossed the land.

And these last—mortal handiwork—frightened her, and she spread her wings and fled into the stars, looking for something that she had seen before and forgotten. Her heart ached with a want to which she could not put a name, a longing she could not describe.

She hung in the void, her wings cutting starlight, her thoughts stilled. She was safe here. There was nothing here that would hurt her. And as the Dance went on around her and in her, she felt strangely comforted, as if here, amid this sea of stars, she truly belonged.

It was still dark when she awoke, and her pillow was damp with tears. She went to the window and looked out, and though the moon told her that dawn was several hours away, she was not tired. Her mind was clear, her body awake, but the stars in the sky made her heart ache once again. There was something . . . something she had forgotten. It hung out of reach like a name that she could not remember.

She turned around and leaned against the sill, seeing the room in shades of lavender and blue, her awareness reaching out like hands, touching the bed, the chair, sensing the minute impressions her stylus had scored in the wax tablet that lay on the table.

She picked up the tablet. The writing was clear to her. *1348—Jaques Alban* . . .

She had planned so carefully, and she had gotten exactly what she wanted. A new body. And maybe a new fate. She could look up, tossing the tablet back on the table, and feel sure that eventually, she could find the man who had committed that last, final outrage.

"I'm going to kill you," she murmured, and she knew that it could really happen. But she wondered suddenly if a sword stroke through his body could make up for all her running, all her suffering, or could lend some sense of validity to the act of desperation to which she had driven herself.

The uncustomary thought shook her. "My name is Miriam," she said softly, looking for comfort in the new, strange litany. "I have red-gold hair. I have green eyes."

But the words were empty, and she started to cry again because her heart was suddenly empty, too.

Chapter Seventeen

There had been a thunderstorm come down from the mountains that afternoon, and George Darci tramped along the edge of the forest, breathing deeply of the fresh, cool air. His green summer cloak caught drips and splashes of water that fell from the overhanging branches, the drops beading on the dense weave until he looked arrayed in diamonds.

He leaned against a tree. If he did not love Anne and Janet so much, he considered, he would gladly throw over Saint Blaise and all that went with it and live in the forest with the Elves. If they would have him. Such a tranquil and quiet life they must lead among the trees! Maybe someday at least he could meet one of the eleven ladies and ask her to teach Janet some of their songs. So nice . . .

"Blessings, George. I trust you have had no further problems with wild boars."

His heart pounded for a moment before he recognized the slender, fair-haired figure that had materialized out of the trees. "Terrill!" he cried. "I'd been hoping to talk with you."

The Elf permitted himself a slight smile. "The next time you send a message, my friend, do not entrust it to a skylark. They are honest and well meaning, but rather feather-brained."

"Skylark?" George vaguely remembered something about a skylark but could not put his finger on it.

Terrill shrugged. "Inconsequential. I am here. Have you a need?"

George nodded. "Advice."

Speak, then."

A large drop struck George's cheek and wound its way

down to his chin like a tear. "There seems to be a move on the part of the Church and the baronage to declare a crusade against the Free Towns." He told the Elf of the words of Thomas a'Verne and Baron Paul, and of what he had found out himself about Aloysius Cranby and Roger of Aurverelle. Terrill looked pained at the mention of the last name.

"The Aurverelle line has given my people much grief," said the Elf. "I have heard of Aloysius Cranby. He calls us heretics. He obviously has no sense of humor or he would laugh at the absurdity of the statement."

"He's an inquisitor," said George. "He's not supposed to have a sense of humor."

"That may well be. But are you people not prepared to defend themselves as they did some years ago?"

"It doesn't seem so." George always felt nervous when talking to Terrill. The Elf had saved his life two years before, when a boar had nearly gored him to death, but George could never lose sight of the fact that he was dealing with an Immortal. Now, moreover, he felt ashamed of his race, sunken as it was in a mire of greed and war. "Now that the Church is involved, it's not a matter of conquest by greedy overlords. It's a spiritual matter. My people are good Christians. They don't want to face damnation fighting against the Church's own armies."

Terrill shook his head in wonderment. "Do your people seriously believe such things?"

George sat down on a stone, heedless of the damp. "Oh, Terrill, I wish it were otherwise. But my people have grown up with the Church, and its ways are a comfort to them. Some might go into the forest at times and listen for an elvish song, but in time of trouble they will turn to their religion. There's no other way for them."

"And what do you believe, George? Are you willing to fight?"

The mayor of Saint Blaise wiped rainwater from his face, but a light drizzle started up and wet it again. "The God I worship enjoys seeing folk get along together and live peacefully. Priests and popes are humans. They make mistakes. I have no fear of my God's judgment on my actions."

"And what do you want of me? My own people have not

fared well in dealings with the Church.'' Terrill folded his arms. His hair was lank from rain.

"I don't know what to do, Terrill, The burghers of my city fear equally for their freedoms and for their souls. As such, they're paralyzed. They spend their days embroiling themselves in technicalities, consulting with priests who are themselves divided. I've even been asked not to communicate any of this to other towns.''

"And so you speak to me?''

"I swore I would tell no man. Upon my oath.'' George smiled wryly. "but I didn't say anything about Elves.''

"And what I do with the information is, as your people say, my own business?''

"Yes, Terrill. Can you alert the other towns?''

"I can. Though I fear that this news may be greeted with no different response than in Saint Blaise.'' Terrill looked meaningfully at him.

"At least I can try. I'm afraid this whole affair endangers the Elves, too. If the crusade is successful, Malvern Forest will be surrounded by hostile people. And the Inquisition . . .'' He mopped his face, not noticing the haunted look in Terrill's eyes. "It's terrible. On my last trip to Hypprux, when I found all this out, I met a little girl in the streets. She healed my ankle. She'd just escaped from the dungeon in the Chateau. She'd been tortured.''

"A small woman?'' said Terrill suddenly. "Black hair? Dark eyes?''

George looked up. "Why, yes. Do you know her?''

The Elf looked off into the trees for a time, then shook his head. "I do not.''

"Well, I pray she's all right, wherever she is. It was terrible, just terrible, what they'd done to her. Her legs were bleeding all over the street.''

"I am sure that she is, in some way, safe.''

"I hope so.''

Terrill considered. "I do not know what to tell you, George,'' he said. "Sometimes force must be met with force. But if your people are unwilling to fight for themselves, then they must surrender. And if you would not surrender, then you must flee.''

George realized what he was saying. "Like the Elves?''

Terrill nodded grimly. "Such was our choice. Fighting does not come easily to us."

George looked at Terrill's sword.

The sky was the color of slate, and it weighed down so heavily on Hypprux that it seemed that only the tall spires of the cathedral kept it from crashing to earth, bringing houses and shops, bridges and walls to ruin. People talked of rain and of a break in these days of heat and leaden clouds, but there was nothing to indicate that the weather had not stagnated where it was, that Hallows or even Christmas would not arrive to find the city still sweltering.

Thomas a'Verne sat back in his bed and went over his notes, resting the tablets on his old, gnarled knees while he reviewed or made notations. His voice whispered as he read, faded as he fell into thought.

If he had been inclined to suspicion, he would have thought that he was being deliberately kept from certain information about the plans of Aloysius Cranby and Roger of Aurverelle. Arrangements, he was sure, had already been made, boundaries drawn, friend clearly distinguished from foe; but no word of this had crept out of either the Cathedral of Our Lady of Mercy, the house of Aurverelle, or the Chateau. Thomas had asked many questions, had received no answers.

"Maybe they think I'm senile," he muttered, taking stylus in hand and crossing out yet another name on his list of contacts. "Maybe they imagine I'll not notice."

Since George had left Hypprux that March, Thomas had received only one message from him. The burghers of Saint Blaise were doing exactly what Cranby and Aurverelle had expected. A combined plot of sacred and secular had been woven about the Free Towns, and its effect was as stultifying as the interminable heat. George was trapped in his town, the captain of a ship on which the sailors, fearing for their souls, had lost the will to fight.

Thomas set the tablets aside and got up. Wrapping a thin robe about himself, he went to the balcony. Across the sea of huddled rooftops—slate and thatched, splendid and sordid—the Cathedral rose, windowed and spired, and the Chateau stood beside it, massive, walled, guarded.

He tugged idly at his gray beard. The Inquisition was at work, a fusion of Church and State, and its power seemed omnipotent. He could only hope that it was not. He thought back to that evening when George had come for dinner, and smiled wryly at the thought of the little healer girl who had somehow defied priest, soldier, walls, bars, and dungeon to make her way to freedom. A miracle it was, but it showed that miracles still occurred, and Thomas took the girl as a sign. When George had left her, she was wearing the ensigns of Saint Blaise and the Free Towns. Maybe there was a meaning in that.

He looked up at the dark sky. "O Lord God," he murmured. "You were a carpenter once. You lived in a little town. Wouldn't you have fought for Nazareth if the Romans had brought an Inquisition there?"

A tightness suddenly in his chest. He stumbled to a chair, sat down, reached for the decanter. It was happening more often during these hot months, but he suspected it was leading to something.

He gazed at the sky. "I'm coming, Judith. Soon now." And he lifted a cup of wine in a toast to her, just as he had lifted one many a time before when she, smiling and blushing, but glad and proud, had been alive to lift one in return.

Miriam knew that something was happening to her. The familiarity about herself had increased, and as the days lengthened and the harvest continued into September, she began to face the mirror in her room with some trepidation. Her need for sleep was diminishing, too: she had finally given up trying to stay in bed and now spent much of the night on the village common, practicing Terrill's dance. During the day, she found herself smiling at times for no reason, as though it took no more than fine weather to make her glad; and she no longer kept her eyes downcast when she walked in the streets of Saint Brigid, but looked townsfolk straight in the eye, wished them a good morning, and meant it.

She tried to find reasons. Perhaps she was merely growing accustomed to herself. Perhaps her work with Terrill had given her hope and self-assurance. Perhaps better health and increased strength had lessened her need for rest. But she sensed that she was fooling herself with such thoughts, that the changes stemmed from matters more profound than attitude or conditioning. And what worried her most was the growing conviction that those same matters were directly opposed to the goal she had set for herself on that terrible day when she had staggered out of the forest, torn and bleeding.

Frequently now, she contemplated that future battle with a helpless feeling of emptiness. The dance she knew and the Dance she was learning were, she had come to realize, patterns that bespoke love, compassion; and as, day by day, they gave her the ability to wield sword, so, day by day, they seemed to want to take away from her any reason for wielding it.

But thoughts of abandoning the idea left her with a bitter rage that cut through any thought of love or compassion like a sharp blade; so she continued her practice. With the exception of a week during which Terrill was off on a sudden and unexplained journey, she was in the clearing every other day, dancing the dance, swinging the wooden practice sword in synchronization with the hidden and omnipresent pattern while the Elf's dispassionate voice commented on her performance.

Each day distanced her more and more from the little victim-healer. There was pleasure in that, but again there was fear, for as she moved further away from what she had been, she moved closer to whatever she was becoming. And she had no idea what that was.

Until, on a day in October, when the leaves were the color of blood, the meadow grass yellowed and dead, the weather cool and crisp and turning, inevitably—in the ever-changing Dance—to winter, she found out.

Her dreams haunted her still, and she awakened well before dawn, her face streaked with tears, recalling little save that she had been striving toward . . . something. A home, maybe. Some place where she belonged.

Her heart ached, and as she wandered out onto the common to practice, she felt for a moment that she would give up anything, even her vengeance, to possess whatever elusive thing it was that she so sought in her sleep.

When she realized the implications of her thought, it was

as though she had been kicked in the belly. She doubled over, and the sky behind her internal stars turned red with anger and suppressed violence. Nausea rose as violently as the power ever had and brought her to her knees.

She was no saint who could immerse herself in a pool of cloying piety and so allow the stranger in the forest to live. Miriam of Maris would strike out, and if she could not cut down all the priests, all the inquisitors, all the barons and cityfolk and brutes, all the mocking, leering faces of her past, then at least she could kill one.

She stood. Putting strength into each movement, each step, her mind taut and focused on the reason she had for such action, such learning, she practiced the dance. And when Terrill came for her in the late morning, she bowed silently and followed him without a word. She would have vengeance. She was committed to it with vows as strong as those that bound Kay to chastity or Roxanne to secrecy.

Terrill did not comment on her silence or upon the grimness with which she took up the wooden sword, but he drove her even more fiercely than was usual, without comment, without criticism. His own silence was an eloquent expression of his disapproval.

Miriam fought hard, placing each stroke with care and cunning. Anger lent her strength, quickened her reactions. Terrill disapproved. Let him. She had work to do.

He finished driving her back to the edge of the trees and stepped away. "You are angry," he said at last. "I would advise you to earth that emotion. It has no place here."

"You haven't hit me yet."

"Still—"

"Come on." She glared at him.

He drove in. Wood met wood. Terrill's blade slid the length of Miriam's and skittered off harmlessly. As he whirled, she saw an opening, and she was angry enough to take it. Pivoting suddenly, she dropped to one knee, swung, and caught the Elf between hip and ribs. Terrill's stroke was already coming, though, and she threw herself flat to avoid it.

When she looked up, the Elf's face wore an expression of unfathomable sadness. There were tears in his eyes. "I had hoped that you would not take that opening."

"Well, I did."

He hefted his sword. "I am sorry."

"Sorry? Sorry that you'd be dead if we were working with live steel?"

"Are you so sure of that?"

She recalled the wound that Varden had received: she had hit Terrill in the same place. Feeling cold, she dropped her eyes. "If you were human, you would be."

"Maybe. But I have spoken to you about anger, and I will continue to do so."

"I still hit," she said stubbornly.

"You did. And you were focused. Too focused, in fact. That is what your anger did to you. You did not see something."

"I saw what I had to."

"Did you? Stand up. Again."

She rose and faced him. Terrill sized her up, nodded, then drove in. Once more, his sword sheared splinters off hers, once more Miriam saw her opening.

She struck. Maybe if she bruised him this time, he would take her seriously.

But the opening was suddenly not there anymore, and her blade was first blocked, then spun expertly out of her hand. Miriam wound up flat on the ground with the Elf's blade hovering inches from her throat.

His voice was heavy with grief, his eyes with tears. "You were so intent on doing me injury that you would have lost your life with a live blade."

Befuddled, she shook her head. "How?"

"I will show you. Stand up."

Shaken, her confidence destroyed, she got to her feet. Terrill sent her off to fetch her sword. When she returned, he told her to hold it in both hands.

"Close your eyes and find the stars. As before."

She did so. She might have been standing among them.

"Now, hold their image in your mind. Cling to it. Then open your eyes, and maintain the vision."

And as she opened her eyes, a door in her mind seemed also to open, and she staggered back a step.

She was seeing everything in all its wholeness, in all its intricate connection. The world was bright and fresh—even the dying leaves and the dead grass—as though created that very instant. But she saw beyond the instant, too, into past and futures. She saw the possibilities inherent in the smallest particle of earth, saw the endless cycles of season and of life and death, the days stretching off behind and before her, weaving through one another and through her in the Great Dance.

She felt herself falling, and Terrill reached forward and caught her shoulder. "Steady."

The word was a command, and she obeyed without question, drawing herself up as straight as the Elf. She let the light fill her, drank it in with her entire body.

"Now," said Terrill. "Slowly." And he lifted his sword and moved in.

Her vision was augmented by the immanent presence of the stars, and a shifting lattice of potentials and possibilities wove about her. She saw the futures and knew where Terrill's blade could strike at any given moment. A finite possibility even existed that he would simply drop the sword and walk away, but as she lived the probabilities, she watched them collapse into the ever-present now and knew that at the last moment, he was going to feint, withdraw a fraction of a pace, and cut at her left side.

Her blade was already moving, flowing effortlessly into the pattern that was forming. The potentials changed again, energy shifted.

Terrill altered his plans. A head shot. Miriam moved, balanced, flowed, and when wood smacked into wood a few inches from her ear, she was already planning a counterstroke.

All the same, though, she had not lost cognizance of the meadow, the grass, the blue sky, and the white clouds. They were all a part of the pattern also, as if only on just this day would the Elf decide to parry her attack downward instead of to the side and step in with his left foot rather than his right. All a part of the Dance.

But after a few minutes, the starfield reasserted itself violently in Miriam's mind, and she faltered, stumbled, and collapsed. Terrill caught her and lowered her gently to the ground.

She opened her eyes again. The world was back to normal. ''That is what you did not see,'' said the Elf. ''Openings, possibilities. Nothing I did escaped you.''

She was too weak to say anything for a moment. Finally: ''What . . . was that?'' she whispered.

''The Greater Dance,'' he said. ''A small part of it. You did not simply look at it, you participated with knowledge. Such is the way of the Elves. Knowledge. We do not consider mere faith to be a great treasure.

She blinked at him. ''But . . . but I'm not a Elf.''

Terrill stroked her head gently. ''When you healed Varden,'' he said with kindness, ''you linked with him, and you absorbed something of his nature. It showed that your being was receptive, and perhaps that should have warned Varden away from transforming you. But he did—you insisted—and you absorbed more.'' He met her eyes. ''Much more.''

''What are you saying?''

''You are part Elf now.''

The blending of starlight and daylight had left her weak, dizzy, and she could not comprehend the import of Terrill's words. All she knew was the stars, the stars that shone brightly within her.

''We will end here for today,'' said the Elf. ''You have much work ahead of you. You will notice that I am not fatigued. The power is yours, but you have yet to learn it. But you will. I have no doubt of that.''

She nodded absently. As he helped her to stand up, she noticed that the world still retained the brightness, the newness. Terrill seemed younger, more clearly defined, and she sensed that his emotions and motives, though still unreadable, had edged toward intelligibility.

But she also felt—suddenly, dimly, but with certainty— that there was more between her and Terrill than the teaching of swordplay.

Chapter Eighteen

As usual, Terrill guided Miriam to the forest's edge. But rather than turning disinterestedly on his heel, he seemed inclined to pause as though he wanted to say something. Words, though, did not come, and after a moment, almost embarrassed, he bowed to her, wished her a good afternoon, and departed.

She remained where she was, wondering, her back against a tree. The fields surrounding the village had been cleared, the harvest gathered in, and the winter sowing of barley and wheat had been finished the week before. Saint Brigid had settled in for the cold season. With no overlord to take for himself the pick of the crop, winter in the Free Town was comfortable, if not luxurious: the houses warm, the food adequate, the feasts many and joyous.

She looked at her hands, held one up against the shadows of the forest, and examined the lambent sheen about it. She turned around, regarded the village, and noticed that perspectives had sharpened, edges were clearer, colors were brighter. She could pick out pebbles on the ground two bow shots away.

Terrill had only told her part of the truth. Yes, she had absorbed something of the elven nature, but what her body told her now, what the stars said as they blazed within her, what the unnerving clarity of her surroundings revealed was that she was still absorbing, still changing. Her transformation had been but a seed, and it had taken root and lifted its leaves in starlight. It was beginning to bud now, and what flower it might bear she was afraid to guess.

She started off toward the town gates, her steps soundless. She did not think about her vow. She was too numb. Whatever lay in the future, she would deal with later—at present she had herself to contend with. But the starlight clung to her, enveloped her, comforted her. She closed her eyes and felt the slowly changing Dance. And that was comforting also.

When she reached the gate, she felt the unease in the village. It hung in the air like a fog, like an odor. She knew these people. They had befriended her and cared for her. She could not help but know that there was something wrong.

Francis waved at her from his forge, just as he always did, but he was disturbed. She met Andrew in the street, and he bowed low, as usual, but there was something on his mind. When she entered the house, she found Varden and Roxanne at the table with Kay. The priest had his face in his hands. The Elf and the witch were both serious, but they smiled at Miriam when she entered.

"Blessings on you, Miriam," said Varden.

She decided to find out just how much she had changed. "The hand of the Lady be on you, Varden."

Varden blinked, startled.

"The whole village is upset," said Miriam. "What's going on?"

"Aloysius Cranby," said Kay, mumbling through his hands. He suddenly struck his fist on the tabletop. "Damn him! Is he trying to buy the papacy with the blood of innocents?"

"Nothing has happened yet," said the Elf.

"But it will."

"Anything is—"

"Yes," said Kay. "I know. Anything is possible. Merely different probabilities. Tell me, Varden, what are the chances of Aloysius Cranby giving up on the Free Towns?"

"I asked a question," said Miriam.

Varden spoke. "The bishop is attempting to organize a crusade against the Free Towns."

Miriam's mouth tightened. "On what grounds?"

"Heresy."

"Heresy? What does heresy have to do with it?"

Roxanne spoke. She was well along in her pregnancy, and her hand rested protectively on her belly. "Miriam, consider the people sitting together at this table."

Miriam understood. Elf, witch, priest of the Church. Such a gathering could not take place anywhere else in Adria—perhaps not in all of Europe. If Cranby needed fuel for the Inquisition, there was plenty of human wood in the Free Towns.

"A man came down from Alm," said Kay. "Cranby's made some kind of deal with the barons. He gets his crusade and they get the land."

"But you fought the barons before," said Miriam. "It might be hard going, but—" The look on Kay's face made her break off.

"It's not just greed this time," Kay said softly. His eyes were bleak. He was a priest of the same Church that Aloysius Cranby served, and he was also a friend of Elf, and of witch, and a loyal citizen of the Free Towns. He would have to choose, and the choice was a terrible one. "It's the Church, too. If Cranby gets his way, then how can any Christian fight against the barons who will be carrying out the wishes of the Church?"

"A rather clever scheme." Roxanne spoke objectively, but Miriam knew—they all knew—that she and her child would be among the first to go to the stake if the Free Towns fell.

Miriam discovered that her hands were clenched. "I'm no Christian," she said.

"Miriam!" Kay looked stricken.

"I'm no Christian," she repeated. "I'll fight. Even if everyone else is scared out of their wits by Aloysius Cranby rattling a monstrance in their faces, I'll still fight. What do I have to lose? You can't see the scars on my legs anymore, but I remember how I got them. And I remember who gave them to me."

"But you're a different person now," said the priest. "No one will recognize you. And you can control your power."

"A little." She leaned up against the closed door, folded her arms. "But I'm still a healer, and I still heal." Her jaw clenched: the old mortal anger came back now in spite of the starlight. "I'm not running anymore."

Varden eyed her. "Do you speak from anger, Miriam?"

She turned on him. "Dammit, Varden, sometimes it's all I've got."

She left, slamming the door behind her.

* * *

Varden was following her. She knew it as clearly as she saw the stars, and she did not know whether to curse the ability or not. At the forest's edge, she stopped and waited for him, then started off once more.

"You are disturbed," he said after they were among the trees.

"Aren't you?"

"I am as I am."

"And I suppose you'll love the soldiers as they tie you to the stake, right?"

She immediately regretted her words, but she could not take them back. When Varden spoke, though, his voice was gentle. "Another move by the Church to exterminate us is not unexpected. We have been persecuted for centuries now, ever since the Council of Ephesus declared the Doctrine of Particular Divinity to be a test of orthodoxy."

"You take this rather calmly."

"I take the changing of seasons rather calmly also," he said. "Summer gives way to autumn, which in turn yields to winter." He gestured at the leafless trees. "It may be that the season of the Elves is ending. We will prolong our lives if we can, Miriam, but if our age ends, we must end with it. We have nothing to complain about."

"And if it's the end of the Free Towns, then the folk who are tortured and burned have nothing to complain about either, right? It's all part of the cycles, right?"

"I did not say that the Free Towns should not battle for survival."

"Of course not. Only that they should do so with love and kindness in their hearts." She turned to him. "Take a good look at where you and your people are, Varden. You used to be all over. You used to wander freely and without fear. Now you're stuck out here in the middle of the deepest forest in Adria, and it's that way all over Europe and probably beyond. You're all dwindling, dammit, and the Free Towns are probably going to get burned to the ground. Maybe it's time you and your people learned a little about being angry. I'm alive today because when I woke up in the forest with blood all over my thighs, I vowed I'd live to kill the man who did that to me. And I'm here. And I still intend to do it. And none of this foolishness about stars and patterns and compassion and . . . and . . ."

She could feel the sadness in him, but she pushed on.

". . . and love is going to stop me."

Varden regarded her for several minutes. The sounds of birds and animals wound around them. Branch rubbed against branch in the cool wind that flowed through the treetops above them, and Miriam sensed that snow was coming—dark, cold clouds building up in the north.

When the Elf spoke, he seemed to be a part of the approaching storm, for his voice was like ice. "What are you afraid of, Miriam?"

The question was direct, precise. But she met his eyes, and for strength she looked not to the old litany that had seen her through torture and sickness, but to the words she had learned from Terrill: *I am here, and Varden is here. We both stand upon the same ground, breathe the same air, see the same stars.*

And she managed to open her mouth, to speak with honesty. "I'm afraid I won't be able to kill him," she said bitterly. "Terrill told me I'm part Elf now. And all I see from the Elves is compassion and love. I can't kill someone I love."

"Are you so sure?"

"You're talking riddles. If I can't kill him, then all this"— she gestured, a sweeping arc of her hands that indicated her body, the forest, perhaps the entire world—will be for nothing. And I'll sit in the forest and smile at the squirrels until the soldiers cart me off to the stake."

Varden said nothing.

"Dammit, don't you ever get angry?"

He turned his gaze away from her. "I was angry. Once."

"Well?"

"Someday," he said quietly, "Terrill may tell you about it. You can judge then."

And she felt the grief in him like a glacier that, cold and glittering, defied the rays of the sun even at the height of summer.

* * *

As Miriam made her way back to the village, she felt Varden standing where she had seen him last, arms folded, eyes on the ground as if searching there for an end to whatever memory it was that eluded renewal. And when she reached the priest's house, she knew that he was still there, silent, the winter forest around him and the air chill.

He had spoken before of the sorrows of the Elves, and she had assumed that such emotions were of a general nature: the persecutions, the losses, the end of a way of life. She had never considered that, like her, Varden and Terrill and perhaps even Natil and Talla might have their own deeply personal griefs, ones that the cycles of the years left untouched, that only the final fading of their race could dissolve.

Immortal regret, Immortal pain. She wondered whether her own anger would go on and on forever, until, in some unimaginable fading . . .

What am I thinking?

She entered Kay's house wanting nothing now but her room, a bed to hide in, and a fire to keep her warm—as though any amount of blankets or heat could drive away the frost in her heart.

Roxanne was gone. Kay was sitting alone at the table, his eyes red, his face pale. "Miriam?"

She realized that the room had grown dark to his eyes. The sun had slid behind the mountains. "Yes, Kay."

"Was it true . . . what you said . . . ?"

She closed the door. "I'll fight."

"Not that," he said. "I mean about not being a Christian any longer."

"It's true," she said. "I can't say whether I believe in anything anymore. But I certainly can't believe in a faith that's hounded me all my life."

She was hurting Kay, just as she had hurt Varden, and she could not do anything about it.

"I'm sorry, Kay," she said, and she tried to put all the care and concern that she felt into her soft contralto.

Kay was not looking at her. She doubted that he could have seen her if he had. "No, Miriam. I'm the one who should be sorry. Aloysius Cranby should be sorry, too, and Clement the Sixth, and all the others. But they aren't, so I have to be sorry in their place." He wept. Miriam stayed where she was, unable to move.

"My God came down to this place once," Kay whispered, his voice hoarse. "And He talked about healing and comfort, just like the Elves. And He preached love . . . and peace. The Church preached love and peace, too, for a while. And then . . . something happened. I don't know what. But it's made us fail you, Miriam. And now you say you're not a Christian."

She watched him silently, felt his tears.

"And I can't say I blame you, my daughter." He sobbed loudly and buried his face in his hands. Miriam went to him, cradled his head in her arms, stroked his thin, blond hair.

"Kay," she said. "It's not your fault. You've tried."

"I've failed."

"No . . ." She bit her lip to stifle her own tears. "It's not all lost. The soldiers aren't here yet. We haven't heard any decrees. We can prepare."

"For what? For battle?"

"For whatever. I don't care what Aloysius Cranby or Clement the Sixth says. If there's anything holy in this damned world, it's not in Rome or in Avignon or in Hypprux . . . it's here in the Free Towns, and I'll fight for it. Dammit, Kay: you're some kind of saint, and if your Church can't see that, then it's not worth spitting at."

"I'm a priest of my Church, Miriam."

"I know. There's no greater irony."

He wiped his tears on his sleeve. "I'm a priest," he said. "I'll do what I can. Augustine delAzri is old, but respected. I'll write to him. And I'll write to Clement the Sixth, too. Maybe there's a chance that he can take enough time away from his statues and his frescoes and his moneylending to pay some attention to a little priest in a little town."

Miriam brought him candles and wax tablets. He began sketching drafts of his messages, pausing now and again to mop his tears. After seeing to him, she went down the hall to her room without taking a light. She had no need of such things.

She crawled under the warm comforter and tried to forget the fact that she would more than likely awaken before Kay finished with his work. Elves, she recalled, did not need sleep.

But she was not a Elf. And yet she could not drive from her thoughts the knowledge that she could no longer consider herself human either.

Chapter Nineteen

The snow came in the darkness, clouds moving across the sky. Before midnight, small, hard flakes were falling, and by the time Miriam awoke, they had turned large and wet.

She wrapped a thick robe about herself and went into the kitchen to stir up the fire. Kay was asleep, his head on the table, the candles burned out. She fetched a pillow and slid it under his head. The snow rattled softly against the shutters. She could see clearly, in shades of blue, the words he had been writing.

"*. . . and so, my most revered teacher, from whose hands I received the three major orders, I do beseech you to use your influence with the barons of Adria . . .*"

She set the tablet aside, threw a blanket over Kay, and made herself a hot drink. As she sat in the dark room, listening to the snow and to Kay's quiet snoring, she sensed that the grass of the common had already disappeared under a blanket of white, and she knew the snow would not stop that day, or possibly the next.

"Early snow, early spring," she murmured, sipping at her tea.

Someone tapped at the front door. Miriam opened up to find Varden. Snow was falling heavily, and he was wearing a gray cloak.

"Blessings," she said.

"The hand of the Lady be on you, Miriam," he returned.

"What are you doing here at this hour?"

"Standing in the snow at present. May I come in?"

"Uh . . . yes, of course." She stood aside as he entered and shook the snow from his cloak. "How is Roxanne?"

"Sleeping," said the Elf. "She is well."

Miriam wondered how much longer the witch would be

able to sleep in peace. In her mind, she saw a lattice of starlight that stretched off into the future, crossing and recrossing in an intricate pattern of possibility. In the web was a strand that was herself, and one that was her revenge, and one that was the man she needed to kill. But she saw also Roxanne, and Varden, and Terrill, and Mika, and the strands blended together in a dense tapestry that she could not comprehend.

Varden's touch brought her back. "Not yet," he said softly.

There was compassion in his touch, and forgiveness. "I'm sorry about what I said to you yesterday," she said.

"Was it untrue?"

"No," she admitted, "it wasn't, but it was cruel. And I've no reason to be cruel to someone who's done so much for me."

"It is what I am here for. Be at peace."

She looked him in the eye. Starlight met starlight. "How on earth do you stand me?"

The Elf considered. "I see you as you were, and I see you as you are now, and I see you as you might be." He smiled. "What is there not to love?"

She grimaced. "Am I going to wind up as mad as you?"

His smile broadened. "Quite possibly."

Kay stirred. "Hmm? Is that you, Varden?"

"It is, Kay. May I suggest that you go to bed?"

"Did you talk to Andrew and the others?"

Varden tucked the blanket around Kay's shoulders. "I did, my friend. Lamps have been burning well into this night. The general attitude of the town council seems to be that freedom is more important than the niceties of dogma."

"Battle?" said Miriam.

"It could come to that. But other paths are still open. The peerage of Adria has profited from the Free Towns. It could be that the barons simply need to be reminded of this fact."

"And if that doesn't work?"

"There was talk of hiring mercenaries," said the Elf. "And of training those who could wield weapons."

Kay spoke. "Mercenaries in the Free Towns? It would be the end of us just as surely as if we were were invaded."

"As I said, other means were discussed."

Kay nodded, rubbing at his eyes. "I have some means of my own," he said. He fumbled with the tablets, and when Miriam remembered that he could not see, she lit fresh candles. "I'll have these letters ready by sext. We need to get one to Maris, and the other has to go to Avignon."

Varden glanced at the writing, nodded. "Good. Someone can carry them to one of the larger cities when the storm abates."

"We don't have any time to waste," said Miriam. "I'll start this afternoon."

Kay started. "Miriam, I—"

"I want to do it."

"But . . . it's snowing."

"True."

"You're a woman."

"I've noticed. So?"

"It's dangerous!"

"Just write the letters."

Varden spoke. "I see no reason to gainsay Miriam's wishes. Traveling alone in the snow is unwise, though. One of my folk will accompany her."

"And do what?" said Kay. "Get burned?"

"Elves can pass among humans for short periods of time. We simply must keep our ears covered. Miriam?"

"That's fine. Who's going with me?"

"I myself wish to stay with Roxanne. I daresay Terrill would offer his company."

Miriam nearly laughed. "So that he can continue my training?"

"Possibly. That is his decision."

She wondered what futures Varden saw. Had he foreseen this situation? Was her offer to take the letters merely a part of an unfolding pattern that the Elf watched as though it were some strange, night-blooming flower? Training, indeed! "Kay, where do you keep your parchment?"

The priest looked almost ready to cry again. "In the green chest in my room. The ink and quills are there, too, and the wax and cord." As Miriam went off down the hall, he put his face in his hands. "What's happening, Varden? I don't understand what's happening. Why is she doing this?"

The Elf laid a hand on his shoulder. "They grow up, my friend," he said. His voice was almost lost in the whisper of falling snow.

Terrill showed up at noon, wrapped in a gray cloak and hood. His eyes twinkled at Miriam. "You desired to travel?" His tone was almost humorous.

"As soon as Kay finishes up," she said. "I'm packed already."

"What are you using for a cloak, Miriam?"

"I have a blue—"

The cloak that Mika had given her was hanging in her room, but she realized that it would not fit her now any better than Charity's diminutive gowns.

"Well, then," she said. "I don't know."

The Elf produced a bundle. "Roxanne is thoughtful and prudent. She sent this."

It was a gray cloak, like those worn by the Elves. "Oh . . ." Miriam held it up. It was perfectly matched to her size, and its clasp was an intricately worked moon and star.

"Natil, our harper, provided the clasp," said the Elf.

"It's lovely." She looked at him curiously. "How am I worthy of this?"

"It is cold, Miriam."

"You expect me to believe that?"

"I do."

Without further comment, she donned the cloak, fastened the clasp, shook her hair back over her shoulders. She had decided to wear her elven garb for traveling, and when Kay came down the hall, the letters sealed with wax and cord and ready in his hand, he stopped short at the sight of her.

"Dear God," he said softly.

"I'll wear human clothes when I'm in town, Kay. This is only for traveling."

He still stared. "Are you sure you can still pass in human clothes?"

She remembered what Varden had said about covering ears, realized that her own were burning, decided not to touch them to find out why. "I'll do my best. The letters can't wait, though."

The priest nodded resignedly and put them into her hands.

"My calligraphy is not the finest," he admitted as she tucked them into a pouch. "I hope Clement will deign to read this."

"I'll try to find someone reputable to carry it to Avignon."

Terrill spoke. "There are ships that sail down River Bergren from Furze and Belroi. Their captains are good men of business. I am sure that one could be entrusted with the missives."

"Furze?" said Kay. "Belroi?"

"I would assume," said the Elf, "that messages sent directly from the Free Towns might arouse interest on the part of Aloysius Cranby or Roger of Aurverelle. Much better that one of the honest rivermen take the letters."

"How soon can we get there?" said Miriam.

"We will travel the forest paths. Two days. Perhaps three."

"In this storm?"

His eyes twinkled again. "Elves are known for being ingenious. Come."

It was still snowing hard when they set off. Miriam hugged Kay farewell and followed Terrill into the bitter wind and driving flakes. She kept her hood pulled close about her face as they made their way along the streets of the town, across the bare, white fields, and into the forest.

Once they entered the forest, though, the wind died, and the path Terrill took was surprisingly free of snow. Miriam almost asked about the change, but as she opened her mouth she felt the soft energies about her. The path seemed to shimmer with magic, and she doubted that any human being had ever set foot upon it until now.

Until now? She wondered.

They journeyed northwest, paralleling the course of the Malvern River, and the sound of moving water blended with the sighing of the wind in the bare branches. But the forest still felt overly quiet, and Miriam had been walking for several hours before she understood why: her footfalls had become as silent as Terrill's.

She estimated that it was close to midnight when the Elf stopped and gestured toward a clearing. "You need to sleep."

Fatigue was indeed telling on her, but she mustered a small laugh. "Maybe, but for how much longer, Terrill?"

"I do not know," said the Elf.

She stood before him. "Are you sure? I've had the feeling these last days that there's a lot going on that you and Varden aren't telling me. Elves can see the futures. What do they tell you?"

He regarded her evenly, a pale, fair-haired figure wrapped in a cloak of gray. "Very little, Miriam," he said at last.

"Do you expect me to believe that, Terrill? I've seen them."

"Maybe," he said. "But you cannot see all of them, nor can I. It is true: there is much that is happening. But you saw many, many possibilities when we fought in the clearing yesterday, and if there are so many in a mere clash of wooden swords, how many more must there be in a life? You make choices, Miriam. You make them sometimes without even thinking. But every time that you do, you alter the Dance. Neither Varden nor I can make choices for you, nor can we predict what they will be. I beg you: consider that before you accuse us of withholding information."

For a moment, she looked among the stars for awareness of the Dance. She saw the strands of starlight that wove together in ever-changing patterns. Strand met strand, potentials split, and split again. She examined the amount of starlight flowing through her futures and knew that no one but an Elf would be so deeply connected with such energies. She pulled out of the vision. Her heart was racing.

"And how much choice do I really have, Terrill?" she said hoarsely.

The Elf turned away and began to kindle a fire.

When they reached the edge of the trees, Belroi was some six leagues to the north. Here, the snow had been light, and the River Malvern cut a trail through dun fields pinto-patched with snow as it ran swiftly toward the city to join the Bergren.

Closer was Furze. "We could reach it by noon," said Terrill, surveying the land with his keen eyes, "but the letters would have to pass through that many more hands. Better we take them to Belroi."

Miriam was changing into a gown. They would be on well-traveled roads now, and she had to appear as human as possible. Terrill had himself donned human dress, and but for the fact that his face was so fair and young, he appeared to be a common countryman bound for Belroi on some ordinary errand.

"Belroi is probably better, then," Miriam agreed, tying her bodice.

But she looked across the fields to Furze, remembering a small house and a woman who lived there . . . alone.

The Elf nodded. "Better. Providing, of course, that we do not run straight into the arms of the Inquisition."

She shuddered. Her legs ached, but she knew it was her imagination. "Do you think there's a chance of that?"

"There is always a chance, Mirya—" He caught himself and stared off at the town as though to avoid looking at her.

They reached Belroi in the late afternoon and entered through the town gates. Terrill's sword was in his pack, hidden, but within easy reach. The Elf received a number of admiring looks from passing women, and the men appreciated Miriam, but otherwise their presence went unnoticed.

Miriam felt ill at ease. This city was much like any other in Adria, like many she had lived in before. There were the same people pressing together in crowds or walking alone and bent under a heavy burden. The cats and dogs were the same, watching lazily from atop a warm wall or running alongside a wagon and barking. Mud. Noise. Shouting. A pot of cold-withered flowers forlorn on a balcony high above the street. A man chiding a woman in an upper room of a squalid house. A woman chiding a man in the dirty market square. A bunch of brown leaves tumbling along the cobbles in a chill wind, turning sodden in the melting snow.

Sadness . . .

She took Terrill's arm. "Courage," he said, laying his hand on hers. "This place has no power over you."

But her awareness insisted on reaching out to the pulse of the town. Sadness. People, young an old, carrying out day-to-day tasks of survival, their exertions mandated by fear:

fear of starvation, fear of penury, fear of damnation, fear of arrest, fear of love or the lack of it . . .

Sadness.

"How do you stand it, Terrill?"

He sighed. "They are human," he said simply, as if that explained it all. "They could, maybe, learn to see as do we, but they turned away from that choice."

"But Saint Brigid? Andrew and Elizabeth and Kay and Charity?"

"They made a different choice," he said. They came in sight of the river. "Their way is easier, or perhaps harder. It is difficult to judge sometimes. But Saint Brigid is not Belroi."

"I've noticed." She felt foreign, and it would not have been much stranger to her had there been—instead of the brightly painted guildhall and the spired cathedral—a cluster of nomad tents, or the onion-domed bulk of a mosque, its minaret pointing toward the sky and loud with the chant of a muezzin—

"Good evening to you, sir," Terrill called suddenly to a burly man leaning against a post by the river. "God bless you."

"Aye, give ye peace," said the man.

"Can you tell me if any ships are to be sailing for Maris tomorrow or the next day?"

"I can," he said. "Tomorrow mornin' early old *Bird of the River* casts off with a last load o' Bergren cheese. Be ye a merchant, sir?"

"That I am not," replied Terrill. "But I would speak with the captain."

The sailor pointed to a rough-looking inn by the riverside. "The Saracen's Head, old Gregory calls it, though if ye ask me he's never been within a stone's throw of a church, much less the Holy Land. Abraham is the captain: he's round as a barrel, with a black beard and an eye for pretty women. He'll be at table in the common room. Mind your wife, sir."

Miriam colored. "I'm—"

"Thank you, sir," said Terrill, squeezing her hand. "Give you peace."

"Aye, sir. And ye also."

They went toward the inn. "Am I so helpless that you have to take care of me?" she sputtered.

"Was it not Augustine of Hippo who said that one can catch more flies with honey than with vinegar?"

"I'm the one who has to deliver the letters."

"Maybe. But I am your teacher," he said, unruffled. "Did you learn anything just now?"

"The captain is glutton and a wencher."

"That is all?"

"Yes."

He sighed. "That is unfortunate. I had meant the lesson to be one in courtesy."

The interior of the inn was dark with the approaching evening, but not to the eyes of the two gray-cloaked figures that entered. Miriam saw Abraham immediately, for he did not so much sit at table as dominate the room.

"Well?" said Terrill.

"Well what?"

"As you so forcefully reminded me, you have the letters," he said. "Go and talk to Abraham. I will have a cup of wine." And with that, he wandered over to an isolated corner and sat down, his back against the wall and his feet up on a stool. Miriam saw him sign to the tapster, but felt his eyes on her. What lesson was this?

She looked at Abraham. The big man was watching her. An eye for pretty women. Staring down at the floor with her jaw set in annoyance, she found her stars and let their energies settle her. Abrahams's size reminded her too much of the man in the forest, and she hoped that this was not another human bear who would try to—

The stars glittered at her. She was used to being small, weak, and at the mercy of those around her, but that did not mean she had to remain that way. With a mental jerk, she pulled her awareness into the present. She could see the stars. She knew the fighting dance. And with a constancy and instinct that still baffled her, she was beginning to sense the Greater Dance that went on about her, that encompassed this city of sadness and the ways of its people, that enfolded in its intricacy even this large riverman who was just now stuffing a large piece of black bread into his large mouth.

With a glance at Terrill, she walked calmly over to the captain of *Bird of the River,* stood before him, and in her soft contralto said with great courtesy:

''God bless you, sir.''

Chapter Twenty

In the name of God, Amen.

I, Augustine delAzri, by the grace of Our Lord now bishop of Maris and the lands around it, being of sound mind and wishing to be at peace with my God and my people, on the twenty-fifth day of October in the Year of Our Lord one thousand three hundred and fifty and in the three hundred fifty-eighth year of the Baronage of Adria, do make my testament in the following manner. In the first place, I bequeath my soul to Almighty God and to the blessed Mary His mother and to all the saints, and my body to be buried in the Church of Saint Giles in the city of Onella, where I was born. And because by a certain form I have arranged for my lands and household goods to be sold and the profits from them to be distributed to the poor of Maris and its surrounding towns and villages, I will that first of all my debts shall be paid, and that to whomsoever I have done any injury, just and due recompense shall be made.

I will that a black cloth shall be arrayed on my body and that five wax candles be burned on the day of my decease, in honor of Our Most Blessed Lady, and that a branch of evergreen be placed in my hands when my body is given into the earth.

I give and bequeath to the Church of Saint Giles in Onella ten florins of gold so that masses may be said for my soul, that my imperfections may not weigh too heavily in the eyes of my God, and that He look with mercy upon me. I ask that my place of burial not be marked in any special or extraordinary way, and that my body be laid to rest among the poor of the community.

And I will that—

So dictated to me, Efram Bougiers, clerk, until the

*strength of the good bishop failed him, and his spirit
departed his body this twenty-fifth day of October, in
the year of Our Lord one thousand three hundred and
fifty.*

The night was dark, very dark. The wind was bitter. The
snows of late November were always harsh, but these were
the worst that George Darci could remember. He could almost fancy the bolts of the shutters straining with the gusts
of the storm, and he instinctively curled up against his
sleeping wife and pulled the down comforter tightly about
them both.

But it was not the wind that kept him awake: it was the
letter that lay on the table at the far side of the room. The
messenger had come that afternoon from the town of Alm,
having fought his way north through five leagues of blizzard
to deliver the sealed parchment into the hands of the mayor
of Saint Blaise. Somehow, the aldermen of Alm had heard
about the threat of a crusade and were asking for a statement
of policy and intent from Saint Blaise. Tomorrow George
would have to stand before the council and ask for a reply.
He wondered what he would get.

It appeared that the Free Towns had been prodded into
action, but the reaction of Saint Blaise, the wealthiest of
them all, was the determining factor. If the burghers decided to fear for their souls, the Free Towns were lost. If
they decided to fight, then . . .

George lay on his back, staring at a ceiling that he could
not see. Even if they fought, the Towns might never be the
same. There was something precious in the Free Towns,
something worth fighting for, but something that fighting
could destroy.

But he had decided, nonetheless, to ask the council to
prepare for war. If what the Towns had was to be lost, then
it was better lost in defense rather than in capitulation.

Anne stirred, cried out, her hands clawing at empty space.
"Janet!" she screamed hoarsely.

George held her. "Anne, you're dreaming. It's all right."

Shaking, she started to weep softly. She buried her face
in his chest. "Oh, God . . ."

"Just a dream," he said soothingly, stroking her hair.

"It was too real," she said. "I saw the town burning. I was watching from the upper window, and the smoke was all about. Then I remembered that I didn't know where Janet was, and I ran down the stairs to her room. She wasn't there. I looked all over."

"Shhh . . ." George rocked her gently. "Remember, it was a dream."

"It seemed so real. . . ."

She wept for a while, and then sleep took her again. Absently, George continued to stroke her hair. Anne did not usually have nightmares, but he supposed that the strain in the town this winter could be affecting her. Still . . .

He wondered, as he often did when he awoke in the dead of night and gazed at her sleeping form, whether he were seeing a faint light about her, an almost subliminal luminescence that allowed him to make out, dimly, the features of his beloved wife.

He had never spoken of it, and he knew that no one else had ever noticed, not even her father and mother. In fact, he normally dismissed it as mere fancy on his part. But now, with the threat of crusade hanging over the town, he recalled certain stories that were told in marketplaces, and at hearthsides, and by wandering musicians. They were stories of liaisons between mortal and immortal, between human and Elf. And he had heard about a woman to the south, in Saint Brigid, who had taken an Elf for a lover and who was now spending the winter in the forest to bear their child among his people.

How much elven blood was there in the land? In whose veins did it run?

He stroked Anne's head. "Oh, my dearest," he said, knowing that she did not hear, "I was honored when you took my hand in marriage. But if what I suspect is true, then am I doubly, trebly honored." He kissed her. "Hail, Fair One."

She stirred, nuzzled at him, and was, once again, asleep.

. . . and so, Your Excellency, as far as I am able to tell, Roderick of Onella, resident of Belroi, is innocent of any connection with the Free Towns. He has, of course, been expelled from the guard because of

the bribe. The whore, Denise, has been handed over
to the civil authorities for punishment.

But Roderick's story raises some questions. Who
were the two women in the cart? Could Miriam of
Maris, the witch, have been the "nasty-looking little
girl" of whom Roderick spoke? If so, then it is obvious that the elven heresy has spread beyond the Free
Towns, for when last seen, the older woman was driving the cart south, toward Furze.

I will make some inquiry in Furze, but will return
to Hypprux before Christmas. I am entrusting this letter to an able river captain named Abraham. I pray
you, Excellency, reward him well, for my supply of
ready money grows short.

Dated this twenty-fifth day of October, in the year
of Our Lord one thousand three hundred and fifty.

Saint Brigid prepared for Christmas, but it also prepared
for war. Word came down from Saint Blaise that the wealthiest of the Free Towns had decided to take up arms if a
crusade were declared, and the other towns joined with it
to defy both secular and ecclesiastical power.

And so, as the Yuletide decorations appeared in the village—bunches of elder, mistletoe, and birch hanging from
door and wall—a sense of expectancy settled about the town
as thick as the snows. Farmers talked about the spring plow-
ing as usual, but they sounded unconvinced, as though
spring might provide, along with green shoots and buds,
the tramp of soldiers and the clang of weapons. Would there
be a harvest next year? Would there be a town?

Near the beginning of the third week of Advent, David
balanced his carvings on an old cart and brought them to
the church. With the help of Andrew and a number of other
men, he set the panels up behind the altar with the canvas
still on. He wanted the unveiling saved for Christmas.

Miriam watched them work as she stood on the snowy
common, her gray cloak wrapped about her and her hood
up to keep the cold from her ears. It had been David's panels that had brought her surety enough to pressure Varden
into giving her exactly what she wanted.

She nearly laughed out loud at the thought. What had she
ever really wanted beyond a dry place to sleep and some

assurance that the morning would not find her in some dungeon, or at the stake?

She turned away from the church, her soft boots noiseless on the carpet of snow. She wore elven garb habitually now. Gowns and skirts lay in the past, along with a good deal more. The clothing was merely an outward sign that signified the profundity of the inward change.

And she felt the Dance everywhere. If she concentrated, she could see the strands of possibility that connected everything around her, weaving in and out in a dense lattice of starlight in which everything, great and small, marvelous and common, fit together in every conceivable combination. Anything was possible. There were only varying degrees of probability.

And among the possibilities, she saw the movements of armies, the mustering of men. She saw peasant set against knight, burgher against man-at-arms, saw the probabilities of battle blur into an indistinguishable mass of potentials. She tried to look beyond the conflict, but the outcomes were many, and the only certainty was that Saint Brigid would never be the same in any of them.

But no . . . there was one in which the town would be spared. Perhaps it could not survive unchanged forever, but for a little while it could maintain its ways. She tried to follow the potential, but it was dim, at present almost insignificant.

There came, from a short distance away, the sound of metal beating on metal. Miriam flinched, looked instinctively for a place to hide. Alarm. The Chateau. The guards coming for her. Her legs bleeding . . .

She shook herself back into the present. At the smithy, Francis was beating out a long piece of steel. The forge glowed ruddy behind the big man, and Michael leaned against the frame of the bellows, his arms streaked with soot and sweat.

They looked up at her approach. "Blessings, mistress," said Francis, but his voice was not as hearty as Miriam had known it in the past.

"Are ye cold, Miriam?" said Michael. "Cam in then, and get warm."

"I'm all right, thanks," she said. She was looking at what Francis gripped in the tongs. It was a sword blade.

Francis nodded wearily. "Aye. 'Tis a sword. 'Tis na the first I made in me life, but I wish 't were na the first I made in Saint Brigid."

"It's necessary, Francis," she said gently. "We may need swords. It looks to be a fine blade."

But when she lifted her eyes, the smith looked away, and Miriam hardly needed the insight of the stars to tell her what Francis was thinking, what in fact many of the townspeople were thinking: *If it were not for the Elves, the Church would not be involved.*

It was not fear, nor was it hostility. It was—and here she was instinctively putting it in terms that had become familiar to her—a yearning for a different path. Somewhere, there had been a future in which Aloysius Cranby had no excuse, fabricated or otherwise, to bring the Inquisition to the Free Towns. *Things could have been otherwise. Why has it happened this way?*

"I'm sorry, Francis," said Miriam. "That's just the way it happened."

He blinked, startled, and she realized that it was rude to read his thoughts. Francis covered his discomfiture by squinting at the blade and rapping out an imperfection in the metal with a blow of his hammer. "And wi' the Fair Ones fight for sic as us? Or wi' they hide in tha forest?"

"I'll fight, Francis. Any way I can."

But when she turned and made her way up the street, she knew that if she fought, it would be because of anger and rage. It would not be because Saint Brigid was her home. She had no home. She stood apart from human beings. As much as the little house of the midwife lay forever out of her reach, so now did the whole of Saint Brigid.

Simon the miller passed her, coughing violently. He was a robust man, but he suffered from weak lungs, and the winter was invariably hard on him. He stumped through the snow on his short legs, but had to stop until the fit passed.

"Simon," said Miriam. "Do you need help?" She could heal. She no longer thought of denying her power in such instances.

The miller gasped a breath, but he shook his head. "I'll be all right in a moment."

"I can—"

"I don't want that," he said quickly.

She saw his thoughts leap forward into a future in which he was answering an inquisitor's questions about his dealings with the Elves. The less that happened, the better. "All right," she said. "Be at peace, Simon."

"And you also, mistress."

He stumped off, drawing his hood up well around his face.

Miriam turned to the stars for comfort. "I am as I am," she murmured, realizing as she did that she was repeating the words that Varden had uttered. Slowly, inexorably, she found herself accepting what she had fought against for months.

She turned toward Kay's house. Charity was in the kitchen when she opened the door, and the young witch smiled at Miriam. "How wonderful," Charity said, slicing a large loaf of bread. "I've just come back from the forest, and now I won't have to repeat everything twice."

"Or risk me muddling everything," admitted the priest. He tried to put on a jovial face, but his eyes were sad. Mortality hung about him like a tattered cloak.

"There's not a great deal to muddle," said Charity. "Roxanne is well. She's having a fine time with Varden and his people. We've all been hoping that the baby would come on the solstice, but Talla looked ahead and said that it's more likely he'll be a few days late." She looked up at Miriam. "Why don't you go out and visit them?"

Miriam was hanging up her cloak. The moon-and-star clasp flashed in the firelight. "I'm not sure I should."

Charity caught her tone. "You know you're welcome there," she said gently.

Kay was getting butter and jam out of the pantry. Miriam looked at the clasp. "I . . . I don't know."

"Miriam?" Kay, too, had heard her grief.

"I'm . . ." The stars had helped her, but they could only soften the loneliness, they could not take it away. "I'm not an Elf," she said. "I don't belong with them. Roxanne is different, and you're different, too, Charity. I'm not quite elven, and I'm not human either. But . . ."

The priest and the witch were silent.

"But villages and towns are what I know. The future . . ." She recalled the flood of starlight coursing through her future, knew that there was a steady stream of that energy through the present. "I can't see all the futures." Slowly, she sat down, put her face in her hands.

She felt Charity's arms, heard her voice. "Stay with us then, Miriam. You're welcome here."

"But for how much longer?" she whispered. The visions of war and blood whirled in her inner sight. "And how much longer will there be a here to be welcome in?"

The snow fell in soft flakes that sparkled in the starlight. Charity and Miriam went hand in hand toward the church. They joined the people of Saint Brigid who came to worship on this frosty Christmas night, their feet crunching through the crust of snow, their cloaks besparkled with glistening flakes. Andrew and Elizabeth were there, and Francis and his family, and Simon and his wife Elanor and their children, and all the others. Women and men, young and old, they came to church for midnight Mass.

Inside, the air smelled of incense and pine, and Miriam sensed the presence of birch and mistletoe, the elder absent since the solstice two days before. Padding softly, she went up toward the front with Charity and stood before David's statue.

Though the thoughts of the villagers were overshadowed somewhat by the wonder of Christmas Eve, Miriam heard them nonetheless. *If only . . . The Elves are good people, but if only they had not come. If only . . .* This was the last Christmas before Aloysius Cranby and the barons would make their move. It could be the last Christmas that Saint Brigid and the Free Towns would ever have.

And Miriam, clad as an Elf, pushed back her hood and let her red-gold hair cascade freely over her shoulders. She stood straight, tall. Terrill's words came back to her: *I will not have you slouching like a human.*

She had gone beyond self-pity, she had gone beyond grief: the relentless changes that stirred her heart had forced her

to accept that these people loved her, each in his or her own
way. Even Simon, fearful as he was of the Inquisition, would
fight for her, as she would for him. And that knowledge
was, if anything, more painful than any rejection, for the
townsfolk were, like herself, torn: wanting one thing, wishing fervently for another.

From one side of the chancel, Andrew sang:

> *"Stella splendens in monte ut solis radium*
> *Miraculis serrato exaudi populum.*
> *Concurrunt universi gaudentes populi*
> *Divites et egeni, grandes et parvuli.*
> *Ipsum ingrediuntur ut cernunt oculi*
> *Et inde revertuntur graciis repleti. ''*

He was looking at Charity, and his voice swelled with
pride, as if he knew that Charity's gaze dwelt upon the statue
of the Lady, as if he had decided, long ago, that that was a
good thing, worthy of praise.

The final cadence drifted up sweetly, with a touch of an
inflection that some who were knowledgeable would call
elven, but when Miriam followed Charity's eyes to the
statue, she was suddenly rooted.

She had seen the statue only once before, when, months
ago, protesting, she had come to the church with Charity to
place flowers before it. She had assumed that it was of the
Virgin. But it was not the Virgin. As was the case with
everything David carved, it was merely burnished and
buffed, but Miriam did not need paint or color to tell her
that Her eyes were gray, Her hair dark, Her robes of blue
and silver. Behind Her, a field of stars went on forever, the
vision taking Miriam beyond the wood, beyond the church,
beyond the world.

"Elthia,'' she whispered, the name coming instinctively
to her lips.

Charity turned to her, eyes bright. "Do you see?"

In truth, Miriam saw nothing else: not the altar, bright
with candles, not the bare cross above it, not the panels that
had been uncovered this night, the wood glowing softly and
depicting the unfortunate Alban. Philip, Andrew's son, who
was serving this Mass, rang a small bell, and Kay entered,
vested in white, the light of candle and lamp glistening on

the fine threads of gold and silver worked into the ornate embroidery of his chasuble, but Miriam was aware of them only because the Dance held their actions and was altered by them. Only on this particular night, with the incense smoke drifting from the censer in just such a pattern, with Kay clearing a fold in the sleeve of his alb in just such a way, would Philip set the bell down as he now did, the clapper scraping ever so slightly on the stone floor.

But her mind was elsewhere, lost in the Lady, lost in the stars. She felt the sheen about her body quickening, felt her ears burning distinctly enough that she gave a shake of her hair to cover them thoroughly. It was only a statue, she knew, but so great was the spirit behind David's skill that Miriam would not have been surprised had She lifted her hand in blessing upon the people of Saint Brigid.

And when the Mass was over—the Mass she hardly heard—she turned to Charity.

"Did you see, Miriam?" asked the witch.

"I did, Charity." She heard the whispers still: *If only . . . If only . . .* But those whispers were faint in comparison to the other voice she heard. *Come,* it said. *Now. Tonight.*

She bent and kissed the witch. "I have to go to the forest, Charity. I don't know what I'm supposed to do there, but I have to go. I don't know when I'll be back."

Without waiting for a reply, she went to the small door that connected the south transept with Kay's house and slipped into the hallway that led to her room.

Kay was still unrobing in the vestry, and it was quiet in the house. Miriam went to her room, wondering if she should take anything with her. For a moment, she picked up the blue cloak that Mika had given her. The garment was absurdly short, but once, months ago, it had fit her perfectly.

She looked down at herself, clad in green and gray, her pale cloak fastened at her throat with an interlaced moon and star. With shaking hands, she hung the small cloak on a peg and left her room, left the house, left the town.

Terrill found her wandering deep in the wood as she searched for something that she did not really know, that she might not recognize even if she found it. Her tears were frozen on her face, and her hands were blue with cold.

For a moment, she looked with unseeing eyes at the Elf.
Was this real? Was it potential? What was real? And how
much of it was going to be lost as the pattern shifted and
choices made many leagues away left the snow spattered
with the blood of humans and Elves?

"Terrill . . ."

"Go to Her, beloved."

"I . . . I can't. I'm not ready."

"Then come with me."

She did not know upon what path he led her. Possibly it
was the same path she had been traveling ever since she had
left the church, maybe ever since she had left her parents'
house eight years before. There was, after all, only one
path: the one she was on. The rest were merely potential.
Maybes. Might-have-beens.

"Where are we going, Terrill?"

"Home," he said softly.

"I don't have a home." The forest, dark in lavenders and
blues, was a confused tangle of trees. Foxes had holes, and
birds had nests, but where could Miriam of Malvern go this
cold Christmas night?

"A place like it, then, Mirya. Come."

For the second time he had called her by that name, and
she saw that his eyes were troubled, that, mixed with the
starlight, there was grief, and loss.

He took her arm gently. "There is warmth and food
there," he said, "and a place to rest. Please."

A part of her noted that he had said rest, not sleep, but
she said nothing. She saw the many paths that were really
only one path, watched the Dance go on and on around her
until, as their steps brought them in sight of a cave that
plunged into the side of the same hill upon which she had
stood with Varden on the Day of Renewal, she heard the
crystalline chime of harp strings, heard also, strong and
loud, the cry of a newborn child, a glad shout of affirmation
amid the bare branches and the white snow.

Chapter Twenty-one

She was not an Elf, but they welcomed her, and she did not hear thoughts of *if only* from them. The past could not be changed, the future was one of infinite possibilities, and the present was now. That was all that mattered.

And so she was not overly conscious of the passage of days. The moon waxed and waned, the sun rose each day, but that was all. Of weeks, or months, or feast days—mere conveniences of a human-created calendar—she knew nothing. Today was simply today.

And today contained the winter forest, and the sky, and the certain knowledge of the Dance that went on around her. With Terrill she wandered through the trees, and together they looked in on hibernating bears and broke the ice of the river for thirsty foxes. One day she found a lamed rabbit, and without thinking, she healed it, the power flowing effortlessly.

It was pleasure. It was very good. And as the days went on, cold and white, the cave warm and filled with firelight and with the presence of the Elves, Miriam allowed herself a luxury that had been denied her for many years: time to forget, time to give up struggles, time to lay aside burdens—for a little while.

Roxanne nursed her baby. Natil played her harp. Talla danced in intricate variations that complemented the shimmering arpeggios of Natil's music, variations in which Miriam detected the patterns of the Greater Dance, variations that she recognized as being akin to the movements she herself knew.

And when, on an evening in that prolonged present into which she had entered, Talla took her by the hand and led her through the subtle twinings of a dance, Miriam moved

with an instinctive knowledge of the steps, as though everything the Elves did—dancing, fighting, breathing, living—
reflected the changing patterns around them, the patterns
they called the Dance, the Dance that was the Lady.

The old, human clumsiness fell from Miriam's feet, and
the shimmer about her quickened again. Talla's dance flowed
into the Greater Dance, and Miriam wondered where one
left off and the other began. Were her movements really
altering the course of worlds? Of stars? How was it that this
little healer had come to enter into the workings of the universe?

When they finished, Talla hugged her and murmured into
her ear: "Ela, Miryai, Elea."

That name again, and with the added inflection that Miriam had come to recognize as an endearment. But she looked
over Talla's shoulder and saw Terrill standing by the entrance to the cave. His arms were folded, and in his eyes
was such a look of grief that she was stricken. Terrill was
more than her teacher. He had, in spite of his demanding
methods, become her friend, and the knowledge of such
sorrow in him made her want to comfort.

"Terrilli," she said, but the Elf was already gone, the
flap of the door falling shut behind him.

She ran across the dry sand to the door, peered out into
the winter landscape. "Terrill!" Her throat ached, as though
she remembered another parting, a long and grievous one,
one she could not name, one that remained only dim bleak-
ness in the back of her mind.

She slumped by the fire, her head bent. Natil came to sit
beside her. "I have tried," said the harper. "There are some
wounds too deep to heal quickly."

"What happened?"

"I may not speak of it."

Before, Miriam's temper would have flared, and she would
have pressed her question. Not so now. She did not speak
for a time. Then: "Is it in the Dance?"

The harper smiled slightly. The firelight caught the silver
in her hair. "Everything is in the Dance," she said. She
took a soft cloth and wiped the strings of her instrument.

"Then I could go back and see what happened."

"You could," said Natil. "But if Terrill is unwilling to speak of it, then have you the right to go and look?"

Miriam watched the flames. "Compassion."

"It is so. Compassion."

For the first time since she had come to this quiet cave, she thought of the many futures that held bloodshed and battle for the Free Towns. Did Aloysius Cranby think of compassion? Did Roger of Aurverelle? Her memory flashed—the Chateau, the Inquisition, the dull throbbing of now vanished wounds. "What good is compassion against an uplifted sword?" she said.

"That can only be answered in the Dance."

"I've looked into the futures, Natil. I can't make any sense out of them."

"Not just the futures, Miriam. The Dance as a whole. Past, present, futures."

Miriam sought to comprehend her words, but if her feet had gained the lightness of the Elves, her mind had not. "It just seems futile, somehow. I must be too human. I can't find any peace in your words."

Natil was still calm. "It takes time. There is time."

Miriam grimaced. Everything was just out of her reach. "No," she said, "there isn't time. Not for Kay, or Charity, or any of the others. Not for the thousand little things that make up Saint Brigid. There just isn't time."

Natil's blue eyes regarded Miriam quietly. There was a peace about the harper that was greater than that of the rest of her people, and when she played, her music spoke of that peace eloquently. "Everything that happens," she said, "happens exactly when it should, happens exactly as it should, because that is the way it happens. We sit beside this fire. That is good. Not because it was foreordained, not because we choose to, but because we are here. That is all. Terrill sorrows. In itself that is not good, but in the Dance as a whole, in all its futures, can you not see that it might be for the best?"

Miriam felt the old anger stirring, dark embers starting suddenly into ruddy life. "And I was raped, Natil. Was that for the best?"

Natil did not flinch. "In the end," she said calmly.

"I don't accept that. Everything only comes out well in the end if there's enough time before the end."

"There is time."

"There isn't," Miriam insisted. What day was this? How long had she been here? "Not for me. Not for Saint Brigid. Not for the Free Towns."

Natil nodded slowly. "I understand."

"But you don't agree."

"I do not."

Miriam passed her hands over her face. "I think," she said softly, "that it's time for me to go back to the town. I came out here for something. I'm still not quite sure what it was, but I think I found it. At least I found as much of it as I can hold right now. I'll be back, though." Natil was smiling fondly at her. "If I'm still welcome."

"There are always returns," said the harper. "To leave is to return. To return is to be welcome." She leaned forward and kissed her. "Be at peace."

Miriam stood up. Suddenly she asked: "What does *Mirya* mean?"

"It is our word for the sudden blooming of a flower," said Natil. "There is a star we call that. And . . ." Her sight seemed to be elsewhere for a moment. "And someone we knew once . . ."

The sky was clear above Hypprux, but the sun gave no warmth. That quality might have been systematically removed from the pale disk that each morning slid above the plains to the east. There was light, and that was about all that could be said.

The River Tordion had frozen over near the first of the year, and now small boys played there, creeping out across the white surface on wooden skates, pelting one another with snowballs, chinning themselves on the large chains that hung from the guard towers on either bank.

Paul delMari, tenth baron of Furze, pulled his hood close about his head as he followed the funeral procession along the Street of Saint Lazarus, the tic above his right eye twitching repeatedly. There was no doubt in anyone's mind about who would be the next chamberlain, for Roger of Aurverelle had already donned the chain of office. Lucky devil! Married right, bribed right, supported right. Although—and Paul looked at the huge man who walked directly behind the velvet-draped bier—the story that Baron Roger had threatened to break the neck of anyone who questioned his claim to the office was quite believable. The baron was not known for gentleness. There were stories about his first wife . . . and about peasant girls found in the forest. . . .

Paul slipped and came close to breaking his head on the cobbles, but the loyal arm of his steward caught him. The baron nodded his thanks to the man as he found his footing, and he reminded himself that his thoughts should be on prayers for the eternal rest of old Thomas.

God, that he himself should live to be so respected and venerable as the late chamberlain! Even Aloysius Cranby had to praise the man who had served the city and the region for over forty years. In fact, the bishop was going to celebrate the funeral Mass himself, although Paul admitted that if he did not, he would be considered discourteous by all, even by his supporters.

And Paul's thoughts returned again to politics. He hoped that George was doing something down in Saint Blaise. But then, George had probably done quite enough already. Those Elves. And witches now, too. He wondered about the letter he had received from Aloysius Cranby the evening before, and had the uneasy suspicion that the bishop had been asking about the old midwife. Another unpleasant thought.

Aloysius Cranby, clad in the purple of his rank, his crozier frosted by the cold but nonetheless agleam with amethysts and—some thought prematurely—rubies, walked at the head of the procession. Flanking the bishop were the two Dominican friars who worked closely with him, and following were the members of Thomas's guild, the Brotherhood of the Queen of Heaven, sevenscore and ten of the wealthiest men of the city who had devoted much time and money to the care of the poor, the outcast, and the unfortunate.

Then the bier, the new chamberlain, and Paul. Behind the baron of Furze marched the other barons who were wintering in Hypprux, the aldermen of the city, and a selection of men from the respected trades. Slowly, the procession wound along the Street of Saint Lazarus, up the Street Gran Pont, and into the Cathedral of Our Lady of Mercy where the choir was already singing. The bells tolled, and a few crows took wing and flapped about the flèche, their cries brittle in the frosty air, their forms dark.

The altar was ablaze with candles, and incense hung wraithlike in the air. After placing the bier directly at the intersection of nave and transepts, the bearers took the black pall away, revealing a dark blue drape with an intricately embroidered device of interlaced moon and star.

Taking his place nearby, Paul knelt on a red cushion and crossed himself. Time to say farewell to an old man.

Every year now, the winter seemed a little harder.

Mika made her way along the road, cloak pulled tight against the cold, booted feet plodding through the snow. Her joints ached, and her eyes smarted. There was a stiffness in her knees that would not go away, she knew, until the weather warmed, and the old twinge in her left shoulder was persisting in spite of herbs and compresses.

"Midwife, heal thyself," she murmured. But even Miriam could not take away the burden of the years, and hers was the most miraculous power of which Mika had ever heard, excepting maybe that of a certain carpenter of Nazareth.

Mika stopped in the road, looked up at the brilliant blue sky. Where was the girl now? Was she warm? Was someone looking after her? Had she found safety? A home?

The wind stung her face. She pulled her hood down low and continued on her way. A crow called harshly from the bare branches of a tree.

"Not much to eat, is there, old one?" said the midwife. "I'll put something out for you when I get home."

The bird flapped its wings once, then settled and fluffed its feathers. Mika took the turning that led to Clare's house and the young mother let her into a warm room that smelled of fresh straw and hot stew.

"It's just in time for supper you are," said Clare. "Will'ee stay?"

"I could be persuaded." Mika doffed her cloak. "How is little Miriam?"

"She's fine." The little girl, ten months old now, toddled up to Mika. The midwife lifted her. Miriam giggled and made a grab for her nose, and Mika laughed.

"She seems fine indeed, Clare. Eyes as bright as silver pennies."

"She's talking."

"She is! What's she saying?"

Clare stirred the stew. "She'll sit on her father's lap, and she'll point to most everything in the room and name it." She laughed. "Sometimes she dan get the names quite right, but that dan seem to bother her!"

Mika smiled. "What's that?" she said to the girl, pointing at the table.

Miriam looked at the table with enormous gray eyes. "Dog," she said seriously.

"It's a table, little sweet," said Mika.

"Dog," said Miriam in a tone that did brook disagreement.

"Well," said the midwife, "I suppose she takes after her namesake."

Clare did not look up from the pot. "Ha' you . . . ha' you any idea where she is?"

"No," said Mika after a long silence.

"The priest asked me questions about her after Mass last Sunday."

"What did you tell him?" Mika's voice was tight.

Clare shrugged, plainly disturbed. "I told him I din't know."

From outside, clearly, the sound brittle in the cold, came the cawing of a crow.

To leave is to return.

There were, Miriam reflected, all kinds of returns, whether to a forest cave and the sound of harp strings, or to a small village in the south of Adria. But as she and Roxanne came out of the trees and saw the rooftops of Saint Brigid poking up above the walls of the town, she knew that her time there would be limited. This was a return, no more. There would be other returns, to other towns, other places. Maybe, in the end, to the forest. It was as if she had passed some midpoint in her life—perhaps on a stone slab at midsummer—as if, from now on, she would only be returning.

She wondered. Would she return to Mika, too? And what about the Chateau? Would she again set foot within its white, polished walls? For what purpose?

So many places to which to return.

Lake, Roxanne's son, murmured softly, and the witch nestled him deep into the folds of her gray cloak. Varden would have come to see them home, but Roxanne preferred to enter the town of her birth by herself, bearing her child in her arms. She had her own returns. Varden, understanding, had not pressed.

"How is he, Sana?" asked Miriam.

"Sleeping," said the witch with a fond smile. "I think he misses Natil's playing already. I'm afraid I'm going to have to take up the harp until he's old enough to hold one himself."

"I'm sure he'll have a good teacher."

"He'll have many good teachers." Roxanne looked up and around at the town, the forest, the snow, the indigo blue sky of evening. Venus glittered in the west, just above the mountains, and the slender crescent of a waxing moon hung nearby. "So many changes," she whispered. "The seasons, the cycles . . . Everything returns, but it all returns changed. I entered this world a child, and I grew into a woman. And now I am a mother. So many changes. So many."

But there had been changes in Saint Brigid also. The opening in the wall was now barred with an iron grille. Roxanne and Miriam stood before it, startled.

"I suppose it was to be expected," said Roxanne. "But it's hard. I've never known Saint Brigid to be locked up at evening."

Miriam pressed her lips together. Though she knew the reason for the gate, it felt too much like a rejection. "I'll get us in, Sana," she said. "You'll have a fire on your hearth this night."

She went to the gate and climbed. Her body was strong and responsive, and she gained the top easily, swung over, and climbed down inside the wall.

"It's obviously Francis's work, Sana," she said. "I've never seen better."

"Who is there?" came the call from within the gate-house.

"Come let your friends in, Andrew," said Miriam. "Sana . . . uh . . . Roxanne's outside with her son."

Firelight spilled into the passageway as Andrew opened the door. "Miriam! You've come back!"

"For a while."

Together, Andrew and Miriam unfastened the catch and swung the gates wide. "Has something happened, Andrew?" said Roxanne as she entered. "Is there danger?"

"No," said the carpenter. "But there may be eventually, and we're trying to get into the habit of locking the town after dark. No one cares for it, but we all know it's probably for the best." He fastened the gates shut. "I'm very sorry. We weren't expecting you to return at night."

"It was the time to come," said Roxanne. "And if the gates were locked, then that was the way they were sup-posed to be."

Lake murmured.

"He's hungry," said Roxanne. "I'll take him home."

Andrew beamed at the child, then bowed deeply. "Bless-ings."

"And on you, Andrew."

The town was quiet, its folk keeping warm indoors. But when they came in sight of Roxanne's house, it was brightly lit. Smoke wafted from the chimney, and lamps burned on either side of the door in welcome. As they approached, the door opened, and Charity stood there, waiting for them.

Miriam did not stay, though. She hugged Charity and Roxanne, kissed Lake on the forehead, and set off for Kay's house.

The gate still hung in the back of her mind like a weight. Saint Brigid was changing, was becoming now like one of the northern cities, like Maris, or like Hypprux. It could never be quite like them, for Miriam was sure that there would never be a Chateau in Saint Brigid, or a dungeon. If there ever were, Saint Brigid would be no more: the land would have other homes on it, houses occupied by strangers with faces scarred by sadness and fear.

She remembered the feeling in Belroi.

She stopped in the middle of the snow-covered common,

cloak clasped about her, hood thrown back. Changing. Changing too fast, in too many ways. Change was inevitable, but did it have to be like this? With gates and bars and bloody wars?

She had struggled to be free of Hypprux so passionately that even though she had been bleeding and mangled, she had dragged herself out of the dungeon and pulled herself through the city's gate. And because there was something precious in Saint Brigid, something worth having, this night she had climbed a gate to enter a town.

She realized that it had been exactly a year between one gate and the other, between the escape and the entering. There were returns. But there were changes, too, and of many kinds. All part of an intricate pattern, a changing Dance.

Swallowing the lump in her throat, she crossed the rest of the common and entered the house. Kay looked up from a frugal meal, and his eyes teared as he watched her take off her cloak and hang it on a peg.

She filled a mug with peppermint infusion and sat down across from him. "Well, I'm back," she said.

Chapter Twenty-two

"Again," said Terrill.

Miriam picked herself up, head spinning with fatigue, hands numb from the unmelted snow that still patched the familiar meadow. Terrill had been attacking her with a practice sword for the better part of three hours, but he had not touched her once. It was exhaustion that had put her on the ground.

With the passing of winter, her lessons had resumed; but—far from becoming easier—they now drained her so thoroughly of energy that she wondered at times if she could summon the strength to crawl to her knees.

And always Terrill demanded more, his voice calm, his gaze piercing. "Stand up straight," he ordered. "Do not slouch. Find your stars, and draw their light into you."

Jaw set, knees threatening to buckle at any moment, she closed her eyes. As she had a dozen times since midmorning, she watched the gleaming stars in her mind for several minutes, drank in their energy. Her knees firmed up, her breathing slowed.

"Good," said Terrill. "Now open your eyes—maintain the vision." And he was suddenly in motion, his sword, as much a part of him as his hand or his arm, sweeping in.

She saw a million potentials in every move that he made, saw which were the most likely to become reality. She moved to counter, blocked his cut at her throat, and swung gracefully around for a quick riposte that almost (a part of the Dance) caught her teacher off guard. He retreated a half step. She felt his approval, but she also sensed his next move.

And all the while, the afternoon progressed around them: the snows melting in the late February sun; the sound of water—dripping from leaves, splashing in puddles, rippling in river and stream—loud in the forest; the animals active, frisking in the crisp air. Only on such a day, with the sun where it was and a crow spreading its wings in the sky, would Terrill approve of her strike and follow up with a—

She ducked and—the devil with it, she was wet and muddy already—rolled out of the path of his sword, aimed a kick at his knee, missed, came back up with a counterstroke that made a shambles of Terrill's further plans. She saw his quick smile—oh, rare expression!—and he backed up again.

All the while, though, her fatigue was growing. A minute into the skirmish, her wooden sword felt like lead. A few seconds later, her vision blurred. Terrill dropped his sword and caught her as she toppled once again, and he led her to a dry, sunlit patch of grass, gently supporting her with an arm about her waist.

"Enough," he said softly.

"I can't do it." She was crying with frustration. "I can't do two things at the same time. I can't hold the stars and fight. That's for Elves. I'm—"

She broke off suddenly.

"Go on," said Terrill.

"Never mind." She found the stars again, breathed. "I can't do it."

"If you continue to say that, it might come to pass. You must continue to work."

"I'm not improving." She crossed her legs, wiped her hands on the grass. She was dirty, sweating even in the cool air, caked with dirt, and her breeches were soaked. In contrast, Terrill was clean, unrumpled, not even breathing heavily.

"But you are," he said with kindness, giving her shoulder a squeeze. It was an open show of affection, and Miriam was almost startled. "You have progressed greatly. Your form is good. Not perfect, but good. And in the space of a few hours, the amount of time you can stay on your feet has increased."

Terrill's face was inches from hers. Miriam tried to speak, could not. The faint memory that had stirred in the cave was stirring again . . . along with something else.

With a gasp, she looked away.

"Miriam?"

"I'm all right," she said, staring hard at a single crocus that had forced itself through the crust of snow, a flare of crimson brilliance against the white. "I can't . . ." She felt Terrill's presence, his arm around her shoulders, the pressure of his hand. "I can't watch you and the stars at the same time."

He sat back. "It is not a matter of watching. You must . . ." He thought for some time. "You must give yourself to them."

Her answer was abrupt, instinctive: "No!" Terrill looked at her, startled. "I can't do that." She had, she thought, given up too much of herself already, torn away bits of her heart and passed them out every day of her life. Mika had cost her dearly. And the brute in the forest had sliced off an even larger chunk.

She felt cold. "Isn't there some other way?" she asked in a small voice. But she knew Terrill's answer already. She was, however, not prepared to lift her eyes and see in his face, once again, the unutterable grief. Nor was she prepared to feel her heart respond to it.

She was back in the clearing the next day, and the next. Each time, each clash, Miriam stayed on her feet a little longer, but she and Terrill both knew that her additional stamina stemmed only from single-minded purpose and iron will. She would return home wet, cold, and frustrated— knowing full well that her teacher was equally frustrated— but though she could soak away the mud in a hot bath, there was little she could do for the underlying problem.

Even with the hot water lapping at her chest, she shuddered at the thought of it. To give up everything. To embrace something so large that it seemed able to swallow not just her heart, but her entire identity. . . .

She had floated among the stars. She had reached out to forest and stream, to town and villager. She had felt herself a part of the Dance. But even when the experience had been most profound, she had always maintained her own identity. She had seen the stars, participated in the Dance, but she had never lost sight of her separateness from both.

And so, every afternoon, she would enter the clearing with Terrill, pick up a wooden sword, and allow herself to be slowly exhausted by the starlight vision.

"Perhaps," said the Elf on a day in early spring, "we should give this up for a time."

Miriam crawled to her knees, shaking her head. "I'll learn."

"Beloved," said the Elf, "this is not something that can be learned. It must be felt."

"I said I'll learn." She almost snapped at him.

It was no longer a question of revenge—it was rather one of self-betrayal. She had controlled her body, and to some extent her destiny, but her heart had rebelled at the task set before it, and its treachery seemed a greater affront than any she had experienced in the past.

When she stood up, shaking, the light in Terrill's eyes was like needles. Lips pressed together, he bent and struck his sword into the ground, point down. "It will end here, then," he said. "I cannot teach you to feel. I cannot teach you to trust. I and my people can and do love. But only you can embrace that love."

"What the hell does love have to do with it?" She leaned on her sword, panting.

"You do not love yourself, do you?" Terrill was impassive.

"I . . . I never thought about it."

"The Church does not encourage self-love," said the Elf. "Those who live under its sway are stunted as a result. Know this: If I do not love myself, that is a clear indication that I am not worthy of the love of others. As I give myself to the starlight, so does it surrender to me. But how can I embrace it fully if I am not worthy? And how can I give myself unless I have myself to give?" He eyed the sword. "I will not continue with this charade unless there is some chance that you can succeed." His voice was gentle, softening the finality of his words, and there was again the flicker of grief.

His sorrow struck her almost as deeply as did her failure. Miriam let go of her sword and sat down on the muddy ground. "So I just give up? I've failed?"

Terrill was beside her in a moment. His voice was heavy with sorrow, and he spoke in his own language as he put his arms about her. *"Miryai, marithae, si altare el eleve ania—"*

"Iye, Terrilli," she replied without thinking. *"Ea sarena a . . . a ombra—"*

The world flickered, and for a moment, she was looking at a different Terrill. He seemed younger, more apt to smile. The weight of years in his eyes had lessened. She realized that she was speaking words she did not comprehend, fell silent.

The familiar Terrill came back, but his eyes were wide, startled. "M-Miriam?"

She passed a muddy hand over her face. "I'm sorry, Terrill. I think I'm just tired."

He nodded slowly.

"But what do I do now?"

"You must . . ." He was watching her as though she might, of a sudden, change before his eyes into someone else, as if he did not know whether he would fear or welcome that. "You must live. You must be. I think that it is time to put aside the swords for a while. Now we must work on you."

She stared at her hands, saw the gleam that surrounded them. She flared. "Work on me? What am I supposed to be now? Dammit, Terrill, what the hell am I supposed to be now?"

He took a deep breath and let it out before he spoke. "You are supposed to be an Elf," he said softly.

"I'm not an Elf!"

"Not yet. You must grow."

"But I don't want to—" She stopped herself short. Could she really say that? Her life before her transformation had become hazy, vague; and although she retained her memories and her hates, she could not but look upon her former self in the same way that a new mother, holding her infant, might regard her own childhood. Changes.

She looked within—at herself, at the patterns, at the Dance—and she found that she was poised exactly at a balance between human and Elf, mortal and immortal.

Terrill's arms were still wrapped about her. She felt her heart stir again. The pattern, the Dance, was altering massively, tipping her into futures that she could scarcely comprehend. And here, in this clearing, with a crow flapping lazily in the sun, with the ground sparkling with spring

flowers, with the scent of life in the air blending with the
rustle of new leaves, with her heart beating as if in response
to the season of new growth come round again as it always
did in the endless cycles, she was at the pivot point of it
all. What she did, what she uttered in the next few moments, would change everything.

And she looked into her changing, stirring heart, and
faced what she saw there with honesty. There was no other
way.

"Teacher," she said at last, "how do I learn . . . to be?"

Market day in Saint Blaise: the snorting of horses and
mules, the cries of vendors and storekeepers, the tread of
many feet. A child's voice rose above the clamor.

"It is the Spring,
Hey, ding-a-ding!
Now all Good Folk do dance and sing."

It was a girlish treble, bright and clear in air washed clean
by the morning's rain. George thought he heard a lute, too,
but he could not be sure as he shouldered his way through
the crush of people at the town gate. Leave them to their
market. It was too fine a day to stay amid stone walls and
cobbled streets.

Outside the town, he stood at the edge of the road for a
moment, greeting the farmers, the merchants, the artisans
as befitted a good mayor. He smiled and waved at those
who recognized him, shook hands with a few. This was the
first of the large markets to which people came from great
distances, even from Maris and Hypprux, and the road was
crowded.

Perhaps there was a crusade in the offing, George thought,
but on a day like this the possibility seemed remote. Everything was too fresh, the April skies as blue as Janet's eyes,
the clouds—all that was left of the rain—glittering as white
as the snow that remained on the upper slopes of the Aleser
Mountains. How could such things as crusades and wars
exist in a world that possessed such skies? Such clouds?
Such mountains? George's heart grew, and his smile, already hearty and full of goodwill, was magnified.

"Good morning to you, brothers," he said to a group of

three friars—Dominicans by the look of them—who were just then passing by.

One lifted his head to expose a ruddy, pink-cheeked face. ''God bless you, sir,'' came the reply.

George tucked his thumbs thoughtfully into his belt and began to whistle as he crossed the fields in which the weeders were already waddling through the crops with hook and fork. Later, he told himself, there was time later in the day to give further thought to defending Saint Blaise from Aloysius Cranby. Nothing could happen today. There was no point in putting the town under siege before there were armies about to besiege it.

George spent the morning in the forest, reveling in the flowers, the grass, the new-leafed trees. There was something precious here, and it could not be found inside city walls. Nor could the richest man in Adria buy it. As ephemeral as starlight, it could slip through one's fingers, and yet it could wrap itself powerfully around one's heart and possess it utterly.

But he seemed to hear Thomas a'Verne talking again. The old ways were dying. And what would come to take their place? Old Thomas himself had passed on during the winter—God rest him!—and had left behind him a world that was shrinking too swiftly from what it could be, from what it once was. Well, Thomas was finished with it.

His thoughts turned suddenly pensive, George returned to the town, his head bent, his mind elsewhere. He was hardly aware of the cries of the people and animals, and though the child was still singing about spring, about flowers and dancing, he did not hear the music.

Yes, Thomas was dead. Roger of Aurverelle was chamberlain now. Suddenly a crusade did not seem so impossible.

To escape the crowds, he took a turning into the alleyway behind his house and let himself in through the kitchen door. Dolores, the housekeeper, was not in the kitchen, but more than likely she was off buying supplies for the year.

Slowly, he climbed the rear stairs to his office. There were maps and inventories waiting for him, along with thoughts of war. He passed the landing that led to Janet's room and peeked in at his daughter. She was bent over a book, reading, and did not notice.

With a fond smile, he finished climbing the stairs and settled behind his desk. He was breathing hard. Maybe it was time to lose some weight.

There was a quick knock on the door to the hallway, and Dolores stuck her head in. "Oh, my lord," she said, her voice low and tense, "I thought I'd heard you come up."

"I'm here, Dolores. Do you need me for something?"

She glanced over her shoulder and shrugged helplessly. "You've visitors, my lord. They want to see you now."

Visitors? George felt his stomach become suddenly queasy. "Uh . . . of course."

Dolores opened the door and stepped back. Three Dominican friars entered, throwing back their hoods as they did so. Two waited on either side of the door. The third stepped forward, holding a familiar green cloak that was embroidered with the ensigns of Saint Blaise and the Free Towns.

George stared at the cloak. "How did—" But his voice failed when he lifted his eyes and saw that the bearer of the garment was Aloysius Cranby.

Chapter Twenty-three

The sense of unease that had possessed Saint Brigid grew along with the crops. Twice a week, there was pike practice on the common for the men and the sturdier boys of the village. The gates of the town were shut just after sundown and opened just before dawn. Francis's hammer rang throughout the day, forging weapons.

There was still talk in the town council of hiring mercenaries, and the names John Hawkwood, Guy Asleman, and Timothy Raydenburn came up frequently. Hawkwood was of particular interest, since he and his followers were just across the French border. Mercenaries would cost money, though, and it was the wealthier Free Towns that would have to make that decision.

But as the days followed one another into late April, there was no word from Saint Blaise. Artisans who attended the fairs held in the northern town reported that the atmosphere there was tense, and that the mayor, George Darci, was silent and, according to some, sad.

It was not an atmosphere that encouraged the forgetting of swordplay, but Miriam tried. At night, she practiced the dance on the common, but she thought as little as she could about what the movements meant. Starlight flowed through her mind and her body, and at times she felt as though she moved at the bottom of a deep lake, felt the liquid resistance of the subtle energies that she pushed and pulled. She was aware of the energies. She was aware of their ebb and flow. She ignored what she might, someday, do with them.

She saw Terrill infrequently. Sometimes as much as a week went by between his visits. He watched her dance when he came, and he nodded in approval, but he said nothing of fighting. Miriam did not ask. She knew that his meth-

ods were obscure and sometimes frustrating, but she trusted
him.

Many days she spent wholly within the town. She had
friends in Saint Brigid whom she had not seen in weeks,
some not in months, and she took time to seek them out.
She chatted with Francis and Hester, spent time playing
with the children, inspected the dog she had healed so long
ago. She helped Elizabeth with her housework and Roxanne
with her baby. And if, in the midst of sweeping, or throwing
a ball, or shopping, the thought came to her that the gown
she wore was not her usual garb, or that she should be out
in the fields with Terrill, she dismissed it gently.

For the first time in her life, she had a goal that went
further than survival for one more day, or more recently,
revenge upon the stranger in the forest. She would survive,
and she would have her revenge, but she was catching
glimpses now of a life beyond both, one that stretched off
into unfathomable futures, one that wove itself into an intricate pattern of strands of starlight. And she knew it, and
she wanted it, and if her heart needed time to heal, then she
would take that time.

Now and again, clad as an Elf, she took to the forest,
spending long, warming afternoons by the side of a brook,
feeling—becoming—the water, the stones that poked up out
of the current, the minnows that flashed silver in quiet pools.
In her mind she mounted up into the air with sparrow hawks,
or knew the musty closeness of a badger den. Often, when
she returned to the town, she felt oddly distanced from the
humans who lived in houses of wood and stone and straw.
But there was nothing wrong with that. It simply was. And
that was good.

When the war came to Saint Brigid, it came quietly, and
unrecognized. Where the townsfolk had expected hundreds
of men, here were only three. Where they had looked for
gleaming mail and thick leather, here were the black and
white habits of Dominicans.

The monks rode up the main street in the early afternoon.
The children ran after them, and villagers looked up from
their work in surprise and curiosity; but there was little about
the three friars to provoke any sort of fear. The brother in

charge of the group looked pleasant enough, with dark hair much streaked with silver and blue-gray eyes that peered about at the houses and shops. Nor did his companions seem at all terrifying, though they were definitely an unmatched set: one dark and thoughtful, the other pink and florid.

They spoke with the children, laughed at the dogs that ran barking alongside their horses, waved at the shopkeepers and housewives. The pink-cheeked friar even trotted over to a window now and again to ask directions or give a greeting.

Francis looked up from his anvil as they paused before the forge. The older man smiled and nodded. "Good day to you, Master Smith."

"Aye, give ye peace."

"Where is the house of the priest?"

Francis eyed him. The man was strong—all three were, in fact—and there was a sense of assurance in the way he moved and talked that seemed uncharacteristic of a humble friar. His hands were soft. The smith distrusted the combination, and he distrusted it all the more when he noticed an arrangement of the friars' baggage that did not quite disguise the presence of at least one sword.

Dominicans with swords? Francis rubbed his black beard. "On as ye come, and left at tha well," he said slowly. "It's tha house hard by tha church."

"Thank you," said the friar. "God bless."

"Aye," said the smith under his breath as the friars continued up the street, "I'm sure He wi'. And She too." He shook his head and went back to work.

Kay opened his door in response to the bold knock, was struck nearly speechless for a moment, then managed to compose himself. Dominicans traveled widely, and there was nothing overtly unusual in their appearing at the door of a priest in the south of Adria. Saint Dominic would certainly not have stayed at an inn: why should his followers?

"God bless you," said the oldest of the three. "I am Brother Louis, and these are my companions, Bartholomew and Hoyle."

Kay nodded quickly. "I'm Kay, the priest. Please, come in." His thoughts were spinning. Maybe—and his hope flashed—this had something to do with his letter to Augustine of Maris.

The three churchmen sat down at his table and accepted his offer of food and drink. Kay tried to control the shaking of his hands as he sawed off large chunks of Elizabeth's bread, but when he dropped the knife to the floor with a clatter, he realized that there was silence in the room. He turned to find that the trio were watching him.

Louis smiled, but his eyes did not change expression. "There is no need to be nervous," he said. "We are on . . . an investigative mission, sent by the good bishop of Maris. He received your letter not long ago and wishes to be of aid."

"Oh," said Kay. "Thank God! We've been terrified here in the Free Towns." The priest's heart leaped, but something about the three friars made him resolve to be cautious. Louis's words said one thing, but his manner said another.

He piled bread and cheese on a tray and brought it to the table. Hoyle and Bartholomew fell to without comment. Louis delicately broke off a piece of bread and looked at it. "Your bread is well made. There is a woman's hand in it, no doubt."

"The bread was made by one of the village women," said Kay. "I do have a housekeeper, though." He did not elaborate.

"Worth her weight in rubies, I imagine." Louis smiled blandly and popped the fragment into his mouth.

Kay felt horribly alone.

"So tell me, Kay," said Louis. "What say the people of Saint Brigid? Aloysius Cranby speaks of inquisition and crusade. He accuses the Free Towns of heresy, and of trafficking with Elves."

"He does indeed." Kay was offering nothing until he was sure.

Louis eyed him thoughtfully. His middle-aged face was incongruously boyish, but his eyes were wary. "You are new to this cure, are you not?"

"I grew up in Saint Brigid," said Kay, wondering at the change in subject. "I have not been priest here long, though."

"Ah, yes. The matter—the odd matter—of your prede-cessor, Jaques Alban."

Kay wondered: what were the sympathies of Augustine of Maris that he would send such an ironic questioner? "Al-ban? He disappeared a few years ago."

Louis was spreading butter on a piece of Elizabeth's bread. "Just so. Disappeared. Odd. We hear of so few priests who disappear . . . just like that." His voice was dry. "They are usually a timid sort who stay around their churches and do not bother with such messy things as disappearing. In-deed . . ." He cut a piece of cheese, peered at it, grunted in satisfaction. "Indeed, one might almost suspect . . . say . . . witchcraft."

Kay felt himself growing warm. His forehead turned moist.

"Witchcraft . . . or maybe Elves."

Kay shrugged and poured himself some peppermint tea. To his relief, his hand was steady. "Alban might have gone into the forest and run into something. A wild beast. A bear perhaps."

"Or a boar, maybe." Louis looked at him over the rim of his mug, his eyes crinkled in a sort of a smile.

Kay set down his tea. "Is there something that you want to say, Brother Louis? I'm a simple village priest, and I don't know the niceties of the city. I call a tub a tub, if you know what I mean."

"Hmmm." Louis left off drinking. "Well, really, Kay, I am not trying to say anything. I am asking questions for Augustine delAzri of Maris. Before he commits to a defense of the Free Towns, he wants to know his facts. Aloysius Cranby is not a man to go up against unarmed. Do you see my meaning?"

"Of course." Why did his stomach persist in churning?

"There have been rumors about Saint Brigid. I would be very surprised if they were true, for if they were, the facts would have been reported to Church officials long ago by the worthy and loyal village priest. But the rumors them-selves are damaging."

"What kind of rumors?" Kay tried to keep his face blank.

Louis chuckled and shook an uplifted finger in the air.

"Aha! The gossip in us all! The simple village priest has a human failing!"

Hoyle looked up appraisingly. Bartholomew grinned. They had said nothing since they had entered save for a murmured *thankee* or *God bless* when handed food, and their watchful silence was unnerving.

"The rumors, though." Louis folded his hands in his lap. "Interesting. Hmmm. The general sentiment expressed is that Alban was the victim of elven magic. That he, as it were, spent the remainder of his days gamboling about on four feet—or rather hooves."

"That's quite a story," said Kay. His hands were still steady. "Do you believe such tales?"

"I'm—" Louis cleared his throat. "Augustine is looking into it."

"I believe I've heard the same fables as you, Brother Louis. Ovid might have believed in such pagan transformations, but I hardly think you and I need to." Kay thought of the years he had spent studying for the priesthood, and as he had watched his tongue then, so he watched it now. "Alban disappeared sometime before I was summoned to this cure, so there's no way I could have firsthand knowledge of the event. From what some of the villagers say, though, Alban was a bit of a pig even before he disappeared, no matter what his eventual fate."

"But it is precisely in his fate that I am interested," said Louis. "Do you realize what has happened, Kay? A priest, like yourself, a servant of Holy Church, has possibly been attacked. Are we to stand back and allow this? By no means!" He lifted a hand as though preaching. "There is a great evil in Malvern. Augustine is aware of it, I am aware of it, and certainly Aloysius Cranby is aware of it. The Free Towns are, I daresay, innocent of any wrongdoing—poor Aloysius; how disappointed he will be!—but they might be unaware of what is happening in the dark shadows of the forest."

Kay forced himself to nod evenly. With studied precision he lifted his mug. With absolute control he sipped.

"There have also been reports of a notorious witch in this area," said Louis matter-of-factly. "A girl named Miriam."

The mug slipped out of Kay's hand and shattered on the tiled floor.

The friar looked from the broken crockery to Kay's face. "Perhaps you've heard of her?"

"I . . ."

"Short. Black hair. Unpleasant-looking wench."

"My housekeeper is named Miriam," said Kay, his resolve firming. "But she doesn't look anything like that."

"We would like to meet her."

Kay met his glance levelly. "She's away right now."

"But she'll be back soon, won't she?"

"Perhaps."

"You should keep a closer eye on your housekeeper, Kay. Women are weak vessels. Left to themselves, they can get into all sorts of . . . mischief."

Kay began to clean up the broken mug, feeling three pairs of eyes on him. "Will you and your companions be needing lodgings while in Saint Brigid, Brother Louis?"

"We had hoped to stay with you, Kay. This is such a fine, large house. I'm sure you have a room or two for us."

"Yes . . . of course . . ."

"And it will give us a chance to become acquainted with Miriam. Your . . . housekeeper."

Kay had to suppress a smile. Given the friar's description of Miriam and his apparent certainty that the village priest's house was being kept by a witch, the maiden's entrance was going to be amusing.

Miriam had finished her housework before dawn that day. Her need for sleep was still dwindling, and she had much time to spend alone, with the village asleep and the streets deserted.

She had practiced the intricate dance on the common, taking time to work on her form, forcing herself to concentrate on the actions in the abstract. Perfection was her goal at present, not the eventual fight. When she had finished, she had stood, straight and motionless, letting the energies settle slowly back into the earth, into the stars.

It was still dark, and would be for several hours, when she—clad as an Elf, her movements silent and unnoticed—climbed over the locked gate of the town. Dawn found her among the trees, and she listened to the rising song of the birds as the sun grew round at the edge of the world and the forest awoke.

She spent the day in the company of the trees and the people of wings and of four feet who made their homes there. At times, she thought she was coming close to understanding their speech, and they in turn listened to her words attentively. There was almost communication, but not quite. She had more to learn, further to go, before she finally became—

She stopped in the middle of a cluster of aspen trees, felt the sunlight, the soft air. She looked at her hands. Day by day, the shimmer about her had grown brighter. When she had first been transformed, it had flickered in soft hues of violet and lavender, but now it had changed to the same silver sheen that surrounded Terrill and his people.

Further to go. But how far? She looked to the patterns among the stars, but they were hideously complicated, a huge knot of maybes and could-bes lying in the very near future. What did it mean?

She was thoughtful as she returned from the forest, but when she set foot in the tilled fields, her head jerked up and toward the town as though she had been pulled by the nose. There was a definite sense of wrongness about Saint Brigid. Something had changed, had changed drastically.

She examined the plexed futures, but the cause of the sudden increase in probabilities eluded her. She reached further into the knot of probabilities, yielding a little more to the ocean of starlight that flowed through her mind as she felt through the strands of choice and action. For the space of a heartbeat, she thought she detected a familiar face, a known voice, but fear awoke, and with a gasp, she brought herself back to the sight of field and village.

Her heart was racing, her hands trembling. Give herself to the starlight? Impossible. So much further to go.

She crossed the fields and entered the village. Francis hailed her from the forge. He told her of the strangers.

"Dominicans?" said Miriam.

"Aye," said the Smith. "They looked peaceful, but—"

"It's the Dominicans who are the inquisitors," said Miriam. Her stomach knotted. "They call themselves the

'Hounds of God.' Most of them are rabid, I think.'' She looked up the street in the direction of the church. ''Have you heard anything from Kay?''

''Nay. Maybe ye'd best stay wi' Hester and me, Miriam.''

''Why?'' She remembered clearly her last encounter with the Dominicans, and the anger that she had so carefully banked began to sputter back into life. Had they tracked her this far? They would be contending with more than a frightened little girl this time. ''I'm not letting a bunch of fat clergymen drive me away from my home.''

She bade the smith a good day and continued down the street. But as she started across the common, she recalled that she was dressed an an Elf, and she entered the church instead, making for the door in the south transept that connected with the house. The late-afternoon light shone in through the stained-glass windows and lit the altar and the carved panels behind it. Alban's fate glowed in reds and blues.

As she turned toward the door, she saw the statue of the Lady and stopped before it. Again, she saw beyond the wood, into the stars, into the face and being of a Woman whose robes were blue and silver. In her mind, the knot of futures pulsed, flickering, minutes away. She would have to enter it, make of it what she could, seek blindly for the best choices. The thought of the task was frightening, and she looked for reassurance and strength in the calm gray eyes that watched her.

''Lady,'' she said softly, looking into Her face, ''You've never asked anything of me. But You helped me. I trust You. And . . . and I'll serve You, if You'll take me.''

She bowed low for a moment, touching her hands to her forehead and opening them wide in the manner of the Elves. And then she took the short corridor to her room and changed into a simple gown.

As she went toward the kitchen, tying her belt, she heard a voice that she remembered well, one that had, months before, condemned her to prison and to torture. She froze, listening to Aloysius Cranby.

''We have it on good authority that George Darci of Saint Blaise has particular friends among the Elves,'' he was saying. ''This is most disturbing. You must understand, Kay, that if Augustine of Maris is to be able to accomplish anything at all, you must tell me everything.''

"I . . .'' Kay sounded dubious, but Miriam knew that he had placed a good deal of hope in his letters to Clement and to Augustine. ''It's rather complicated . . .''

Futures were shifting, strands of starlight branching into potentials that terrified her. She ran for the kitchen.

Chapter Twenty-four

When Miriam stepped into the room, Kay fell silent as though relieved. But Miriam was looking at the middle-aged man who, clad in the habit of a Dominican, was just lifting his hand as though to admonish a refractory village priest.

Aloysius Cranby, bishop of Hypprux. She wished that she could kill him where he sat, a piggish look of bland astonishment on his face.

But forcing itself through her anger was an awareness of the patterns that were forming and reforming. There was a safe passage through this encounter, but it did not lie in exposing herself or in attack. She had to be calm. The stars shone within her, and she reached for their light. Slowly, Cranby became a problem to be solved rather than a temptation to rage.

"I am Miriam," she said evenly, not forgetting to drop a curtsy. "Kay's housekeeper."

"Miriam," said Kay, "this is Brother Louis, and his companions, Brother Hoyle and Brother Bartholomew. They've been sent by Bishop Augustine."

Miriam cast a quick glance at Kay. Did he really believe that?

The priest looked noncommittal and slightly afraid. "They'll be staying with us for a week or two."

A week or two? In the same house? She began to wish that she had indeed killed Cranby on the spot. She stifled the thought.

Brother Louis grinned. "A fine woman you have here, Kay. I can see that you are not without taste. Ha-ha! A simple village priest . . . more human than simple it seems!"

Kay blushed crimson. Miriam took a deep breath. *Go*

ahead and play, you bitch's whelp. She glanced at the friars, felt through the potentials that now surrounded her, sensed the thoughts of the Dominicans. Although they were surprised by her appearance, there was also an element of lust in their perceptions. She set her jaw. "Do the good brothers have need of anything?" Her contralto was firm, soft.

"Attend to our horses, woman," said Louis abruptly. "Because of your absence, they've stood outside all this time."

The anger welled up, but the potentials held it back as though their message were written in letters of flame: *Say nothing. Do nothing.*

"As you wish . . . Brother Louis."

"And bring our baggage in," Louis continued. "Kay, will you show us to our rooms? There will be time for more talk later on." He glanced at Miriam. "Why are you standing there, girl? I told you to attend to our horses."

Miriam did not reply. She merely walked across the room and went out through the front door. Behind her, she heard Brother Louis' voice: "Is she simple, Kay? Or does she only understand the uncultured patois spoken down here?"

She shut the door behind her. Perfectly balanced, the futures hung before her, intricate and treacherous. Cranby was exploring, assuming the guise of a not-so-humble Dominican friar so as to find out what went on in the Free Towns. When he returned with a Church court, he would know exactly what questions to ask, and of whom to ask them. If he even bothered with such formalities.

Does Kay know?

It took her only a minute to lead the horses to stable, unburden them, and set them to feeding. They were fine beasts, rather gentle, and she could not but smile as she stroked the strong back of the dapple gray. If their masters were evil, the horses could not help it.

But she was fretting: she had to talk to Kay, she had to warn him. If he did not realize the identity of his guests, he might at any moment say something unfortunate.

She had no clear idea of what she was going to do, only a pressing need to do something. In the same manner in which she had once found a skylark in flight above the forest, she now cautiously allowed her awareness to envelop the priest's house. Slowly, a new perspective took shape around her: she could see the kitchen as though she stood on the tile floor, and she passed into the corridor, following the sound of voices that came to her as though from a great distance.

"There's probably some truth in the rumors, Brother Louis," Kay was saying. "Rumors have to start somewhere, after all."

"But what truth, Kay? As I said, you must be willing to cooperate with Augustine."

She felt the baldness of Louis's lie as she peered into the guest room. Augustine was dead. Kay's letter to him had been intercepted. She knew it as surely as she knew, months ago, that Roxanne was pregnant.

But Kay had started to speak, and she sensed that he was going to say something about Varden and the Elves. *Kay,* she shouted in her mind, *that's Aloysius Cranby! Don't tell him anything!*

And, abruptly, in the middle of his first word, Kay shut his mouth, looked a little astonished, and made an excuse for leaving the room. The friars did not appear to have heard anything.

In the stable, Miriam sagged against the wall, frantically pulling her awareness back into herself. The vision had taxed her, and her physical sight was still blurry when Kay burst in.

"I heard—" He shook his head as though to clear it. "Was that you?"

"Aloysius Cranby," she whispered. "That's him."

Kay stared. "Are you sure?"

"Dammit, Kay, that bastard tried and sentenced me!"

The priest was fumbling with his thoughts. "But what's he doing here?"

"What do you think?"

"O dear Lady!"

"We need to warn the villagers. The Elves too. And it would probably be a good idea to get Charity and Sana away."

They heard Charity's voice then—"Miriam! Miriam!"— and looked out the stable door to see her running across the common, skirts flying, dark hair streaming behind her. She made directly for the stable. "What's happening? I heard you shouting something about Aloysius Cranby."

"You heard me?" Miriam breathed the starlight. Her knees stopped shaking.

"Anytime you make that much noise between the worlds, Miriam," said the young witch, "we're *all* going to hear you. Roxanne would have come, too, but she's nursing Lake."

"It's just as well she didn't come," said Kay. The day was not overly warm, but his brow was dripping. He fretted with his sleeves. "Cranby's here in disguise. He's looking for information."

Charity's eyes flickered. She has become quieter since she had been made a priestess. On the surface, she was still Charity, still full of sunlight and flowers; but within her, doors had opened, depths had been explored, knowledge had been won. Miriam would not have been overly surprised if Charity now knew about her past.

The witch shook her head. "He won't get it."

"You and Sana should probably go and stay with the Elves until he's gone," said Miriam.

"Sana, maybe," said Charity. "She has Lake to think about. But I'm staying. This is a fight for all of us: pagans, Christians, Elves . . . whoever. We need to be sure that the bishop doesn't find out anything of any use to him."

"We need to alert the village," said Kay.

"I'm on my way," said Charity. She kissed them both and departed.

Miriam rubbed her eyes. She was still struggling with her emotions, was barely succeeding in keeping them in check. Her strength was returning, and she absently gave one of the baggage packs a disgusted prod with her toe.

In a moment, she was on her knees beside the pack, untying the fastenings.

"Miriam!" cried Kay. "Leave it alone!" But when she threw open the flap and lifted out a sword, he slowly put a hand to his mouth. "That's . . . that's horrible. What's going on in Hypprux? Churchmen aren't supposed to carry weapons like that."

"Supposed to, Kay?" Disgusted, Miriam put the sword back. "*Supposed to?* Churchmen aren't supposed to lie and hate either. They're not supposed to condemn innocent people to death. They're not supposed to do a great many things.'' She stood up, brushed the dirt from her gown. ''Unfortunately, it also seems that they're not supposed to pay any attention to the religion they claim to practice.''

''Miriam . . .'' Kay sounded hurt, and Miriam realized that her words had turned cruel.

''I'm sorry, Kay,'' she said. ''All this is . . . it's too close.''

''I know.''

''I wish Varden were here.'' She picked up two of the packs, and Kay took the third. ''We might have a few more pigs in the forest, but at least we wouldn't have them in the house.'' She broke off suddenly and caught her breath. ''We've got to get those panels out of the church, Kay,'' she said hastily. ''The ones that David carved.''

Kay hardly reacted. His eyes clouded, and perhaps his shoulders became a little more stooped. ''It's too late, Miriam. They were going down the hall to the church as I left the house. They've already seen them by now.''

But Brother Louis and his companions did not comment on the panels. Kay and Miriam did not doubt that they had seen the carvings, for they looked very knowing at supper that night. Knowing, but maybe a little afraid, too. Miriam brought them food, filled their wine cups, tended to their wants, and she sensed the worry in them. *If that happened to Alban . . . then . . .*

That night, their swords were by their beds. That night also, Roxanne and her son left for the forest, and the town council gathered at Andrew's house after midnight.

''You're sure of this, Miriam?'' Andrew asked.

''I'm sure.'' Firelight and candlelight cast dark, wavering shadows of the men and women on the walls. Miriam felt their eyes on her as she stood before them, her elven clothes gleaming softly like a forest at dusk. ''I met him during my trial in Hypprux. He questioned me, and he ordered the soldiers to torture me. I saw him several times because they brought me to him every day to see if I'd be more cooperative.''

"Yer absolutely sure?" said Francis. "Ye were in pain. Mightn't ye—"

"Dammit, Francis, I'm sure."

The smith thumped his large hand on the bench where he sat. "Then we'd best be rid a' 'em. And quick."

Elizabeth caught his meaning. "Kill them?"

"Aye," said the smith. "Kill 'em and be done wi' it."

"They haven't done anything," said Simon.

"But they will."

Andrew spoke quietly. "I have no wish to murder sleeping men."

"They'd do ye in a trice."

Miriam stood up. "If we kill them, then everything falls apart. Cranby's friends in the northern towns know where he is, and they'll also know what's happened if he disappears. It would be one more reason for the Inquisition."

"How do you know this?" said Simon. He sounded suspicious.

"I . . ." How could she explain? The strand of potential that gave Saint Brigid safe passage for a few more decades still shimmered tantalizingly amid alternate futures of battle and war, and though she did not know how to make it more real, she knew that the immediate murder of the three clergymen would extinguish it altogether. "I . . . just know. Think about it, Simon."

"The Elves got us into this," said the miller. "I'm not sure they'll get us out."

Miriam knew what he meant. Since she had ceased denying it to herself, for how much longer could she deny it to others? Simon knew what he was seeing. She felt the distance between herself and these humans about her, but she loved them all the same. "All right, Simon. If I am an Elf, then listen to me as though I am." She was almost frightened by her audacity, but she pushed on. "I'm seeing more. I know more. My people brought something to Saint Brigid years ago, and now you're in danger of losing it completely. Listen to yourself talk. All I hear is distrust and suspicion. It used to be that the Elves were friends to this ground. Now . . . Well, what say you?"

Francis spoke. "I'll listen to ye, maiden. Ye speak wisely."

Simon's face was grim. "You're probably right," he said at last. "But then what are we supposed to do?"

Andrew spoke. "We must make certain that the three friars find out nothing." The carpenter's voice was quiet in the darkened room, his tone thoughtful. "We have to be sure that there are no contradictions in what we tell them. We need to send word to Saint Blaise and the other towns about who they are."

And so it was that in the ensuing days, when Brother Louis wandered through the town, stopping now and again to chat with a housewife or a shopkeeper, he found that all the villagers were ignorant of any dealings with Elves, witches, or demons of any sort. "We're all good folk here," he heard frequently.

Miriam, her awareness focused on the trio, found in them an increasing sense of frustration. Where were the Elves? Why did no one know about the panels in the church? Why did everyone seem to think that it was just a funny story? There was even talk of dedicating a plaque in the church to the memory of Jaques Alban, for the serene repose of his immortal soul. . . .

Maddening!

Miriam was cleaning the stables, and she was sure that someone was watching her.

She saw a quick flash of white over by the house. She went on with her work, but a short time later, she saw it again, this time closer, near the woodpile.

Mechanically, she forked hay into the mangers of the four horses, her mind shifting into starlight, her awareness slipping quietly out to the woodpile. It had been a week since the friars had arrived in town, and the villagers had, as far as she knew, held out against their questioning. Cranby's disguise, while allowing him anonymity, had its disadvantages, for he could not press for information as he could have if he had come as an official of the Inquisition.

Her awareness reached, surrounded the woodpile.

Hoyle?

As she worked, she watched him. Hoyle had been the most silent of the three churchmen. Obviously, he had his opinions, but he was not going to reveal them. Louis spoke at length, often patronizingly, and Bartholomew giggled and laughed like a schoolboy, sometimes mimicking members of the town or animals, so that even the most cautious had to laugh. But Hoyle . . .

A hot flash of lust exploded into Miriam's mind. Hoyle, it seemed, had needs that he was attending to.

Miriam broke off the contact, tightened her grip on the pitchfork. "Bastard," she muttered.

Thinking back over the last few days, she realized that Hoyle had been watching her a great deal. He had always made sure that he was near her on some pretense, whether she was occupied with housework or merely arranging flowers in the church. Now, when she finished up in the stable and reentered the house, he followed her.

The kitchen was deserted. Hoyle entered behind her. "We need to talk," he said.

"About what?" Instinctively, she dropped her hands to her sides, relaxed but ready.

He pulled a chair away from the table and sat down. "All sorts of things," he said. "About Elves . . . and witches . . . Things like that. I assume you want to help your village."

"I do what I can," she said.

"Hmmm . . . just so. I'm sure you can do a great deal."

"What do you want, Brother Hoyle?" The starlight was telling Miriam more than she really wanted to know.

He steepled his fingers, looked at her appraisingly, "We've come to know much about this town," he said softly. "We know, for example, that a witch with your name journeyed down to this area about a year ago."

"I'm not a witch, Brother Hoyle."

"Oh, I'm sure you're not. But don't you see? You bear her name."

"There are at least ten other women in this village named Miriam." An edge crept into her tone.

"I'm sure there are," Hoyle continued. "And we'll have to talk to them also. But you could make everything much easier for yourself—and them—if you became . . . a friend of mine. I'm in a position to help you."

Miriam felt nothing but contempt.

He did not notice. "You have to understand, Miriam.

Witchcraft is a serious charge, difficult to disprove. Witches are capable of using the most evil forms of magic to conceal the truth, and in order to be sure that you are not of their company, we might have to . . . question you strenuously.''

She kept her face a careful mask of calm. Starlight.

Smiling, he held out his hand. "I can help."

She met his eyes. "Go to hell." She turned and left the house, feeling his rage beating on her back in hot waves.

That night, at dinner, Hoyle kept his eyes sullenly on his food, but Miriam knew that his thoughts were elsewhere. Nevertheless, she served him politely; but she was still relieved when the three friars retired to their rooms.

Kay leaned back in his chair, wiped his forehead. "I don't know how much more of this I can take. Something's going to slip eventually."

"Something has." Miriam told him about Hoyle.

Kay nodded slowly. "Yes, that's one of their methods. If they can't find Elves, they'll fall back on witchcraft."

"Why are they so sure I came here?"

"They're not totally sure, and of course they haven't recognized you, but Brother Louis—Cranby—mentioned to me that they have some fairly reliable information. He asked me about it."

"What did you tell him?"

Kay considered for a moment. "I told him the truth, Miriam," he said gently. "Charity helped me decide what the truth actually was. I told him that, yes, Miriam of Maris had come to the village, that she was injured, and extremely bitter, and that, in despair, she had eventually taken her own life."

Miriam stared down at herself, stunned. "Dear Lady," she said. "Is that what I did?"

Kay looked at her somberly. "I think it was, Miriam."

She sat down. She had never thought of it in that way.

"The story seemed to mollify him," Kay went on after a time. "Though I did see him poking about in the churchyard. Of course, the lack of a grave marker proves nothing: commoners' graves aren't marked, particularly if there's suicide involved."

Miriam was still half in shock. "But how did they know I came to Saint Brigid in the first place?"

"Louis said that a witch was taken some distance from here. She was questioned, and she said that she knew you."

"A witch? I don't know any witches . . . I mean, except for Roxanne and Charity."

"Well, Louis called her a witch. Actually I suspect from some things he said that she's really a midwife."

Miriam went cold, dizzy. "Wh-where?"

"Up around Furze. Miriam? What's the matter?"

She stood up and grabbed him by his soutane. "They're still holding her? Is she still alive? Where is she?"

"Miriam!" Kay gasped. "Please!"

Letting go of his cassock, she forced herself to find the stars, breathed, dragged herself toward a semblance of calm. "Kay . . . that's Mika they're talking about. That's the woman who nursed me back to health." She pressed her hands to her temples. "And Aloysius Cranby's got her. There's no need to ask where: Hypprux. They're torturing her, maybe getting ready to kill her. I have to get help, Kay. I have to get her out of there."

"But . . . but how?"

Anger was not helping. Painfully, she flooded it with starlight. She felt the tranquillity expand, and she yielded to it a little. Her identity began to slip, but she fought her fear and opened herself to the light. She could not give herself totally yet, but she had to try, for she was going to need what the stars could give her.

She looked at Kay. There was a gleam of starlight in her eyes. "Elves," she said, "are known for being ingenious."

Chapter Twenty-five

Since the friars had come to Saint Brigid, Miriam had not left the village; and when she set foot among the trees that night, the forest, with its odors and sounds, its sense of quiet life, filled for her what had become an almost physical need. Her elven clothing glimmered darkly in the shadows, and the shimmer about her quickened as though her arrival in Malvern was something of a homecoming.

She saw the forest in shades of blue and lavender, but though the path she trod was clearly visible, it was not the path she wanted. The path that led to the Elves remained hidden. The Elves could see it, she knew, but she knew also that she could—she must—find it and walk it herself.

Standing on one path, searching for another, she felt anger and tears welling up along with starlight. She closed her eyes.

"I am a kinswoman here," she murmured. Holding to the vision of the stars, she opened her eyes and saw the forest as though it were new-made. Potentials shifted around her with every breath, and a path—previously hidden, shimmering with starlight—led off into the trees. Straight. Secret. With a brief thought of the Lady to whom she had pledged herself, she stepped onto it, unaided, and felt the magic tingle questioningly on her skin.

You've helped me. I know You've helped me. Help me now.
The magic accepted her. She moved on.

She walked silently, passing unnoticed within inches of sleeping deer. Owls watched her without comment. A quick-moving fox accompanied her for a few minutes, and where the path twisted and forked, she followed the animal. It left her when the way was straight again.

Thank you, she thought.

But the vision that had allowed her on this path was sapping her. She was growing dizzy. She leaned heavily against a shaggy oak, and the entire history of the tree flashed though her mind, but she paid little attention, for she was trying to keep from falling. Fighting with her instinctive fear, she clung to the stars. As though she lowered herself into a deep abyss, so did she carefully inch into the light, playing out her sense of identity as though it were a lifeline.

Please help me. I'm afraid, but please help me anyway.

Her consciousness slipped and slid further into the light.

She saw someone that was her, and yet not. Tall, slender, with hair of red gold and eyes the color of emerald, she walked through a springtime forest of green leaves and yellow flowers, a sparrow hawk on her shoulder and a sense of youth in her features that had nothing to do with days or years. And for a moment, Miriam became her, knew herself by another name, another lifetime, another Dance.

Mirya.

The pain in her hands brought her back. She had been gripping the oak so tightly that she had splintered her fingernails. Rubbing blearily at the wounds, she pushed herself away from the tree and stumbled down the hidden path. The fatigue was yet with her, but it was tempered now. She could manage.

And when she stepped into the firelit clearing where the Elves were gathered, she stood, trembling, until they were all looking at her, then bent and touched the ground with her bleeding fingers. "I claim hearthright," she whispered. She staggered to one side.

Varden was on his feet instantly. "Well said," he murmured as he caught her.

He guided her to a seat by the fire. At her side was Terrill, still examining her every movement as though this were simply another test he had devised. Other Elves were there also: Talla and Natil, and some she did not recognize. Roxanne smiled quietly at her from across the fire, and Lake nuzzled at his mother's breast.

Gently, Terrill took her bleeding hands in his own. "Varden," he said. "Please."

Varden touched her hands. She felt a moment's warmth

and did not have to look to know that her fingers were sound.
"Thank you, Varden," she said. "Be at peace."

"Terrill," said Varden, "what have you been teaching
Miriam?"

"What have I been teaching her? An odd question, my
brother. I have been teaching her the way of the sword."

"More than that, I am sure."

"She has natural gifts, Varden," said Terrill. "You more
than anyone should know that."

The light in Varden's eyes flickered. "And you?"

Terrill met his gaze for a moment, then closed his eyes
and sighed. "I know."

"What is your errand, Miriam?" said Varden.

She shuddered at the thought of what the midwife was
enduring. "I need help," she said. "For the sake of love
and friendship."

Varden regarded her for some moments. "Love and
friendship," he said with wonder. "Until now, I do not
think I have heard you utter those words with anything but
contempt."

"I've changed." Her voice was sharp. 'I've learned. The
midwife who nursed me after I escaped from Hypprux has
been taken as a witch. She's being tortured."

Terrill sat back, his eyes on fire. "Human ways are not
ours," he said with an effort. "I agreed to teach you, Miriam, so that you could have your revenge. That, I thought,
was the extent of my involvement."

"What about Saint Brigid? Information they've tortured
out of Mika has brought Aloysius Cranby and his dogs here
looking for me. The town's been implicated, and they've
seen the panels in the church."

"Human ways." Terrill was obviously struggling with his
memories. There was grief in his voice.

"Elven ways," she said defiantly. "Aid? Comfort? Don't
you care?"

Varden was staring at Roxanne. The Elves called her Sana,
as though she were elven herself. But though she had taken
on many of their ways and attitudes, she was human, frail,
mortal, and there was a sense of fragility about her as she
sat, wrapped in a gray cloak, nursing her baby.

He spoke softly. "We care." Slowly, he removed the pendant he wore and held it up in the firelight. Finely worked in silver and gold, it was in the form of an interlocked rayed star and crescent moon. He hung it about Miriam's neck. "I will help you, Miriam of Malvern."

"Varden, you cannot," said Terrill. "There will be fighting, and though you have skill, it is insufficient for such a venture."

Varden deliberated. "How have Miriam's lessons progressed?"

"She is almost ready for steel," said Terrill, "though there is much more for her to learn. But . . ." He seemed to fight with himself for a moment. "But I will go with her to Hypprux, and together we will rescue the midwife."

"Very well," said Varden. "I will remain and help Kay. The friars doubtless have some ideas in their heads."

There was a sense of import to his words, and Miriam instinctively looked into the lattices. She saw another knot of futures ahead, ready to unfold, ready to demand choice and action.

"But there is another matter," said Terrill. "Miriam will need a sword."

Varden and Terrill were silent for a long time. The fire hissed and crackled: dry wood, gathered from the forest floor. The Elves would not cut a living tree.

"Is that your wish?" said Varden at last.

"It might be good. I do not know. It might teach her."

"Very well." Varden rose and walked away from the fire. Miriam watched as he opened a bundle. When he returned to the fire, he was carrying something long, narrow, cloth-wrapped.

He produced a fine sword in a dark blue scabbard. "Many years ago," he said. "I wore this. I do not wear it anymore. Perhaps it would suit your hand. . . ." He offered it to her, and when she slid it out of the sheath, it blazed in the firelight as though it were itself made of flame. Miriam caught her breath.

"It is called *Eltieviel*," said Varden. "That means: Rainfire."

She hefted the sword. Rainfire seemed alive in her hand, as though it could fight without anyone having to wield it. The handle was an intricate tracery of lapis set in lignum

vitae, the crosspiece a crescent of bright metal. The blade
was smooth, flawless, with a watered look as of the finest
Damascus steel.

"Magnificent," she said. "How is it that I am worthy of
this?"

"Need makes many a worthy," said Terrill, but Varden
shook his head.

"There is much in you, Miriam," he said. "I think you
are beginning to know that. Bear this sword well. You are,
I believe, deserving."

As she looked at the sword, she felt its past, felt Varden's
hand merge with her own as, long ago, he had wielded it.
There was grief there, deep grief, and Rainfire had been put
away.

But she saw the futures, too: a network of interlocking
possibilities that led off beyond her comprehension. She saw
the strands of starlight again, and she saw that Rainfire
traced its own path toward the eventual confrontation between her and her rapist.

They made plans quickly, deciding to leave the next night.
The Elves would need time to gather the necessary supplies,
and in any case, the friars would be asleep and would not
know that anything unusual was taking place until well into
the following day.

Without comment, Terrill guided her to the forest edge in
the predawn darkness, bowed, and departed. Miriam felt
that he was almost afraid. Afraid? Of what? Certainly not
of battle. *I once cut a man through the spine with a wooden
sword.* Her hand fell to her side and came to rest on Rainfire's pommel. She wondered what Terrill could do with live
steel.

Whoever kept watch at the town gate this night did not
notice Miriam's arrival any more than her departure, and
she climbed the iron grille silently, the weight of the sword
at her hip at once unfamiliar and comforting.

Even at a distance, she felt the alien presence of Aloysius
Cranby, Bartholomew, and Hoyle in the otherwise smooth—
though anxious—flow of the town. A thickening complex of
lifelines wove about them, indicating an eventful day.

And as she crossed the common, a sudden blow on the

back of her head sent her staggering across the grass. Before she could find her balance, another put her on the ground.

She felt a hand feeling for the fastenings of her garments, and the white-hot rage that surged up within her eclipsed the stars as though a nova had kindled among them.

She locked her fists together and swung up and out, catching her assailant in the face. With a grunt and a curse he fell back, and Miriam had time enough to pull herself to her feet, recenter on her stars, and let the energy flow. Her vision cleared instantly, the pain in her head faded. She was not overly surprised to see Hoyle getting to his feet a few yards away.

He was wiping blood from his mouth. "You could make it easier for yourself if you submitted."

"So you can fuck me before you burn me?" she said. "Is that what you have in mind?"

"You'd better come with me, woman."

"Touch me if you dare, man."

He drew a sword and started to move in. Rainfire slid out of its sheath eagerly, flashed in the growing light. The friar saw the elven blade, hesitated, then came on.

With a blink, she was in the starlight vision, examining Hoyle's every move with inhuman awareness. On this pale morning, at this particular time, with the set of his foot just so, Hoyle was going to move to his left and attempt to grab her arm while deflecting her blade. It was a reckless move, one that showed that he had no respect for the combat abilities of a woman.

He was about to learn respect.

Hoyle's sword was spun to the side. Rainfire slashed in toward the friar's throat. He nearly broke his neck as he lurched away, and Rainfire cut through the air a finger's width from his face. Whirling, he changed his tactics, approaching her more cautiously now.

But he seemed clumsy to Miriam. Dancing to one side, she let his blade flick by, and as she watched, she saw the beginnings of a roll. Openings flashed through her mind, but just as Terrill had been open once, so she was now open. Her side. Potentially.

Hoyle rolled, struck.

She leaped, kicking out and down, flattening Hoyle's arm

to the ground. His sword caught in the grass. Miriam was already on his other side, but Hoyle swung as he rose, putting his whole weight behind his sword, trying to batter her down.

Miriam knew that he could indeed batter her down. Stepping back, she let his strike expend itself in the empty air. He had left her a clean opening.

Rainfire flashed, lancing out. Just as the rim of the sun blazed at the horizon, touching the steeple of the church with pink and gold, the blade ripped through Hoyle's throat.

A fine spray of blood. A glazed look on the friar's face. He sprawled onto the dew-spattered grass.

The fighting had weakened Miriam, and she lost no time in pulling herself out of the starlight vision. Moving slowly, she went to Hoyle and found that he still lived. His blood, though, was reddening the grass, and his eyes were unseeing. The gash in his throat gurgled and sucked. Miriam's healing power flickered in response, but the stars in her mind burned clear and cold, and the heat subsided.

"No," she said softly. "I will not heal you."

In her mind, she saw the lattices that indicated futures and maybes. Hoyle's line was fading, terminating, his choices ending. When he jerked suddenly and lay still, his line winked out, leaving behind a void. There was no future for him now, only a past.

Rainfire was stained and red, and she wiped the blade carefully before sheathing it. She was still breathing hard, and she worked slowly, methodically.

Terrill spoke up suddenly from behind her. "Well, *healer*, are you satisfied?"

She whirled. The Elf folded his arms.

"You've taken life."

She found her voice. "He wanted to kill me."

"Maybe. Do you realize what you have done?"

"I saved myself."

"It is not that simple. How do you feel about this hunk of dead meat on the ground?" He stepped forward until Hoyle's body was between them. "You can see how everything is connected, how everything has its potential. I know you can, for you could not fight the way you do if you could not."

"What the hell are you trying to do to me, Terrill?" She nearly shouted at him. "This bastard wanted to rape me, then haul me off to the torturers and the stake. And you're worried about philosophy?"

"There was always the possibility, Miriam, that Hoyle could have been persuaded to forget the entire affair. If you had spoken more kindly to him earlier, he might not have been prodded into such a fatal course." Terrill spoke dispassionately. "Such probabilities are very small, to be sure, but can be made larger . . . if one is clever."

Miriam glared at him.

"You had the audacity this night to claim hearthright with the Elves. When you set foot on that path, earlier on, you had the cheek to call yourself a kinswoman. I heard. You cannot deny it."

Her weakness was ebbing slowly. "I won't deny it. Is it your duty to eavesdrop at the forest's edge?"

"It is my duty to teach you, Elf."

Miriam started.

Terrill nodded slowly. "I will give you the dignity of that title, though to my mind you have yet to earn it. Let me say this: You can see as we do, and you can kill. You took away every one of this man's futures by slaying him, be your reason good or bad, and you created others, for futures spring up to fill the void of a death. By your actions, you take on responsibility. You have much to learn about who and what you are, Miriam of Malvern, but let this be your first lesson: You are responsible as no human can possibly be, for you can see the past, and you can see all the futures. You are not ignorant, and therefore you have no excuse."

She made herself breathe evenly. Outbursts were doing her no good and—she was beginning to understand—never really had. "So," she said, "you're berating me for saving my own life?"

"I am not. I watched. You did well. As well as I expected. Even better. Had you been in danger of losing, I would have killed him myself, for when he fought you, he found out too much about your nature. Aloysius Cranby might be looking for a witch, but he would have found an Elf. All the better for his plans."

"His plans? We have a dead body to explain, Terrill."

Terrill looked down at the sprawl of flesh that had been Hoyle. "Just so. I will lug the guts into the forest. Hoyle's simple absence will be less troublesome than his corpse."

Miriam was seeing probabilities again. Terrill was right: the void left by Hoyle's death was being filled. There were choices ahead, actions. She saw Aloysius Cranby and Bartholomew, Kay's frightened face, Charity lying in the street.

But nothing was certain. Nothing was ever really certain until it happened. There were too many choices, too many maybes. The Elves could see everything and, as a result, could see very little at all. Only the intense focus of the starlight vision allowed anything resembling surety, and that only seconds before the actual event.

She nodded slowly. "You're right. Better get him out of here. The town gates will be open by now. I'm sure that no one will say anything if they see you."

"They will not see me." Terrill picked up the friar's body easily, though it must have been nearly double his weight. Slinging it on his back, he turned to go.

Miriam's hand rested lightly on the pommel of Rainfire. "Why doesn't Varden wear this sword anymore?" she asked.

Terrill turned back for a moment. Hoyle's corpse hung grotesquely over his shoulder. "For the same reason that I always wear one," he said at last, and his inflection told her that he would not elaborate.

She had hoped to be able to return to her room undetected, but seconds after she had closed the door, it was flung open again and blocked by two figures. "Have you any idea," said Brother Louis, "what has become of our dear Brother Hoyle?"

She stood, clad as an Elf, a sword at her hip. Louis, she knew, was perfectly aware of what had happened to Hoyle. In the space of a few heartbeats she retraced the strands of the past and saw Louis watching the fight on the common. She traced a little further back and heard skillfully placed comments and innuendos that had goaded Hoyle's sense of pride until he had gone looking for the woman who had defied him. He had prowled through the streets of the village all night, until . . .

"Oh," she said innocently, knowing that Louis would not believe her anyway, "has he disappeared then?"

"We've known you from the beginning, witch." And Miriam saw that Louis and Bartholomew were both armed with swords. She caught a glimpse of Kay's agonized features behind them.

"Brother Louis—" began the priest.

"Silence, man," said Louis. "You've been bespelled, can't you see? You'll follow her to the stake along with all the others if you're not careful."

"I'm not going to the stake," said Miriam evenly. Her hand grazed Rainfire's pommel and hung, ready.

"You are an Elf and a witch," declared Louis.

Very consciously, Miriam relaxed. "I am not a witch," she said softly, "but you are Bishop Aloysius Cranby of Hypprux, and we have met before. And you accused me of much the same things then; but this time, wanting me and having me are two very different things." Her tone was cold, the starlight holding back a weight of anger that could have riven mountains.

The bishop shook off his surprise and motioned to Bartholomew. "Arrest her in the name of God."

Bartholomew stepped forward, his ruddy features set. Rainfire flashed once, and he fell to the floor and did not move again.

Miriam turned, pointed with her blade at Aloysius Cranby. "You have two tears now, Your Excellency. Elven magic, and elven swords."

"If you kill me, it will bring the Inquisition down on this entire town," he said. "No one will be spared."

"As if you intend to spare anyone in any case," said Miriam. She took a step forward. "This way, I'll at least have the satisfaction of seeing you dead. You shouldn't complain. You wanted Hoyle to die, just like you wanted something to happen to Jaques Alban. You've wanted excuses to bring the Inquisition down on the Free Towns. Well, now you have them. Several of them. And I'll be more than happy to give you one more."

Her sword leaped, and the bishop parried, but he did not stay to fight. Shoving Kay brutally aside, he vanished down the hallway toward the front door.

Miriam started to follow, but Kay grabbed her tunic. "No more, Miriam," he cried. "Please, no more. There's been enough killing today."

"Dammit, Kay: let me go. He's heading for the stable."

"Please, Miriam!"

If she had struck him, his grip would have loosened, but she could not bear to hurt the priest. Slowly, she pried his hands from her clothing and pushed him away as gently as she could. Kay was sobbing helplessly.

She ran to the door, but she was too late. Cranby was already horsed and was galloping across the common. There was no way she could catch him, and the village gates were open.

But the carpenter's house was near the gate, and someone lived there who could hear her. "Charity," she shouted among the stars, "have the men close the gate! Quickly!"

And, again too late, she realized what was going to happen, saw what her words and her actions had done. In her mind, she saw the probabilities unfold, watched helplessly as the young witch left her house. Charity saw the bishop approaching at a gallop, and having no time in which to reach the gate, she leaped for the horse's bridle.

Cranby did not slow or turn aside. Instead, he simply rode her down and continued on through the gate and into the open fields. When he returned, he would bring the Inquisition.

But Miriam was not thinking of the Inquisition. She was running across the common, screaming, her mind blank save for the image of Charity lying broken and crumpled in the street.

Chapter Twenty-six

Night and day had blended together into an uninterrupted blackness, pocked upon occasion by the glare of torches red as her own blood, the touch of iron and wood to her naked flesh, and a change in the quality of a pain that had by now become habitual in spite of its intensity, that caused her screams to float ambiguously between madness and torment.

And when her cries now and again faded into whimpering and then into harsh gasps, she could hear the distant wails of other prisoners, the scurrying of rats, the steady drip of foul water. She smelled mold, rot, excrement; and her mouth was filled with the taste of her own blood, retched up hot and metallic during those hours in the blinding torchlight. But none of these—nothing—told her whether or not the sun or the stars shone, or how long she had been here, in this dungeon, on this rack, chained to this reeking pallet. . . .

Always she heard the questions, the ostinato litany of interrogatives that dinned in her ears even when there were no lips to speak them.

What did you do with the Elves?

She had never known the Elves, had never looked into compassionate eyes that were filled with starlight or heard the melodic language that had been formed to describe the creation of a world. She wished that she had, for those memories might have contained enough strength for her either to endure the endless day-night of pain and horror or to force herself into the shadowy release of death.

You have been sodomized by the devil, haven't you?

The questions rang in her ears, mingling with her screams and the screams of others, and all she had with which to

fight them were gentler, more human recollections of pregnant women, the painful glory of birth, the chubby, reaching hands of an infant, the first flush of returning health in
a pale cheek.

Tell us everything.

One by one her allies had fled, for they were no match
for the glowing tongs and the blood-corroded spike. The
balance between madness and torment was, minute by minute, scream by scream, becoming more precarious, and she
could not deny to herself that she was glad that she was
slowly tipping toward the former.

White fire blazed up Miriam's spine, incandescence filled
the space behind her clenched eyes, and the pain was such
that she breathed in shallow, miserly gasps, but she did not
complain: she almost relished the onslaught of the healing
power, rejoiced in its magnitude.

But Charity, still and bloody on the ground, seemed an
abyss of damage. Aloysius Cranby had ridden directly over
her, and the heavy hooves of his mount had crushed her
skull. By the time Miriam had arrived, the young witch had
seemed dead. No breath, no heartbeat, massive blood loss.

Still, Miriam had fallen on her knees beside her, letting
the power flow, taunting it, dragging it from her spine in
ever-increasing amounts. She had healed plague. She had
brought men back from near death. Surely she could save
one frail young woman.

The power surged, and her head seemed close to splitting
with the light. *For Charity. I'd not do this for anyone else.*
She remembered the little priestess as she had been: whole,
complete, with a quietude that bespoke vast depths of
knowledge and at the same time a merry laugh that was the
essence of an early, flower-filled spring. *Charity!*

No answer. And Miriam's seemingly inexhaustible stores
of power were suddenly nearing their limits.

She felt her shoulders gripped. "Moderate it, Miriam,"
came Roxanne's voice. "A little with control is better than
a great deal without."

The smooth, even energies of the witch blended with her
own. The healing flow subsided into a firm, strong current

through which Miriam could sense Charity's presence. *Sana, she's here!*

"Steady," said the witch.

"Find your stars, Miriam," said Varden, and she felt the touch of his hands on hers, the blending of starlight with the white-hot healing.

Carefully she searched for, found the firmament within. The stars were bright and clear, and they, too, added their energies. Miriam felt a massive balance, as though of life and death, tipping slowly. The abyss was filling.

"Vardeni," said Roxanne. *"Ei astael Cara ami circalmi."*

Miriam picked up her meaning. *Astael.* Starlight. Charity could be profoundly changed, the immortal radiance altering the very basis of her existence. At the moment of Miriam's transformation, the starlight had flooded into her. And she had changed. . . .

The balance hung, frozen. "Carai," said Varden, his soft voice echoing among the stars, "you must decide."

Miriam's pain was still intense, but she held out against it. She saw the girl's hand and her own gathering flowers for the statue of the Lady, scattering crumbs for the birds. . . .

"To stay or to go," the Elf continued, "as you wish. You are aware of the possibilities."

Charity's voice was soft, calm, almost matter-of-fact. It befit a trained priestess who had already faced death and rebirth twice in the course of one lifetime, who would now face it again with equanimity. Miriam felt Roxanne's pride.

"I have work to do," said the young witch. "I will stay. If I am changed, then so be it."

And the three healers, Elf, witch, and one who was not quite either and yet, maybe, a little more than both, loosed the energies that, for a moment, they had held in check.

Miriam opened her eyes. Charity was still bloody, but her wounds were healed, and the terrible rent in her head was no more. Miriam felt her squeeze her hand, a gentle thank-you.

"Better sleep, Carai," said Varden, and the young witch nodded, sighed, and drifted off.

The Elf's face was gray. His voice had been soft, but the

light in his eyes was hot and bright, like the edge of a newly
blooded sword. He stood up slowly, his sight seemingly
elsewhere, as though he looked into the past.

Terrill was standing with a crowd of villagers a little to
one side, holding Lake. Near him, Elizabeth and Andrew
were crying, and Francis had his big arms about them both.

"My brother . . ." said Terrill.

Varden did not reply. Terrill handed Lake to Roxanne and
took him into his arms. Varden shuddered, wept softly.
"Once again, Terrill," he said. "Once again. Mirya, now
Cara . . . Who next? Sana? Elizabeth? Andrew? Kay? Who
do we love best? *Ai, ea sareni, Elthiai!*"

After a minute, Varden sighed, his tears spent. "Go on
your errand," he said to Terrill and Miriam. "I will attend
to other matters. Alone."

Terrill regarded him in silence, examining, evaluating.
Then: "He has a sword, dear brother."

"True, Terrill, he does. And I have only my hands. But
they will be sufficient."

Varden knelt beside Charity and kissed her on the forehead, then rose, turned, and departed, his garments of gray
and green dark in the bright sunlight.

Together, Miriam and Terrill picked up Charity and carried her into her parents' house, where Elizabeth and Andrew cleaned the blood and dust off the pale face and put
her in her own bed.

Miriam stood at the unshuttered window, her jaw
clenched. Terrill was at her side.

"We will be able to leave by noon," he said. "We need
not delay."

"How long to Hypprux?"

"Three and one half days," the Elf responded.

Below her, there were dark stains in the street. Charity's
blood. "He could have turned," said Miriam. "He could
have turned and still made the gate."

"That is so."

"He rode her down deliberately."

"True."

She pushed herself away from the sill and faced him.
"Let's go kill some humans," she said.

The Elf's grief was evident, but he did not say anything.

He reached out as though to touch her cheek, but appeared to think better of it. He bowed and departed, his feet noiseless on the stairs.

Miriam knelt by the side of Charity's bed, took her hand, and pressed it to her lips for a moment. The shimmer about the witch was plain to her. So much starlight they had put into such a small woman! And what would happen to her now?

She noticed that Charity's eyes were open.

"Miriam."

"Cara."

Charity hovered on the borders of sleep. "Try, Miriam. Please try." Her eyes closed.

Andrew looked at Miriam, puzzled. "Try?"

Miriam nodded, rose. "Try to love," she said simply, and her voice broke. Her feet, though, were as silent as Terrill's as she went down to the street.

Terrill tapped at the door of the priest's house just at noon. He was wearing his gray cloak and, as usual, his sword. Kay, who had answered the door, bowed and gestured him in, and after considering a moment, the Elf entered.

He found Miriam in her room, buckling on her sword. "Be at peace," he said.

Her words in Andrew's house had pained Terrill, had even frightened him, and she felt herself examined again, this time in great earnestness. "Be at peace, Terrill," she said reassuringly. "The hand of the Lady be on you."

Terrill was still tense. "And on you."

"I'm ready."

"It is well. Everything is prepared. And I can tell you that Cara is well. She is awake." He smiled slightly. "And she is very hungry."

Miriam smiled also.

He turned to the play of leaf shadows on the window. "She can see the stars."

Miriam had been bending over her pack, but she straightened. "Will she . . . do you think . . . ?"

"I cannot say. It is too early. Much will depend upon her own reactions and inclinations. Varden could tell more, but he is not here."

In her mind, Miriam saw Malvern Forest stretching north and east, league after league. She saw the road that ran along its western flank, bare dirt in some places, ancient Roman pavement in others. "Cranby has a horse."

"My brother is quick," said Terrill, "and he knows the paths of the forest."

"What will he do?"

Terrill was silent for a time. "Varden has his choices."

Miriam picked up the pack and slung it over her shoulder. "So do we." She stood beside Terrill at the door and again felt his earnest, almost fearful analysis. She laid a hand on his arm. "I'll try, Terrill, if only for Cara's sake. But it's not easy."

The Elf bowed deeply to her in the manner of his people. "The horses are waiting."

"Horses?"

"We will need them. Mika does not have our endurance, and we may need bursts of speed that two legs alone cannot give us."

Kay was waiting at the front door, wringing his hands. He had not slept the night before, and his eyes were red from both fatigue and the death he had seen that day. It pained Miriam to see him suffering, and she embraced him. "I'll be all right," she said. "I'll be back, don't worry."

He lifted his eyes to her. "Fair One . . . I . . ." He could say no more, and he simply hugged her. Miriam could feel that he was weeping.

Fair One. There had always been distance between them. Kay did not know hate. He did not know the kind of fear that made life a furtive hell. All that was enough to separate their worlds. But since her transformation, and growing as the months passed, there was something else, too. *Fair One.*

"Kay," she said. "It's still me. I'm still Miriam."

He peered into her face. "Yes," he said. "I know."

It was not quite a lie for either of them.

Terrill's voice was factual. "It is time."

Miriam touched Kay's head. "You haven't asked," she said, "but you need this. May the hand of the Lady be on you, Kay, now and always." It was as much of a blessing as she knew, and she kissed him and followed Terrill out into the noon sunlight. She turned back once. "You'll take care of Esau, won't you?"

Kay stood at the door, a slight figure in a black soutane. Almost boyish. But his eyes . . . "I will."

Terrill had continued on, and when she caught up with him, he extended his hand, and she took it.

Evening. The road lay blank and bare. The sky was tinged with rose and red in the west, with violet and indigo at the zenith. Varden waited at the edge of the trees, watching the distant mounted figure that trotted steadily northward: a part of the pattern that shifted—incrementing, decrementing— with each breath, each thought.

The futures promised little hope for the Free Towns, but there would be none at all if Aloysius Cranby lived. The bishop carried north with him the knowledge that Saint Brigid was frequented by Elves, that his companions had been killed by an elven blade, that the priest's housekeeper was of that race herself. Any one of those facts was enough for the Inquisition, and the combination thereof would bring the baronial armies to the Free Town as surely as the warm summer sun brought bees to the flowers of the fields.

But if the bishop were no more, then there would be time, for his lieutenants would battle for power and alliances would have to be remade. The Elf saw that the most probable future was one in which the Free Towns had a reprieve of only a few months, but much could happen in a few months. Anything was possible. There were only differing degrees of probability.

But he could still see Charity lying in the street, her head crushed.

He put his face in his hands, trying to banish the vision, attempting to find in himself the love that he needed this evening. Anger had given him nothing. Hate had emptied his heart. He had to love.

When he looked up, the man on horseback was much closer, but the horse had been ridden too hard, and it was tired. Its head hung as it slowed from a trot to a walk despite the urgings of its rider.

Varden stayed under the trees, looked at his hands. He had not killed in over three hundred years, not since that terrible night when he and his brother had descended upon the cluster of farmhouses near the town of Aurverelle, driven by anger to precise and exacting butchery. Their swords had flashed, and when they were finished, they had returned to the clearing in the forest where the tall, slender body lay, her red-gold hair cut short by the humans who had called her demon, her features nearly unrecognizable.

With Talla and Natil, they built a pyre with their bare hands, taking wood from the forest that the trees had given up willingly and laying it tenderly about the remains. A bolt of summer lightning had kindled a small blaze in the forest, and with that flame they fired the wood.

Natil laid her harp on the pyre, and as the fire grew, brightening, consuming the wood and the body, the instrument suddenly cracked, strings snapping loudly, sparks showering through the night air as bright as stars.

When it was done, they had scattered the ashes. Varden had put away his sword. Natil had not touched a harp again for many years.

Aloysius Cranby was very close now.

Who was this tall, slender stranger then, come now with red-gold hair and eyes the color of emerald? Why, when Varden had manipulated the energies of the universe to re-shape the body of the ill-tempered healer girl, had the strands of starlight woven and interlocked themselves into a matrix that had given her such a form as she now wore? Was it merely an accident brought on by his own memories and regrets?

He could not believe that. Nothing happened by chance. But whatever purpose Miriam fulfilled, it lay beyond his comprehension, lost in the interweaving of past and future that contained everything: Saint Brigid, the Free Towns, Adria, the Elves. . . .

Even Aloysius Cranby, bishop of Hypprux.

Varden stepped out when Cranby was a few yards away. The bishop saw him, drew sword, spurred his horse.

But the animal was tired, and Varden simply ducked to one side and lashed out with a foot. The bishop toppled, falling heavily into the dust.

Varden saw the potentials shift. There was always the

chance that Cranby would give up his plans, his ambition. The chance was absurdly faint, but it had to be offered.

"Your Excellency," he said. "War is not good for your people. There will be much suffering. Your own Savior preached peace. I most humbly ask you to reconsider your plans regarding the Free Towns."

Aloysius Cranby stood up, lifted his sword. "You should know about my Savior. You tempted Him in the desert."

"I did not. You know my people have only brought healing. Why—"

Cranby moved in, slashing. The Elf rolled out of the way. "All the killing could end here, Your Excellency. Your people and mine could live in peace, without fear. I ask only that you reconsider your plans."

"The Inquisition is here for a purpose, Satan." The bishop's voice was a flat monotone, his words a pronouncement. "If the Free Towns are a part of your unholy empire, then they must perish. You killed my companions, and now you want to kill me. But I have a sword, I am unafraid, and I am strong in my faith. You cannot win."

Varden listened. He could not say for sure whether the churchman believed his litany of condemnation or not. Perhaps it was only something to believe in, a depiction of a sure, definite opponent in a world that had none, an objective that gave some purpose to lives that were not so much lived as endured.

Sadness. Sadness in the world of men. Sadness in Aloysius Cranby. Varden felt the human pity stir in his own heart. Sadness in Varden of Malvern.

"I am sorry, Your Excellency." Here it was, happening once more in spite of his vows, his promises, his sorrow. *Arae a Circa.* Day of Renewal. It was indeed the first of May, and his hands were seconds away from blood.

Cranby moved again, swinging, doubling back quickly, his sword flashing in the twilight. Varden saw his moves, knew what was planned even before the bishop himself did. He simply stepped aside. "Forgive me, Aloysius," he said softly.

"Damn you!" Cranby screamed, but his words were cut short. Varden slid in behind him, hands blurring. The sound

of two dull cracks hung in the still night air as the bishop's spine snapped.

The horses went on its way and the road was once again deserted save for a solitary corpse that stared with unseeing eyes at the evening sky. The first stars began to appear.

PART THREE

Alba

Chapter Twenty-seven

Bright flowers graced the formal gardens of the Chateau. The weather had been warm since early spring, and roses were blooming alongside hyacinths, tulips were brilliant and stalwart, hawthorn glistened like coral.

Roger of Aurverelle poked idly at the base of a daffodil with the toe of his boot. The effeminacy of this city still rankled him. It was all very well to build a keep, or a palace, or a chateau. Such things were necessary. But then to ornament them like drabs tricked out in gutter finery . . .

He had given up complaining about it, or about the courtiers and the sycophants with their perfumes and their fine clothes and their pretty manners. Such things would change. He was chamberlain now, and with the support of the baronage that would come from a successful conquest of the Free Towns, he would eventually be able to do as he wished.

"Lord Chamberlain . . ." The voice was a cultured blend of the urbane and the ironic. Roger looked down at Brendan a'Lowins, marshal of Hypprux, who held a letter cylinder in his pale hands.

"What do you want, mouse?" Roger hated the man. Brendan's long hair was elaborately curled and perfumed, and the drooping mustache he had cultivated seemed less a mark of anything masculine than a faintly humorous incongruity.

"A letter from Saint Blaise, messire." As though to distance himself as much as he could from this rough forester who had dressed himself up first as a baron, then as chamberlain of the city, the marshal had cultivated the very precise accent and dialect of Maris. "One of the bishop's archers delivered it to the porter, and as I was on my way to see you, I brought it with me."

Poison, thought Roger. Poison in my food someday. A woman's trick. That's what the likes of this waterfly has in mind. As if anything could spring from his loins except cabbages and eels. "Is it from Cranby?"

"I believe so."

Roger took the case and shoved it into his belt. If it was from Cranby, then it would be in Latin, and he would have to get a priest to read it. The bishop appeared to enjoy reminding him of his comparative illiteracy.

He looked up at the cloudless sky, longing to be away from the city for a time. He could head south, down to one of the peasant hamlets, and he could find a woman there. That was what he needed: his leathers, his sword, a woman. She would have good solid earth under her thighs, and she would know what it felt like to be covered by a real man. Oh, she would scream and fight, to be sure, but he would have his way. He always had his way.

His shoulder throbbed. No, not always. There had been one occasion . . .

"The archer said something about the good bishop traveling south with his friars," said the marshal.

"Whatever the good, stupid bishop wants," said Roger. "Just so long as the good, stupid bishop is back here for the mustering. We need him."

"Just so, messire."

Contemplating the marshal, Roger could think only of mice. "Get away from me. Go attend to your embroidery."

The marshal flared delicately. "My Lord Chamberlain, I am an officer of this city."

Roger was about to laugh in his face when a flash of movement caught his eye. It was a young woman with hair like flax. She wore a gown of pale blue and was wandering through the gardens reading a book. Her head was bent low, as though she were trying to ignore her surroundings.

"Who is that?" he asked abruptly. "I've never seen her before. Is she with this household?"

"Her name is Janet Darci, messire," said Brendan. "She was sent up from Saint Blaise as a . . . guest." He coughed politely.

There was a grace about her that reminded Roger of another girl-woman he had once seen. What was going on in those Free Towns?

His shoulder throbbed again. "She's very pretty," he said as she passed out of sight around the corner of the curtain wall. "I must meet her someday." But the ache from the old wound shifted his thoughts to the Free Towns, to the indignity he had suffered in the forest just outside Saint Brigid. The Towns would pay for that. So would the Elves. "Have you found out anything more from the witch?"

"I spoke with Brother Karl last night. She is delirious and must rest for a day or two before we can have another"—he coughed again—"talk."

"Let her rest. And then find out what we need. When Cranby returns, he can finish his work on the proclamation. With any luck at all, we can be ready by midsummer." He looked at Brendan. "And by the way, Lord Marshal, you'll be traveling with us."

"Me? Messire, I—"

"Get away from me. And learn how to use a sword for something more than spearing fruit."

White-faced, the marshal departed. For a minute, Roger debated following Janet, but decided against it. He needed to have the letter read. And there would be time for Janet later on.

Terrill and Miriam rode north through Malvern Forest, following hidden paths beneath new-leafed branches that dappled them with May sunlight. Once again Miriam traveled upon these secret, elven ways by the permission and strength of another, but that did not matter to her, for she had put aside considerations of pride and achievement and had focused instead upon the woman who lay in the dungeon of Hypprux, upon what had been done to her, upon what might be done in the near future.

Torturers' methods varied with their personalities. Perhaps Mika had been given over to one who had taken pity upon the old midwife and had only shown her, time and again, the instruments he would use on her body unless she told the inquisitors what they wanted to hear. Perhaps Mika was still unharmed.

But the lifelines and the lattices told Miriam that other

probabilities were greater. Torturers were frequently only interested in money. Usually they were actually sadistic. Every joint of the mortal body was known to them, and they would, if necessary, dislocate each one in pursuit of what the inquisitors considered to be the truth. Feet would be converted to pulped masses of bruised flesh and pulverized bone. Compound fractures. Veins removed one by one. Blood . . . Eyes . . .

She was no longer looking at the forest path, but at the niter-encrusted walls of the dungeon in the Chateau. She saw herself strapped into the chair, saw Mika shackled beside her, saw an incongruous flash of red-gold hair as a tall, slender Elf maid was methodically dismembered.

With an involuntary cry, she fled back to the forest. The sun shone warm on her back, but the roots of her hair were damp with sweat. Wiping her face, Miriam centered herself on the stars, recalling that although her memories were human, her body and her heart were not. She could weigh, she could plan, she could act.

Varden worked his magic and his healing. Terrill fought with terrible precision. Talla danced. Natil played her harp. And the energies of the stars flowed through their abilities and quickened them, so that the flame of talent turned blue white with stellar fire. Now she herself, Miriam—once of Maris, but now of Malvern—partook of that light, that energy; and as she looked into the many futures, she saw her actions drive into the potentials like shafts of lightning.

Night came, but they still traveled. Beneath her, the horse trotted on. Before they had started on this journey, Terrill had brought her to the mounts that he had tethered at the edge of the forest and had told her to introduce herself. "Horses," he had said, "bear us of their own will. We must ask their permission." And he had gone off to inspect their packs then, leaving her alone with the animals. She knew instantly that the dapple gray was named Cloud, and the roan, Nightflame.

The two mares regarded her curiously. Miriam almost felt that they looked within her. "My name is Miriam," she said. "I'm . . . a healer."

Cloud and Nightflame waited.

"And . . . and . . . I'm an Elf . . . in a way. It's hard to explain.'' The horses' brown eyes held her. There was too much happening. Her anger still raged, but it battered impotently against the starlight.

When you can love him . . .

Sympathetically, Cloud nuzzled her.

"Will you . . . will you bear me?''

The horses deliberated, but when Cloud took the sleeve of her tunic in her teeth and shook it softly up and down, Miriam did not need the physical confirmation. She had already heard: *I will.*

Near midnight, Terrill signaled a halt. "There is a clearing ahead,'' he said. "We will rest there.''

"I'm not tired. I don't think I have to sleep.''

"You did not sleep last night. The circle of waking has closed for you, but I think it would be wise for you to take an hour or two. In any case, we must have a care for those who bear us.''

He touched Nightflame and moved on. Miriam followed him to the clearing, and together they brushed the horses and found them grass and water. After a simple meal, Terrill spread a thick quilt on the ground and gestured Miriam toward it.

Miriam spread her hands. "I really don't think I can sleep.''

The Elf examined her for a moment. "You were thinking about Mika some distance back, were you not?''

She looked away. "And about myself.''

Terrill gestured again at the quilt. "I will fetch your cloak. Sit. It is May, but the earth is cold under the trees.''

He wrapped her in her gray cloak, threw his own about himself, and sat down before her, cross-legged, knees almost touching hers.

"You have been losing your need for sleep ever since Varden changed you,'' he said, watching her. "You are . . . still changing.''

She met his eyes. "I know.''

"How do you feel about that?''

She hesitated. "It's hard to say.''

"Are you frightened?''

"Not anymore.''

"Happy?''

"Yes."

Terrill's eyes flickered. His fair hair, falling softly to his shoulders, framed a face that, like Varden's, would not have been out of place on a woman. "I will ask you to sleep later on. For now, I want to teach you something else. Give me your hands."

She did so, and when he took them, she felt a warmth spring up within her: a gentle, golden glow.

"Now find the stars."

She closed her eyes. There they were, clear and bright, as always.

"Miriam . . ." she heard his voice in her mind. "Miriam, your nature has changed. I called you Elf this morning. I do not think that I was overly premature in doing so. Before, just after Varden transformed you, you fought both the starlight and yourself; but you grew nonetheless, and as you slowly accepted yourself, you grew more quickly. You seem to be able to do many things instinctively, which is good, for I would not know how to teach them to you. But there are some things I can teach: I can show you something of what we are . . . of what you are now. Here, though, I work somewhat blindly, because what has happened to you has never happened before. It is an indication that your nature was, from the beginning, receptive to ours. And I think it is also a mark of the Lady's favor."

"Who is the Lady?"

"Simply: everything," said Terrill. "That is part of what I want to teach you this night. Are you afraid? Will you go where I take you?"

She watched the drifting starfields. Growth. Changes. She found that she was smiling. "I trust you."

"I do not think I have heard those words from you before."

"I've been thinking them. For a long time."

The stars drifted in silence. Then: "It is well. Find a star that pulls you in its direction."

Mentally, she turned, searched. The gleaming patterns of light shifted and settled. There was a bright, blue spark ahead of her, calling. "I see."

"Reach out to it. Do not fear: where you are going, you are safer than you have ever been in your entire existence."

"All right . . ." She reached, and the star reached in return, grew quickly until it filled her sight, blanketed her in incandescence. There was a sound like the roaring of ocean waves, and then she was standing in the midst of a grassy plain. Above her, a night sky blazed with unfamiliar constellations. Before her stood a Woman who was robed in blue and silver. Her hair was dark, Her eyes were clear and gray.

The Lady looked at Miriam, and the healer bowed deeply to Her. She felt Terrill beside her and was grateful for his presence. "We call Her *Elthia Calasiuove*," the Elf said softly. "She is . . . everything. The trees, the horses, the ground beneath us, the sky above our heads. I am She, as are you. But you know this."

"I . . . I know now." Her throat felt dry. She had seen Her before in David's carving, but that encounter had been, for all its immediacy and power, distant. Here now was immanence. Here was divinity. Here was the reified existence of compassion and love made manifest.

"She wears this form for our convenience," Terrill continued. "In this, we are privileged, and we love Her dearly. As She loves us."

"But . . . what . . ."

The Elf's face was tranquil, as though here, under this strange sky, in the presence of this embodiment of immanent love, he could forget past grief and old pain. "She made us," he said simply. "She *is* us."

Miriam turned to her. "You've helped me," she choked. "In the forest, and before. I think You've been with me from the beginning, but I didn't know it. In the church, I said that I'd serve You. And I will. But now that doesn't seem like much to give You. It's all I have, though."

The Lady spoke. "In giving yourself, child, you give everything. And therefore am I honored." She came forward and stood before Miriam, her gray eyes mirroring starlight.

"My Lady . . ." Miriam gestured at herself. "I . . ."

"It is well, child."

She was slowly becoming an Elf. And that was good. Everything was good. "Do you . . ." Miriam's vision blurred with tears. She felt Her hands upon her head.

"Be at peace . . . Mirya."

When her vision cleared, she was sitting with Terrill on the thick quilt. Stars twinkled through the canopy of leaves. Terrill's face was calm, peaceful.

"As I said," he murmured, "we are privileged." He released her hands, and she felt suddenly tired, as though sleep were, after all, a good thing, something that she needed in order to absorb what the Lady had given her, to progress a little farther on this strange journey that had started on a stone slab under the moon, or even before. . . .

Terrill went on. "Because of what we are, because of our nature, it is good that we see Her in this way. Elves do not merely believe: we know. And what you have seen tonight is the knowledge. But do not forget this: She is you. She is I. Everything that you touch, everything that you see is, at once, both part and totality of Her. Because She loves us, She wears a particular form, and we can go to Her. But do not be mistaken. She is everything, and everyone." A smile softened his face for a moment. "But you know this."

Head tilted back, she was looking at the stars. Yes, she knew it. She could never forget now. "I think I'll sleep for a while."

She saw everything.

The world was before her, intricate and varied, changing from moment to moment in the Dance that went on in all things. She saw the lives of people, of plants, of animals; saw the teeming, human built cities and the slow, graceful fertility of forest and lake.

A fish leaped, and the ripples that spread out upon the waters of Lake Onella mirrored the trembling of the wine in a chalice lifted in that moment by an aged priest celebrating his last Mass in a hamlet in Ireland, were mirrored in turn by the unfolding petals of a flower passed—dying even in the act—from the hand of a Poor Clare to the hand of a priest in a garden in Sicily. And in like manner, the ripples of lives spread, expanding in interconnected lattices of starlight more intricate than any flower, than any ripple of water, than any liquescent trembling of candlelight upon wine.

And, as if she were a falcon rising above the land, her awareness expanded, her keen sight perceiving everything in every minute detail: soldiers lighting torches in a barracks; molten gold in a crucible; nervous horses rubbing against one another; a harsh-voiced tinker throwing a pot at a mud-spattered woman; a palace built of marble in the alpine highlands; Russian peasants gathered around a stove, drinking . . .

. . . trees, stretching off and away for miles, giving way to grasslands that in turn gave way to the sea. The world turned beneath her, an immense, imponderable weight that she suddenly held in her mind as though she held a ball in her hands . . .

. . . and then, further, the sun glowing behind her and the moon to her right, wheeling with the days, the months, the seasons. The stars were above her head, beneath her feet. She turned and looked into a universe that went on forever.

And she felt it all. She was the fish, the ripple, the poor Clare, the flower, the gold, the soldiers, the horses, the forest, the grass, the sea, the earth, the sun, the stars, the infinite.

For a moment she understood. The Lady was an emblem only. Miriam knew that. But she knew also—she did not merely believe—that She was absolute reality: a part, the totality, of everything . . . including Miriam of Malvern.

But even as she strove to grasp the unity and love that was offered her, she felt them both slipping away, the connections riven apart by white-hot wedges of passionate rage. In moments, the width of her vision had narrowed once again to herself: bundled in a cloak, curled up on a warm comforter under the trees, memories of rape and torture burning in her mind.

She awoke sobbing.

Chapter Twenty-eight

It was still dark, and as Miriam's tear-filled eyes cleared, the faint swirls that swam in her sight coalesced into stars. She was in the clearing. An hour had passed since she had lain down, perhaps less.

"Beloved?" Terrill knelt beside her, concerned.

She shook her head, passed a sleeve across her face. "I'm just an idiot. That's all."

"Can I help?"

She shook her head. "It's me. It's just me." As usual, she had passed from sleeping to waking without any transition. She was simply conscious once again of the clearing, the trees, the scattering of leaves about her, the breathing of the horses a few yards away. She felt Cloud's thoughts: *Blessings on you this day.*

Smiling in spite of her sorrow, she looked up to the stars. One glowed with the hue of a summer rose. "What star is that?" she said suddenly.

Terrill turned his head, his pale hair whispering in the night air. "We call it *Mirya,*" he said. "It is named after a word we use for the sudden blooming of a flower. It is something of a flower itself, for it changes in brightness day by day."

She remembered then.

"That's the star Natil talked about," she said. "It's what you've all been calling me on and off. And the Lady called me that last night."

"I heard."

"What did that mean?"

"She confirmed your name." Terrill stood and picked up a corner of the comforter, and Miriam rose and helped him fold it. "Miriam is a human name," he said. "Mirya is

Elvish." He put a last fold into the comforter and tucked it into a small bag. "It is fitting: the sudden blooming of a flower."

Miriam stared at the star. *Mirya.* "Terrill," she said suddenly, "am I going to have anything left of myself after all this?"

"Meaning?"

"My body's changed. My mind's changed. Now I'm losing my name. What else?"

He was tying up the packs. "I am not sure you will like my answer. You will have to lose your anger and your hate."

It was as though he had read her dreams and knew precisely what had dragged her away from love and union. She felt the tears start again, stifled them. "I know."

"I will help as I can."

But his words, though sincere, were infused with a feeling of impotence, as though Terrill knew well how little his assistance was really worth in the face of a task that she had, in the end, to do herself.

They let the horses rest for several hours more and set off just at dawn. As the lavenders and blues of Miriam's night vision yielded to the vivid colors of the day, she noticed that they were now not far from the forest's edge. Where the trees thinned, she could see the North Road that led through Alm and Saint Blaise and wound among the scattered villages.

"What about the other Free Towns?" she said. "Do your people visit them, too?"

"Rarely. But we will stop in today. Saint Blaise is an hour's ride ahead, and the mayor there, George Darci, knows me a little. I saved him from a wild boar once. Do you know him?" Terrill glanced back, one eyebrow lifted.

"No. We've never met."

"All right." The Elf turned back to the road. "He is still frightened of us a little, Mirya. Pray, do not speak sharply to him, for I do not wish to see him melt."

"I . . . I'll try to rein in my tongue."

Terrill smiled over his shoulder. "There is my good Elf."

After a while, Terrill turned off the hidden path and passed onto a human trail. Across broad fields filled with a springtime growth of crops, Miriam could see Saint Blaise.

Saint Brigid was a town, a village. Saint Blaise was a city. The northernmost of the Free Towns, Saint Blaise was the connecting link between the independent cities of that region and the feudal territories to the north. Traders of every sort met in its marketplace, and as its fairs had year by year grown in size and revenues, so had Saint Blaise grown in wealth and esteem. The purity of its coinage was a standard throughout Adria, and only the most hardened inquisitor could find any objection to it.

Miriam touched Cloud, and the horse halted at the edge of the trees. Her lips pursed in wonder, she stared at the bright tiled roofs of the city, the spires of the guildhalls, the colorful banners that flew from the top of the council and mayoral buildings.

And then she caught the sense of fear.

"Terrill."

The Elf had halted beside her. "I feel it. I suppose we should not be surprised. Aloysius Cranby's journey to Saint Brigid doubtless included a stop here."

"What do you think it is?"

Terrill did not answer for a minute. Miriam knew that he was looking to the stars, feeling through lifelines and probabilities. "There are strangers in the town," he said after a moment. "They are unwelcome, and armed. I think the war may have already begun, but I want to find out more. If we are traveling north, I do not wish to have difficulties at my back. To my mind, a town in the grip of the Inquisition is a very palpable difficulty. I will talk with George."

"Is it wise to go in there?"

"It would be unwise not to." He dismounted. "Fear not: we are Elves. We are known for . . . being ingenious."

From their packs they took clean but nondescript garments without elven devices of any sort. Miriam looked with distaste at the gown. "I'm supposed to wear this?"

He smiled. "You are becoming spoiled, Mirya." She noticed that he used her elven name freely now. The Lady had confirmed it: the matter seemed settled for Terrill. "You will have to put off your sword also. Be at peace: fighting is not what we want right now."

She had become used to the weight of the sword, and she felt naked without it. The idea of entering a potentially hostile town without a weapon frightened her, but reluctantly, she wrapped Rainfire and put it with her pack when Terrill hid the baggage.

"Are you not well?" he said.

"I don't like this." She gestured at her hip. "This isn't Saint Brigid."

Terrill thought for a moment. "Perhaps you are right." He reached into a side flap of his pack, took out a long dagger, and handed it to her. "Hide it among your skirts. Once, I made the mistake of leaving myself unarmed. I will not do so again, nor will I allow a friend to."

Dressed simply as a young husband and wife, they crossed the fields, came upon a road, and approached the south gate of the town. There were many people going in and out, and the men at the gatehouse seemed bored with their task. Miriam did not have to turn to the stars to know that they were among the strangers Terrill had sensed.

"Shake out your hair, Mirya," said Terrill. "Make sure your ears are covered." Miriam reached up unthinkingly and realized that Terrill had cause for his words. Hurriedly, she arranged her tresses. Terrill himself gave a flick of his head and his hair settled evenly.

"Casually, Mirya. Find your stars, and watch the gate-keepers' inattention. It is time you learned fine control."

The life of the town was a complex knot among the webs, but Terrill guided her awareness to the strand in question. She watched it fade in and out, and when it dimmed to near invisibility, Terrill calmly took her by the hand, flicked the penny toll into the basket by a guard's arm, and led her past the men's unseeing eyes.

On the surface, the town seemed quite normal: vendors hawked their wares, shops were open, housewives chatted beside the well. But the fear was there. It stuck in the back of Miriam's mind like a sooty cloud, glowed in her aware-ness like a hot stove. One of its focal points, she saw, was the mayor's residence.

In many ways, the mayor of Saint Blaise was just another citizen, and his house was neither overlarge nor ostenta-tious. At present, the windows were unshuttered to let in the fresh air, and Miriam caught a glimpse of well-made hangings in one of the upper rooms.

"Glance at it, Mirya," said Terrill softly, "but do not stare. Observe, instead, the men lounging against the wall on the far side of the street."

There were two there, dressed rudely, like poor city folk. But Miriam saw the webs that connected them with the house. "Spies."

"It is so. Come. Up a street, and then to the right. We shall approach from the back. And keep your ears covered."

Miriam was surprised by the alley. In contrast to the reeking, open sewers that made up the back ways of the northern cities, it was quite clean. The kitchen door of the house did not appear to be watched. Miriam examined the webs and found nothing. Terrill, approving, confirmed her observation.

The Elf knocked at the door. It was opened after a minute by a serving girl in a brown smock, her face flushed from the cooking fire and her dark hair tied back severely.

"Good morning," said Terrill.

"I'm sorry, sir. We have no positions open." The girl was nervous. She was not looking at them, and the fear clung to her like oily smoke.

"Dolores," said Terrill, allowing his Elvish accent to come through plainly, "be at peace."

Then the girl actually saw them, and her eyes grew round. "Oh, dear God! Terrill! Oh, God, please come in!"

They entered, and she shut the door behind them. She leaned against it and passed a hand over her face.

"There is fear in this house," said Terrill. "What has happened?"

"Oh, Fair One," said Dolores, "the churchmen have been through the town, and their soldiers came in disguise. They've been questioning people, and Mistress Janet is up in Hypprux, and the mayor and his lady are left without their daughter—" The words tumbled out, sliding over one another in her haste to be rid of them. "—and I'm so worried about Janet. She's but a mite of a girl, and what would they want with her in Hypprux?"

"Easy, maiden." Terrill laid a hand on Dolores's shoulder and helped her to a stool. She buried her face in her hands.

"It's been dreadful here. His lordship won't talk to any-one about anything. Stays holed up in his study, he does. Lady Anne won't eat. The house is so . . . so . . ."

"It is the fear." Terrill spoke gently. "Now, did you tell me that George is in his study?"

"I did, Fair One."

"Take us there, please."

"He won't see anyone, kind sir."

Miriam spoke up. "He'll see us. Don't worry."

Dolores stared at her, frightened, then rose and curtsied deeply. "You do us honor, my lady."

"Just take us to the study."

Dolores led them up two flights of stairs to a wooden door. "All right, Dolores," said Terrill, "thank you. You can go back to the kitchen. We will do what we can."

She nodded at them and scampered down the stairs. Ter-rill knocked at the door. "My lord!"

"Go away, and have done with you," came the reply. Miriam wondered: the voice sounded vaguely familiar. "I gave orders that I was not to be bothered."

Terrill shrugged and lifted the latch. The door swung open on well-tallowed hinges. A man sat at a desk, his back to them, his head bowed.

"Orders," said Terrill, "sometimes grow outdated."

The man turned, almost as startled as Miriam. This was the fat man that she had healed on a cold, rainy night in Hypprux, who had given her his money and his cloak. The mayor of Saint Blaise! No wonder his cloak was so fine! No wonder it bore the insignia of the city and the Towns!

George, though, did not recognize her. How could he? The little healer who had mended his ankle had been dead for almost a year, having taken her own life out of de-spair. . . .

The thought gave her a queasy feeling. She had an aware-ness of the Dance, but here was someone from the past come back again, as though a familiar partner, swept away by one turn of an estampie, was now back with a new step, reaching out a hand for her to take once again.

George has risen quickly. "Terrill." He came forward and took the Elf by both hands. He looked wasted, wan, as though sleep had been elusive for many days and grudging with its rest when it actually came. More lines had been added to his face, and they had not come from laughter. "Unlooked for and in time of sorrow you come," he said. "Forgive my harsh words."

"Forgiveness is found within yourself," said Terrill. He took Miriam by the hand. "Mirya, this is George Darci, mayor of Saint Blaise. George, Mirya is a kinswoman of mine and a healer."

The greater status that Terrill's introduction had accorded her was not lost on Miriam, nor was the mayor's deep bow. But she was still flustered by this apparition from her past. "Blessings on you," she stammered. "How is your ankle?"

"My ankle?" George was genuinely puzzled.

Miriam shook her head slightly. "No matter. Be at peace."

"Would that I could."

"Speak to us," said Terrill. "You spoke of sorrow. Was it brought by Aloysius Cranby?"

George sat down on a carpeted chest. "That bastard. That bloody bastard." He looked for words, and in the silence, Miriam heard, through he door at the other end of the room, the sound of a woman sobbing hoarsely. "It was on the first large market day after the thaw," the mayor said. "There were many people come here from all over the country, and since we hadn't heard of any overt preparations against us, we were caught unawares."

The sobbing continued.

Terrill spoke. "From what Dolores said, I assume that the bishop and a number of soldiers infiltrated the town."

George nodded. "Quite a lot of soldiers. Swiss archers, many of them, but many more are of the sort who never wear mail, but spend their time in the taverns and the town squares, listening. Cranby and his two friars came up here and told me that they knew of my dealings with Elves and witches. They brought some fairly irrefutable evidence with them."

"Evidence?" Miriam was almost afraid to ask. The Dance was turning spiral-wise, cycling back to the beginning. She realized with a sense of unease that her purpose in this northward journey was to enter the very dungeon from which she had escaped months before.

George pointed to a peg on the wall where hung a familiar dark green cloak. "I gave that cloak to a little lass in Hypprux," he said. "She was a healer, and she'd been tortured. She healed my—" He stared for a moment at Miriam, who was transfixed by the sight of the cloak. "Healed my ankle."

Terrill gently slid his arm around Miriam's waist.

"I had no idea whether she got out of the city or not, but obviously, she did. Cranby's men found my cloak in the possession of a witch just outside of Furze. Apparently, the girl had stayed with the witch."

"She's not a witch," said Miriam. Trembling slightly, she took down the cloak, examined it, felt again the warm wool, ran her slender finger over the embroidery. "She's a midwife." *Oh, dear Lady! Mika!*

"As I thought," said George. "In any case, they confronted me with the cloak, and there wasn't much that I could say."

"And what is the situation now?" said Terrill.

"The soldiers are still here. And the spies. And Janet . . ." His lip quivered, and he covered his face with his hands.

Miriam put the cloak back on the peg and knelt beside the man, her arms around him. "Easy, my friend."

George sobbed. "They've sent my daughter to live in the Chateau in Hypprux. Ostensibly as a guest. Ostensibly to further her education. In truth, she is a hostage. To ensure my cooperation."

Only half-aware of what she was doing, Miriam closed her eyes, let the light of the stars fill her. She realized suddenly that she was giving the mayor strength. George's sobbing quieted slowly, and he regained control.

"Peace, friend, peace." Stars. She felt the flow and soothed as she could, healing him for the second time. *And he's part of Her, too. Everything is. . . .*

When she opened her eyes, George was looking at her. "So I am required to be a spy myself," he said, "or my daughter will take the consequences."

"To whom are you to report?" said Terrill. "The men in the street?"

"Are they still there?"

"They did not see us."

"The soldiers at the gate?"

Terrill snorted softly in reply.

George nodded, relieved. "Actually, one of Cranby's agents stops in once a week. He's due soon."

Miriam stood up. "It may be the bishop himself who is due soon," she said, regretting for the hundredth time that Kay had not stayed her hand.

Terrill regarded her levelly. "Do not expect Cranby to return. He is dead."

It took Miriam a few moments to understand. "How do you know?"

"Varden is my brother. I know."

Miriam thought of Varden. The healer. The Elf who had put his sword away forever. In seconds, any joy she felt at Cranby's demise was eclipsed by her sorrow at what that action must have cost Varden. "Oh, dear Lady."

She went to the cloak again, took it in her hands. The Dance was infinite, infinitely varied. A single step was enough to alter it. She had played her part. So had George. Mika was a partner, as were Varden, and Terrill, and Janet, and Charity. . . .

The list could have gone on forever. Indeed, the list would have had to encompass the universe in order to be complete. "Tell me, Lord Mayor," she said softly. "If you had known what would come of your gift of a cloak to a little, mutilated girl, would you have, nonetheless, tendered the gift?" The golden threads in the embroidery glistened at her, weaving, crossing.

George looked as if he were trying to guess the meaning behind the strange actions and questions of this Elf maid. "My lady," he said, "I would have, regardless. The girl was cold. She needed help. She had given me help. How could I do anything but give in return? Dear God, if she had been willing, I would have taken her into my own house!"

The emblems had blurred to Miriam's eyes. Slowly, she put the cloak back on its peg. "I am sure, my lord, that the girl, in her own way, is grateful to you."

Again, from outside the room, came the sound of weeping.

"And who is that?" said Miriam. She noticed that Terrill was watching her, examining her, analyzing her; but this time the look in his eyes was one of tenderness. *A little further,* he seemed to be saying. *Only a little further. Please . . .*

George bent his head. "Lady Anne. My wife. Janet's mother. It's been hard on her." He hesitated. "I would guess that you are traveling north. Toward Hypprux, or maybe beyond. Could you . . . is there any way that you could see that our Janet is well?"

Terrill answered dispassionately. "How much of what we have said here will you tell to Cranby's agent?"

George's head snapped up. "Upon my word, nothing."

"In spite of the fact that if you are discovered, Janet will suffer?"

"Terrill!" cried Miriam. "What are you doing?"

"It is well, my lady," George gasped. "He has a right to know. No, Terrill, I will say nothing to the bishop's agent. But I will trust that you and Mirya and the powers of your race will see to it that you leave unnoticed so that I will not be found false."

"So be it," said Terrill. "We do indeed travel to Hypprux. Other matters call us there."

"And we will see that Janet is safe," said Miriam. "I give my word."

Terrill glanced at her. His eyebrows lifted for an instant, then settled. "Let us go then."

In the other room, Anne sobbed again.

"A moment, please," said Miriam. She had touched George's heart, and she felt that her own had widened as a consequence. When she looked about the room at the cabinets, the desk, the racks of carefully rolled documents, she saw in everything beginnings, potentials. Even the rushes on the floor were full of promise.

There was need in the other room.

She went to the door, opened it, and stepped out into the hall. Anne's crying was louder now, and it came from behind a curtained doorway. Miriam paused. She was intruding, but . . .

Lifting her hand, she pushed aside the green velvet drape and entered the bedchamber. Anne was lying facedown on the white bedspread, her head cradled in the fold of her arm. The window was open, and the air was fresh, warm, scented with early spring.

Miriam shook her hair back so that her ears were visible. Calmly, she let the starlight take her, felt her identity begin to slip, did not fight. In the back of her mind she saw a flicker of blue and silver. "Lady Anne," she said softly.

The woman lifted her head. Blond and blue-eyed, she reminded Miriam of Elizabeth, and when she thought of Anne's daughter Janet, hostage in a strange city miles to the north, she consistently visualized Charity in that role.

Anne caught her breath. "Fair One . . ."

"Be at peace," said Miriam. "I'll see that Janet is safe. But for now, let me help you." She extended her hands, and after a moment, Anne pushed herself up and grasped them.

Chapter Twenty-nine

The day was growing hot when Terrill and Miriam turned their horses once again onto the hidden path that led northward. The trail here was broad enough for two to ride abreast, and Miriam remained at Terrill's side as the sun passed noon and westered. Terrill was thinking, his sight turned within himself, and he appeared to be paying little attention to her, but he spoke up suddenly near the middle of the afternoon. "What did you do to Anne? For that matter, what did you do to George?"

Miriam herself had been silent since they had left the city. She felt subdued, calm. The starlight had flowed through her instinctively, and the widening she had felt in her heart had remained. She felt as though the morning's ride toward Saint Blaise had been made by a different person.

She looked at her hands and wondered for a moment whose they were.

"What did I do?" she said. "Strength. Comfort. Aid." She tipped her head back, looked at the leaves against the sky. "What else are we here for?"

"I am . . . impressed." There was affection in his voice. "And grateful. I watched you give yourself to the light."

A little further . . . only a little further . . .

"I gave myself a little," she said, "but it wasn't really much. Healing comes easily for me. I've done it all my life. Fighting, though . . ." She shrugged, tossed her hair back over her shoulders.

Terrill rode in silence for a while, then reined in his horse. "We have not eaten. We should stop for a moment."

"We won't make very good time if we do."

"I have some preparations to make."

His voice was as analytical as it ever had been. Miriam

noticed the chill of the light in his eyes. She shrugged again and they dismounted where the trees were thin. Miriam was doffing her pack when Terrill's voice rang out harshly.

"Mirya! Elf!"

The urgency of his tone made her to drop her pack and whirl. A wooden sword was streaking at her head, and she only just managed to get her hand up in time to catch it.

Terrill was already leaping in, and Miriam had but a fraction of a heartbeat in which to link with the stars before he was upon her. As she watched the potentials change and shift, she realized that he was moving at full speed, that his strokes were going to be at strength.

Which made Hoyle's swordplay seem infantile in comparison.

Terrill's face was a mask of indifferent concentration as she parried his blow. Her wooden sword splintered along its edge, and she winced. Terrill spun to follow up. Head shot. Parrying again, she swung Terrill's sword down, kicked it away, and swept her foot behind the Elf in hope of catching him off guard.

No luck. Terrill leaped clear. At the same time, he was swinging for her open side. Irritated, Miriam blocked hard. This time it was Terrill's turn to flinch.

But in the back of her mind, Miriam was almost frightened. Terrill's charge had come out of nowhere, and all that told her that he was not bent on taking her life was the fact that he had tossed her a wooden sword instead of challenging her with steel.

She was angry also. By what right . . . ?

Terrill was driving in again, and her anger flowed into her block. Both blades splintered and broke.

Terrill flashed out his sword. "Draw, Elf."

She had no choice: his first stroke was already coming. Rainfire slid out of its sheath just in time to block a cut at her neck that would have taken off her head. "What the hell are you doing, Terrill? Dammit, this is live steel!"

"So it was with Hoyle, Mirya." He was moving, turning, feinting, attacking. She could not believe his skill, but she had little time for belief or disbelief. Terrill somersaulted back, rolled to his feet, cut at her legs.

The starlight saved her. She danced out of the way, but

the vision was draining her strength into an abyss of fatigue, and her sight was blurring at the edges. Terrill, though, showed no signs of letting up. She knew that he could go on like this for hours. Was he going to kill her then?

"Elthia!" she cried, bringing up a sword that seemed of a sudden to weigh tons. *"Me ya ciryo!"*

"You are picking up the language. Interesting." Terrill was not even breathing heavily. Miriam was gasping.

She had no strength for anger anymore, for every particle of her being had to be given over to the Dance and to her sword. She lost cognizance of everything save Terrill, the changing potentials, the stars.

Feint, parry, stroke, counterstroke . . .

. . . leap . . .

. . . and she forced herself on through the weakness that mired her feet and weighted her arm. She dragged starlight into her body as she dragged air into her lungs.

There was no time for anger, no time for anything.

Too weak to attack, reduced to parrying, she doggedly blocked Terrill's battering swings one by one. Nothing escaped her. But if she weakened more . . .

And she knew she would weaken more.

Her mind blurred into the Dance until she was no more than an expression of the pattern that went on in and about everything. As she reached for more starlight, she reached out to a larger portion of the Dance. She felt her heart widening again, expanding, filling.

A blue-white star burned in her mind. Or maybe it was she that burned within the star. She did not know. But what awareness of herself she had left she threw into it, and the flare nearly knocked her unconscious.

But everything came back then. Terrill, the forest, the grass under her feet, the blue sky, the sound of running water a half league away, the moon, the stars . . . the Lady . . .

She was no longer Miriam. She was the Dance, and Terrill was the Dance also, and as her sword came up, weaving in and out of the shifting pattern of life and death, Terrill's blade was leaping forward once again. Effortlessly, she blocked . . .

. . . and counterattacked.

Sword to sword, face-to-face, they fought in the middle of the clearing, dancing in and out, matching speed for speed and strength for strength. There was no fatigue, there was no advantage to either: the Dance was flowing with itself, and there could be no victor.

Simultaneously, they stopped. Terrill nodded, bowed, sheathed his sword. "Good."

Her fatigue was gone. The forest went on around her. The world, the universe went on around her. But though her awareness returned and she could again call herself Miriam, she was not, she knew, the Miriam to whom Terrill had thrown a wooden sword.

She felt the starlight moving through her. Change . . .

"What . . . was that?" Her voice sounded odd. A different inflection had, it seemed, become a part of it. Memories floated in dim recollection. Something about a sparrow hawk, and about Terrill when he did not sorrow . . .

She shook her head, trying to clear it, but it was already clear.

"Now you know what it is like to fight without anger," said Terrill. "I wanted you to know. I wanted you to lose your fear of giving yourself. I wanted you to learn to use the starlight vision so that it would not drain you. But it was your anger that most concerned me."

"I'm not giving anything up," she said. She had focused too long on her goals, and her responses were almost automatic. "I have things to do."

"I have no objection," said Terrill. "I ask only that you act without anger." He smoothed his hair with a flick of his head. He was not even sweating. "This was the last chance I had to teach you. I am sorry the lesson had to be so forceful."

She was surprised that she was not more angry at the form the lesson had taken. She felt, instead, rather calm. "Try what? To dissuade me?" Still, she heard the alteration in her voice.

The Elf's mouth tightened for a moment. "I wonder sometimes if you ever listen to me. You killed Hoyle, and you intend to kill again. But each time you draw sword you create a potential for your own death, and anger makes that potential all the greater. I have done my best to fulfill my responsibility not only to you, but also to those whom you may fight, for in teaching you, I have a hand in their fates. So."

She felt the grief in Terrill clearly now, the starlight linking them, opening lines of sympathy and communication. For an instant, for the first time, she could read Terrill, and the emotion she saw there shook her.

"Know what it is that you contemplate, Mirya," he said softly. "Life is precious. Any life. Maybe the Elves realize that more than humans because we are fading. Men come and take away our homes. And they take away more than that also: they take away our world, our time. We are immortal, but we will fade, dwindle, dissolve. Our lives will end in a manner that humans cannot understand." He looked up at the sky, absently felt the back of his neck. "We will eat and move on. Nightflame and Cloud must forgive us."

She still felt the emotion in Terrill, and it made her feel empty, unfinished. *"Ea sel—"* she blinked, fumbled for words that she knew. "I'm sorry."

Terrill had bent over the packs, but he straightened at her first words, and the look in his eyes made her wonder who he was seeing. "I had to do something once, too. I will tell you this: It brought me no happiness."

"Did it bring you anything?"

His eyes were sad. Softly, he touched her cheek. "It brought . . ." He faltered. "It brought me sympathy for you."

She put her hand to his.

"That is why I agreed to teach you."

"Terrill." She looked into his eyes. Starlight and starlight. Potentials wove together, split, reformed. She felt them, contained them all within her widening heart. "Thank you."

"I hope you can say that when your tasks are accomplished." Leaning forward, he kissed her lightly. "Be at peace."

"I . . . I can't say what I'd like to say. I wish I knew your language."

"Our language," said Terrill gently.

Miriam dropped her eyes. She understood now what inflection it was that had entered her speech.

"I will teach you." He went back to the packs. For a moment, before she went to help him, she stood with her hand against her cheek.

Chapter Thirty

Dusk: the sun gone down behind the Aleser Mountains two hours since; and Malvern Forest darkly shadowed, leaves turning into gray and silver shimmers among the branches, streams fallen into darkness. The evening star was rising in the east. Saint Brigid was full of candlelight shining from unshuttered windows.

A single lamp burned in the church, and Kay was kneeling just within the spill of light. His eyes had grown no less red since Miriam and Terrill had departed, and his hands were sore and blistered from digging graves for Hoyle and Bartholomew.

His voice rose softly in the darkening church as he intoned an antiphon that he had learned long ago from an old Cluniac in Maris. Feeble but genial, the last of an order that had been dissolving in a haze of gracious ornament for over a century, the old man had sat him down in the deserted choir of the cathedral and had taught it to him slowly, showing him how to coax the last small nuance out of the rising and falling syllables of the chant.

It had always had a place in Kay's heart, but these days he was singing it constantly; and he had made one small but potent alteration in the words that held as much significance as the fact that ever since that terrible last morning with Aloysius Cranby, he had chosen to kneel not before the altar, but rather at the feet of David's carefully wrought statue of the Lady.

"A porta inferi,
erue Domina,
animam meam."

Over and over, the words followed one another. Maybe through this plainsong he could find some solace in a world that was speedily going mad. Or send strength and protection to a young woman traveling far away on a journey that could not but end in blood—her own or others' he did not know . . . was afraid to think.

A hand came down on his shoulder so softly that he did not even start. Charity stood behind him. How quiet her footsteps had become these last two days! His voice trailed off into the whispering silence of the nave.

"You have not eaten today, Kay," she said.

"I haven't?" He blinked at the statue. "I guess I've forgotten."

"Your father thinks you will blow away in the first strong wind. He wants you to come home for dinner."

"Has Varden come back yet?"

"He has not." The priestess tugged at Kay's soutane, and he rose, rubbing the tears from his cheeks. "Sana has not heard from him."

"Do you think that the bishop . . . ?"

"Aloysius Cranby is dead." Charity said the words without either joy or sorrow. Her eyes flashed in the lamplight, and Kay knew that the starlight was growing on her.

"He's dead?"

"It is so."

He put his hands to his face again. "Then we're lost."

"You don't know that for sure."

"Everything's going to hell. Everything that makes up the Free Towns is being lost."

Charity only watched him.

"There are too many changes . . . everything's changing . . ."

"I am aware of that, Kay." She smiled, and the flashing of her eyes turned into a twinkle.

Kay stared at her. Yes, she had changed. "How do you do it?" he said. "You've gone through—what?—two transformations in your life—"

"Three," said Charity. "I worked leather once."

He had never heard her refer directly to her previous existence, and her calm tone shocked him.

Charity led him out of the church. "You need to eat."

"What about you?" said the priest, frightened. "Did that go away? Are you still human?"

"Human enough," said Charity. Her smile was warm, and though it was tinged with starlight, it was still mortal. Human enough.

"How do you stand it?"

They walked down the street that led to the smith's house. "How do I stand it?" Charity mused. "I never thought about having to stand it," she said after a time. "I'm here, and there's a reason for me to be here in just this way. If I don't know that reason, then obviously I'm also here to learn it."

The indigo sky was deepening to velvet black, and she looked up at the stars shining above them. She smiled again, as though her meaning were plain for Kay to grasp and have for himself if he would only reach out and take it.

"There are many things I have to do," she said. "And I can do them. There's meaning in that. Meaning enough for me."

Meaning. Varden was watching them, listening to them, his awareness slipping through the quiet town as it had drifted through forest and field a short time before. For a moment, he lingered at the door of the smith's house as Kay and Charity entered a warm room filled with firelight and lamplight, and then he returned to himself, to a hill that rose above the trees and gave him a clear view of Malvern from north to east to south.

Once, he had brought a broken-spirited healer girl to this same place and had tried to tell her about renewal. He had failed. He had come here tonight to try to tell himself about the same thing. And he had failed.

Meaning.

The very nature of all his kind cried out against the mere marring of a leaf, and yet he had, swiftly and deliberately, left a corpse lying faceup on the road. Cranby's spine had fractured with a dull vibration that he could still feel in his hands. He could still see the bishop's face filling with a mild surprise that ebbed away into the blankness of death. And most terribly of all, he could look at the Dance and see an emptiness that would more than likely be filled by warfare and blood.

Meaning.

Charity was right. Of course she was. But what meaning was there in these interlaced webs of maybes and might-bes that he could see weaving through himself, through the Free Towns, through the world? Varden looked ahead and saw the webs branch into futures so numerous that their images blurred with complexity. He saw the end of the Free Towns, watched the face of the land change as cities grew and highways leaped from one settlement to another.

It did not matter what he or Miriam or anyone did: the time of the Elves was drawing slowly to an end. Varden could see plainly the lifelines of his people fading, growing weaker with each passing year until they were only a soft, dissolving shimmer among the stars. There would be legends among humans, of course, and stories, and confused and puerile tales of beings who dwelt in sylvan immortality until, for some reason, they were no more; but the Elves would be gone, the forests empty.

Meaning.

What meaning could there be? What meaning was there in Charity lying in the middle of the street with a fractured skull? What meaning in a lecherous friar with his throat torn out on the village common? What meaning in a fat priest turned into a pig? What meaning?

And yet it all led inexorably toward a future without his people. The world was leaving them behind.

His own failure combined with the fate of his kind, and he rested his head on his drawn-up knees and wept for everything that lived and died without any certainty that it would live again. The darkness that was not obscure to his eyes grew around him, and the moon rose in the east.

And as the wash of moonlight spattered the hill and the forest with silver, he felt arms about him, and a head was pressed to his.

"Why do you weep?" She said.

He tried to gather his feelings into words. "I weep," he said after a time, "because we seem to be at the end of everything. Humans will go on, to be sure. But for Elves— what we care about—it seems to be the end."

"The same could be said of summer roses when the cold season threatens."

"Roses do not think as do we."

She was silent for a time. Her arms remained about him like protecting wings. Together, She and Varden looked off across the forest to the plains, and beyond to the moon that was ever rising.

"What is it that you want, my child?" She said finally.

"I have lost the meaning," he said. "It was all well when Elves were everywhere and the land was fertile and humans lived upon it in peace. The meaning was clear then. But humans grow and increase, and Elves fade. I cannot comprehend Your pattern, my Lady."

"Humans and Elves are two, Varden," She said. "But both are my children. Look ahead. Far ahead. Not one of my children shall be separate from Me. I have been with you all from the beginning, and that shall not change. Look, Varden. Follow the Dance into the future, and know that I love You."

She left him then, Her steps silent; and he did as She had asked, reaching his awareness out to the corners of the world, tracing the Dance in all its complexity and variants.

The Elves faded. The world changed, changed terribly. Skies turned gray, forests vanished. Men fought wars that spanned continents. Machines conquered the land. Humans sank into a mire of their own making.

Darkness grew on the horizon of future ages, but it was not the quiet, safe darkness behind the stars. This was unlight, denial, and ending from which nothing could ever arise again.

Yet, in the face of that blight, there was a gleaming. In a far country of blue skies and high mountains, the starlight flickered into life, and men and women who had thought themselves human suddenly found that there was old blood in their veins, blood that was awakening, blood that had been spread throughout humanity through the love of Elves and humans here in these last days.

Meaning. Winter into spring.

Roxanne was nursing Lake, getting ready for bed, when she heard her front door open and turned to find Varden taking off his cloak. He came to them quietly, smiled, and wrapped his arms about them both. She noticed that in one of his hands was a wood rose, and when she met his eyes, she saw a single tear make its way down his cheek and fall on Lake's forehead, where it glittered, a small pearl in the firelight.

Toward midnight, Terrill and Miriam reached the northern border of the forest. Beyond, the land was rolling and grassy, spotted with small stands of trees, patched with plots of cultivation. Farther on, the grasslands gave way to the immense flax fields of Hypprux.

"We have a full day's ride before us," said Terrill. "The road is straight and well tended, but we will have to be careful when we use it. If we can reach Hypprux by tomorrow evening, we can set about finding Mika. With the Lady's blessing, she will be safe by sunrise."

"Tomorrow evening . . ." Miriam stroked Cloud's neck absently. "That won't give us much time to prepare."

"We will be prepared enough."

"What about rest?"

"Rest? Terrill smiled. "Mirya, how tired are you right now? Are you sleepy?"

"No, not at all,' she said, and then smiled self-consciously.

"We are stopping now only for the sake of the horses."

They found water and sweet pasture for their mounts, and then they walked out into the grasslands and watched the stars together. A cricket chirped nearby, and Miriam felt it as much as she heard it. Her perceptions were still expanding, but they were becoming so natural to her that she hardly noticed.

She held Terrill's hand. "Will I be immortal, Terrill?"

A long pause. "You will. As immortal as our people can be in this age."

"That frightens me."

"Really? Many humans would give great wealth to be immortal."

"That's because they don't think they can really get it."

"I had not thought of it in that way." Terrill sounded relaxed, as though any thought of breaking into an armed keep the following night was far from his mind.

The night wind was cool, the skies clear. They lay on

their backs with their heads almost touching. Miriam saw a familiar star.

"Look, Terrill. There's *Mirya.*"

"You will notice that she appears brighter tonight."

She glanced at him for a moment, detecting double meanings in his words. but his face was serene. "I do," she said. "But . . . " She reached out and took his hand again. "But it looks as though she could do better."

"True."

"And . . ." What did Terrill think of her? She recalled the grief that hung about him, the time he had rushed out of the Elves' cave. But she remembered also the stirring she felt in her heart and the touch of his hand on her cheek. "And what happens when she reaches her full brilliance?" she said softly. "She fades?"

Terrill rolled over and looked down at her. "I . . . I pray not."

Right now, she did not want to kill, she did not want to hate, she did not want to fear. Simple existence was her goal, and indeed, she had attained it. "You pray," she said. "For her or for me?"

He did not meet her eyes. He was resting on his elbows, and he stared off at the forest a thousand yards away.

"You lost your beloved, didn't you?"

His lips moved soundlessly for a moment. Then: "She was murdered before my eyes. I could not save her."

"And you . . ."

"My brother and I planned and executed vengeance. We were most exacting. Afterward, Varden set aside his sword forever. And I retained mine."

"Forever?"

"Until I can find renewal." He put up his hands and rested his face in them. "She was tall, beautiful. She could heal, and she could sing. We grew together over the years. We were inseparable. And then one day we were captured by men of Aurverelle. We were unarmed. They had their sport with us."

Miriam went cold. "Did they . . . ?"

"That," he said into his hands, "and worse. And then they killed her slowly. I managed to escape only after she was dead. I bore her body away with me."

"But you went back."

"I did. And Varden and I slew them." He dropped his hands, looked down at her again. "Her name was Mirya."

"Terrill . . ."

"Now you know why I counsel you against your actions. I have slain in anger, and I am no happier as a result."

"And if you hadn't acted, how would you feel?"

He did not reply.

She touched his cheek. "I'm a healer."

"My wounds are beyond your powers."

"I care about you, Terrill."

His eyes were misty. He seemed to look beyond her. And she knew now what he was seeing. "And I about you, Mirya."

Gently, she reached up, took his head between her hands, and brought his lips down to hers.

Just at daybreak, they bathed in a swift stream that passed near the forest on its way east to join the great River Bergren. The water had tumbled down from the heights of the Aleser and retained the chill of its origins in the glacial melt. Gasping from the cold, mildly chagrined at having forgotten her hairbrush, Miriam sat on the bank and dried her hair with her fingers as she watched Terrill standing motionless and naked in the stream, tracking fish and, she imagined, talking to them.

The day was warming up when they rode north. Miriam was wearing, once again, her brown shift, and Terrill was in the garb of a country man, a broad straw hat on his head. Clad as he was, his elven face looked ridiculously young, and they both laughed about the children being allowed out on the road.

At sext, they heard the crisp peal of distant church bells. They rested the animals at the side of the road and lunched on bread, wine, and cheese. Hypprux lay under a hazy cloud in the distance, and they could smell the odor of the retting pools, dank and pungent. Terrill wrinkled his nose. "I cannot understand how anyone would want to live in that stench."

Miriam was looking at the city. She had seen it in much this same way when she had first journeyed toward it on her way down from Maris, skirting the shores of Lake Onella, sleeping in ditches and in the decaying wrecks of abandoned outbuildings. She had been fleeing persecution in the north then, living with the constant taste of fear. Now she was returning, changed.

She shook her head ruefully. "It's the seat of power for this part of the land."

"The seat of *their* power, maybe."

"Do you know the city, Terrill?"

He gazed at it with a sense of weariness. "In a way that is of no help to us. I visited it once."

"I don't understand."

"It was centuries ago. The city was much smaller then, and less preoccupied with power and wealth. There was another time also, but that was before it was even called Hypprux, when its folk lived in houses built on log pilings set into the river."

The idea seemed outlandish to her. "When was that?"

He thought for a moment. "About thirty centuries before the establishment of the Church." He took a drink of wine from the skin and passed it to her. "You know Hypprux much better than I. Tell me."

She picked up a stick and drew on the ground. "Hypprux is built on either side of the River Tordion. It's also surrounded by a wall."

"We will have to scale the wall."

"Is that wise?" She drank. "Wouldn't it be better to enter the city through the gate, watch the Chateau for a day or so, and find out the ways of the place? I got out by sheer luck, and I'm sure getting in will be no easier."

Terrill took the wineskin back from her. "Such a course of action would take time. I daresay neither of us thinks that Mika has that time."

"I know, but—"

"We will scale the wall tonight." He tipped his hat down a little to shade his eyes. "You have never explained to me how you escaped."

She shrugged. "The guard forgot to lock me in one evening. He thought I was unconscious. But I crawled out and found my way to a sewage pit. When a man came to empty it, I hid in his cart along with the turds. Before he tossed everything in the river, I climbed out.''

Terrill took her hand gently. "You have a great heart," he said. "You are very brave."

"Bravery had nothing to do with it," she said. "I had nothing to lose, Terrill."

He seemed to see beyond her for a moment, then: "What about the river?"

"There are chains across the river," she said. "But they're for boats."

"Guards?"

"Well . . . yes, guards."

"Are you skilled at rope climbing?"

"I don't know. I haven't tried it recently. I've changed. I'm sure you've noticed." She grinned at her own joke.

"It will be difficult," said Terrill. "Do not doubt that. It will take all our skill and knowledge. Have you given any thought to Janet Darci? We will have to look for her also. Once inside the keep, though, we should be able to slip about somewhat."

"But how do we do that without knowing the routines?"

"Elves are known for being ingenious."

She knew that he was laughing at her a little, but she did not mind, because it was the kind laughter of a friend and a lover.

A few miles from the city walls, there was a small wood. There they cared for the horses, ate, and waited for night-fall.

Miriam sat with her back against a tree, watching the city, idly fingering the pendant that Varden had given her. The last time she had entered Hypprux, she had been a prisoner: completely at the mercy of the men who bound her and, later, mocked and tortured her. Now, however, she was re-turning changed, armed, taking power for herself.

Hypprux was an opponent to be weighed, examined, judged; an intricate set of puzzles that she—dispassionate, cautious—had to solve, one at a time. But she could do it. She knew she could. Mika would not die. The dungeons of Europe had claimed too many wise-women, too many heal-ers, too many witches. Perhaps she could not do much, but she could save one. Years before—and how many she was afraid to guess—Terrill's lover had been tortured and killed. Miriam was about to even the score.

In spite of her feelings of dispassion, she knew that her anger still existed, but she had begun to understand that it did not stem solely from her violation. Rather, it grew out of her society as a whole: the Church and the overlords who controlled, violated, raped the body and soul both; the serfs and commoners who consented to the abuse. She herself had once consented, but no more. She had withdrawn her permission, had, in fact, withdrawn herself from the human race. She was connected to the mortal world still, as she was with everything, but she would not allow it to direct her.

"And tonight, Miriam," she murmured, "we do some directing of our own."

Miriam. Her name. She turned it over in her mind, pushed thoughts of anger and revenge aside, examined it dispassionately. Terrill had been calling her Mirya for the last day, and though she had not complained, neither had she really accepted the name as her own.

Out across the flax fields, the city of men rose up, hazy and prosperous. She felt herself opposed to it, distant, even disdainful.

"I am Mirya," she said suddenly. The name settled into her mind, and something else settled, too. She felt more herself, and she had a greater sense of her own presence. Yes, she was here, under this tree—the grass beneath her, the air about, the sun above—an essential part of the webs, the patterns, the Dance that formed the being of the Lady.

"Mirya," she said again. She nodded; a short punctuation. It was done.

Chapter Thirty-one

Elven, silent, clad in forest hues of gray and green, seeing by starlight, shimmering softly in one another's eyes, Mirya and Terrill approached the walls of Hypprux. They skirted the silent masonry until, at some distance from the main gate, Terrill laid a hand on Mirya's arm. "Here," he said under his breath. "Before we proceed, find your stars and give yourself to them. Your life will depend upon them for the next several hours, perhaps for the next several days."

She understood. When she had asked about learning the ways of the Chateau earlier that day, she had been thinking as a human. As an Elf, she moved with the Dance, aware of all its intricacies. What need had she of learning when she could reach out and be?

She slid into the vision of the stars and saw a lattice of interweaving lifelines, probabilities, potential futures. She felt the guards on the parapet, felt also that inaction had dulled their eyes. Patrolling the walls of Hypprux, it seemed, was a job, nothing more. Safe, secure, routine.

Terrill reached back to the small pack he was wearing and extracted a grappling iron and rope. When the guards were distant, he threw the hook silently, expertly. It lodged in the crenellations sixty feet above their heads. He gave the rope a good pull to make sure it was fast and then put it into Mirya's hands. "We have a few minutes before the guards come back," he said. "Take your time. Be gentle with yourself."

With a silent prayer to the Lady, she hauled herself up foot by foot. She surprised herself: her ascent was silent, though slow, and the guards' attention was still dull and distant when she pulled herself over the top. Terrill followed in a third of the time, and he coiled the rope and put it and the iron away.

"It should be relatively simple now to reach the street level," he whispered.

"True. Providing we don't meet anyone on the stairs." She put her hand to Rainfire for reassurance, though a fight was not what they wanted.

"Do you know this area?"

"The walls? No. I know the streets, though."

Keeping to the shadows, they skirted the inner parapet until they came to a gap. Stairs led down. There was a small fire at the bottom, and men sitting around it.

"Armed too," said Terrill. "I hope this is not standard practice in Hypprux." They continued around the wall.

The second stair they found was better, but there was a man coming up. Mirya did not need Terrill's gesture to know that the guard would not look at a small corner at the base of a tower. They hid in the darkness. The man passed them by.

The stairs led to a back street, unlit, the houses shuttered and quiet.

"One of the poor sections of the city," said Mirya. "This street to the first turning, right, then all the way to the Street of Saint Lazarus, then left to the heart of the city and the Chateau. The Cathedral of Our Lady of Mercy—" She paused at the name, shook her head, continued. "The cathedral is hard by, and the dungeon is beneath the keep. There's an outside wall to the Chateau grounds, and an inner curtain wall to the keep, then the outer wall of the keep itself. We'll have gates to pass."

"Walls we can climb, and gates we can pass," said Terrill, "but we do not want to stroll openly along the Street of Saint Lazarus. Do you know the back streets?"

"Given my previous status, I know the back streets best."

Mirya led Terrill through alleyways and passages between dank buildings and squalid houses. They paid little heed to the sounds of people arguing in the upper rooms, men laughing and shouting, the complacent snoring of a justified sinner; but then, ahead, they heard scuffling footsteps.

"Someone," hissed Terrill.

Mirya had already seen the strands of starlight shift into

new futures. She stepped into the darkness of an enclosed
church porch. After glancing at the crucifix and hesitating
a moment, Terrill followed.

It was only a drunkard. He staggered by without noticing
them.

Mirya peered after him. "I have to keep reminding myself that they can't see in the dark."

They moved along winding, crooked streets that were
clotted with refuse and dung. The way opened out a little
as they drew near to the Street of Saint Lazarus, but they
waited long minutes before they could be sure of crossing
the main thoroughfare unseen.

With Terrill following soundlessly, Mirya found her way
along more streets and alleys, picked up the shore of the
River Tordion, and came at last to the northwest side of the
Chateau. The outer wall was coated with a layer of white
plaster and was higher than that of the city. And better pa-
trolled.

"The palace grounds are large," she said, "and there are
many outbuildings. Here, we're closest to the keep." The
river flowed at their backs, muddy and polluted. She found
herself wishing for the quiet streams around Saint Brigid.

"The gates are shut for the night," said Terrill. "We will
have to climb again. Although . . ." He indicated a small
door in the wall. It was of heavy oak studded with bronze
nails. "We might keep that in mind for our departure. We
will most likely be carrying Mika."

"I'm a healer."

"Can you heal minds also?"

The question hung. Mirya thought of what weeks of torture might have done to Mika's soul. But she recalled George
and Anne and what she had done for them. "I think so . . .
now. . . ."

"Let us bear the door in mind, though. I can see that it
is barred, but not customarily guarded."

They waited long minutes before it was safe to throw the
grapple. As it was, Terrill missed the first time, but he
caught the iron without a sound. The second time, the hook
held. "Again." He gestured to Mirya.

She climbed faster now. She was learning the trick. In

another minute, she and Terrill stood on the wall, looking down into the torchlit grounds.

The spring gardens were bright with flowers of all kinds, the paths carefully tended, the grass immaculate. Mirya wrinkled her nose. The studied formality of the design seemed an affront to the plants that grew there. But across ninety feet of essentially open ground was the granite curtain wall of the keep.

They followed the parapet around to the front. It looked easy: the gates were open.

Mirya consulted the webs. Just within those gates was a maze of intersections of high probability. Images and futures blurred into one another. "We'll have to climb again."

"Not so," said Terrill. "We must take the gate. Look."

She felt around the top of the curtain wall, then checked the lattices. Climbing, she discovered, would bring instant discovery.

"I still don't see how we can get in the gate."

"That is because your training is not complete. We must descend, though. Guards are coming."

They found stairs, descended quickly, and hid among some sacks of gravel piled at the edge of the gardens.

In contrast to the surrounding city, there was activity in the Chateau. Government, machination, and plot all worked throughout the night here, and when sunlight failed, torch and candle supplied illumination. Mirya knew that they would be seen by human eyes if they were not careful.

As they crouched in the shadow, the main gate of the Chateau opened briefly. A man entered, minced up the walk, and entered the gate in the curtain wall. He was a dainty fellow, with elaborately curled hair and a droop of a mustache.

"Probably breaks the hearts of the court ladies," said Mirya.

"Or the bones of the prisoners."

"How do we get in?"

"Watch . . . watch the patterns."

She settled back for what she assumed would be a long wait and allowed the webs to shine clearly. She felt the ongoing life of the keep pulsing, moving, shifting. Far within its walls, though, there was something that disquieted her. She started to follow those strands to their source, but Terrill's voice brought her back.

"You will notice that there is an opportunity a short time from now. The probabilities are not good for us, though. We will need better."

"So, what do we do?"

"We make them better."

For a moment, Mirya thought that he had gone mad, but a distant star blossomed and flared. She snapped back to normal sight long enough to see that Terrill was deep in concentration, his fists clenched, and when she went back among the stars she found that he was feeding light into the matrix of ifs and might-bes, shaping the future subtly but distinctly to his own ends.

There was suddenly a short gap in the vigilance of the gate guards. Terrill opened his eyes. He was shaking.

Mirya stared at him. "What . . . was that?"

"Something I did not show you before."

"I didn't know you could do that."

"I can, and you can also." Terrill took a deep breath, and his strength returned. "But think before you do it: what is it that you intend to accomplish? And are you willing to take the consequences and the responsibility for altering them?"

Someone started laughing riotously at the main gate of the outer wall. Two men walked out of the keep's guardhouse and strolled across the garden to see what the matter was.

"Now," whispered Terrill.

Even the torchlight seemed to flicker and die down slightly as they raced for the gate, bent low, taking cover behind the rosebushes. Terrill passed through the entrance first, grabbed Mirya's arm as she arrived, and pulled her farther into the courtyard and down the wall.

"Mere moments . . ."

The laughter continued and a soldier walked out of the door to the keep, across the court, and through the gate they had just passed. He was smiling, as though he anticipated hearing a good jest, which, Mirya knew from the webs, he would.

In a moment, they were in the keep, down a short corridor, and at the base of the tiled stairs that led to the upper floors.

"I know this place," said Mirya. "I was hauled up and down these stairs many times." The memory made her legs ache and her spine tingle.

"The ladies' quarters?"

"Up. The floor above the council chambers and the judgment room."

As they ascended, they heard music. Trumpets, horns, drums. The music grew louder as they passed the kitchen level and the sitting rooms. A third level. "What is this?" said Terrill.

"Dining room. Servants' quarters off to the side. You can smell the reek of dinner."

"I can."

"Council chambers are the next level, then the sleeping rooms." Again, something in the lattices made her bristle unconsciously.

She had little time to puzzle over it. The music peaked at the council chamber level, but the lattices had altered, the futures had shifted, and on the floor above and the floor below, a whiff of torch smoke entered the stairwell. There was movement on the steps.

"One coming up, one coming down," said Mirya, catching her breath. She saw that the fourth-level corridor was vacant. There was no time to judge better, and Terrill was already moving. They darted down the corridor and into a window embrasure.

Hearts beating, they leaned against the marble wall. Ascending and descending torches drew near, paused, and passed. The music rose behind a door ten yards down the hall. If the men on the stairs said anything, it was lost in the din.

When the stairwell was dark again, they prepared to continue, but a sudden fanfare of trumpets and horns blared into the hallway. The doors were thrown wide. Bright light spilled into the corridor.

Terrill glanced through the open window. "Outside, quickly. There is a ledge."

They scrambled out and perched. The ledge was shallow, but the wall was dark. They would not be seen. "It is good to know that this is here," said Terrill calmly. He made himself as comfortable as possible and examined the layout of the surrounding courts and walls.

Mirya settled back into her stars, and her heart slowed. Inside, the fanfare ended and men began passing down the hallway. Again, she felt the strange discomfort. Very close now.

"Baron Roger," came a smooth, urbane voice.

"What do you want, mouse?"

Mirya stiffened, eyes wide. Terrill glanced sharply at her.

"The papal legate, Monsignor Gugliemino, has been pressing for information. The letter that Clement received from the priest in the Free Towns was obviously effective in arousing a certain amount of suspicion, and the legate is not at all satisfied that Bishop Cranby is unavailable for questioning."

"So? What of it? The bishop is most certainly not available. For all I know, the bishop may be lying in the middle of some road with his throat cut."

"Dear Lady." Mirya's fists were clenched, and she was staring, unseeing, into the night.

"Mirya . . . what is it?"

"That's him." She was whispering, but there was savagery in her voice.

The men who were speaking stopped by the window. "A pleasant night, Baron."

"For us, maybe." Roger of Aurverelle laughed, and Mirya's anger flamed white-hot.

"I intend to have her questioned further tonight."

"Do that. And tell that Hound of God to get some results. Gugliemino wants a reason for Clement to sanction the crusade, and so we have to give him something."

"I will see to it." The accent was of Maris: cultured, urbane, a trifle ironic.

A dry laugh. "You don't have much choice. Do you, mouse?"

"My lord, I would ask—"

"That I speak to you as an equal, *mouse?* That I actually treat you like a man?"

"Baron Roger, I do have recourses. Conceivably, the Church would be grateful to one who—"

There was a thump, and the man started to strangle.

"You will have me to deal with should any thoughts of that nature come into your head," said Roger. "Do you understand?"

A muffled, choking sound.

Do you?"

The sound of a body falling, then: "Aye, my lord."

Mirya was fighting herself, for her instinct was to plunge back through the window, sword drawn. But that would have been the action of a fool, and she did not need the lattices to tell her that. Painful though it was, she held herself in check, eyes blazing, knuckles white.

"Are you certain?" said Terrill.

She nodded, shifted her weight a little, peered cautiously into the corridor. There, a few feet away, she saw the man who had raped her, the man she had sworn to kill. He was dressed in blue silk and red velvet. His surcoat bore the arms of Aurverelle, his gold chain of office those of Hypprux.

The man with whom he had been speaking slowly picked himself up off the floor. No one moved to help him. Mirya recognized the dandy who had entered the keep. "I shall be downstairs," he said.

"Be sure you get something out of that whore tonight," said Roger. "Monsignor Gugliemino doesn't sound like a patient man."

The hum of idle conversation arose once again. Roger and the fop moved off down the hall, the music resumed, and the corridor cleared.

Mirya crouched on the ledge, unmoving, rigid. Terrill examined her uneasily. "Mirya?"

"I'll be all right," she said softly. "Now I know."

Chapter Thirty-two

They climbed back into the corridor when the last footfall had died away. Mirya stood, forced herself to relax, searched for the stars from which she had been torn by the sound of a terribly familiar voice. Her anger burned in her belly like a mugful of vinegar, and her hand dropped to the pommel of her sword.

"Servants will be coming along soon," said Terrill. "We must act quickly."

Mirya was still fighting herself. The man's unexpected appearance had taken her completely off guard, and she was stumbling in her efforts to regain balance. The stars. Where were the stars?

Terrill touched her. She did not notice. With a glance at the hall and the doors, Terrill put his head to hers. Mirya's night sky blossomed suddenly, and she sighed. "My thanks."

"You will have to get over that," he said. Footsteps in one of the rooms. "Come."

Their feet were silent on the parquetry and on the stone stairs. Up one level were the sleeping chambers and the women's rooms, but they paused to examine the lattices and to listen.

The upper floors were quiet. "Sleeping or vacant?" whispered Mirya.

"It is hard to tell. Ah, there is a guard."

There was indeed, but something seemed odd about him. Mirya wondered for a moment, then: "He's asleep, the idiot."

"Have you any idea how you will look in on Janet?"

She shrugged. "I've got an idea. It's not very subtle, though."

Terrill smiled. "Whatever is appropriate is good."

"The guard is asleep. I'm . . ." She looked at him as though for permission. "I'm an Elf. . . ."

Terrill nodded.

"I should be able to avoid waking him."

"More than likely," he said. "Be at peace."

Words came to her lips unbidden. *"Ai, Elthiai, ea sarena . . ."*

Terrill's eyes flickered at the Elvish words. "Have no fear. When you are in the room, call up your memories of George and Anne and find Janet's lifeline through them."

She climbed slowly, cautiously. Her soft boots were soundless, but accidents could always happen, and no amount of attention or foresight could guard against every possible permutation of future potentials. She chose her steps with care, kept a hand on Rainfire.

She watched the guard's awareness. He was deeply asleep, beginning to snore. Images flashed by her: a hard day sweeping out the stables, a heavy dinner, a little too much wine. . . .

Silently, she slipped by him, pushed aside a thick hanging, and entered the large room. Curtained couches lay against the walls, and the sleepers were breathing softly.

I am here in the Chateau . . . and George and Anne are in Saint Blaise, but we are all a part of the Dance . . . we all stand upon the same earth, breathe the same air, partake of the Lady. . . .

She let her mind drift back to her memories of the mayor and his wife. Gradually, George and Anne became as distinct as if she were looking at them. They were sleeping, Anne curled up against her husband. Her head was on his shoulder and his arm was about her.

She realized that she was seeing them—across distances, miles, forests, rivers—as they were at that moment. *Peace. Be at peace. The hand of the Lady be on you.*

For a moment, she wondered at the faint shimmer that seemed to surround Anne as she lay with George, then she descended into their thoughts and waited quietly until she saw Janet. In moments, she saw—felt—the girl's birth, her growth, her joys, her sorrows . . . the sparrow she once kept as a pet. . . .

Shaking herself away from individual memories, she concentrated instead on Janet, examined her life, felt it until it was familiar and easily recognized.

She slid back to the present and the Chateau and cast about in the room, sorting through the patterns of the sleeping women. For a minute, she was afraid that Janet was not in the chamber. But then she saw the familiar weave of her life, and she slipped silently down the length of the room and stood over the sleeping maiden. Janet was safe, and as Mirya scanned her potential futures, she saw that the girl probably would continue to be so. It was impossible to be sure, but she had done the best that was possible, even for an Elf.

Janet slept soundly, and Mirya was reminded strongly of Lake at those times when the half-elven infant dipped into human sleep. But there was another similarity, too, for Mirya became aware of the shimmer about Janet's body, like the one that had surrounded her mother. And standing in a darkened room filled with the sounds of the even breathing of many women, Mirya knew that in some time long past, there had been love between mortal and immortal, that Janet and Anne could trace some part of their heritage back to the same blood that now flowed through her own veins.

But just before she broke her link with Janet, Mirya saw one future that broke away from the others, crossed a complex network of lines and probabilities, and finally entered a knot where all potentials became obscure and muddled, the same knot in which she would meet her rapist for the last time. Shuddering, she let the vision go and wound up staring at the wall above Janet's couch where hung a small painting of the Virgin.

Blue and white. Blue and silver. She nodded to the painting, remembering the starlight in Her eyes, and slowly, without a sound, she left the room, passed the sleeping guard, descended the stairs. "She's there, and well," she said to Terrill.

"Good. Mika now."

Mirya remembered the dungeon well. It was reached by a back flight of dingy stairs that spiraled steeply down from the ground floor. A guard was stationed at the bottom, always present, watching the juncture of the two corridors that led away from the stairs. At the farthest end of the north passage, around the corner of a short crossing, was the torturer's chamber, large and well equipped. It was located at a good distance from the stairs so that any screams that leaked out from behind its thick door would stay at dungeon level.

Mirya and Terrill left the upper floors of the keep, scanning ahead down the stairwell. Empty. Quiet. The man guarding the entrance to the keep was eating a cold pasty in the porter's lodge just off the doorway. He was vigilant, but he did not see them as they slipped down the stairs and around to the back of the keep.

The door to the dungeon stairs was thick and stoutly bound with bands of iron. Mirya examined its latch and hinges. She did not need the lattices to tell her that they were rusty and would squeak if opened.

"We'll have everyone in the castle down our throats."

"Peace," said Terrill. "Humans, it is true, might, but . . ."

His voice trailed off as he took hold of the latch and paused. Mirya thought that he was waiting for a break in the probabilities of discovery, but it finally dawned on her that Terrill was moving the latch so slowly that it would make no sound.

She marveled at both his patience and his control. In five minutes, he had lifted the latch, and he proceeded to slowly open the door. When there was room, they slipped through. Noiselessly, with agonizing deliberateness, he reclosed the door.

In the fetid darkness of the stairwell, he straightened, wiped his face, pointed down the curving walls. Only then did Mirya notice the cries drifting up from the lower level. They were muffled, distant, almost inaudible, but they were obviously those of a woman.

With anger that had abruptly turned to ice, Mirya centered herself, found her stars, and moved down the stairs. Terrill followed, and he made no comment when she drew Rainfire. He had, in fact, already drawn his own weapon.

Even at a run, they were as silent as they were lethal, and the guard at the foot of the steps looked up just in time to see the flash of an elven sword. He did not even have a chance to cry out. Sprawling into a pool of stagnant water that mixed swiftly with his own blood, his headless body rolled over twice before it stopped, twitching.

Beyond the single stroke that she had placed with calculated efficiency, Mirya paid no further attention to him. She listened, followed the warp and weft of the lattices, then pointed—as she had feared she would have to—up the north corridor.

Screaming. Louder. Demented. But also, in the lulls, there was the incongruous sound of impassioned speech.

Dear Lady!

Ahead, the webs contracted into a blurred knot of indistinguishable events. They could know nothing of what would happen until they were well into it.

"Heavy fighting." Terrill commented almost casually.

The corridor was dark only to human eyes, and they ran northward, reached the crossing, turned in the direction of the screams.

In another lull, they heard a man's voice, shouting, commanding, imperious.

"Confess, woman! Weren't you sodomized by the Evil One? Haven't the Elves shown you how to use this sack of corruption that is your body, this carrion bag of mucus . . . ?"

The iron door reverberated with the sounds. Mirya knew it well. They approached, the nexus of existence and future unwinding in their minds. Moments from now, the crisscrossing strands of starlight turned into hazy nebulosity.

Terrill put his hand on the latch, looked at Mirya. "Are you afraid, Elf?"

She stared at him, incredulous. The screams continued.

"Are you?"

"No."

"Are you angry?"

She could have chiseled through the iron door with her anger, but she forced her voice to be even. "I don't believe that's a legitimate question."

Terrill looked at her. Calm. Analytical. Dispassionate.

Her eyes said it: *Dammit, Terrill, open that door!*

Terrill moved, swinging the door wide. Ruddy torchlight

poured into the corridor along with the stench of vomit, urine, and old blood, but Mirya was already springing through the opening, driving at the men who were suddenly looking up at an unexpected and frightening attack, driving toward the body of a woman stretched on a table in the middle of the room.

The men were clustered, and the first went down within seconds. Webs parted and shifted, potential futures were examined, rejected, or chosen. Mirya kicked an unarmed man away because there was a method to her task, and those opponents who held weapons had priority.

The dandy who had spoken with her rapist a short time earlier was coming in quickly, sword drawn, and his skill had some subtlety: he could be a formidable opponent.

But he had his weaknesses, and Mirya knew them immediately. Bending, she slashed his legs out from under him, then straightened and caught him across the throat. As the spume of blood spattered the room, she spun and slammed Rainfire's pommel between the eyes of the torturer, a man she recognized from her own time in the dungeon. "Old scores, you bastard."

He looked uncomprehending, but his skull had been shattered. Eyes glazed, he slumped to the floor.

Mirya was no longer concerned with him. She was focused instead on the man who was about to hew off the prisoner's head with an ax. Before she had time to move, though, a blur of motion streaked at him, and Terrill ended the threat, doubled back, and finished off a soldier who was bolting for the door to raise an alarm.

Mirya turned and opened a gash in another soldier. He looked down at his wound unbelievingly, as though he would weep. Rainfire ended his sorrow in the next moment.

There was a Dominican present, and he had fled to the far corner of the room. Mirya assumed that he was the interrogator. He was a pale, intense man with dark rings around his eyes from long nights of reading or, she guessed, questioning.

She pointed at him with her sword. "Your time is coming." Then, crouching, she put her entire weight behind a thrust that severed the spine of a captain of the guard that

Terrill was fighting. At the same moment, Terrill's stroke went through him from the other side.

The battle lasted only a minute. Mirya was abruptly aware that the only sounds in the room were the dull whines of the bloody figure on the rack.

"Cut her loose, Terrill, please," she whispered as she turned to the friar. "I'll help in a moment."

She stepped deliberately toward the Dominican, sword ready.

"I will shout," he suddenly declared.

"Shout then," said Mirya as she advanced. "This chamber is deep and isolated so that those above us cannot hear."

He stepped back and bumped against the wall.

"Do you know who you have been interrogating, man?"

"She is a known and confessed witch."

"She is not. Her name is Mika, and she is a midwife and a healer. She is one of the only flakes of gentleness and nobility in a land otherwise infested with men."

The friar held his ground. "You are not going to kill me."

Mirya stopped in front of him. He embodied everything she hated.

His eyes widened with realization. "Please—"

She slashed expertly, economically, reflecting almost with bitterness that he would feel very little pain.

When she turned around, she became aware that the white fire of her healing was burning fiercely. Terrill was trying to comfort Mika, but he looked up as Mirya approached. "Bones broken," he said softly. "Many. She is bleeding within and without. She has lost sight in her right eye, and the hearing of her left ear. She has been burned over most of her body. She is dying."

Mirya shook her head. "The torturer was skilled: he would not have let her die."

"But she is old."

"Yes, she is old."

Her power was coming up fast, burning along her spine, and she had no intention of gainsaying it. She searched among the stars until one called to her, and when she reached Mika, she wrapped her mind about it and put her hands on the mutilated flesh.

A searing burst of passion and energy rocked her, white

light so intense she thought she might go blind. Her hands
were burning.

"*Ai, Marithiai!*" she cried. "*Hyrialle a me!*"

Then she was falling through darkness so profound that
even her elven eyes could not pierce it. In an instant, she
felt Mika's pain and fear, felt the crack of bones, the pain
of red-hot tongs, the agony of dislocated shoulders. But she
was aware also of the star that she cradled in her mind, and
she clung to it, embracing the power and the love.

"*Elthiai!*"

A flash of blue and silver, and the room came back. She
pulled her hands away from the warm, sound flesh that
she had created. Terrill was staring openly at her. "Mirya!"
he said in awe. "Fair One! Healer!"

The midwife's eyes were unseeing, for Mirya had tended
to her body only. Mika whimpered, her pain having become
too habitual for mere physical healing to eliminate it. Terrill
gathered her into his arms, trying to soothe her, but she
strained against his grasp as she had once strained against
the ropes that had held her.

"Be at peace," he said. "You are among friends."

"She doesn't hear you, Terrill."

Grief was heavy in his voice. "I know."

There was another kind of heat glowing within Mirya now,
one that she felt in her heart. It filled her, eased her, comforted her, made her want to reach out to Mika as she had
reached to George and Anne. And she knew that she could.

"Hold her steady, Terrill." Her hands were gentle as she
placed them on Mika's head, and Terrill's eyes widened
again when he realized what she was doing.

Almost immediately, Mirya lost cognizance of Terrill and
of the room. The blackness she had experienced in the physical healing was nothing compared to the infinite and impenetrable void that had opened in the midwife's mind. If
Mika were falling through this, she might well fall forever.

The dark closed around her like a fist. She felt Mika's
terror, felt, redoubled now, the pains and the tortures.
Darkness . . . but there was blood everywhere, and it reeked
in the back of her throat.

Mirya was starting to grow angry, but she caught herself,

quelled it, forced herself to confront the dark, searched for the stars.

Faintly, she heard Terrill's calm voice. He spoke as he had on that first day in the meadow when she had stood before him, tired, frustrated, angry. "Center yourself," he said. "You are here, and I am here, and Mika is here. We stand on the same earth, breathe the same air. . . ."

She was drifting through a night sky then, the stars cold and clear and infinitely powerful. A web flowed among them, but not the web of future and past. Mirya looked at the strands, examined the weave, recognized it as Mika. Her totality. Her being. Parts of it were fragmented by fear and madness, but most of it, the greater part, was intact, beyond the reach of men.

But the parts that were shredded, Mirya could touch, could heal. She seized strands, called upon the stars for strength, and began to reweave the pattern. She worked by instinct, feeling parts of Mika flick by as she fused the lattices, the midwife's memories flowing into her own when she touched them.

Hyrialle a me!

And as she worked, she saw that she had taken on yet another responsibility: for as she could heal, so she could also change. She knew what Mika's pattern should be, and for now, she merely blunted memories and softened the torments. But had she so desired, she could have made Mika eternally joyful, or a genius, or a musician, or . . .

She paused, the last strand mending in her hands.

. . . or elven.

She saw the stars shining through the web that was Mika and knew how she could fuse one into the other and remake the woman's being from the very core. Varden had not changed her own nature deliberately, but for a moment Mirya saw as he must have just before whatever power that burdened him flared into incandescence and bent his will to unknown ends.

For a time, Mirya let herself rest among the stars, soaking up their light and peace, reflecting upon the profound and unlooked-for effects of her transformation. And when at last she came back to the dungeon room, she looked into Mika's clear eyes and sighed softly. "Be at peace, Mika."

"Fair Ones," said Mika, staring with wonder. "Why have you done this for me?"

There was not a shred of recognition in the midwife's eyes. Mirya smiled a little sadly. "Because, wise one, whether you know it or not, you helped me once. And Elves do not forget."

Terrill's eyes were haunted. "It is true," he said softly. "We do not."

Chapter Thirty-three

The cathedral bell tolled matins in the quiet night that had blanketed Hypprux. Giuseppe Gugliemino started up from his couch at the sound, and his thoughts whirled for a moment before he remembered where he was.

He had not been sleeping soundly, and he knew it would be some time before he could drift off again, so he got up, lit a candle from a torch in the hall outside his room, and began to read his office, his voice whispering dryly through the room.

But his mind drifted beyond the words. There had not been a night he had spent in the Chateau during which he had slept well. Clement's suspicions regarding Aloysius Cranby were not popular here in Hypprux, and the closeness of the keep, the surreptitious murmurings, and the tension between Roger of Aurverelle and the marshal all made Gugliemino wonder about poison in his food or a convenient accident.

Who cared if Cranby's mentor had been Jaques Fornier! If Benedict had won fame for burning a few thousand Cathars, what of it? Did Cranby honestly believe that the Throne of Peter was to be bought with blood?

Probably. After all, it had been before.

The candle flickered. A gust from the open window blew it out and left him wrapped in the amber and rose torchlight that the courtyard walls reflected into his chamber.

He gave up on the book. He had been lax with his office for the last eight years, and he could think of no particular reason to become ambitious now. Drawing a bench up to the window, he settled down to watch the burning torches and the movement of men who were just now changing the guard.

Jaques Fornier—that old bloodgutter. And Cranby . . . Clement was probably right: the Elves were an excuse, nothing more. True, they were something to worry about, for even at best their beliefs could only be called heretical, but the demand of the bishop of Hypprux for a full-scale crusade sounded as though it were engendered by thoughts more of gold and glory than of grace.

The stout monsignor had never met an Elf, though he had read the legends and had heard the stories. Here, in Adria, there were said to be many of that immortal race left. And here also, he recalled suddenly, the toll of the Black Death had been felt the least. Most of the people of Adria had been untouched—some had never even heard of the Plague. Demons? Gugliemino doubted it. A mystery of God? Who knew? Perhaps in some mysterious way, the workings of Divine Providence had, for a moment in eternity, settled here in Adria.

Maybe we should just leave them alone.

Up—high up—above the roofs and infinitely beyond the light of the torches, the stars burned, eternal, illimitable.

Mirya's powers had been growing steadily stronger: Mika was neither cold nor tired, in spite of the massive healing she had undergone.

Her clothes, though, were a mess of bloody rags, but Terrill had foreseen the need. He went through the pack he was wearing and extracted a thin, dark blue gown and a pair of soft shoes. "The gown is of wool challis, madam," he said. "The night is not cold, and it should be all you need."

Still half in wonder, Mika nodded and dressed quickly. Mirya went to the door and listened, then watched the patterns forming in the potentials of the keep. She sensed a change in the near future. A glance from Terrill indicated that he had noticed also.

"We have overstayed our welcome," said the Elf softly. He opened the door into the corridor. The sword belt of a dead guard clanked as Mirya shoved the body aside.

Both Mirya and Terrill kept their swords in hand as they escorted Mika down the hallway. Near the base of the stairs, a decapitated body lay in the shadows. It was visible to a human, but Mirya did not call Mika's attention to it. "Wait

here," said Terrill. "I will go ahead and open the door."
He disappeared up the stairwell. Mirya sensed the lattice
changing, and she saw that the probabilities of discovery
were increasing. Multiple futures held the promise of combat within the next hour.

"My lady," Mika whispered.

"Mistress?"

"Do I . . . do I know you?"

Mirya smiled slightly. Was there anything recognizable
about her now? She was no longer even human. "Probably
not."

"There's something about you. . . ."

Mirya sighed, recalling the little house near Furze, evenings under its warm thatch, Mika's poultices, and the anxious look on her face when she bent to change the dressings
on the mutilated legs and raw hands of a healer girl. "We
met once. But I'm sure you don't remember me."

"It must have been a long time ago."

"Ages."

She heard Terrill's voice within her mind. "Get ready."

She took Mika's arm. "Come. The hand of the Lady be
on you." She led her past the inert body of the guard and
up the stairs. Terrill was easing the door open a last inch.

"Through," he murmured.

They slipped into the tiled corridor, and Terrill closed the
door behind.

"Do you see the webs, Terrill?"

"I do. We must choose our paths with care."

As he spoke, someone came up the walk to the keep and
entered the porter's lodge. Voices drifted to them.

"Time to take over, eh?"

"Aye, but he'll want to share my wine, I imagine."

"Harry's always willing to take advantage of a friend!"

Laughter. Footsteps. Terrill pointed around a corner, and
Mirya and Mika slipped out of sight while he, under cover
of the loud steps, whisked open the door and vanished back
down into the dungeon.

Harry's relief approached the door, swung it wide. "All
right, you black devil, I'm coming. You can run into the
arms of that whore you call a wife." He plunked on down

the stairs without waiting for a reply, and the door crashed shut behind him.

The webs were in motion, shifting quickly. Mirya did not like it at all.

The guard from the porter's lodge called out suddenly. "Hannes!" When he did not receive an answer, he also made for the door to the stairs. "Forget his damned head if someone didn't remind him," he muttered.

Pulling the door open, he stuck his head into the stairway just in time to hear a clatter as Terrill dealt with Hannes.

"Wha?" He was drawing his sword when Mirya launched herself at him, Rainfire bright in her hand. A quick stroke, and she kicked the body down the stairs and closed the door quickly. She waited for the muffled thumping and crashing to die away.

After a minute, the latch lifted slowly in her hand. Terrill opened the door. "They must be changing the guard," he said. "We have little time."

"We can go out the same way we came in."

"With Mika? She cannot do what we can."

Mirya grimaced. The defenses of the keep and the Chateau, designed to keep hostiles out, were quite adequate to the task of keeping them in. "What do you suggest?"

"The upper corridors will be clear for a while. At its closest, the curtain wall is about twenty yards from the building proper and is as high as the windows of the third level."

Mirya saw the pattern that Terrill was building up in the lattices and she did not like it any more than the movement in the futures. But they could not repeat their stealthy run through the gates with a human in their company.

They led Mika up to the third level and entered the windowed hallway that passed by the council chambers. There was random motion in the webs, but nothing that indicated a problem . . . as of yet.

Mika looked out and down, paled. "Mother of God." Her hands tightened on the sill and she swayed against Mirya.

"What is it, madam?" Terrill's voice held no impatience.

"I'm afraid of such heights."

"Well," said Mirya, "there's not much else we can do. Can you bear with it?"

Mika looked panicky.

"Mirya," said Terrill, "can you help her?"

She knew what he was asking, and she shuddered. Perhaps Natil could justify altering memories and thoughts, but Mirya wanted no part of it.

Terrill regarded her seriously. "It is the only way."

Mirya spoke with her eyes averted. "Mika, I can help you. I can take away your fear of heights, but I'll only do it with your permission."

"Fair One," said Mika without hesitation, "you rescued me. How can I not trust you? Of course you have my permission."

"Proceed, then," said Terrill. He was extracting his climbing hook and stepping to the window.

With a look of apology, Mirya placed her hands on Mika's head and turned within. She went through the darkness, centered herself, and felt through to the webs that were the midwife. In a moment, she had done what she had to, and she blinked at Mika, who stood serenely before her, smiling. "Thank you, Fair One."

Such trust. Sweet Lady, let me never violate such trust.

Terrill had thrown the hook and made the line fast. A taut rope stretched sixty feet through the air to the curtain wall, and Mirya could foresee that no guards would be along for a while.

But then, looking ahead, she saw the webs explode.

There was an urgency to Terrill's manner when he turned to Mika. "I shall go out first. When I am ready, climb upon my back."

Carefully, Terrill took the old woman. Hand over hand, he made his way across to the vacant curtain wall, then beckoned for Mirya to follow. She did, quickly, confidently.

"We will need the rope," said Terrill. "I will go back and untie it. Mirya, please draw it in, and I shall be along shortly."

"How far can we push this?"

He shrugged. "As far as we must."

"You've seen what happens to the webs."

"I have. But we need the rope. Fool that I am, I did not bring extra."

Without waiting for an answer, he stepped out, balancing on the line like a wire walker, and scampered back to the third level. In a moment, the rope went slack, and Mirya gathered it in.

Minutes went by. Mirya tried to track Terrill through the webs, but the crossings and recrossings were too random, too confused. Even their position at the top of the curtain wall was doubtful. When they had first entered the keep, they had avoided the wall because of the uncertainty, and now, later, the situation was but little better.

A cry. She stiffened, but then there was laughter from the main gate of the outer wall.

More minutes. She understood that Terrill was waiting for a break in someone's attention.

Then, out among the stars, he was talking to her again. "Take Mika down to the outside ground as fast as you can. Use the grapple and rope. Hurry."

Carefully, she fastened the hook and took Mika on her back. The midwife seemed light to her as she inched down the wall in the semidarkness. Mika held on trustingly, and Mirya dropped the last foot and found cover behind the shrubbery. A flick of the rope, and the hook fell into her hand.

But as they waited for Terrill, another voice drifted to Mirya. It came from a window somewhere above her head, from a room within the curtain wall, and it was the voice of Baron Roger of Aurverelle. He was saying something about the guards.

Again, she stiffened, her anger blotting out the stars, and for a minute, she was nearly beyond control. She clenched her hands and bit her lip to keep from shouting curses up at the unseen baron.

I can't afford this. Not anger. Not now.

Terrill was elsewhere. She was on her own. Roger's voice went on, complaining, threatening. Mirya fought herself. The anger was a raging column of fire that twisted through her, enveloped her, tried to force her to its will—

Like her power.

Like Roger of Aurverelle.

The thought was a sharp smack in the face, and it made her fight. Deliberately, she turned her thoughts away from the baron. She thought of Kay. Of Varden. Charity. Terrill . . . of that last night on the borders of Malvern Forest when they had both realized how closely they were linked by the Dance and by their hearts. She closed her eyes, felt Terrill's arms about her again, saw his face above her. Behind his head, high above, glittering like many-colored gems, were the stars.

The stars. In her mind they suddenly flashed again in an endless night sky. Her fists unclenched. The baron's voice went on and on, and there was a sound as though he had struck someone. Mirya would not have been at all surprised if he had. The baron, she knew now, liked his sport, whether it was hawking and hunting or murder and rape. And he was willing to travel for it, whether to the gaming grounds in Beldon Forest ten miles to the north, or to the Free Towns to the south.

Terrill appeared beside her a few minutes later. "I have opened the door in the wall that leads to the river. It took time. I regret delaying so much."

Bent low, the torchlight flickering across the garden paths and playing among the spring flowers, they crept along a narrow avenue toward the river-most section of the Chateau wall. Twenty feet from the door, the lattices gave way.

"Guards! Ho! Intruders! Seal the gates!"

Terrill and Mirya each grabbed one of Mika's arms and hustled her forward. There was no time for subtleties, and both knew that for the instant, all eyes in the Chateau would be turned in the direction of the shouting man who stood at the gate of the keep.

"In the dungeon! Make haste!"

"The fools," said Terrill. They passed through the door. He turned, closed it, wedged it shut.

"The streets of the city will be crawling with soldiers," said Mirya.

"No matter: we take the river. Mika, can you swim?"

"Nay, master."

"Then hold on to me. Mirya?"

"I'll be all right."

In the Chateau, the guards were roused and the reserves

called out. The inner and outer walls were quickly manned, but the soldiers were too late to see three figures slip into the reeking waters, kick out to midstream, and drift, with the current, out of the city, past the chains, and into the open countryside.

Chapter Thirty-four

The first light of dawn found them fleeing southward on horseback, Mika seated ahead of Terrill and held by a strong arm. Nightflame and Cloud were forgiving and understanding both, for though they had been ridden hard for the last several days, still they ran freely, lightly, as though they felt neither fatigue nor resentment.

Occasionally, Mirya glanced back, half-expecting to see some kind of pursuit. There was none. The soldiers of Hypprux had apparently assumed that the intruders were still within the city walls.

Before the morning was half-done, Terrill called a halt for the sake of the mounts, and they rode into the cover of a small wood through which a clear stream flowed. The horses ate and drank, and Mika, worn out from memories and flight, slept soundly. A smile was on her lips, and a dappling of sunbeams flickered across her with the tossing of the branches above her head.

Mirya saw to Cloud's needs, then methodically stripped and washed both her clothes and herself in the stream.

"Hypprux is a pisshole," she said as she worked a stubborn bit of tar out of her hair. "and its river is no better."

"Our point of view is different from that of humans." Terrill looked with disgust at his smeared arms. In the hot sun, the pollution was becoming fragrant, and after checking once more on Mika, he joined Mirya in the stream.

"You say *our*," said Mirya. "In the dungeon you called me Elf. Once you said that I'd have to earn that title. What do you say now?"

He glanced at her, then plunged his head into the water and scrubbed. When he surfaced, he cleared the hair from the back of his neck.

Mirya had waited. "Well?"

"Anger?"

She worked at the tar. "What about you? You still wear that sword after Varden put his away. You fought beside me in the dungeon."

"I was not angry."

"It looked like anger."

Terrill's skin was fine, white, like ivory. He washed slowly, sitting in midstream. "It was not. Someday, you will understand. There is anger, and that is not a good thing. There is also wrath, and when I say wrath, I mean something that empowers, something that ennobles. Anger knows only how to hate and kill. Wrath can choose. I was wrathful. Something precious was in danger of being destroyed, and I had to save it. I had little choice as to my methods, but if I had been given any, I would have considered them carefully."

Mirya still fought with the tar. "Why didn't you just change the futures?"

He laughed suddenly, his hair scattering water in a shower of sunlit drops. "Ah! Why not indeed! I will tell you this, Mirya: every future must be accounted for, and you must take responsibility for all of them. So, as I said, consider carefully what you want before you change the futures." Clean at last, he stood up and brushed water from his body. "But, in answer to your first question . . ."

The tar finally gave way and she tossed it into the bushes. She looked at him expectantly.

He let her wait for a moment, then: "What do you think?"

She dropped her hands into the water in exasperation.

"Well?" He was smiling at her.

"I am as I am. I'm still angry."

"Maybe. But I have been angry also. And in spite of your anger, you acted with dignity and kindness; and you risked your life for love. You healed, Elf."

She felt a tightness in her throat. "Thank you, Terrill."

"It is well." She was clean, and when he reached a hand to her, she took it and stood up. The sun shone warmly and flashed in Mirya's hair. "You have," Terrill said, "farther to go. It will not be easy. But I will call you Elf, and if you claim hearthright, I will not accuse you of audacity."

"It means a great deal to me."

"We all need to belong somewhere."

She dropped her eyes, nodded slowly. A playful trout approached and nibbled at her toes. She thought she recognized it: maybe, once, it had leaped high above the waters of Lake Onella, the ripples it created mirroring the petals of a flower in Sicily. Laughing, she bent and shooed it away.

"What will you do now?" Terrill asked softly.

She knew what he meant. Roger of Aurverelle was in Hypprux, and, apparently, had a good deal to do with both the city and the plots against the Free Towns. "I . . . I haven't decided yet."

"Will you be returning to Saint Brigid?"

"I'll be going as far as the north edge of Malvern."

"You cannot find peace among us?"

"No more . . ." She swallowed with difficulty. "No more than you can, Terrill."

His mouth worked. He met her eyes. "I may . . . I may be looking at my peace right now."

She passed her hands over her face. "I—"

"I do not wish to . . . to lose you."

Even though he did not utter the word *again*, she heard it in the tone of his voice. She stumbled to the shore, sat down on a rock, and mechanically ran her fingers through her hair to help it dry. Slowly, as though shamed by his admission, Terrill followed.

"I'm not she, Terrill."

His eyes were haunted once more. "Are you certain?" he said softly.

"I'm too different."

"Are you certain?"

She understood. She had seen flashes of image and memory that had not been a part of the life of Miriam of Maris. Snatches of the elven tongue came to her at times. Her healing powers seemed no longer something alien, a cruel burden that she was forced to bear, but rather a part of her, a genuine gift. "No," she said at last, "I'm not certain. But I can't find peace through you."

"I know that now."

"Am I ready to fight him?"

For an instant, Terrill looked pained. He sat down beside

her, thought deeply. "I have watched you fight. I have fought you myself. I know what you can do. You have talent that I have only rarely seen before, and then only in the best. And yet, unless you lose your anger, I cannot say. You had difficulty in Hypprux because of anger: you lost your stars."

"I found them again." She told him of the second time that she had heard Roger's voice, what she had done.

"That is good," he said when she finished. "It gives me some hope."

"But you're still not sure."

"I am not. I am afraid."

"You want to see me again."

His voice was barely audible. "I do."

She moved closer, rested her head on his shoulder. His arm went around her. "You will," she said.

"I would like to see you happy." His arm tightened. "I would like to see you at peace."

Once, Varden had offered her paradise: Saint Brigid could have been a haven for her. But she had turned away. Now, something else she wanted was being offered her, and again she had to say: *Later. I can't now. Later.*

Somewhere among the futures, Roger of Aurverelle stood, sword drawn, facing her. She had fought to come this far, and she would not turn back.

"I'll go with you as far as Malvern," she said. "I'll head north then. After a while, I'll come back. That's all I can do."

He watched the stream for some time, his arm still around her, *"Ilme mari yai, Miryai,"* he said at last.

She did not need him to translate. *"Ilme mari yai. Me ya ciryo."*

He turned, held her tightly. "I am," he said. "And I will, someday, again."

She recognized his last statement as a prayer.

Monsignor Gugliemino folded his hands on the table. Roger tried to read him and found that this damned churchman was keeping his expression very carefully neutral, the picture of dispassion, of objective analysis.

"My Lord Chamberlain," said the monsignor, "I find this

very curious. The so-called witch that you claimed held the key to Bishop Cranby's investigation of the Free Towns is no more. Do I hear you correctly? Has she died?''

Roger had tried on many occasions to intimidate this man from Avignon, but even sheer physical size seemed to have no effect. Gugliemino was, Roger assumed, so inured to the plot and counterplot of corrupt papal politics that simple threats held no terror for him. ''No,'' he said, trying to conceal the anger, ''she has not.''

''Well then—''

''She was rescued—taken out of the keep.''

Gugliemino allowed himself to look mildly astonished. ''Rescued? From an armed keep?''

''Elves. It had to be Elves. Those demons can walk on water if they put their minds to it. Bishop Cranby can tell you more about them. He's been collecting information for years.''

''I'm certain that he has.'' The day would be a warm one. Air fragrant with the scent of flowers in the formal gardens poured in through the window, and moisture beaded the legate's forehead. ''But don't you see, my good baron: His Holiness Clement the Sixth sent me here to investigate this matter personally—''

''On the basis of one damned letter from a heretical priest!''

Giuseppe Gugliemino looked genuinely concerned. Roger forced himself again to be silent. If only Cranby would return! Men, women, animals: the baron knew how to deal with them. But these eunuchs, these spiritual castrates who went about in women's clothes—they were something different. Cranby came the closest he had ever seen to being a real man, and that was, perhaps, why they could work together. But the others . . .

The monsignor wiped his forehead with a sleeve. ''I will have to consider all of this, Lord Chamberlain. I was hoping to be able to speak with the witch myself. Personal confirmation is always a good thing to have, as I'm sure you'll agree.''

Roger got up, leaned across the table. In truth, he wanted to shake the miserable priest by the throat. ''Don't you see, Monsignor? This is all the personal confirmation you need.

The marshal is dead, as are several soldiers. Even the inquisitor, Karl son of Hanno, a man of the cloth like yourself, was slain. And who but Elves could get into the keep without raising some kind of an alarm?''

"I believe, Lord Chamberlain, that an alarm was indeed raised.''

Frustrated, Roger sat down.

"And what evidence is there that the deed was not committed by individuals within the castle?'' Gugliemino continued. "Perhaps they are among your soldiers? This would make sense: after all, soldiers would be able to move about the keep without arousing suspicion, they would be familiar with the grounds and rooms of the Chateau, they would—''

"Shut up.'' The words were a muffled rumble.

"—know its routines. I had occasion a year or so ago to speak with a very learned Franciscan, William of Ockham—''

"Shut up.'' The rumble neared the surface, threatened to erupt.

"—who very wisely had said once that entities—''

"Shut up, damn you!" Unthinkingly, Roger grabbed the heavy table and flung it across the room. It fetched up against the granite wall and cracked in two.

If he had been less angry, the chamberlain might have noticed that Gugliemino had paled by a shade or two. Breathing heavily, Roger turned to the window.

"I would like you to speak to Baron Paul delMari,'' he said, forcing the words into some semblance of calm. "The witch practiced her infernal craft in his district for many years.''

Gugliemino cleared his throat. "I have already spoken to the baron. He indicated that he had been paying her to stay in his region as she was a midwife of most incredible skills.''

"Skills gotten from the devil!''

"Skills gotten from her teacher, and from her teacher before her. Baron Paul indicated to me that he did not in all honesty know for sure if the woman were a witch or not. He commented that he had to be guided in the matter by the superior wisdom of . . . Aloysius Cranby.''

The baron leaned on the stone sill, his face thrust out into the sunlight. His head ached, and the light hurt his eyes, but he stayed where he was, because he was not sure that he could look at the churchman again without killing him. "Thank you, Monsignor," he managed. "We will just have to get along without the approval of His Holiness."

"Am I to understand that—"

Baron Roger turned around. *"Get out!"*

The legate rose, bowed calmly in spite of his renewed pallor, and departed. Roger went back to the window. Outside and below, among the gardens, resplendent in a gown of light blue samite, Janet Darci of Saint Blaise walked. Reading as usual.

Behind him, the door opened. "What is it?"

The voice of his page answered. "My Lord Chamberlain, a man has just arrived from Saint Blaise. He reports that Bishop Aloysius Cranby has been found dead on the road south of that city."

Roger kept his eyes on Janet. "Is that all?"

"Aye, my lord. Do you wish to speak with him yourself?"

"Later."

"As you wish, my lord."

Light blue gown, hair like flax, skin like ivory. Janet Darci walked among the flowers, a flower herself, and her image burned in Roger's brain. He did not even notice when the page withdrew and shut the door behind him.

Mika rose in the late morning, and Terrill and Mirya let her bathe and eat before they called the horses and resumed the journey. They pushed on throughout the rest of the day, and by evening they were within the northern marches of Malvern Forest. A short distance away, the hidden path glimmered, but only to the eyes of the Elves.

Mika was tired, and they spread the comforter for her and watched her as she slept. "Kay will need a housekeeper," said Mirya.

"You are not returning to his house?"

"Could I? My way doesn't lie with humans anymore."

"True."

He took her hand, and together they walked under the trees. Mirya looked up at the interlacing branches. Mind, body, and heart, she had changed, and the trees were inviting. She could spend the rest of her existence beneath their leaves, beside a fire, listening to Natil's harp, watching Talla dance. There remained but one last task.

They came to a small clearing, a forest meadow, its grass deep and lush. The starlight glistened on the wildflowers.

"I could ask you once more," he said, but her silence was her answer, and he sighed softly.

They said their farewells then, in the night, and in the morning Terrill took Mika up before him on Nightflame. Even from a distance, Mirya saw that the starlight of his eyes was uneasy, troubled. He nodded to her, and she waved. He turned the horse onto the elven path without looking back.

Mirya stepped up to Cloud.

"My friend," she said, "will you bear me? It's an uncertain journey at best."

Cloud watched her.

"There's a battle ahead of me. I hope it's my last. Will you?"

The brown eyes were sad as they answered: *I will.* Taking up her pack, Mirya mounted and started north.

Chapter Thirty-five

Out along Street Gran Pont, then down the Street of Saint Lazarus to the southwest. A quick turn that led among darkly clustered buildings built over two centuries before, then along a street—little more than an alley, actually—with a plaque at the corner that, under a layer of soot and dust, read DOMINO CROSSING.

Paul delMari picked a path through the puddles of excrement and piles of refuse until he came to a small, run-down church with a green lozenge roughly daubed on both pillars of its tiny porch. Wary of beggars, he kept the rough, brown cloak pulled tightly about him until he was through the door.

The light in the nave was dim, as much from the congestion of buildings pressing up on all sides of the church as from the soot that covered the windows. Above the altar was a crucifix done in the Spanish style, and the half-rotted eyes of the Corpse seemed to follow Paul as he made his way up the nave. He wished for some light, but the only flame he could see was the lamp in the sanctuary burning red as a clot of blood.

He nearly fell over the black-clad figure who stood at the side of the Little Mary. Eyes like jet glittered in the dimness. "Baron Paul delMari?"

"I am he."

"Follow, please."

As Paul followed the Benedictine into a passage behind the altar, there was a momentary lightening of the gloom: a large, roughly dressed man opened the main door, entered, and knelt. Perhaps he was a poor laborer who came to pay his respects to the divine this May morning.

The Benedictine escorted Paul to the vestry, then through

a low archway, and into a small office. A man wearing robes the color of amethyst waited there, small and tensed. Paul's tic throbbed, and the wine he had drunk that morning burned and sloshed in his otherwise empty stomach.

"Bishop Clarence," he said.

Clarence a'Freux bowed slightly. "I'm very glad you could come, Baron Paul." He extended his ring.

Paul pretended not to notice. "I assumed that anything that would take a newly appointed bishop away from his see and bring him to"— he half smiled, indicated the dingy surroundings—"to Hypprux must be important."

Clarence rubbed his hands. "I'm glad you're interested. Please sit." He indicated a chair near the hearth and with his own hands he brought Paul a cup of wine before he dragged up a stool for himself. He sat, poised, like a cormorant inspecting a river for fish. "You were not followed?"

"I assume not." Paul looked into his cup. The wine was dark, venous, and he set it aside, untouched.

"Assume?" The bishop looked incredulous.

"I do not habitually look over my shoulder when I walk abroad," said Paul. Clarence made him itch as though he had scabies. And that one by the door! By Our Lady! "There was no reason for anyone to follow me."

Clarence ran a hand back through his thin blond hair, cleared his throat. "Let me begin, then. My predecessor, Augustine delAzri, was more interested in the hereafter than in the here and now. I differ with him. If the work of Holy Church is to be done, then by necessity it must be done on earth. Therefore we must take no little interest in the affairs of state that go on about us."

Paul smiled. "You would be well received at Avignon."

"Thank you. I was." Clarence glanced sharply into the flames of the fire, snapped his gaze back to Paul. "Word has come to Maris that Aloysius Cranby is dead."

"I believe that's well-known by now. It's certainly no secret."

"What is also known is that Aloysius had very interesting plans regarding the Free Towns. He shared those plans with Roger, Baron of Aurverelle."

"So I . . ." Paul hesitated. After his conversation with

the papal legate about the midwife, he had hoped that his part in this whole affair was finished. He was having bad dreams about it: screaming in the darkness, pleading eyes regarding his own from inches away. His wife would not sleep in the same bed with him now. "So I have heard."

"The thought has come to me, Baron Paul: what will become of those plans now that our dear brother in Christ, Aloysius, has departed us?"

From somewhere outside the room came a noise like the scraping of a boot on the floor. Clarence looked at the Benedictine, and the man slid into the hallway like a shadow.

"I take it you have something in mind," said Paul.

"I do." Clarence chose his words. "I see no reason why the bishop's carefully laid plans should come to naught. And it seems to those in Maris that perhaps Hypprux is striving after too much power in the south. This threatens to upset the balance that has been maintained for the last four centuries. This could lead to"—his milky blue eyes blinked at the baron—"disorder. . . ."

"The here and now," Paul commented dryly.

"Exactly. I am beginning to establish contact with the southern barons regarding this matter. You, my lord, are baron of Furze. Your city would be threatened by an increase in the power and influence of Hypprux. I know that you have some disagreements with Aloysius Cranby's methods. I can assure you that an alliance with me would not be unprofitable."

"You forget something."

"And what is that?"

"Baron Roger of Aurverelle."

Clarence smiled thinly. "I am not overly worried about Roger. He is a brutal man, canny in his own way, but he was only one-half of a team of horses. And his mate lies dead in the harness. He will give us no trouble."

"I should not like to be wrong about that," said Paul.

Clarence shrugged. "Are you with me?"

Paul let the silence grow. The fire crackled and spat with the exuberance of unseasoned wood. The tall Benedictine reentered, took his place by the door, shook his head in reply to Clarence's questioning glance.

"Well?"

Paul got up. "I don't want any part of this. I delivered an old woman up to the torturers a while ago, and I haven't been sleeping well since. Call it the weather. Call it a whim. Call it—" He thought of George, smiled in spite of himself. "Call it the farting of birds. I'm not interested. I'm glad she escaped. The devil take you all."

Without waiting for a response, he stood up, pushed past the Benedictine, and found his own way down the hallway and into the nave.

He was already out in the street when he remembered that he had left his cloak behind. With a shrug at the loss, Paul continued on his way, his feet finding their own way through the garbage. He brooded on the midwife, but mixed up with his hopes for her were images of Clarence's face, smooth as melted wax, watching him expectantly, waiting for his reply. Another one like Aloysius Cranby. And, no doubt, he would find another like Roger of Aurverelle, and so there would be two factions of nobles fighting over the Free Towns. If there would be much left to fight over after a few months of battles and sieges.

He was so absorbed in his thoughts that he did not hear the tread of heavy boots, nor was he sensible of the bulk of the man behind him until he was seized—a strong hand over his mouth—lifted bodily, and borne into a dark cul-de-sac.

He was spun around as though he were a sack of grain. Roger of Aurverelle's face was inches from his own. "Carrying tales to the legate, eh? Plotting behind my back, eh? you little effeminate worm . . ."

Paul delMari felt only the first blow of his head against the thick stone wall.

Mornings grew around Mirya: bright, clear, the grass gleaming with dew. The days were full of sunlight and blue sky. Evenings were quiet, with stars like double handfuls of diamonds scattered across the firmament.

She did not don a disguise, but she did not ride upon the road either. She kept to the grasslands, traveling up and down rolling hills, crossing streams at shallows. She went slowly. The lattices told her that haste for now was not important.

She stopped often, both to rest Cloud after the hard riding of the recent past and to give herself time alone, apart even from the horse. While Cloud grazed, Mirya wandered. At times she cast herself at full length to contemplate a flower, as if now, with Terrill's final benediction, she was able to see the bloom for the first time in all its presence, all its potentials, all its futures. At other times she merely sat, the sun warm in her hair, wondering.

Her hands, lying lightly on the ground, felt more than the soft grass of spring. They felt the individual plants, the earth beneath them, the webs that wound through all. And when she stood up and gazed across the miles to the city that was no more than a brown smear of haze on the horizon, she found herself ever more distanced from it. It was walled, roofed, polluted, the muddy streets bounded by houses and overhung with the pall of woodsmoke. Windows opened into dark rooms of battered furniture, cracked paneling, frayed hangings; rooms in which money changed hands, conspiracies were framed, wise-women were condemned to the rack and to the stake.

Directly or indirectly, she had felt the effects of those rooms. She had been pursued, captured, tortured, and condemned. She knew what it was to flee, what it was to feel fear as an intrinsic part of existence—like breathing, or eating. She knew the fire of red-hot tongs and the touch of the iron spike.

And yet those same dark rooms, rank with the odors of human sweat and the sickly decay of mortality, held people who loved her. She could have spent an hour naming them all: quiet people of the Free Towns and elsewhere who gave of themselves, who fought for those things they found precious not because they would gain or profit from the spoils, but because precious things were worth saving.

Those same rooms, dark and human though they were, could come alive with candles and rushlights in the night, with warm hearth fires that illuminated a mother nursing her newborn or a rough but gentle father telling stories about someone—Elf or human, it really did not matter—who, regardless of the Cranbys and the Albans and the Baron Aurverelles of the land, had preached about kindness, giving, healing.

She saw Hypprux, but she knew Saint Brigid, knew
those rooms, candlelit and filled with the simple, homely
love of human beings, one for another. Once she had
wanted some of what they contained. She had departed
from Hypprux in torment, and she had left Mika with a
final vision of denial and fear, despairing, believing that
she would never have those candlelit rooms, that gentle
man. And indeed she would not. Ever. The rooms were
gone, left behind, grown out of; and she had entered into
a world of forests, quiet evening fires, and the eternal,
ineffable light of the stars.

She reached the edge of the flax fields at the end of the
fourth day. The land was flat here, with only a few hills,
and she skirted the fields and found herself traveling
northwest, toward a curve in the Aleser Mountains that
cupped a large valley where a forest grew and was sheltered. It was there, to Beldon Forest, that the noble and
the wealthy went to take their sport chasing deer, or boar,
or in the hilly, unforested region hard by, hunting pheas-
ant and quail.

"A little farther, Cloud," she murmured as the sun slid
behind the mountains. "Then you can have a long rest."

Toward midnight, she passed under the trees. Beldon Forest was of another sort than Malvern. It was tamed, friendly,
and open . . . to humans. Paths and trails—not hidden—
crisscrossed through it, but farther in, it was a little wilder,
and Mirya knew—as only an Elf could know—that she would
be undisturbed. She found water and grass for Cloud, and
after she brushed the mare carefully and saw to her needs,
she let her run free.

She walked in a night that was not dark to her eyes. No,
this was nothing like Malvern, but it was nonetheless her
home, as forests and glades and rivers and streams would
always be her home. Forever . . . or until the end of her
race claimed her. She stepped into a meadow, looked up,
and saw Vega glittering fiercely near the zenith. It seemed
both a beacon and a promise.

She found a tree that felt right and sat down at its base,
leaned against it, wriggled until she felt comfortable. Closing her eyes, she watched the silent stars until one called to
her, and then she reached out, wrapped herself around it,

held it in her mind. For an instant, before the rushing filled her ears and the star bloomed like an immense flower, she heard a nightingale singing in Beldon Forest.

Then she was standing on a grassy plain, facing a Woman robed in blue and silver. She regarded Mirya quietly for a moment. "Child . . . '

Mirya knelt at Her feet. "I . . . I'm sorry," she choked. "I have to. Please forgive me."

The Lady's gaze was compassionate. "Forgiveness is in your own hands. I am here: I have been with you from the beginning, and I have always loved you. But forgiveness is yours alone, to grant or to withhold as you choose."

Mirya looked up into the gray eyes. "I'm torn. I've changed . . . but I can't be free until I do what I have to."

"Are you asking My approval?"

"I don't think I believe You'd give it."

The Lady knelt, took Mirya's head in Her hands, peered into her face. "Child, I can neither approve nor disapprove. You are responsible for your own actions. You can see the futures, and you can see the past. You do not act in ignorance."

"Can't You help me?"

"Not in the way you want, Mirya. I can tell you that I love you, and that I will love you regardless of your actions. But with regards to those actions, I Myself am helpless."

Mirya looked at Her, incredulous.

"I can love," said the Lady. "I can cushion a fall . . . sometimes. Perhaps I can bring comfort and strength. But in the end I must fold My hands and watch, helpless, while My children do what they must. I cannot violate your free will, nor that of anyone else."

Mirya was crying again. "But what do I do? I'm still angry. I still want to kill."

"Sorrow, guilt, regret, hate, anger: you take them on of your own free will, and you put them off also. They are not Mine to give or take."

"I know." Mirya hung her head. "I . . ." She felt empty, hollow.

"Be at peace, child."

Beldon Forest blurred into existence about her once

again, and Mirya sat for a few minutes. She had not expected approval or encouragement. She had not even expected love, but she was given it freely, without question or condition.

But she had to put the love aside for a time. Roger of Aurverelle was waiting somewhere among the futures, and tonight she had to find him, to plan how her vengeance might be accomplished.

She closed her eyes again, steeled herself, let the stars shine. Carefully, unsure of her powers, she felt through the rolling world, balancing past and present in her mind, weighing both against events that were even now sliding toward reality. She followed her own past back to Malvern, then northward to Hypprux until, once again, she crouched under cover at the base of the curtain wall, listening to Roger of Aurverelle upbraid one of his officers.

The sound of his voice rattled her, but she reminded herself that all her actions would be in vain if she could not control that refractory anger. Clinging to the stars for strength, she managed to center herself, held on to the images.

Carefully, she followed Roger's actions, watched where he went and what he did. She kept herself from blenching when the gate guards were flogged, and she shuddered when the baron—now chamberlain of Hypprux, she realized—gave orders for a house-to-house search. Something similar had occurred when she had escaped from the keep by herself, and she recalled the screams, the pounding on doors, the miserable townsfolk driven into the freezing rain.

She knew that torture and perhaps death would result from Mika's rescue. And she knew also, because she had acted, because she had chosen, because she had played a distinct part in a shaping of causality that was no less definite than Terrill's alteration of the webs by other means, that she was responsible.

I'm sorry . . . I'm sorry. . . .

She could not blame herself for everything, though: Roger of Aurverelle had his own choices. He could have dropped the investigation. He could have been less harsh. But he was determined, and he was brutal: he had his own responsibilities.

Roger raged and questioned. His plans, Mirya noted with some satisfaction, were eroding, and from her vantage among the stars, she felt the entire pattern of Adria and Europe changing, the result of comparatively insignificant actions that had expanded and enlarged like the ripples of a pond or the petals of a flower.

Jaques Alban had been nothing more than an expendable lackey. The plan had been all along that he would vanish and in so doing would provide an excuse for investigation and, later, inquisition. But the investigation had gone awry, for it had led to Cranby's death and thence to the difficulties in which Roger was now embroiled.

And Roger himself had played a part in the disintegration of the plan, for as the result of a casual rape, he had created an angry healer who had become an elven maid with a sword. And she, in turn, had arrived just in time for Cranby and his followers to come into conflict with her so that she might play her own part in the collapse of the plot.

And Cranby had ridden down Charity. . . .

And Varden, who had transformed a healer girl into an elven maid, had ended the bishop's life. . . .

And . . .

The web grew in Mirya's mind, intricate, plexed, the relations between events blurring into obscurity, leading her awareness even farther from her, but she reached her limit of comprehension, pulled out the mass of interconnections, and focused instead on Roger, tracking him through the days that followed.

She watched as he eavesdropped on Paul delMari and Clarence, watched him batter the small man's head against a wall until Paul's features were an unrecognizable mass of pulped meat and gristle.

And Paul had betrayed Mika to Cranby. . . .

And Mika had . . .

Focus. She shook herself away from the connections. She saw the discovery of Paul delMari's body by a wandering soldier-turned-pilgrim named Roderick. She saw documents—wills, codicils—passed from hand to hand. A young clerk with a roll of parchments began to climb a flight of stairs up to a council chamber where Roger waited as the strands approached the present.

Suddenly Roger's life branched into a matrix of interwoven futures of varying potential, and Mirya sorted through them, allowing them to pass before her like the pageants of a mystery play. Coloring all, though, was the anger that mounted steadily within the baron of Aurverelle: he was looking for something or someone to strike out against, and his inmost thoughts were a welter of blood.

Shuddering, she searched for a way to confront Roger alone, sword to sword. A second entrance into the city would be futile: there would be no way that she could have Roger to herself. She plodded through the potential. Would Roger leave the city, either by himself or with a suitably small company?

The complex braid that was Janet Darci wound through one of the futures. Mirya backtracked. The baron's eyes had been lustful at the sight of the hostage. Doggedly, Mirya traced forward again, approached the knot of possibilities in which her own future entered the picture.

Strand by strand she sorted through the lattices. As a result of Roger's attraction for Janet, there was a future in which he would go hawking with her . . . and with two attendants who could be trusted to become lost at a convenient time.

You son of a bitch.

Grimly, she centered herself again and watched the pageant unfold. Roger, with only the unsuspecting Janet and the attendants, left the city and headed for—dear Lady!— Beldon Forest. And after a while, Baron Aurverelle suggested that he show Janet the beauties of Beldon. Without the attendants.

A few minutes after, one of Mirya's potential futures intersected theirs, and the potentials became confused.

A future. Uncertain probability. Mirya found the stars and began to channel starlight. Power flooded through her. Funneling the starlight into the webs, she filled the desired future with energy, rammed into it her wishes and her will.

When she finally opened her eyes, she was gasping for breath. Her clothing was damp with sweat, and her hands trembled so violently that for some minutes she could not lift them to wipe her dripping face. She was stiff, cold, and hungry; but she had succeeded: the day after tomorrow, Roger of Aurverelle would leave Hypprux with only a young woman and two attendants for company.

And he would ride to Beldon Forest.

Chapter Thirty-six

Codicil the Second:

It being that my dear wife and I were not granted a son until comparatively late in our lives, at which time we were given our most beloved Charles, and said Charles—who by the grace of God shall be eleventh baron of the House of delMari and of Furze—being but ten years old at this date, I, Paul delMari, baron of Furze, make herewith this second codicil to my will.

I hereby command that should I die before my eldest son reaches his majority, George Darci of Saint Blaise shall be regent and executor of my will until such time as said son shall come of age and assume the rights and responsibilities of his title and house. George Darci shall have, until that time, control and command over my estates, lands, possessions, chattels, and trusts, excepting of course those of my wife (should she survive me).

I adjure George Darci, as my friend, confidant, and milk brother, to have a care for the wishes and desires of my wife and eldest son and to listen carefully to their advice, for they are not without wisdom and knowledge, notwithstanding sex (in the case of my wife) or age (in the case of my son).

Should George Darci not survive me, I assign all rights and offices enumerated above to the town council of Saint Blaise, under the same conditions, limitations, and terms.

I command that copies and records of my will and codicils thereto be kept at my house in Furze, in my castle at Shrinerock, and in the record house of Hypprux.

With my own hand do I write this codicil, and do sign and date it this twenty-first day of March, in the

Year of Our Most Blessed Lord, One Thousand Three
Hundred and Fifty-one.

Roger sat without moving for some time after the clerk
read the last word to him. It was well after midnight, but
candles provided a ruddy light that flickered in an amber
wash over the big room.

Suddenly he moved, sweeping the candle holders from the
table before him in a jangling mass that hit the flagstones
of the floor with a clatter, rolled, and lay still. In the half
darkness left behind, Roger pushed back his stool roughly
and turned to clerk.

"Is that what it says?"

"It is, my lord."

"That traitorous bastard!" Roger stood, fists clenched,
jaw working, wanting nothing right now so much as revenge. But what revenge could he have against a dead man?

"Shall I return this to the record rooms, messire?"

Roger did not answer. He was occupied, casting his mind
about, considering the consequences of the insignificant bit
of parchment. Furze under the control of the Free Towns!
It seemed incredible. Milk brother! Why had no one told
him about that?

"My lord—"

Roger turned, snatched the parchment from the clerk,
backhanded him off his stool. The young man fell among
the rushes and lay stunned for a moment before he tried,
weakly, to rise. His hands and feet scuffed futilely on the
tile floor. His robe tangled with his legs and he cried.

His hand shaking with impotent anger, Roger held the
manuscript above the flame of a remaining candle until it
caught. When his skin stung with the flame, he tossed it
into the fireplace.

The clerk was sitting up, whimpering, his hands pressed
to his face. Blood seeped from between his fingers.

"Get out," said Roger.

Groping, the clerk made his way out the door and into the
corridor. His sobs faded slowly into the distance.

Burning Paul's will, Roger knew, accomplished nothing.
There were copies stored throughout the land, and doubtless

the most official of them was in the keeping of Paul's steward.

The crusade was steadily slipping away from him. First Gugliemino, then Paul delMari, and now, on top of everything else, that jackal of a bishop of Maris, Clarence.

And his mate! *Damn him!* Dead in the harness!

Cranby's body had been brought back to the city for examination. Aside from some wounds left postmortem by wild animals, there was not a mark on the bishop. The cause of death, though, was obvious: Cranby's spine had been broken twice, the fractures created with the skill of a surgeon, precisely placed.

Elves.

Roger left the room abruptly, slamming the thick door behind him. His shoulder throbbed as he made his way down the hall. Even after a year, the wound still reminded him of its presence, of the Elf that had given it to him.

The Free Towns would pay for that, one way or another. He would see to it. He wished that he had the time to journey down to those despicable little cities and begin exacting the cost immediately, but he had to put off his departure for the wilderness yet again, for now affairs in Hypprux had to be handled with great delicacy. Not only was there a chance that the whole plan would fragment, but Clarence was there on the fringes, hatching his own plots, eager to pounce if given the chance. And Furze of all things. *Furze!*

He leaned his elbows on the windowsill and rubbed at his face. When he opened his eyes he noticed, on the narrow ornamental ledge that ran just below the level of the window, the print of a boot in the dust. The foot that had made it was small, slender, and Roger had a distinct feeling that he knew to what race it belonged.

And had he not stood at this very window on that very night? Could it be that only a yard or so from him—

He pulled away from the window. Lusting for revenge, he had to content himself with the thin gruel of patience, for there seemed to be no one in Hypprux against whom to strike. Impotently raging, he folded his arms, leaned against the wall.

A stray thought intruded into his anger: a fair girl, with hair the color of flax, reading a book. He hesitated, weigh-

ing the thought, weighing other thoughts . . . balancing. . . .

Kay made his way home through the dark streets of Saint
Brigid. There was an empty pyx in his bundle and, in the
house he had left a short time before, a vacancy that would
ache for some time.

The stars shone down brightly, and the air was warm and
clear. Dawn was some hours away, and he carried a lamp
so as not to stumble. He stumbled anyway: the lamp was
dim, and he was too preoccupied to look at his feet.

A porta inferi . . .

The words clung to him, dogging his steps along the treet,
over the cobbles, across the grass of the common.

. . . *erue Domina* . . .

"Deliver me," he mumbled, fatigue slurring his words.
"Deliver us all. The shepherds have thrown in with the
wolves, and who shall care for the sheep?"

He was not making much sense, even to himself. His
God? Who, or what, was his God anymore? *Erue Domina.*
Deliver me, Lady! Had he not been chanting that antiphon
over and over for the last ten days? And by what right did
he then don the stole of Christian priesthood and visit the
house of a dying man, bringing the oil and the wafer and
guiding him into a kingdom of which he himself had lost
sight?

Domina!

The Elves knew Her, saw Her, spoke with Her. As did
Roxanne now. Charity too, he did not doubt. And they all,
without exception, faced with equanimity and calm the future that crested above them like a wave. Whatever came
was—how had Varden said it?—acceptable. In whatever form
it took. There was no other way.

He stood on the soft grass, bereft, betrayed, traitorous to
his own creed. The casual and oft-made promise of eternal
life in heaven seemed a paltry thing indeed when held up
to the imminent threat of war, burning, death, and torture.

Sitting at the kitchen table with a cup of peppermint tea
before her, Mika had told him what they had done to her in
matter-of-fact words. The midwife was a middle-aged
woman with a kindly look about her eyes and a deftness to

her hands, and Kay had found himself listening with horri-
fied fascination to her stories of methodical torment. Miriam had raged, and her anger had dissipated some of the
force of her words; but here was a simple peasant woman
talking simply of burning flesh, broken bones, rape, red-
hot—

He sat down on the grass and covered his face with his
hands. He had committed sacrilege this night, and no one
knew it except himself.

I can't believe anymore. I can't.

Faith was not enough. Faith was what his Church had
demanded of him, and he had tendered it devoutly, with his
whole heart and soul. He had clung to it, preached it, guided
others by its light, made it so much a part of his own life
that it had taken on the form and substance of absolute fact.
God loved. Heaven was there. Salvation was attainable.

But since his faith was based, of necessity, not upon direct experience, but on the teachings of those he assumed
were wiser than he, it tottered and fell when those teachers
flouted the very doctrines they preached.

He dropped his hands. Eyes streaming, he looked up at
the stars. "Oh, My Lady," he breathed. "How long have I
been such a fool?"

The stars twinkled in the clear night air. The village was
dark and silent, and he pulled himself up slowly, his bones
aching, his heart empty. Wiping his eyes on the sleeve of
his soutane, he discovered that the once familiar garment
now seemed alien, strange, ill-fitting.

His lamp had gone out, its oil exhausted. Groping, he
picked it up and made his way across the common. His legs
felt weak; the world seemed unreal, thin, as though it could
be torn away of a sudden to reveal something different,
something he did not expect, something he could not comprehend.

He could not see anything—and probably would not have
seen even if his lamp had been working—and it was not
surprising therefore that he stumbled over a pile of stones
that the men had left before his house so that they could
repair the wall the following day.

His foot caught on a large block and he fell into the darkness, his empty lamp clattering across the hard ground, but

he was caught by strong hands. "Are you not well, Kay?" said a woman.

He did not recognize her voice. "I'm . . . all right. . . ." He regained his footing and groped for the lamp, but the woman had it in her hand already. There must have been a little oil left, with enough of a spark in the wick to ignite it, for the lamp was burning again, and Kay could see a fair face, almost elven, framed by dark hair. "Charity?"

"No," she said. "A friend, though." She took his arm and guided him toward his house. "Come. You look tired."

There was something familiar about her, as though he had seen her in the village many times before, but he could not place her. Someone's cousin?

Kay poked up the fire in the kitchen while the stranger hung her cloak on a peg and accepted his offer of a seat by the hearth and something hot to drink. Her eyes were clear and gray, and her gown, like her cloak, was blue. Her hands were graceful, and when she took the peppermint tea from him, they cupped his own for a moment and held them. "Thank you, Kay."

"God bless," he said. Her hands were still about his, as though this passage of a simple herb infusion from one to another was as sacred as the giving of a consecrated host. He looked into her eyes. "Do . . . do I know you?"

"You do," she said. "I'm in Saint Brigid often."

"It's very late for you to walk alone."

"Saint Brigid is safe. There is something precious here."

"That's true," he admitted.

She released his hands, took the cup, sipped. Her eyes watched him over the rim. "You're disturbed," she said.

Kay turned away, folded his arms inside his sleeves, looked at the fire.

"Well?"

"Yes," he said. "I just discovered that I've lost my religion."

She set the cup aside, clasped her hands loosely in her lap, leaned back in her chair. "Lost it? Are you certain?" Her voice was compassionate. "It has been my experience that nothing is lost without there being something offered in its place. It is the way of the world. Or am I incorrect? Do you have a hollow place in your soul now?"

"It feels like it. Everything I've believed in has gone away." *I don't even know this woman. Why am I telling her this?*

"Everything?"

"Well . . . there's still the Elves, what they've taught me. But you have to understand—" He turned around, and she looked so utterly familiar that he was surprised that her name did not spring immediately to his lips. "You . . . have to understand. . . ." He seemed to live among shadows, real and unreal, dancing hand in hand. "I've spent all my life becoming a priest. To leave it now is . . ." He gestured helplessly.

She leaned forward, her elbows on her knees. She reminded him of Roxanne. "Change is frightening," she admitted. "But to live is to change. And maybe one spends all one's life preparing for each change as it comes along."

Like Roxanne. Like an Elf. A suspicion was growing on Kay, but he tried to dismiss it. It was too incredible. Yet Varden's words, spoken long ago when David had first unveiled the panels for the church, came to him unbidden: *Someday, my friend.*

"So what am I doing, then?" he said, his voice shaking a little. "I've spent my life becoming and being a priest. So that what? So that I can give it up?"

"So that . . ." She considered for a moment, eyes thoughtful. "So that you can put it into perspective. So that you can see all your life as a part of what you are, but not all of what you are. You were a priest. And you still are, I think. That is a good thing. It has opened your sight to the spirit, to the unseen, to the holy. It has played a part in shaping your soul, in making you what you are. Now you feel empty and hollow. Perhaps that is a good thing, too, because it is shaping you once again."

"Shaping me? To become what?" *Someday, my friend.*

She shrugged slightly. "You know best, Kay. Maybe to become a better priest. There are difficult years ahead, and the people of Saint Brigid will look to you for assurance that their faith rests upon a man from Galilee and not upon a throne in Avignon. You may have to become a little more than what you have been. You may have to stand in two worlds. As for yourself, you've grown beyond faith."

"Grown beyond it? What do I have instead?"

Someday . . . He was afraid of the thought, it thrust itself at him. Where had he seen this woman before? How did she know all this? Neither human nor Elf she was. Something else. Something more.

She stood up, regarded him levelly. "What do you have instead, Kay? You have direct knowledge."

"How?" He took a step toward her, his eyes beginning to mist over.

Someday, my friend.

She was smiling. "By looking, Kay. By hearing. By feeling." Her smile broadened. "Do you understand now?"

Dawn began to brighten the windows. The light found its way in through the shutters and streaked the walls of the kitchen. Birdsong. The earth awoke, breathed. Faintly, Kay heard Charity's voice lifted in an elvish song, sweet and clear on this spring morning:

> *"Ele, asta a mirurore,*
> *Cira a ciraie,*
> *Elthia Calasiuove,*
> *Marithae dia."*

"I understand," he said. His voice was an awed whisper. "I understand, My Lady."

Breakfast was hearty: good porridge, black bread, honey and butter, milk straight from the obliging cow. Monsignor Gugliemino ate at the big common table in the downstairs room of the inn at Alm. The shutters had been thrown back and the warm light of the just-risen sun streamed in and glowed golden on the wooden floor.

Artisans and merchants, farmers on their way to work who had stopped in for a bite to start the day, fellow travelers whose names he did not know—all regarded him curiously, for the cut of his clothes and the papal insignia on his cloak marked him as anything but a local resident. But in spite of the threat of war and inquisition that hung over the Free Towns, he detected no hostility. He could raise his head from his plate and smile, and the smile would be returned—a little nervously, perhaps, but genuinely.

The innkeeper approached him, wiping her hands on her

apron. She was a tall, stately woman who wore her long blond hair in heavy braids. "Is there anything else I can get you this morning, Monsignor?" She seemed genuinely friendly.

He finished the last of his milk and looked out the window that gave a view of the forest. A skylark fluttered to the window and perched there, unafraid. "This is a wonderful place," he said. "How could anyone—" He broke off, not wishing to spoil the morning.

"I believe I'm finished here, madam," he said with a smile. "If you'll give me my reckoning and ask your son to fetch my horse, I shall be departing shortly. Can you tell me how far it is to Saint Brigid?"

"Saint Brigid? About a half day's ride. Are you going there?"

He nodded, wiped his mouth, and stood up. How could he not go there? He was not only legate, he was investigator also, and he was sure that Roger of Aurverelle would never dream that he was not returning directly to Avignon, but was instead journeying south to look for the humble priest who had written so eloquent a plea to Clement. Gugliemino had seen the parchment himself, the calligraphy shaky, the Latin stilted. And yet the words were simple. From the heart. *"My dear Holy Father!"* Fit to soften even the jaded soul of one accustomed to papal politics. There was something in Saint Brigid, and Monsignor Gugliemino was going to find out what it was.

And something about that was giving him hope, a gentle sort of hope, a hope that fit in very well with this May morning and this common room with its sunlight and view of the forest, and a wind rustling through the trees and a skylark singing on the windowsill. . . .

Chapter Thirty-seven

Mirya spent the rest of the night among the stars, bathing herself in their light, resting. In the Chateau, Terrill had rewoven the lattices only slightly, and the action had left him—experienced though he was—weak and trembling. Mirya had done more, much more, and it was not until dawn approached that she found strength enough to stand. As the horizon brightened, she walked slowly to the top of a hill that rose above the level of the treetops. A golden arc sparkled on the rim of the world and then grew swiftly into a disk. She raised her arms and let the light fill her.

The sun was a star, and it was warm and close. It dried the dew that had fallen on her and took the last of the chill from her bones. It, too, was a part of the Dance, a part of the Lady, and Mirya found within herself a well of gratitude that she had not thought existed: deep, clear, overflowing this morning, responding to the day, the sun, her memories of the Lady's hands gentle upon her face, her certainty that she was loved, that she would be always.

She was happy as she had never been before. Running, hiding, torment; there had been no room for joy. Now there was room, and more room. And it was filled. Love, a home, a people—everything seemed to be coming to her. And she nearly laughed at the idea that it was through pain, despair, and violence that she had, at last, come to herself, to fulfillment.

And then the sudden thought, like a mailed fist: she stood this day on a hill and greeted the sun—elven blood coursing through her veins and the stars bright within her—because Roger of Aurverelle had raped her on a spring morning over a year ago.

The causality was absurdly simple: rape, anger, transfor-

mation, growth; all linked, all following one from another,
a series of free choices that had come to form the core of
her present existence.

All the sunlight in the universe could not warm her now.
She had not eaten, but the nausea that gripped her buckled
her knees.

Roger of Aurverelle was an integral part of the pattern of
her life. But for him, she would still be a little fugitive
healer, would in all probability still be running. How precious a gift he had given her, and in how strange a fashion!

But I have to kill him.

She could not rationalize, and she could not equivocate.
She knew what she would do on the following day, and she
would take full responsibility for her actions. There was no
other way.

"I'm sorry," she whispered. "I'm sorry." And in the
back of her mind, she admitted that she might have been
talking to Baron Roger of Aurverelle. It was a disturbing
thought: she did not know whether she deserved praise or
condemnation.

The sun was well into the sky when she at last stood up.
She would not turn back. Regardless of what she had gained
in the last year, Roger had still raped her. That was his
responsibility, and he had to deal with its consequences.

Away and below, the forest moved, branches and leaves
tossing in a mild east wind. Jaw clenched, holding off tears,
she walked back into the forest and, for the rest of the day,
prepared for her task. Slowly, she took herself through the
fighting dance that Terrill had taught her and had drilled
into her brain until it left off being learning and turned into
instinct. Movement by movement, she let the stars take over.

As she moved—turning her hands just so, and bending
her knee at the proper time—she felt her connection with
the clearing in which she danced, the forest around it, the
land stretching off for miles around, the world and everyone
in it. Lattices. Webs. And there was one in particular: the
one that enfolded her and Roger of Aurverelle, George and
Anne, Janet, the Free Towns. . . . It wove and turned and
fluctuated about her as if she stood poised at some incredible focus of tension and stress.

The responsibility was crushing, but she could not escape

it. The lattice she formed and balanced was not to be altered
with any amount of starlight, but was held, and shaped, and
changed, simply by her existence. Action or nonaction
bound her equally. She could not beg off.

She finished her dance, drew Rainfire. She cleaned and
polished it, checked its edge, then sat with it unsheathed in
her lap, meditating. It was a sharp blade, very keen, very
fine, and it could easily cut through flesh . . .

. . . or futures.

The lands south of Alm were a pleasant combination of
shadowed forest, rolling grassland, and in the distance,
craggy mountains that soared up to summits white with
snow. It all reminded Gugliemino strongly of his home in
Italy: the alpine foothills rich with farm and vineyard and
forest and a scattering of villages that, from above, looked
like a child's toy left out upon a piece of green velvet.

He stopped his big bay horse in the middle of a stone
bridge, the water rushing under him, crashing over rocks;
the mingled sounds of mist, rain, spray, a million drops all
gathering together into what was almost a voice.

The monsignor could understand why this place would
arouse the greed of a man like Roger, and it would be easy
to underestimate the readiness of these people to defend
themselves. In Alm, in all the villages through which Gugliemino had passed, he had never heard a harsh word or felt
anger or hostility. If he had detected anything, it was no
more than a quiet, tragic regret: *It all could be so different.*

But there was determination present also. It could indeed
be different, but if it were not, then pity poor Roger of
Aurverelle, for the monsignor felt certain that beneath the
regret slumbered a wrath that would rise up to defend what
the Free Towns deemed precious.

He breathed deeply of the sweet air. He had talked with
priests and with layfolk. And this morning he had met a
young man clad in green and gray who had pointed him
along the right way when the road had forked. He had noticed the flash of starlight, but he had also noticed the courtesy.

It all gave him hope. He no more wanted this land laid
waste by men and arms than he desired the quiet valleys

about Montalenghe and Ivrea plowed up and sown with salt. In Hypprux, he had been entertained by men who claimed to be his friends, men who uttered veiled threats, who spoke of war and killing with casual indifference, men among whom he was afraid. Here . . .

There was hope here. There really was. Gugliemino had been lax with his office for the last eight years. He had plotted and connived with the best. He had even, at times, doubted the reality of his own faith. But it seemed to him, in this land of the Free Towns, where, regardless of fear and the imminent threat of inquisition and war, there was still room for courtesy and even—miracle of miracles!— friendship, he had found something that could make up for his plots and his laxness, something to counter his doubts, something to cling to when the world felt cold and the smiles of those about him seemed terribly, terribly false.

And if that something edged ever so slightly into hetero-doxy . . . well . . . no one had ever questioned the goings-on at Monscrrat, and Hildegard had pressed her mysticism at Rupertsburg well beyond any kind of orthodox boundary. Did it make so much of a difference that the Free Towns were not enclosed by a monastery wall, but instead lay open to the blue sky and the bright sun that reminded him so much of home?

They could so easily have hated me.

He wanted to talk to Kay, but he knew already what he would hear; knew, in fact, what report he would give to Clement VI.

Mika arose shortly after dawn to find Kay at the table, his head on his arms, sound asleep. There was a smile on his face that reminded her of a contented infant, and as she led him to his own room, he came to himself just enough to murmur: "Don't forget your cloak."

"My cloak?" she said. "Am I supposed to go some-where?"

"No . . . never . . ."

And he drifted off again as she tucked the sheets up under his chin.

There was no cloak in the kitchen, though there was a half-finished cup of peppermint tea on the table and a chair

was drawn up to the fire as though Kay had entertained a
guest during the night. Doubtless, he had met someone on
the way home from bringing the Sacrament to Simon's father and had eventually decided that no sleep was better
than an hour's worth. Nature, obviously, knew better.

After breakfast, she finished her morning chores, then
took a moment to peek in on Kay. The priest was still asleep,
curled up, a smile still glowing on his features.

*Would that I had such easy memories and such peaceful
dreams.*

With a sigh, she closed the door, resolved not to wake
him unless it were absolutely necessary. She had only been
in Saint Brigid a few days, but she was picking up the routines, and life here was not so much different than in the
little hamlet south of Furze. It was still a matter of shopping, cooking, cleaning, of people watching out for one
another, of babies coming and old folks going. Kay could
sleep.

She entered her room and poured out water to wash.

But then there were the Elves, and that made for some
differences. Here in Saint Brigid the priest did not cross
himself when they were mentioned: he had them in to dinner instead. Here, too, Miriam had stayed as a welcome
guest. In this very room, in fact.

Mika dried her face. Had Miriam been happy in Saint
Brigid? Was she well? Where was she now? Mika had asked
all these questions of Kay, and the young priest had answered them all in the affirmative, but with an inflection to
his voice that told the midwife that there was more involved
in her questions than a simple yes or no could address. He
had not offered to elaborate beyond saying that Miriam was
off on a journey, though, and Mika could only hope that
here, in the safety and tolerance of the Free Towns, Miriam
had found some kind of ending to her pain.

She changed into a gown that Elizabeth had lent her, and
just before she left to go to market, she picked up the brush
that Miriam had left behind. What luxury this was for an
old woman who had so recently lain upon the rack: safety,
a bit of mirror, and a real brush . . . and her own room!

"She must have been happy here," she said to herself.

Her eyes fell on the brush she held in her hand, as though

through it she could touch the girl she had come to love. Tangled in the bristles was four days' worth of her own hair, dark brown and shot with silver. But some of Miriam's was there also.

She squinted at the brush. Red gold? Mirian's hair had been black.

She took the brush to the window and drew out one of the near-blond strands. It was long and fine, much finer than any hair she had ever seen on a human head. Only once had she seen this color before, and that was on the head of the Elf who, with Terrill, had rescued her. Terrill had called her Mirya, and she had seemed, at times, so familiar.

We met once. But I'm sure you don't remember me.

Tall, slender, hair the color of red gold, and eyes like emeralds that flashed with all the light of the stars on a summer night. Mika remembered her clearly. How could she ever forget someone like Mirya?

Mika puzzled over the connections for some time, but the link did not come to her until the early afternoon, when, as she dozed on the bench at the side of the house, nearly asleep, vision and memory suddenly fused together into a coherent, incredible whole, and she started awake with a cry.

Kay had just then come to the front door and was blinking at the noon light. He scratched his head as though wondering where most of the day had gone. Mika ran to him and grabbed his arms. "It's true, isn't it? Mirya is Miriam . . . isn't she?"

Kay listened quietly to her frantic questions, his eyes peaceful, and that soft smile still hanging about the corners of his lips. Slowly, he nodded. "It's true. It's a long story."

She thought he was going to tell the tale right then, but she felt a presence behind her and turned around to see a big bay horse with a stout man sitting on it. He was a clergyman, a monsignor at that. A gold ring was on his finger, and the brooch that fastened his cloak was in the form of a papal crest.

"Oh, dear God," she said, "they've come."

The stout man bobbed his head at them. "I am Monsignor Giuseppe Gugliemino," he said, his voice lilting with the accents of Italy. "I am from Avignon. Clement received your letter."

Mika stole a glance at Kay. The priest's face was still peaceful. "And what is the news from Avignon, Monsignor?" His voice was calm.

Gugliemino swung a foot over the horse's rump and slid to the ground. "What news?" He looked at the house, at the church that was too large for the village, at the lush grass of the common, at the children coming toward him at a dead run as they laughed and shouted and challenged one another to be the first to touch the stranger's fine horse. "What news? I cannot say what it is now, but I can tell you what it will be, Kay. Aloysius Cranby was an ass, and a bloodthirsty one, too. And Roger of Aurverelle is a greedy boor." He approached, stuck out his hand, smiled broadly. "Or maybe I am wrong?"

Kay let his arm encircle Mika's shoulders as he took Gugliemino's hand. "Welcome to Saint Brigid, Monsignor."

Chapter Thirty-eight

Even at a distance of three leagues, Mirya could see clearly the four riders trotting toward Beldon Forest. The lattices were regular, even. There was nothing for her to do but wait. Unless she changed her plans drastically, she and Roger of Aurverelle would meet shortly after midday, when the baron would decide to add to his appetite before lunch.

She felt oddly impassive, as if the past days and her recent realizations had drained her of emotion. Her hand, resting lightly on Rainfire's pommel, gripped the sword for a moment and loosened it in its sheath, but she had hours ahead of her, and she shook her head and walked down the hill into the forest.

Her conscience twisted a little for having involved Janet in the execution of her vengeance, but she was not overly worried about the girl: she knew the webs too well. At least she knew them up until that moment when they twisted into the bewildering knot that represented her encounter with Roger.

The sun rose toward the zenith. She was sitting under a tree, off among the stars, examining the knot. It loomed ahead of her like a sea of light in which she could make out the flickerings of half-formed images. Anything was possible. In one potential future, she even saw herself healing a dying Roger of Aurverelle.

When she shook herself out of that particular vision, she was gripping her knees so hard that her knuckles had turned white. She rose, rubbed the stiffness out of her hands, called Cloud with a sharp whistle. It was time.

Closing her eyes for a moment, she felt through the present and saw that the attendants had lost themselves, that Roger and Janet were moving deeper into Beldon. The baron was talking soothingly to the girl, telling her tales of what he had done on past expeditions.

Mirya touched Cloud and the horse started off. She was certain that Roger was not going to tell Janet about everything that he had done in Beldon.

But Janet was listening attentively, and Mirya felt suddenly unclean at the thought of dragging her into even a potential danger. She had used Charity as a means of pressuring Varden, and now she was using Janet to reach Roger. In spite of her transformation, her growth, and her changes, was she really any different? But it was too late to change anything.

As she expected, she was exactly on time. There was a small meadow a mile or two into Beldon, carpeted with lush grass and sparkling with flowers. Mirya had noticed the flowers, as, she knew, would Janet. Roger would see nothing in the meadow save a flat, open space where he could put a maiden on her back.

Roger and Janet were approaching. The knot grew ahead of her inner sight until it eclipsed everything else. Mirya took Cloud to the edge of the meadow and halted, screened from sight by a cluster of poplar trees.

Wait.

A flash of color at the far side of the meadow, and Roger and Janet rode into view. Janet was laughing, a sunny, girlish giggle. Roger added a harmony with his bass. He looked as though he had in mind nothing more than a quiet lunch in the grass.

Wait.

"Are there really still boar in this part of the country?" Janet was saying. "I thought they were only in Malvern."

"Ah, my lady"—Roger laughed—"I myself have taken boar here. But I have to tell you that we've run out of them and have to . . . import them . . . from Malvern. Piggish though they are, they cannot keep up with our demands."

Wait.

They dismounted near the middle of the clearing, and Roger spread a blanket. At least, Mirya reflected, he planned to have Janet on the blanket: considerably better treatment than a small ragamuffin healer had received at his hands.

Wait.

As Mirya expected, Roger sent the horses off a little distance, far enough so that he would not be able to offer mounted combat.

Wait.

Janet was standing by herself. She reached down and picked a bright yellow flower, smelled it, put it in her hair. She was a fair girl, blond like her mother. Mirya passed a hand over her face, recalling the shimmer about Janet's body. Dear Lady!

Wait.

Roger stepped toward Janet, took her by the arm, embraced her, and forced her to kiss him. Mirya felt her sudden surge of fear.

Wait.

Roger smiled as Mirya had seen him smile before. He carried Janet toward the blanket.

Wait.

"My lord!" cried Janet.

Wait.

He tore at her gown.

NOW.

Mirya rode into the clearing. Rainfire was already in her hand. The bright sunlight glittered fiercely on the polished metal of the blade.

Janet was struggling, but though she was no more a match for Roger than a small woman named Miriam had been, she kept his attention occupied, and he became aware of Mirya only when she was almost upon him. With a cry of surprise, he released the girl, spun, and drew sword. Janet fell, weeping hysterically.

Mirya dismounted ten yards from Roger. "We meet again, Roger of Aurverelle."

"I don't know you," he said flatly.

"Months ago. In Malvern." Here was something she had not considered. Of course he would not recognize her. "I've changed since then."

He grinned. "I don't believe I've had the pleasure of making love to an Elf."

"Love had nothing to do with it." With a blink, Mirya shifted into the stars, watched the webs pulsate and increment. She had no time to be angry right now. She had too much to do.

"I don't know you, woman," said Roger, "but if you insist at playing the man with a sword, I'll teach you a lesson."

"I've vowed to take your life, man," she said. "I'm not here to talk."

She moved, quickly, lightly. Roger found her almost on top of him before he had a chance to get his sword up. It was a free shot, and she took it as best she could, but he parried. He would be on guard now, fighting with speed and strength. And Roger of Aurverelle, Mirya knew, was an excellent fighter.

Futures shifted as he swung at her. She dodged, feinted, and swept a foot behind him to trip him; but Roger was as light on his feet as he was strong. He evaded her trap, and Mirya had to backflip to avoid a crushing counterstroke. She found herself suddenly wondering how this battle would actually end.

Minutes went by, blades flickered in the sun. Mirya was not breathing hard, nor, she noticed, was Roger. Any man who could walk away from a fight with a sword in his shoulder had reserves of strength beyond belief.

The patterns shifted as Roger set himself, ducked under one of her counters, and spun. Mirya could hardly believe it, for now Roger's blade was coming overhead, and her feet were set completely wrong for any ordinary defense. Bending back, she raised her sword and caught the blow squarely on its edge. It was not an elegant movement, but it worked, and she saw respect on Roger's face when she backed to give herself room.

"Yield," he said. "Yield and I'll spare you."

Mirya forced a laugh. "After you rape me again?"

"Why do you want to die? I don't even know you."

It was true. He did not. Feeling hollow, Mirya faced him. "In Malvern Forest, when you'd been mauled by a bear, I healed your arm."

He stared, bewildered. "That couldn't possibly have been you."

"I've changed." She saw a momentary slackening of his guard, and in an instant she had evaluated the futures and struck. Roger parried . . . barely. Rainfire's tip streaked a line of blood across his cheek.

"First blood," she said. "Don't bother to yield."

His shock turned to anger. "Damn you, woman."

The returning blow almost numbed her arm. Mirya sought the stars and poured strength into herself. The lattices were hazy with potentials leading off into various futures, various outcomes. She was near the middle of the knot of probabilities that formed this battle.

Down. Up. With a lcap, Mirya side-slipped a thrust that would have removed her ribs, turned in midair, kicked Roger's sword arm away, and went straight for his throat.

It was a calculated risk, and she lost. The webs shifted and Roger backhanded her. She staggered, caught herself, then dropped flat onto the ground as Roger's sword whistled through the air where her neck had been.

Quickly, she riffled through the futures and saw very few options other than being spitted on Roger's blade. She chose, rolled onto her back, and swung. Rainfire impacted on Roger's right leg and cut deep.

"Elthia!"

Her cry mingled with Roger's curse as she sprang to her feet. Flailing with his free arm, Roger tipped and fell heavily on his side just as Mirya's sword cut into his throat. She saw the gush of blood and knew that the battle was over.

She stood over him. If he had known her, she would have enjoyed the sight, but she was a stranger to him. As far as he was concerned, the battle had been without reason, and that one simple fact made everything—the battle, her training, her sacrifices, her transformation—meaningless.

She dropped to her knees beside the dying man, anger seething through her. "Damn you," she screamed. "Damn you! *Don't you know me?*"

He simply stared at her, eyes glassy, uncomprehending.

Bending over him, she seized his head, reached for the webs that made up Roger of Aurverelle, let the memory of the rape flow into him. She felt his terror, but she persisted, forcing the experience on him. She was raped, and he was raped, and she knew that he would die with full knowledge.

But grappling as she was with the lattices of Roger's psyche, she could see that he was sick, that he had been for a

long time. She saw his illness—brutality, grief, loss—etched
unmistakably in the weave of his existence, and she knew
something of why he was cruel, why he killed, why he
forced his anger upon the bodies of women.

Just as she knew a little of why she herself manipulated,
plotted, hated; why she had, in despair, decided to vent a
lifetime of outrage upon the body and soul of one man.

She stepped back mentally, feeling weak, sickened. About
her, potential futures swirled like a pearly mist, and she
was moderately surprised: the fight was over. The knot
should have been behind her.

But she saw what she had not seen before. She was indeed
at the focus of a lattice that stretched between the Free
Towns and Baron Roger of Aurverelle, for the void left behind by Roger's death would give free rein to those who
would rush in to fill the vacuum. Clarence had his own plans
for the Free Towns. So did the barons who would join with
him. So did those who would remain loyal to the baron of
Aurverelle's plans.

The futures were absurdly clear now: at least two armies,
sieges, towns captured and recaptured, fields burning. All
of Adria would be involved.

She had killed Roger, she had exacted her revenge; and
in doing so she had destroyed the Free Towns.

She sought a way out of the dilemma and found nothing.
Living, Roger would have allowed the Towns to continue in
a bastardized state, with much of their population intact.
Aloysius Cranby would have pushed for a full inquisition,
but Roger would have controlled him. Cranby's position was
now filled by Clarence, but Roger's would be empty. Dead,
he could do nothing.

Living, though . . .

Roger's blood had puddled around his opened throat, and
his breath was a shallow frothing, almost nonexistent. There
was one future—Mirya had seen it that morning—in which
she healed him.

I can't do that.

But what future would the Free Towns have if she did?
Even if Roger lived, they would be in his power, paying
tribute to him or to his representatives. Perhaps he would

use them as he used Beldon Forest: a fine place to hunt unusual game.

Living . . . dead . . . or maybe . . .

She had to choose. She looked through the futures, weighed them, felt the delicate strands of causality and potential. Something precious was in grave danger, and she felt the awakening of what Terrill had called *wrath*.

Deliberately, she allowed her power to flame up her spine, searched among the stars for the one that she could tap, and let its energy flow through her. It was several minutes before she was done, for Roger had been very near death. She had to drag his life back to his body, ram it home, and weave healing about it to keep it in place. But when Roger was alive and well again, she did not stop. Wrathful, she had made her choice, and she was doing now what she had once vowed never to do.

For a while, she examined the web that was Roger of Aurverelle. Then, carefully, she set to work, changing strands, altering patterns and perceptions, transforming his existence. When she was through, he was still Roger of Aurverelle, but some parts of him were new, and some were different, and the weave of the futures he would create had been remade.

She sat back shaking. As terribly as she had been raped by Roger, it was as nothing compared to the magnitude of the violation she had perpetrated upon him. If souls had ever been taken, she had taken his; and the clarity of his eyes when he sat up and blinked at her did nothing to diminish her horror.

"Fair One." He licked his lips, looked uncertain, dropped his eyes in shame. "Do I know you?"

Wearily, she shook her head. "You do not. We have never met. Ever."

He passed his hands over his face. "Please excuse me," he said. He nodded in Janet's direction. The girl had wrapped herself in the blanket and was staring at them, frightened. "I fear that I've done this maiden wrong."

"It might be well—" She broke off, noticing that the elven inflection in her speech had redoubled.

Farther to go. But there was no farther to go now, at least not in terms of Elf or human. She let the words choose themselves.

"It might be well for her to return to Saint Blaise," she said. "I will take her."

"Yes . . . perhaps that would be best."

He stood up and stretched. He was still Roger of Aurverelle, still prideful, still violent, but his bent was now toward different ends.

He looked about as though he saw the world for the first time. With a manly grace, he stooped, picked a flower, and offered it to Mirya. "If I have affronted you, Fair One, my apologies."

"Perhaps." She took the flower, but she felt ill. She was seeing a mechanical contrivance go through its preordained motions. "You have been conspiring against the Free Towns."

"Aye." He looked bemused. "I've been wrong. The Church meddles too much. So do the barons." He ran his fingers across his cheek where Mirya had cut him. The wound was gone now; he felt the skin abstractedly. "I'll have Janet's belongings collected and sent after you to Saint Blaise. Cranby is dead, and I'll see that Clarence's plans come to nothing." He laughed in a warm basso. "The silly ass."

When they went to Janet, the girl shrank away from Roger. He looked hurt, but seemed to understand. Mirya knelt before Janet. "Do you wish to return home?"

"Fair One . . ." Janet's eyes were wide, wondering. "I . . ."

Mirya forced a gentle smile through her pain. "There is no need to fear me."

"My father told me about the Elves, but I did not think I would ever meet one."

"Be at peace."

"It would be nice to go home."

"Then you shall."

Roger looked concerned, sympathetic. "Fair One," he said, "I feel as though I owe you something."

Mirya felt bleak. "You owe me nothing, sir."

"Still . . ."

"Only make certain the Free Towns are spared and I will

be satisfied." As she turned away, she murmured to herself: "And then maybe everything will not have gone to waste."

She was an Elf; and like Varden, like Terrill, like all beings whose burden of immortality gave them more than ample time to reflect upon such things as consequence and responsibility, she wondered desperately about renewal.

Chapter Thirty-nine

Southward again. Beldon Forest fell behind, turning first into a haze of green, then into a dark line on the horizon. Hypprux lay to the east, veiled in smoke. The grasslands rolled gently, crisscrossed by streams. The presence of humans was manifested only rarely—a scattering of huts, an occasional village—and Mirya stayed far away from it.

Janet sat before her on Cloud, eyes still wide with wonder at seeing, talking, touching this immortal being; and even the violence she had suffered could not stem her curiosity or silence her questions. Where are you from? How do the Elves live? Are all the elven ladies warriors? Do you have a lover?

Mirya smiled tiredly at the onslaught. She answered when she could, what she could, but she was more often than not silent, almost brooding. Janet was wise enough not to press for answers. In fact, she seemed perfectly happy to let her questions hang while she sat with one hand on the immortal arm that encircled her waist as though to reassure herself that she did not dream.

But she did dream at times, and Mirya would stay nearby while Janet slept, watching the stars overhead and within, watching the visions that came to the girl. The violence and the fear would surface, and Mirya would soothe them away.

Healing. Comfort. Varden had talked about them, as had Terrill. She was beginning to understand. She could give, and by that giving she herself was increased, was able to give even more. There was joy in that.

Janet's face was pale and lovely in the starlight. "Mirya," she said once after the Elf had banished a nightmare, "I . . . I love you."

Love. It was something of a miracle. Mirya answered in

Elvish, the words coming to her effortlessly as the girl slid back into more peaceful dreams. *"Ilme mari yai, Yaneti."*

She leaned back on her elbows, her long legs stretched out on the grass, and the thought came to her that sleep was, at times, a good thing, something to break the continuity of the days, to put distance between oneself and painful events.

But oblivion, even temporary, was no longer possible for her; and she spent the hours of darkness within herself, among the stars, pondering.

There was not much else I could have done.

Weighed in some objective balance, Roger's violation was a small thing compared to the horror that would have fallen upon the Free Towns as a result of his death. And if he had lived untouched, the Towns' lot would have been little better. The balance was true . . . if she wanted to believe it. She could have absolved herself . . . if she wanted to believe it.

But she could not believe, and the memory of what she had done was a raw ache in the pit of her stomach. Varden had talked of renewal, and he had tried to show her how to achieve it; but she wondered if Varden himself had ever found any renewal, even on those countless days when he had stood on a hilltop and greeted the dawn. Terrill, she knew, had not, save in his love for her; and that was a tenuous thing indeed, based as it was on his memory of a long-dead Mirya who had, seemingly, returned.

But she was not at all certain that Terrill's conviction was untrue. Hour by hour, since she had healed Roger, since she had finally done away with the conflict in her heart, her language, her gestures . . . even her memories had been changing. If Terrill had been with her to say *"Ele, Miryai. Manea,"* she would have, without thinking, answered him: *"Alanae a Elthia yai oulisi, Terrilli,"* flicking her hair out of her eyes with a toss of her head that had been so characteristic of . . . someone else.

Like Charity, she had been reborn. But her rebirth, unlike Charity's, had been a bitter one, sought without regard for responsibility or consequence until both had risen up and overwhelmed her.

She went out among the stars, found the one she was

looking for, and went down on one knee before the Woman robed in blue and silver. Her gray eyes were untroubled, serene, and Mirya wished that she could have some of what they contained, because what she saw was the past, the present, and the countless futures fused into a simple Being in which grief, sorrow, and pain had no place.

"Be at peace, child."

"It is not easy to find peace," Mirya whispered. "I hate what I did."

"I know."

"How do I leave it?"

"You accepted it. That was the first step. Remember this: Your pattern, your dance, meshes with many others, and your path is shaped by what it crosses. Would you want sovereignty over all?"

Mirya bent her head. "I would not."

"It is well. If you had killed Roger, by your own admission you would have failed. In a way, you triumphed."

Mirya's eyes flashed in spite of her tears. "Triumph? How do I live with my triumph?"

The Lady turned half away and watched the stars for some minutes, then sat down on the grass beside the Elf. "There was a maid came out of Maris, once upon a time," She said. The light glistened in Her eyes, and Mirya wondered if She wept. "She was burdened with great powers. She was filled with anger and hate, and she would turn those emotions on others, whether they were deserving or not."

"Lady, I—"

"Hear me. But she is not angry anymore, and the only hate she feels is directed at something she did . . . once. This is not ideal, but it is an improvement." She looked at Mirya. "And how did she arrive at this improvement?"

"I grew, Lady."

"In spite of yourself. Now, knowing what you are doing, you may find your way easier. Take comfort in that. I cannot say *Deny your pain.* There is no life without pain. But use it. Grow beyond it. And do not deny your joy, either, for without it, life has no meaning."

"Varden was right then."

"About being on a path?" She smiled. "He was indeed.

But then, everyone is on a path, so it was an obvious conclusion.''

Mirya and Janet entered Saint Blaise the next day: openly, undisguised. Mirya brought Cloud to the gates, tossed the penny toll into the basket in front of the astonished guard, and rode on, her red-gold hair tucked carefully behind her ears and her sword at her hip. The man at the gate stared at her as though he had got a fish caught in his throat.

The cries started up before they were fifty feet from the gate.

"Janet Darci! She's back!"

"Fair One!"

People ran to windows. Women stood on tiptoe, shading their eyes against the sun. Men climbed up on wagons to see better. A flower vendor hastened to put together a spray of her finest blooms and presented them to Janet with a deep curtsy.

"Mistress Janet's back! With an Elf!"

Mirya nodded in acknowledgment, but kept to herself, to the stars. She had paid a high price for these cheers, and so had Janet.

The news had already reached the mayor's house by the time they stopped before the door. George and Anne ran to meet them, and Mirya handed the girl down into the arms of her startled father.

"When I asked you to look in on Janet, Fair One," George gasped, "I had no idea. . . ."

"It seemed the proper thing to do." Mirya replied. "Janet was not needed in Hypprux anymore."

"Not needed? What about—"

"There have been some changes." Mirya considered the sound of her voice, shrugged. "You will be hearing from Roger of Aurverelle soon, my lord. Treat him with respect."

"But—"

"It is possible to be the friend of a bear," she said. "One only has to keep one's hands away from the bear's mouth. The Free Towns will be safe. Fear no more."

George looked as though he had been struck. "But . . . but what happened?"

Mirya did not answer. She looked up at the snowcapped mountains, then down at the people who crowded around her. They were human, mortal, limited in their understanding and their sympathies, but she loved them; and it was so easy to give, to aid, to heal. "I grew up," she said.

"I don't understand."

"Nor do I." She started to move off, but Janet broke away from her parents, ran to her, and reached up. Mirya bent and pressed her head against Janet's, felt soft arms encircle her neck.

"Will you visit?" said Janet. "Please?" Her eyes were bright and blue, and Mirya saw the faint starlight in them. A kinswoman.

She had involved Janet in her revenge, and the girl still suffered from that. How much love would it take to soothe away the violence and the nightmares?

As much as I have to give. Mirya smiled and kissed Janet's forehead. "I shall. Soon. And often."

When she passed through the gate again, the soldier was still staring. "Where are you from, sir?" Mirya asked.

He found his voice after a moment. "From Zurich."

"It might be well for you to return there. Your services are no longer needed in Adria. God bless you." She rode on, feeling his eyes upon her. The fish was back in his throat.

She spent the night in the forest and resumed her journey in the early morning. She stayed on the hidden path and made good time. With her promise to Janet, the aching had left her stomach, if not her heart, and it was comforting to be under the trees again.

Just at evening, she left the woods and followed the road across the fields to Saint Brigid. The gate was open, and she rode up the street, circled the grass of the common, and came to the house of Kay, the priest. "Wait for a moment, please," she said to Cloud.

Kay opened the door and stood transfixed for an instant. "Oh, dear Lady! You've changed, Miriam."

"Be at peace." She entered and looked about. The kitchen was as she remembered it, but though its sense of mortality was tempered by a deep tenderness, it was still a room built by humans, and she needed the forest.

"I cannot stay long," she said softly, the Elvish accent strong in her voice. "I have come to say good-bye. And to thank you for your kindness . . . and for putting up with me."

"Terrill stopped in a while back. He said you wouldn't be living here anymore."

There was acceptance and peace in Kay's voice, and Mirya saw the difference in his eyes. The despair was gone. "You have changed, too, Kay."

He nodded. "I had a Visitor."

She understood, bowed low. "Blessings upon you this day."

"And there was a man from Avignon here, too. Clement will give us no trouble. So much for the Inquisition."

"How is Mika?"

"Fine. She's in bed. She doesn't sleep well yet—bad dreams and all—but she's getting better."

"I hope the arrangements are satisfactory."

"More than satisfactory."

Silence fell as human and Elf searched for words. But words were limited, and in any case, what they wanted to say, Mirya realized, would best be conveyed over time, when touch and tenderness, sympathy and love would transcend any difference of race or lifetime.

"You're . . ." Kay fumbled. "You're not human anymore, are you?"

She shook her head.

"Did you do what you wanted?" He sounded almost afraid to hear the answer.

"I am not sure. I am not entirely sure that I knew what I wanted in the first place." She laughed at herself, smiled at him.

One last look about the room, then.

"I must go," she said. "I do not belong here."

There was a noise in the hallway. Mika was standing there, wrapped in a blanket. "Miriam! I thought I knew you."

Forgetting the blanket, she ran to Mirya and hugged her tightly. "My girl. You've changed so much."

Mirya held her, stroked the graying hair. "You were right, Mika," she murmured. "I did find an ending."

* * *

She knew the path well. It shimmered invitingly in her vision, and she followed its twists and turns effortlessly, her soft boots silent on the forest floor. The moon floated in a sea of stars, and its light dappled the ground.

Her ears were burning again, but this time with a sense of coming home to friends and family. With few exceptions, she did not know them, but she loved them, and she was, she knew, loved in return.

And there was one in particular. . . .

When she saw the firelight ahead, she sent Cloud off to find Nightflame and sweet pasture. Alone, quietly, she entered the clearing. Terrill was there, and Varden, and Natil and Talla, and others. She touched the ground. "May I still claim hearthright?"

Varden stood up slowly. She knew whom he was seeing, and could not say that he was wrong. "It is not necessary for family to claim hearthright," he said, and he led her to the fire and sat her down beside Terrill. A cup of wine was put into her hands by an Elf maid. Mirya looked up at her.

"*Ele, Miryai,*" said the witch.

"*Manea, Carai,*" replied Mirya. "*Alanae a Elthia . . .*"

Terrill was watching her, the analysis fled from his eyes. Mirya saw fear and knew that he had not looked into the Dance to see what decisions she had made. He was not wearing his sword.

"Did you kill him?" he asked finally.

"I did worse," she said. The firelight glistened in the clear wine of the cup that she lifted for a moment like a chalice, offering it to the Lady before she sipped. "Worse . . . or maybe better. One of these years, perhaps in the early spring, on a Day of Renewal, I will know which. Until then . . ." She shrugged, looked at Terrill, then at Varden. "But I think I won, finally."

Setting down the cup, she put her hands to her waist and unfastened the sword belt. Rainfire was light in her hands as she offered it to Varden. "I do not think I will have to wear this again," she said.

Varden shook his head. "Keep it all the same. Swords have their place."

She let it rest in her lap. She could see that Varden was still in pain. In fact, now that she was among her own people, she sensed that they all had their own pain, that year by year, they came to know it, to put it into perspective, to understand how it fit into the larger pattern of their lives.

She had taken life, and she had given life, and each action had implied the other. Each action always implied the other. Both were a part of the Dance, a part of the Lady. And though there was pain, there was joy also.

Elthia Calasiuove.

Terrill had been right. She had been ready to fight Roger of Aurverelle, for she had killed him, and yet, in the end, she had loved him.

Her vision was blurring with tears. Terrill took her hand and kissed it gently. She heard Natil begin to play her harp. It was a healing melody, and she welcomed it.

ABOUT THE AUTHOR

Gael Baudino grew up in Los Angeles and managed to escape with her life. She now lives in Denver . . . and likes it a lot.

She is a minister of Dianic Wicca; and in her alter ego of harper, she performs, teaches, and records in the Denver area. She occasionally drops from exhaustion, but otherwise can be found (grinning happily) dancing with the Maroon Bells Morris.

She lives with her lover, Mirya.

Her short stories have appeared in anthologies by DAW and in *The Magazine of Fantasy and Science Fiction*. The first book of a trilogy, *Dragonsword*, has been released by Lynx Books, to be followed by a second volume in late 1989. Paradise Music will be publishing a primer she wrote for the wire-strung harp at about the same time.

27 million Americans can't read a bedtime story to a child.

It's because 27 million adults in this country simply can't read.

Functional illiteracy has reached one out of five Americans. It robs them of even the simplest of human pleasures, like reading a fairy tale to a child.

You can change all this by joining the fight against illiteracy.

Call the Coalition for Literacy at toll-free **1-800-228-8813** and volunteer.

Volunteer Against Illiteracy. The only degree you need is a degree of caring.